Adva...

"*One Night Gone*'s ... everything is fragile, unstable and under th... freedom and Allison's hard-won recovery t... ...ricate framework of relationships and hierarchies that underpins life in the small seaside town. It makes for a subtly but relentlessly unsettling book."

—TANA FRENCH, author of *The Witch Elm*

"A heart-wrenching and suspenseful novel of betrayal and revenge. A stunning debut!"

—CAROL GOODMAN, Mary Higgins Clark Award–winning author of *The Night Visitors*

"Allison is a recently fired television meteorologist who becomes entangled in an affluent beach town's missing-girl cold case. Featuring a brilliantly executed dual timeline with two unforgettable narrators, Tara Laskowski's *One Night Gone* is a timely and timeless mystery, one that will keep you obsessively reading well past your bedtime."

—PAUL TREMBLAY, author of *The Cabin at the End of the World* and *A Head Full of Ghosts*

"Absolutely gripping. This multi-layered and gorgeously structured tale of betrayal, murder, and redemption will haunt you long after the book is over. The talented Tara Laskowski, with her confident hand, beautifully drawn characters and unique style, is sure to be a major voice in crime fiction."

—HANK PHILLIPPI RYAN, bestselling and award-winning author of *Trust Me*

"There is so much to love in Tara Laskowski's *One Night Gone* that I don't even know where to start. At its core, it's a mystery, and a perfectly paced, well-plotted one at that. But it's also a beautifully lyrical coming-of-age story that depicts the socioeconomic divide of small beach town life, with all the 1980s flavor to go with it. Laskowski is a truly gifted storyteller with that 'X-factor' you look for—but rarely find—in a debut author. Spectacular."

—JENNIFER HILLIER, author of *Jar of Hearts*

"With evocative p... ...nister hall of mirrors, br... ...efuge for the wealthy, s... ...thirty years ago."

...elling ...sh For

ONE NIGHT GONE

A NOVEL

TARA LASKOWSKI

GRAYDON
HOUSE

GRAYDON
HOUSE

Recycling programs
for this product may
not exist in your area.

ISBN-13: 978-1-525-83219-2

One Night Gone

Copyright © 2019 by Tara Laskowski

GraydonHouseBooks.com
BookClubbish.com

Printed in U.S.A.

For Mom

ONE NIGHT GONE

The little mermaid kissed his hand, and felt as if her heart were already broken. His wedding morning would bring death to her, and she would change into the foam of the sea.

—"The Little Mermaid," Hans Christian Andersen

PROLOGUE

Opal Beach
Summer 1986

The girl tried not to look up into the hazy summer night, the seagulls circling overhead like giant paper airplanes. They made her dizzy. She focused on the horizon, the dark ocean churning, its vastness broken up by milky froths.

Thomas, the guy from the party, was pressed up against her, his thighs tight against hers. She could feel the heat in her cheeks, but at least it was cooler here at the end of the pier, away from the lights and sounds, from the constant *pop pop pop bling bling* of the arcade games and the deafening roar of the Zipper, a ride she'd thrown up on last year and then sworn her friends to secrecy.

Thomas dipped her back over the railing—not too far, but enough that she felt the danger, felt that if he just shifted his large hand an inch or so off her back she'd fall, tumble like a tragic mistake. He laughed, pulling her back, his dewy breath catching in her hair.

"Stop it," she said, batting at him, though she wasn't sure she meant it.

She liked him. She liked the way he made her feel—important. Funny. Sexy. At the party, he'd said he was from the cornfields of Indiana, a state—she would never tell him—that she wouldn't be able to point out on a map. He was tall like a cornstalk, she thought, and let that bubble up into a giggle on her lips as he swayed into her again and kissed it away.

Their friends were on the other side of the pier, drinking beer they'd poured into empty soda cans, chattering away and tossing a Frisbee. The guys flicked the disk so fast and low that she was afraid it was going to soar over the edge of the pier.

It was as if they were all in a delicious dream that might never end, a pause on life, a stop-freeze on a late-summer moment where everything still felt good. Right. *Forever.*

And this guy. This cornstalk Thomas, with white-blond hair curled by the salty air. His arms long and warm and his breath in her hair and his tongue filling her mouth and *oh.* She was drunk, that was for sure. That had been their mission, all of her friends. One week before college. Get wasted. Let your hair down. Wasn't that what everyone came here for?

She closed her eyes.

When she opened them, a fluttering on the nearby post caught her attention. It was a piece of paper, tattered, clinging by one small piece of remaining tape. The wind slammed it back flat across the post, and she saw a girl's face, black-and-white, the word *Missing* scrawled across the top.

"Thomas," she said low, trying to push him off her. "Thomas. Look."

She couldn't quite make out the girl's name, printed in small type below her photo, but the girl's face—well, her eyes stared right at her, it seemed. Smiling shyly. A yearbook photo, perhaps. *Remember me always forever.*

The paper fluttered again, a pathetic flag rippling, weak.

"Someone's missing," she said. She tore her gaze away as Thomas untangled himself from her neck. He was smiling at her, his teeth so white. She pointed to the poster and he reached out and steadied it for her. Now she could read it. The girl had gone missing the summer before. How long had this paper been hanging here? She straightened her thin bra strap. *She could be any of us. She could be me.*

"No reward, though," he said, tapping the poster with a thick finger. Behind them, one of the guys hooted, and a peal of laughter echoed in the night. Thomas crinkled his nose. "How do they expect anyone to care without a reward?"

The girl's eyes widened. Surely he was joking, this guy who just earlier, at a crowded party, had shamefacedly admitted he didn't know how to swim. Who had seemed so crushed she was leaving in only a few days to go home.

"Oh, come on," he whispered, burying his face in her neck. "No time for being sad. Not now."

"Maybe she was already found," she said, more to herself than him.

Thomas muttered what sounded like a *yes* in her ear. His fingers snaked into her shorts and she wondered how far they would go tonight. And where.

Another gust of wind, and the missing poster freed itself from the post, whipped around the pier for an instant and butterflied into the darkness. The girl watched as it flitted to the ocean, wavered on the choppy surface. She closed her eyes, and when she opened them again, the paper had disappeared.

1

━━━━━●

ALLISON

September 2015

*Y*ou'll feel like a new woman.
    That's what Annie said. The perfect opportunity to reinvent myself.

Annie was raving excitedly, brushing her hair away from her face as we sat outside on the patio of Chez Monsieur, a name that sounded way fancier than the actual restaurant. Perhaps that was why I was skeptical of her enthusiasm—I was uncomfortable, distracted by the sucking sound that came each time I pulled my forearms off the sticky plastic tablecloth. And that loaded term: *new woman*. Was Annie suggesting that I was damaged?

Perhaps I was skeptical of everything. Nothing worked out to be perfect. There was no perfect, no happy-ever-after. No happy *ever*, it seemed.

Still, my younger sister was almost the only thing I had left, so I nodded, sipping my water from a filmy glass with only a few chips of ice still withstanding the late-summer Philadelphia sun.

"The off-season at the beach," she said wistfully, staring off into our very un-beach-like surroundings as a taxi driver honked his horn and tossed a select finger at another driver trying to back into a space on the narrow street. "It's a great opportunity to relax, recoup—recover." She smiled reassuringly. "And the house—oh, Allison. It's divine. You won't even believe it."

I tried not to roll my eyes at my sister's undying optimism. "And I'm sure these heavenly people are just going to hand me over the keys, right? Without even checking up on my… background?" I asked.

A large cumulus cloud whipped over the sun, dimming the patio and turning the strong wind cold. *An omen*, my mom would say, but I quickly dismissed it.

"No, no, no." Annie leaned forward, and I caught my reflection in her large lenses—a hunched-over, thin waif of a person with hair too long for forty. Ever since I'd gone off-air I'd let it grow past my shoulders, though vainly I still dyed it every five weeks. I could never stand the gray roots.

I sat up straighter, adjusted my chair. Annie was still going. "Like I said, my friend Sharon knows the couple really well. And the town—she grew up right near there. I can vouch for you, no problem. They want someone they can trust—not just someone off the street. Oh, Ally. It's so perfect for you. A chance to get away from…from all this."

I thought about making a snide comment along the lines of, *you mean get me out of your apartment*, but that would've made her feel self-conscious about Mike, and I didn't want her to feel guilty for having a stable relationship. So instead I said, "Do you think I could really ever get away from any of it?" Because, contrary to what Annie believed, despite the protests she was now making at my negativity, I didn't need to become a new woman—I needed to get back to the old me. The me I was before. Before it all crashed.

Yet in spite of my sarcasm and doubt, already, *already* the idea was beginning to appeal. An oceanfront home, rent-free for the winter. The couple had just bought the place last year, but the wife's job was unexpectedly calling her abroad and they didn't want the house to be vacant for that many months. But they also didn't want to bother with the mess of renting the place out—distrustful of random strangers trooping in and out of their home week after week. All those horror stories you heard about people renting their homes through Airbnb on the internet—

"Do they use Google?" I asked, half joking.

Annie just shook her head at me. "Allison, please don't."

"YouTube? I'm just being practical."

"You just need to see this house," she said, ignoring my comment.

My sister had a talent for ignoring subjects she didn't want to discuss. It came as part of her nurse package—cute kitten-adorned scrubs, a cheery sing-song voice and a no-nonsense attitude for dealing with grumbly, pessimistic patients. *The best medicine is a positive attitude*, she always said, and I mostly admired it, though sometimes I wanted to do what one of her patients once did—dump a filled bedpan on her. She put up with a lot, but she always did it with a smile.

"Four bedrooms, a back deck, a sunroom overlooking the ocean. You could use the time to relax. Or you know, figure out your next steps. The beach is a great place to study weather, right?" Annie snaked her hand across the table to squeeze mine, but I picked up my water glass and watched her pull her hand back. "Besides, you're doing much better."

"Well, according to everyone else, that bar is pretty low, isn't it?"

Annie ignored that, too. She knew where this conversation

was headed. It was a relief, really. I didn't want to talk about Duke anymore either—the same ground over and over again.

"Just think about it, okay? We'll take a look tonight—they've got pictures. We have to act fast, though, because someone's going to snatch this up, I just know it. It's like a dream come true."

●——————●

It turned out that Annie wasn't exaggerating. *Divine* was a good word for Patty and John Worthington's beach house. Cozy, but also lavish. The place looked like it had morphed out of an issue of *Architectural Digest*. Wooden siding on the outside, cute A-frames. On the inside, an open living room with a ceiling that stretched to the top floor. A sunroom off the back with views of the ocean and a second-floor back deck with sun chairs.

"Built in 1986," the online ad read. The house had an opulent charm, and I immediately fell in love. It was exactly what I needed. A chance to get away. A place of beauty to run to.

"See? I told you." Annie squeezed my arm, shaking me until I broke into a grin. She squealed like she used to when we were kids and pressed snails or earthworms we'd found near the neighbor's pond into each other's palms. Or later, as teenagers, when we'd slip into each other's beds after a night out and whisper secrets about the guys we'd met, the way their clove cigarettes had smelled, sweet and smoky, the way their hands had nestled onto the smalls of our backs. Annie would giggle, her face pressed into her pillow, then sit up, hair streaming around her, eyes gleaming in the moonlight with all the possibility. We'd always been each other's ears, there to absorb both the delights and the horrors. So when Duke betrayed me, Annie was the one to help me pick up the pieces.

Annie kissed the top of my head and jumped up from the couch. "I'm going to call Sharon."

I sat back and closed my sister's laptop, staring up at the ceiling of her little apartment in Manayunk. My home for the last nine months.

This was not where I was supposed to be. This was not in any of the New Year's resolutions I'd sketched out each year in my leather-bound planners. I was supposed to be in Annapolis, living in a large, single-family home not far from the water, giving the morning weather report on *WDLT Annapolis* with a beaming smile and a jaunty flair, married to Dennis "Duke" Shetland. I was supposed to be finding tile to remodel our kitchen, planning a trip to Greece, fighting with my mother about not having kids. In other words, turning forty with a husband, house, job and friends—like everyone else I knew.

Instead I had regular appointments with a divorce attorney, sleeping pills, antidepressants, jaw pain and a tiny bedroom my little sister let me crash in while I sorted out my life. Instead, for the first time in my adult life, my compass was twirling around and around, unable to find direction.

Maybe the house *was* the solution. A chance to prove I was just fine, to show everyone—including myself—that I was no longer the Allison-puddle-toxic-hot-mess that I had been for the past year. In a new space, I could get perspective. Annie's apartment had its charm—with her stacks of dog-eared paperback books, colorful afghans over every chair, cross-stitch framed inspirational quotes posted slightly askew in the halls *(You can't see the sunshine with your eyes closed!)*—but it was nowhere close to the breathing room I'd have in a three-story house right on the coast.

I tried not to, but I started to get excited. An actual new start. The possibilities were whirling inside me, gaining momentum like a tropical storm gathering strength just off the coast. I could use the time to figure out my next steps, as Annie had said. Repair the self-confidence that Duke had systematically filed down to a small sliver. Find a new job or take a class. I could start a blog—my lawyer had told me to bump up my online presence with good things, positive things, that would push the bad stuff down in the search results.

Page two, my lawyer had chanted. *Your goal is to get them to page two. Do you know what the percentage is of people who click to page two of the search results? It's low, Allison. Very low.*

How sad my goals and aspirations had become.

2

ALLISON

October 2015

Opal Beach was about a two-hour drive without traffic from downtown Philadelphia. It was somewhere
halfway between Ocean City and Atlantic City and way
less touristy. The beach always reminded me of vacations as
a kid, running barefoot on hot sand, creating lopsided sand
castles with plastic buckets, breaking crab legs and sucking
out the meat. But there was also a sense of slowing down,
of taking it all in, and I needed that now. I could feel the
air change, the way it clung, coated, opened everything up.
Through the car windows, the October air was shockingly
cold but also reviving. The salty air had always bothered my
mother and sister, who complained it was too humid and
their tongues felt strange, but I loved the way it worked its
fingers into my hair and curled around the tendrils. It made
me feel a little wild, a little different. Untamed. Like anything could happen.

Was I really doing this? Was I really pressing on this pedal, steering, guiding these four wheels to a stranger's beach house, where I would live for the next three months alone? It had all happened so fast. A blur, really. Annie's friend Sharon, with that same nurse-like efficiency that Annie had, set it all up so quickly that I'd barely had time to adjust to the idea before it was actually happening.

But I was used to life messing with me now, used to tripping over a curb or forgetting to eat breakfast or chipping a nail, waking up only to discover that everything I'd known to be true was suddenly different. So in some ways this journey, the picking up and leaving behind, felt like an emerging. Like Rockefeller, the hermit crab I'd bought on our family vacation one year at a boardwalk shack, I was crawling out of a dingy shell and moving into a shinier, larger home. (Unlike Rockefeller, though, I hoped I wouldn't die from the soap residue that was left inside the new shell when someone tried to clean it too vigorously before setting him inside the cage.)

I drove down a two-lane road just off the ocean, the main drag for all the beachfront houses. I could imagine that on a weekend in July it looked like a parking lot as families navigated in or out of town, canoes and coolers tied up on their roof racks. But now it was eerily vacant, and I had the sense I was the last woman on earth, that in my quiet drive alone the rest of humanity had vanished. I was trying to decide if that was a good thing or not when a giant orange Hummer zoomed into view behind me and passed without slowing down. "Well, so much for that. Asshole," I said.

The houses were dramatically large and looming, blocking what otherwise would've been a magnificent view. You could tell which ones were just rentals—the monstrosities with thirteen bedrooms and a six-car garage that five families could rent out at once. But farther down the road, the houses had more style and character. The kind of places—lots of windows, big porches, nice landscaping—that would make your mouth water even without the lush ocean backdrop as icing on the cake.

I slowed as my GPS indicated I was getting close, but even so I almost missed the tiny driveway and its faded, weather-beaten road sign declaring my new mailing address: Piper Sand Road.

I had made it.

The long gravel drive split off halfway up, with one side leading to the Worthington house and the other side to their neighbor's. When I'd first met the Worthingtons for my "job interview" just a few weeks before, I'd been so nervous about the whole thing that I'd taken the wrong driveway and parked in the neighbor's lot and stared at it for a good minute before realizing the house number was wrong.

But now, pulling into the correct driveway slowly, it felt like an adventure movie soundtrack should be swelling. *And our heroine finds her destiny.*

I could imagine Annie's reaction when she finally saw the house in person. It was stunning. The surrounding homes were propped up on beams, like old ladies hitching up their skirts so they wouldn't get wet in the surf, but that just gave the Worthingtons' house an understated effect. It stood confident and modest between them, a beach gingerbread house right out of a fairy tale, with light blue curtains and sweeping eaves.

I parked right at the porch steps and got out, wrapping my cardigan around me to stave off the whipping wind. The front porch was small but quaint, with two wooden rocking chairs and a white table with flaking paint. I ran my palm along the back of one of the tall chairs, and it creaked from my touch. The chairs seemed to be more for decoration than sitting.

Dolores, Sharon's sister who lived in town, was supposed to be meeting me to hand over the keys. Yet it seemed I'd arrived first. I'd had to come one week sooner than planned, as Patty and John had been whisked away to her mysterious assignment in Eastern Europe a little earlier than expected. Patty had called me from the airport with the news. I'd pictured her in her white visor and tennis sneakers rushing through the terminals, bags bouncing off her lower back as she breathlessly gave me instructions.

Still, I half expected to see Patty inside as I squatted down and peered through the window. It was hard to see with the bright sun glaring at my back, but I could make out the shadowy silhouette of the large island counter in the middle of the kitchen. Beyond that room, I remembered, was the living room, with doors and stairs leading to all the many nooks of the house.

All empty now, waiting for me. A shiver curled from my spine up to my neck, unwinding inside me. *Calm down, you idiot*, I told myself. Not everything is a trap. Think positively, and positive things will come.

You'll be safe here, Patty had told me that day in the kitchen, leaning up against the counter, popping a grape into her mouth and patting me on the shoulder. Her voice, otherwise booming, had been low, possibly so her husband couldn't hear from the next room.

"Sharon told me…well, she told me you were having…she mentioned the divorce."

"Oh, well, thank you, but—"

Patty held up a hand. "No *buts* here. Just *ifs*. I didn't mean to say anything to you—it's all your business. You don't have to explain anything to me. I know every situation is different. I don't need the details. I just know that Sharon said a friend could use some escape, some time to recoup from a major life change, and this is what we want."

A crunch of gravel brought me back to the present. I turned. A car was coming up the driveway, its headlights cutting through the thin mist of the afternoon. A small, beat-up red Toyota, music blaring. The car jerked, stopped messily behind mine, and I could see Sharon through the windshield, waving her hand at me. But no, it wasn't Sharon. As she got out, her car door squealing in protest, I realized it was a punk version of Sharon. Her hair looked almost purple, curled in tight ringlets around her face. Her nose stud sparkled, and a tattoo peeked out from the neckline of her black sweater dress. This must be Dolores.

She gave a wave, and I left the porch to meet her.

"I'm sorry I'm late. We were just closing up at the gallery and someone walked in. Can you imagine? We get no one for days on end this time of year and the one time I've got somewhere to be, we get a customer." She extended a thick hand. "I'm Dolores. You must be Allison."

"Thanks so much for doing this," I said. "I'm sorry to put you through the trouble."

She made a noise in her throat and waved her hand in dismissal. "No trouble at all. Patty and John are good people, as you know. My father is an artist here. Jim Gund. Patty loves his work. They are probably our best customers."

"I can't wait to see the gallery."

She slammed the car door and patted all her pockets, finally fishing out a tiny silver key, which she held up. It glinted in the sun.

"That tiny key unlocks *that*?" I asked, gesturing toward the house. I had the sudden urge to giggle.

"What this? No, this is my diary key." Then Dolores did giggle, bending over herself in a fit of *hut-huts*, the first and only resemblance to her sister. She composed herself and glanced over at my car. "Just kidding, of course. Can I help you with anything?"

"What? Oh. No. I mean, I don't have anything with me. Yet. My sister's meeting me later with her truck. She couldn't get off work in time." Only Annie had a Ford pickup truck in the city—it was a sight to watch her try to park it on the narrow cobblestone streets of Manayunk on a weekend.

"Oh. Well, good enough. I can't really go in their house anyway."

"You can't?"

Dolores shook her head. "Not rich enough."

I stared at her for a moment, wondering if I'd heard right. Then Dolores bent over again, erupting in another laugh. "You should've seen your face. No—" she swiped playfully at me "—no, no. I'm allergic to cats."

It was then that I remembered Catarina. Patty and John had sprung it on me during the interview—their cat couldn't come with them. It would cost too much, thousands of dollars just to fly her over there—and so would I mind? She was such a good cat, I'd barely even know she was there, gosh, they barely even knew she was there half the time. And so it was that I was also responsible for a living being in addition to my house duties.

"You want a tour of the town?" Dolores asked. She'd been checking her phone, but she locked the screen and slid it back in her bag. "My evening appointment just got canceled, so I've got some time."

"Sure," I said, trying to recapture the excitement I'd felt driving in the car. *This is your new house, your new town. Embrace it, Allison.* "I would love that."

"Well, I could start you right here," Dolores said, clapping her hands together and then spreading them wide like a tour guide introducing a historic property. "Here, in the middle of the 1 percent of Opal Beach. Old money, for the most part, though right next door you've got the *Bishops*." She said the name with an exaggerated reverent hush, leaning forward. "They own the biggest seafood restaurants in the area—the ones that the mums and dads and their sunburned kiddos flock to so they can sit outside and drink cans of beer and crack their crabs with a hammer." She made the motion with her hand. "The biggest one is right at the end of the pier."

"Oh yeah," I said. "I think I saw the sign—"

"The giant crab light?" Dolores nodded. "Can't miss it. They say if you find the giant crab and the giant clown, then you've found Opal Beach." She leaned forward again. "The Bishops are *it* around here. You'll see. They could buy you an island tomorrow and have it furnished by Friday. I'm sure, being their neighbor and all, they'll take very good care of you."

I nodded slowly, looking up at their gigantic home. "Well, I wouldn't turn down an island."

Dolores chattered away while we drove. I let her talk. I felt thrown off guard and was trying to figure out why. Then it hit me: I wasn't used to people treating me like a normal person. For the past ten months, everyone seemed to act as though I was going to snap angrily at any moment or burst into tears and never stop, tiptoeing around any subjects that might remind me of my marriage or the wreck of it. But Dolores—*she didn't know.* Any of it. She didn't know about Duke, about the fallout from everything. It was a glorious feeling, to be freed of baggage. To not feel that I was being judged.

I felt myself calming as we approached downtown. Opal

Beach seemed mellow, I took that much in. It was smaller in scale and tackiness than Ocean City. The central downtown area was cross-sectioned by a pier that stretched out into the ocean with the famed Bishop restaurant at the end and a giant Ferris wheel and all kinds of French fry joints, arcades, bars and gift shops that I'm sure were packed full of tourists during the height of the season. The main drag—Atlantic Avenue—had a post office, a movie theater ("They show the classics on the last Thursday of every month," Dolores noted, and seemed pleased when I expressed my appreciation for that), a couple of coffee shops and restaurants, and a library that looked more like a shack. Since it was the middle of the week, there weren't many people milling about, but enough to get the general idea of what the place was like. Low-key, friendly, casual.

"Always plenty of parking in the off-season," Dolores said. "You'll have no trouble skipping down here for a nip or whatever." Despite her quirks, Dolores had a cool factor about her. A style and a confidence that went beyond the tattoos and the nose ring. I realized I wanted her to like me.

"So you're from here?" I asked.

"Oh yes. My mom moved to Delaware years ago after the divorce, and Sharon, of course, moved to the big ole city to be a fancy nurse, but Dad and I have stayed. Probably always will. It has its flaws, don't get me wrong, but it's a great place to be, especially in the off-season." She glanced sideways at me, and each time she did, she also turned the steering wheel, causing the old car to veer off the road. I clutched the door handle a bit tighter.

"So you don't get lonely after everyone packs up and leaves for the summer?" I said, only half-joking.

Dolores laughed. "It's not for everyone, that's for sure. But we locals, we like it when it's quiet. When you don't have to worry about idiot frat boys shimmying up the light poles or pissing in your flowerpots."

"Yeah. I can see that."

"But you know, when that wind howls in the winter...it can freak you out, that's for sure." Once again, the car swerved. "Sharon and I used to scare the pants off one another when we were kids, reading all those terrible ghost story books you find in the local bookstores."

"Ghosts, huh?" I asked. "I suppose every beach town has to have some."

We drove off the main street, turned away from the ocean onto a larger two-lane road where the sand dunes got higher and the buildings got farther apart. "You can probably tell, we're entering a different section of town now." At the end of that road, another layer of shops appeared, more modern and fancy than the main drag.

"This is Parkins Plaza," Dolores said breezily, with a hint of sarcasm. "It's a new development. You'll find your designer clothes—Lilly Pulitzer and the like—" at this her nose crinkled in disgust "—and organic food stores. They just built it a year or two ago. It's clearly for the ritzier class, if you know what I mean." She rolled her eyes, tucking her curls fruitlessly behind her ears where they had slid forward again across her chin.

Dolores circled around the shopping center and headed back toward the house. We drove in silence for a while, and I took in the scenery, trying to make a mental map of the area. My new home.

When we passed a field of thick reeds I thought I recognized, Dolores slammed on the brakes, jerking us both forward. "Sorry," she said, flustered, backing up the car on the two-lane highway. I looked back to make sure that no cars were coming fast around the corner. "For whatever reason, no matter how often I get up here, I always miss the turn."

I'd missed it, too. The faded road sign: Piper Sand Road. We headed up the long driveway to find Annie's pickup truck parked behind my car, and Annie sitting on the porch steps chattering away on her cell phone. She waved as we approached.

"Home sweet home," Dolores proclaimed.

3

• ━━━━━ •

MAUREEN

June 1985

The boy with the slicked-back dark hair returns for a third time to try his hand at the Stop 'n' Throw. He grins at me, slaps down his ten cents. "This one's for my future girl-friend. Which prize do you want?" He said that the other two times, and it wasn't funny or charming then either. I take his money, though, and smile back. Wide, broad. Really feeling it actually. You see, I already decided that this place is mine. Ever since our bus pulled into the empty field a few days ago, settling crookedly into a ditch, I've known that Opal Beach is it. My destiny. Where magic will happen.

I hand the boy a Wiffle ball. He is a boy for sure, the im-maturity fluttering around him like the velvety fins of the beta fish in Jacqueline's booth. It doesn't matter if he is try-ing to win me over or just making fun of me for the sake of his friends, who all hang out just outside the perimeter of my booth sharing a burned funnel cake balanced on a flimsy paper plate. The guys are wearing their Easter-egg-colored polo shirts with turned up collars and trying to hide their acne with skin-colored Clearasil. The bunnies are all Madonna wannabes—ripped mesh gloves, belly shirts, chunky crucifixes around their necks. It's all bad bleach highlights and twenty-dollar bangs around here, lighters struck too close to their hair.

No one in this town understands. They can't feel the pin-pricks of possibility in the air, the tides of fate tugging us around, tossing us in one direction or another. They're like all the others in all the other beach towns, so concerned about who's looking at their legs that they can't take even one minute to think about who they are and what they want from this great, wide, insane world. They have it easy, and they don't even know it.

I lean forward to set up the pins for the boy, lining them up on the target areas, taking my time to give him a glance at the tops of my breasts when my shirt gives in to gravity. He may not know or care what he wants beyond a taste of candy apples, but I do. And one thing I've learned from working these towns is that rich boys love the carnival girls. We are the elusive, exotic prize on the top shelf, the one that it seems urgent to win in the moment, even if it will be forgotten and tossed away later. Sometimes during that moment, when you're still shiny and new, you can benefit. Shift up the social ladder a few notches, get a glimpse of the other side of things.

"I guess you already know the drill," I say.

"I do, but I love to hear you say it," he says. Up close his teeth look green, but that could just be the lights from the Ferris wheel reflecting off them. Clyde's pumping old disco through the speakers. Everything's about *doin' it right, doin' it right, doo doo don't ya know,* and the air still smells of suntan lotion and grease. There's the circus music and the screeches from the Tilt-a-Whirl, and it's so summer I can almost bite into it.

I step away to the side of my booth and watch the boy squint, concentrating hard. One of his friends calls out, "Let's go, Nolan Ryan," and all the Material Girls tittle. Another says, "Don't blow it again, man." My boy ignores them, winds up and throws the Wiffle ball. He doesn't even get close. He misses all three pins, his worst performance yet.

"Guess third time's not the charm," I say cheerfully. Clyde's got it fixed so that the last pin is heavier than the others, making it nearly impossible to knock over with something as light as a Wiffle ball. Wouldn't want everyone winning the cheap stuffed frogs and bears, of course.

From across the way I catch Jacqueline's eye, and she raises her brows in a question, but I don't take the bait. She's got all softness inside her, that Jacqueline—too nice for her own good. She's a dove. Always in bed right after the carnival shuts down for the night, reading love stories and stretching her hamstrings. She has no interest in playing the rich boys' games. Says she's seen it all and none of it is pretty.

"I've spent enough money here to get your name, though, haven't I?" the boy asks.

"Maureen," I say, before I can think to lie about it. This boy's not my destiny, but I don't care. The path to destiny can take some detours.

●———●

We end up in the Hall of Mirrors. The carnival has closed down, the rest of the people slowly shuffle to the gates for the night, but I know it's not final call until Clyde cuts off the music.

The boy tells me his name is Barron. His friends are waiting for him outside the gates, but he lingers. He likes the Hall of Mirrors. I tell him he's got to count to five and then come and find me. If he catches me, he'll get a surprise. I can see by his face what kind of surprise he thinks I mean.

I leave him at the entrance, eyes closed, hands shoved tensely in his shorts' pockets, counting to five too quickly. He likes games. That's one thing we have in common. Too bad for Barron that I know the Hall of Mirrors as well as he knows his fancy childhood mansion. I know about the secret passages that allow the workers to slip quickly from one part of the hall—which is really not any larger than a garage—to another. I've got the upper hand in this game, which is how I like it. The world is one giant game after all. You just have to know how to play. What doors to unlock. What moves to make.

I lift a mirror in the front room and hop up the three steps to the top floor, peek through the tiny black hole in the wall to watch Barron stumble in, his eyes adjusting to the bright lights of the entrance hall. He's got no choice here but to look at himself. I wonder what he's thinking. Endless reflections of Barron staring at Barron staring at Barron. But he doesn't pause for long. He's a man on a mission.

In the grand hallway I let him catch a glimpse of me. There's a two-way mirror, and I stand in front of it, pretending I don't know he can see me. I turn around slowly, like I'm listening for him. I can feel him on the other side of the wall, watching me. He's grown quiet, but I can almost hear his breath. He thinks he's got me now. He thinks he knows something I don't, and I let him. I bite my nail, brush back some hair. I shove my hands in the back pockets of my shorts.

Then I run.

In the next room, before Barron has a chance to follow, I slip behind the giant floor mirror and through a short passage that leads me to a central room—not even a room, smaller than a closet—where I stop. I can hear Barron getting frustrated. "I'm coming for you, Maureen," he says.

In the echo of the hallway his voice sounds menacing, and I suddenly regret all of it. I feel tired. I don't want to play anymore. I don't want Barron's sloppy hands pawing. I don't want to hear about all the people he can buy weed from. I just want to go back to my trailer with Jacqueline and have her read aloud her stupid quizzes and fall asleep to the sound of the waves.

"Alright, you've had your fun. Let's go," our hero calls.

I slide out, peer through another hole and see him yanking on some of the mirrors, trying to find another path. I wonder, if I did leave, how long he'd stay there, tearing up the secrets of the Hall of Mirrors.

But I know I won't leave. There's still a chance he has something to offer.

I wait for him in the last room. It's the room of distortions. In one mirror I look tall and thin, my neck giraffe-like, my face like it was pressed through the salt water taffy machine. In the next I am Humpty Dumpty, feet like pegs, my tummy and ass like a large ripe pear.

In another it looks like I have two faces. In the last, no face at all, my head decapitated. It's here where Barron finds me, grabs me from behind in a violent bear hug, like he's afraid I'm going to slip away again. "There you are," he says, but I can't see his face or mine. We are just bodies, a tangle of arms and legs. He's finally won the elusive prize. I let him win. This time.

─────●───────●─────

I learned long ago to trust my intuition, to let the universe in when it comes knocking. That's how I got the gig for C&D Amusements in the first place. I'd been crashing at a friend's pad for a few days and could tell she was getting all get-out-tired of me, when I decided to wander down to the bus station, hop on one and see where it took me. Instead, I saw the large trailers and trucks with C&D printed all over them, framed by a silhouette of a tall roller coaster and tangled messes of bumper cars. And Jacqueline getting off a bus. I'm not much for starting conversations with strangers, but I let her bum a cigarette, and she introduced me to Clyde, and that was it. It's not a bad gig. Clyde hires some locals to fill the spots, but we are the core crew that travels. The season picked up in late spring, and we did a few quick two-week carnivals, and then in early June we settled in Opal Beach for the summer to feed people terrible food and make them queasy on shitty rides. After Opal Beach, Jacqueline tells me, we move on to state fairs and harvest festivals, but this is only a temporary gig for me, something I need until I can figure things out, start fresh.

"Sure," Jacqueline says in her sweet sarcastic way. "Melvin's temporary, too. He's been here seven years now."

"This could be the place," I say, ignoring her, refusing to think about Melvin and his sad eyes. I open our trailer window and let the salty air inside. "There's a magic here. I can feel it."

"What's so special about it?" Jacqueline asks me from her bed, where she's painting her toenails a pale pink color that reminds me of a tongue. She waves her fingers, and the scent of varnish overtakes the ocean air. "It looks and smells the same as all the others."

"I don't know," I admit. I flop down on my bed and pull out my notebook, start doodling. "But I think I'll figure it out."

Jacqueline rolls her eyes. "That's what everyone says. We're going to figure it out. Get our shit together. Right? But yet, we're all still here."

She wants a story. Everyone wants a story. The folks here at C&D trade stories like they're baseball cards. One night in the last town we were in, Jacqueline told me about her daddy. She said the night he broke her finger was the night she left. *Who are you running from?* she asked, because everyone at C&D was running from something. I could've told her then—about my mom, or Gwen, or the dirty needles I'd have to be careful not to step on barefoot in the middle of the night, the red and blue lights twinkling through my bedroom curtains. I could've told her my Sad Story—we all have them, we all carry them around like precious little pets—but I know it's never good to let anyone see you vulnerable.

So I don't talk about it. Which is why everyone thinks I'm a hard one (read: bitch) around here, and why Clyde's brother, Desmond, hates me like I'm a parasite. He never pays anyone properly, but he especially likes to dick me over. It's like he knows how important the money is—what measly pay they give us, anyway—and purposefully taunts me. Jacqueline's said more than once I should never let myself be alone with him. He's older and dumber than Clyde, and I suspect Clyde only keeps him along because he's family. He's just there. A heavy presence that makes your skin crawl whenever his eyes flick over you like a lazy lizard with poison in his teeth.

"Don't let the sunshine fool you into thinking you belong here, girl. You'll just be disappointed, like the rest of us," Jacqueline says.

But Jacqueline is wrong. We've been in Opal Beach for almost a week, and I can already tell it's got a something. It's not the people or the smell or the sound. It's more like a vibration, a sense, like the electricity in the air just before a violent thunderstorm. I can feel its pulse, calling to me, soothing and delightfully exciting and terrifying, something new and life changing and yet as old and familiar as a battered, lonely seashell. Whatever it is, I've been waiting for it. And I'm ready.

4

◆——————◆

ALLISON

One year around Christmastime, our parents took Annie and me to Ocean City. The off-season at the beach was magical. The ocean waves whipped in the breathtaking air, delivering slush to our booted feet as we shivered on the sand. Full, bright moon. Salty snowflakes. And the quiet. My mother had thought that all the closed beach shops and outdoor crab shacks had looked sad and abandoned without suntanned, laughing people sitting at the wooden high-top tables sipping cold drinks and tugging at bathing suit straps. The big red clearance signs and the sagging beach towels in the windows of the surf shops had depressed her.

But the rest of us had been enthralled. It was like stumbling upon an amusement park that you had all to yourself. It had felt powerful—like the speckled, worn boardwalk, the birds diving and fighting and pecking, the dark alleyways between the lofty hotels were hiding secrets, waiting for us to peek under or inside and discover them.

In the same way, the Worthingtons' house felt like a giant box to be unwrapped, a gift holding a promise for the future. It didn't take long for Annie and me to move my stuff inside because there wasn't much—a few cartons and two suitcases, a cooler full of groceries, and my longtime plant Linus who took up most of my backseat and was about the only thing that I had left of my marriage. No kids, no cat, but a plant larger than an ottoman that I'd managed to keep alive for twenty years.

After we brought it all inside, I gave Annie a tour. We started upstairs. Reclining beach chairs lined the top porch, facing the ocean. A roll-out minibar was parked just inside the doors for when the Worthingtons were entertaining. On every shelf or nook sat a statue or vase or trinket that suggested Patty and John had done a lot of travel in their time. We started opening drawers and dressers, peering into the many closets and cabinets in the house. There were little odd-shaped doors and slanted ceilings, giving the house a fairy-tale quality, like at any moment a series of elves or gnomes or fairies would pop out from the walls and braid ribbons into our hair.

In almost every room, John had left a detailed to-do list. Downstairs, I picked up one notebook from a table near the doors to the back deck and read aloud to Annie. "Because we are on the water, there is so much more maintenance to do. The salt water coats the windows. The air rips around our flags, tears them to shreds. The plants need constant attention, although I suppose not so much in the winter."

The main level was the most elegant part of the place, with a hallway on the top floor winding around above our heads, flanked by a wooden railing. Half of one wall in the living room was lined with wooden paneling, suggesting the house's age, but everything else felt updated and modern. It was still hard to believe it was all mine.

In the kitchen, John wrote about the particulars of the

dishwasher and the stove, meticulous about which cleanser to use and how hard to scrub the surface. Patty had lined the refrigerator with notes in her loopy script—suggestions of where to eat ("Bishop's Seafood is a must-do! For Italian, try Giuseppe's in Jasper!"), what to do ("Parkins Plaza has some new boutiques!") and how to work various appliances ("Our blender's on the fritz, so whatever you do, don't push the pulverize button!").

"I can't wait to see the list of instructions on how to flush the toilet," I joked.

Annie raised her eyes. "You're in for it, Mongoose."

⸻

I selected the smaller of the two upstairs bedrooms. The room was long and thin—the bed took up most of the width, but I didn't mind. It was cozy. There were lovely exposed beams on the ceiling, and the walls were painted in a quiet pale aqua. Catarina was curled up on the end of the bed—the first real glimpse I'd had of her—but she leaped up when she caught sight of me and ran out. *Well, at least you'll be easy to take care of,* I thought sadly. Duke's cat hadn't been much of a lap cat either, but at least she hadn't been terrified of me.

Above the bed was a large canvas. A silhouette of a whole beach carnival, the Ferris wheel looming over it all, and the backdrop of the ocean, with the sun setting into the horizon. It was one of Dolores's father's paintings, I realized. Jim Gund, the gallery downtown.

That first night, Annie and I ate dinner, drank daiquiris and, before we knew it, we were on the couch in our pajamas, yawning. Hanging out with Annie was comfortable and familiar, but I kept thinking ahead to the end of the weekend when she would leave. We weren't roommates anymore. She wouldn't be just a thin apartment wall away. I would no longer hear her padding footsteps outside my door late at night, coming home from her hospital shift. She would no longer be able to chide me for eating too much licorice.

But it was going to be fine. I was the woman who once chased down a tornado in my Dodge—watching as it chewed up the roof of a T.J. Maxx. I was tough. I just needed to get used to living alone. I'd always had my family, or a roommate or two, then Duke, and then Annie. It was natural to be nervous.

"Whatcha thinking about over there?" Annie asked, poking me with her toe. She always had a good radar for my mood shifts.

"I was thinking how much you're going to miss me and feeling sorry for you," I said, poking her back.

"I *will* miss you," she said earnestly, and quickly sat up. "Listen, I've got something to tell you. But you can't get mad at me." It was the same tone she used whenever she got on her soapbox about how I should try a neti pot when my allergies flared up. That *I'm right, but you're not going to like it* voice that, as her older sister, always annoyed the hell out of me.

"I'm already mad," I said.

She frowned. "No, listen. It's good. So there's this guy, a patient of mine at the hospital…"

"Annie, for god's sake, how many times have I told you I'm not ready for any dating nonsense?"

"No, no. I mean, he *is* quite handsome—and single—but no, that's not what this is about. Yet. He's a producer at WTXF in Philly." She put her bare feet up on the couch and took another sip of her drink. "He said he wants to talk to you. About a possible job. Once he gets out of the hospital and back on his feet."

"Is he in the loony ward?"

"Oh my god, you are impossible. No, doofus. He hurt his back. Doing some kind of work on his house or something. Nearly destroyed one of his vertebrae. It's not pretty, but he will walk fine again after rehab." She glared at me. "But did you hear me? This could be a good lead for you. A start-over."

"Yeah," I said. I wanted to be more enthusiastic, but I just couldn't muster up the energy. I imagined Annie bulldozing over her poor patient, trying to get him to agree to humor me with a talk. "Maybe. We'll see."

"We'll see?" Annie groaned. "I thought you'd be a little more excited than that."

"I'm thrilled," I said, and when she didn't react, I leaned forward. "Seriously. Thanks. You always look out for me."

"I do nothing that you wouldn't do for me in a heartbeat." She clapped her hands and sat up. "Now, to celebrate, we should play hide-and-seek!"

I made a face.

"Come on, it'll be fun. Don't you remember we used to do that in the beach house we rented as kids?"

I nodded. "Sure, yeah. When we were ten. But I'm too tired for nonsense games right now."

She scrunched her nose in disapproval. "Don't be a poo. This house is crazy. There are all kinds of places for us to hide." She threw her arms up like she was going to do jumping jacks. "Come on. You first." She pinched my arm.

"Ow," I said crabbily, rubbing my skin. "I'm not playing."

"One. Two. Three. You better hide, Mongoose. Four, five."

I got up, sighing heavily. "This is stupid."

"Six. Seven."

I walked out. Annie's bedroom was on the main level of the house and would require the least amount of effort. I went over to the far side of the room and slid in between the nightstand and the bed, crouching down and waiting.

I heard Annie call, "Ready or not, here I come," and felt it then, that tiny bit of excitement deep in my gut that I used to get as a kid whenever we'd pull out our Ouija board or say Bloody Mary in the mirror. Summon up the monsters under the bed. I bent over to look under the bed and make sure there wasn't a gremlin.

No gremlins, but there was a bunched-up piece of fabric. I fished it out and held a colorful silk head scarf up to the dim light. It had a green-and-blue paisley print that shone like a mermaid's scales. I loved silk and couldn't help but run my fingers over it. It seemed brand-new. Was it Annie's? I rubbed the scarf gently between my fingers and reached up and tied it around my hair like a headband, letting the long ends of the scarf trail down my back. I heard Annie coming. "I smell you, Mongoose," she said, and then she was in the room, flicking on the lights. She jumped on the bed and peered down at me from above. "Gotcha."

"You're so good at this," I said, standing up. "It's like you're a whole twelve years old."

"Whatever." She cocked her head. "Cute scarf."

"Is it yours? I found it on the floor."

"Nope. Finders keepers, though. It looks good on you."

I walked over to the mirror and stared at myself. It did look nice. Something different, anyway. Patty must've forgotten it. I told myself I would just wear it for a little while. That I could always get it dry-cleaned for her before she got back. She would never know.

●━━━━●

It wasn't until the end of the weekend, when Annie pulled out of the driveway, waving out the window as she disappeared behind the tall reeds, that my thoughts started to consume me.

"What am I doing?" I said aloud, rubbing my palms across my jeans. My voice seemed to echo in the tall expanse of the main room. The house, which seemed so luxurious that weekend, now felt too large and cold and imposing. A giant tomb.

I flopped down on the sofa in the living room with a novel that Annie had lent me. But I couldn't focus. I threw down the book, giving up, and started pacing. When I'd been on-air at WDLT, my schedule had been so hectic. Navigating unpredictable, rotating twelve-hour schedules, getting up at 3 a.m. for morning broadcasts, staying late to work on graphics, filling in for others—there was no such thing as a regular day. Duke had always complained that I didn't have weekends, even though when I was home on a Sunday, all I did was *interrupt* his sports-watching schedule. My mom and dad, my friends, everyone had always talked about taking it easy. *Don't burn yourself out*, they'd say. *Take a vacation once in a while.* But the truth was, I *liked* being busy. I thrived on having a project, a job, something to focus on. Maybe this job prospect Annie had mentioned would work out, but in the meantime, I needed to train myself to relax, get used to a new place, new surroundings.

Before I went to bed, I forced myself to walk around the house, to warm it up, in case it wasn't quite ready for me and I wasn't quite ready for it. I thought of my mother, who always liked to smudge new spaces with her weird sage sticks, "clearing the energy," as she called it, imagining her wandering around, jutting smoky wisps on the Worthingtons' Russian nesting dolls and decorative bowls. Part of me wished she was here. Annie and I had both pursued professions that soothed our logical, rational sides—Annie with her thermometers and blood pressure machines, me with my anemometers and weather satellites—and yet occasionally our mother's influence, her crystals and horoscopes and meditation, creeped in, as much as we resisted it. An ongoing joke between me and Annie involved blaming everything on "auras."

I stopped at the top of the stairs to the basement, looking down into the darkness. "Don't be a big baby," I said into the silence and walked slowly down. When I made it to the bottom, I immediately felt foolish. There was a strong smell of mildew, but the rec room was actually quite comfy with its large sofas and big-screen television. John had hung a British dartboard on one wall, and I could picture the Worthingtons entertaining friends or curling up under blankets with a bowl of popcorn to watch a movie.

No, I corrected myself. I could see *me* curling up under blankets here. I ran my hands along the back of the couch, leaning into it. This was mine now. At least, for the next few months. I turned and surveyed the room, nodding. Yes. And wouldn't Duke be surprised if he could see me now—living in a place that even his parents and their high-society lifestyle would be envious of.

A big TV. A fancy deck. A whole beach and ocean, for goodness' sake—and loads of time to take advantage of it all. I strode across the room, checking out all the books on the shelves and a stack of DVDs, when I was distracted by another piece of Jim Gund's art on the wall. I stopped in front of it. Another Ferris wheel, this time painted on top of torn book pages—a kind of mixed-media collage. The Ferris wheel, a bright yellow blur in motion, looked like it was going to spin right off the wall. There was something about Jim Gund's paintings that felt alive.

Something cracked through my thoughts then. I felt faint, and I had to grab on to the back of the couch for support.

I was his lobster baby—

A voice. A woman's syrupy voice, a hint of a laugh but somehow cold and sinister, too. With the combination of the damp smell, which seemed to be getting stronger, I felt a little ill. I shook my head to clear it.

Lobster baby. Where had I heard that before? A movie? Something someone had said to me? It was there, just around a corner of my memory, but it flicked away as soon as I tried to focus on it.

5

•——•

ALLISON

When you're married, you start to take certain things for granted. You get into routines, ruts, and the grooves run so deep and slick you might not even realize how hard it is to get out. Duke always paid our bills, filing them in neat piles in a teak organizer next to the KitchenAid mixer. He took out the garbage and killed spiders. He had driven most of the time we'd gone anywhere because I hated getting lost. He did most of the cooking, too—planning the meals, shopping for the groceries, picking out the wine. We didn't have dinner together very often because of our work schedules, but when we did I knew he'd take care of it. He enjoyed all that.

Unless Annie was around, my meals now consisted of packaged soup or Hamburger Helper or pasta with jarred sauce. But I was determined to be more health conscious at the beach. It was part of my resurgence—learn to cook. I'd even brought several books with me with intimidating titles: *Novice Gour-*

met, Fit and Flair, and the slightly demeaning, though vaguely satisfying, *Cooking for One.*

I made a delightful and thorough list of groceries—soy milk, chicken thighs, avocados, bananas, yogurt, eggs, wine, cat food—taking pleasure in adding foods that no one liked but me—lime Kool-Aid, whipped cream from a can, tuna fish—and dividing them all into categories so it would be easier to shop.

I turned on Patty's Keurig to fuel me for my first foray into town. If I listened to omens, then the grinding whir that came from the inside of the machine was a bad one. So was the blinking red error light. And the brown water that spit from the machine and splattered my white sweater before the whole thing died.

Okay, then.

Patty and John had left a list of local businesses on the refrigerator and had underlined Sweet Spot coffee as *the best.* I was skeptical it would be any better than my favorite Italian espresso shop in Philadelphia, but Keurig breakers couldn't be choosers, so in my car I went, surprising myself by remembering how to get downtown without using my GPS.

The town was so quiet I half expected tumbleweeds to start rolling in front of my car. I stopped at the Opal Beach Library and got out to check the meter. I was still reading the parking restrictions when Dolores's car pulled up behind me. I could hear Bruce Springsteen blasting even though the windows were closed.

"Don't bother," she said as she got out, waving her hand. She wore a snug-fitting, long-sleeved black T-shirt with Chicks Rule in silver across her chest. "No one pays during the off-season."

"But it says Monday through Saturday."

"Trust me. No one checks it now. That's just for the tourists." She rummaged in her car and came out with a bunch of large blank canvases from the backseat, juggling them and kicking the door closed. "If you get a ticket, come find me in there." She nodded at the gallery. Art—Jim Gund. "But you won't need to. I know Horace, the sheriff, and he treats the off-season like a long vacation."

"Thanks for the tip," I said.

"How are you making out up there in that house all alone?"

"Oh, I'm fine. It's colder than I expected, I guess. But I'm used to braving the elements."

"It goes up and down," she said. "In November we'll have some days where it feels like June. Just the way it goes."

I said goodbye to Dolores and headed across the street to The Sweet Spot. Inside, a woman stood behind the counter, cleaning up the mess from a coffeepot that had turned over on its side while she chatted over her shoulder with two customers. Country music was blaring—Dolly Parton singing about love—so the store seemed lively despite there hardly being anyone inside. A few wooden tables lined one side of the shop, and beat-up–looking canvas couches faced each other in the back. In the corner opposite the couches sat a turtle-shaped sandbox and a bunch of kids' toys. I lined up at the register.

"Right with you," the woman behind the counter yelled over the music and the humming of the coffee machines.

The two customers in front of me were talking loudly. The woman, short with painfully dyed blond hair, practically squawked, "Oh, sugar, you are just too much," at the policeman standing with her. She giggled and adjusted her tight suit, then spotted me and shuffled over to the side to clear room. I wondered if the policeman was Horace, the sheriff who treated the off-season like a vacation.

A large wide mirror hung above the wall behind the counter, and I could see myself in it, hunching over, a bad habit I'd adopted since going off-air. During broadcasts, the crew would always remind you to stand up straight, shove your shoulders back, but these days, without the need to force that winning smile, I often felt loaded down. It was starting to show.

I adjusted Patty's scarf in my hair and, just as I did, the woman behind the counter glanced up and saw me in the mirror. She froze, her eyes wide. She turned quickly. "Can I help you?"

The cop and the lady had also stopped talking, and I could feel their eyes on us.

"A latte?"

She fiddled nervously with her apron. "What size?"

"Large." The cop and the woman started chatting again, though I could sense they were still listening to us. Then, in the spirit of my new adventure, I added, "Can you put a little scoop of ice cream in it?"

She flinched, and now I knew it was not my imagination. I took a step back.

"Ice cream?" she asked.

"I mean, gelato. That stuff…" I wavered, gesturing to the containers lined up behind the counter. "Never mind, that's weird. Just cream and sugar is fine." I blushed, embarrassed. This whole trip into town was already exhausting me.

"You okay, sugar?" the lady customer asked, the smile on her face clearly forced. "It just—forgive me—you just seem a little peaked."

"I'm fine, thanks," I said. Her strong musky perfume overpowered even the chocolatey smell of espresso beans.

"Just visiting?" Her head cocked to one side in a way that reminded me of Bobo, the dumb parakeet we had as kids. I missed Philadelphia, or downtown Annapolis, where you could faint on a packed city street and no one would acknowledge you.

"I'll be here for a while," I said.

Behind the counter, a spoon fell and clattered against the tile.

"Well, if you're looking to buy, I'm your woman." She thrust out a manicured hand with vicious pointed nails. Each tip had a silver jewel in the center. "Mabel Halberlin." She handed me a slightly bent business card with her professional glamour shot on the front.

The cop chuckled. "Always the saleswoman."

I sat down at one of the tables, nervous. The barista—had she somehow recognized me? I pulled out my phone. The internet signal was spotty at the house but here I had a strong connection.

No new emails. Not a one. I couldn't tell if that was a good or bad thing.

My phone beeped with a text from Annie: This is the first day of the rest of your life!

I chuckled, and when I looked up, the barista was standing there, holding out my coffee. "You're her sister, aren't you?" she said.

"I'm sorry?" I shut off my screen and put my phone down on the table.

"Or a cousin?"

The surprise must've shown on my face. She breathed out heavily. "You're not...related to Maureen?"

I shook my head. "I don't know a Maureen."

"You didn't—come in here to see me?"

I took the cup of coffee from her and saw, with satisfaction, that there indeed was a lump of ice cream bobbing frothily inside it. "Everyone's been recommending your coffee. But I can leave..."

She burst into a short giddy laugh. "Oh god," she said, her shoulders visibly relaxing. "I'm so sorry. I thought you were—" She seemed bewildered. "You look—you reminded me of someone."

"Oh," I said, relieved myself. "I get that all the time."

I still sensed the unease in her face, but she seemed to be warming up. I'd thought at first she was young, but now I could see the fine lines around her eyes and the slackness in her neck. She had freckles, tons of them dotting her nose and cheeks. She was pretty now, but I bet when she was younger she'd been gorgeous.

"It's just so odd…she used to put ice cream in her hot chocolate. And your hair."

I pulled the scarf out and stuffed it in a ball in my hand. "I don't normally—I just found this."

"That's so…funny." She held out a hand that looked chapped, like she washed it a million times a day. "I'm Tammy." She was flushing now, her skin bright red beneath her freckles. "I didn't mean to be rude. She was an old friend… she used to wear her hair like that, is all."

"Oh. I'm sorry. Did you lose touch, then?"

"Something like that." Tammy's smile fell a bit.

"Have you tried to find her? I mean, with Google and Facebook and all—I found this friend of mine from elementary school that I hadn't talked to in decades. It's kind of crazy. And now, seeing all her nutty political posts, I kind of wish I hadn't found her, you know? You can almost know too much about someone these days." I was rambling. *Google her?* Had I really just given that advice?

"I couldn't find anything," she said. She bent over and started wiping my table with her dishcloth.

"Oh, don't worry about that. I'm not going to stay."

"Please do. I don't want to run you out." She put a certain *oomph* into the cleaning, using the weight of her entire body to scrub the table, working in straight rows across, not missing one centimeter of the surface.

"I'm not—you aren't. I was just, I have some errands to do."

"Just stay, at least to have your coffee. It would make me feel better, after the way I behaved." She finished, folded the cloth in a neat square and tucked it in her apron. "Are you in town for long, then?"

"I'm house-sitting."

"Oh really. Where?"

It took me a second to remember the name of the street. They all sounded the same. "Piper Sand Road?"

"Nice area up there."

"Beautiful. It's kind of crazy. I feel quite lucky."

"I bet." She smiled. "So what? Are you a writer or something?"

"A writer? No, no. I'm a meteorologist. A weather geek, my dad likes to say."

"Oh," Tammy said, her eyebrows raising. "That's really neat. On television?" She seemed genuinely interested, not in a fake way like the real estate agent had been.

"I used to be, yes. For a few years. You don't get that news here, though." I stopped, suddenly grateful that my former station wasn't broadcast this far up the coast. I'd been counting on the fact that my…infamy might not follow me to Opal Beach, and so far it had worked. I needed to be careful, though. I had a feeling in a town this small, one innocent Google search and my whole sad story would spread around like a bad cold.

"Wow! Still, you're famous," she said, and I tried not to flinch at her words. "At least by Opal Beach standards," she added. "Unless you count our mayor getting on some travel website's list of Best Small-Town Mayors—he was number 97—we don't really get much in the way of celebrities around here."

"Hardly a celebrity." And then, because Tammy was still smiling enthusiastically, I added lamely, "This is great coffee."

She seemed to snap back to life. "Well, let me know if you need anything else." She left to attend to a machine buzzing incessantly behind the counter.

My phone lit up again. It was Annie following up.

Don't have too much fun there, sis.

6

•━━━•

MAUREEN

Turns out Barron is useful for something. He and his friends know where all the good parties are. After I get off my shift at the carnival, I meet up with them. Sometimes the parties are in smaller beach houses with tiki glasses and coolers, old smelly rentals filled with college boys who eat cereal right out of the box. Or in fancy houses with long winding driveways and sculptures of nude women flanking the porch, one nervous boy or bunny wandering around encouraging people not to break things or fall off balconies. I swipe free food and drinks and occasionally a few dollars when no one's looking. The best parties are right on the beach, the spontaneous ones, where someone starts a bonfire and beer appears and it's that magic again.

Like tonight. No one knows what time it is. The ocean is a beast. She roars and complains, and the salty air makes my hair all fancy. I let it loose, drape it over my shoulders and arms and lean forward. Flick my imaginary tail. I'm a mermaid, just like my mom used to call me. *My little mermaid,* she'd say, brushing my hair until it shined, clasping in little plastic shell barrettes to hold it off my face. Back when things were good.

I stare into the bonfire's flames, trying to melt my mother from my mind.

"They say if you look close enough you can see every color of the rainbow in a fire," I say. I'm talking to the boy next to me, even though I don't know him. He seems startled I've broken the silence, and I smile slightly, but I still focus on the fire.

"Oh yeah?"

I nod, twist my hair off to the side and start braiding it. "I've found everything but green and purple."

We both sit for a while, searching for those colors. Instead the fire spits orange and yellow and black *snap pops.*

"Maybe it depends on what burns," he says. He digs into the sand and sifts the grains through his fingers.

Barron and his friends are down at the water's edge, a bunch of untrained puppies daring each other to do stupid things. This boy is also friends with Barron, I know, but he seems different. Gentler somehow. He's not interested in showing off, playing games, and I find his solitude strangely intriguing.

The fire warms my bare shoulders and my nose. I bury my feet under the sand and ripple my toes out.

"I'm Clay. Clay Bishop," he says. He's got long blond hair that he keeps tucking uselessly behind his ears, and from the way his legs are folded in front of him I can tell he's pretty tall.

A girl plops down next to me, kicking sand up on my skirt, but I don't say anything. I talked to her briefly before, when I was getting a beer from the cooler. She'd asked where I got my bracelet.

"You're wanted down at the water," she tells me now, slightly out of breath like she'd run all that way just to deliver the message.

"I'd go if you could tell me they even remember my name."

She widens her eyes at me. She's pretty—red hair and freckles all across her nose that I bet she hates to pieces but which make her seem dewy and sweet. She's wearing a ruffled off-the-shoulder crop top that completes the farm girl look, but the lines under her eyes betray her. She's not so innocent either. "They didn't say your name."

"Carnival girl?" I shrug to show it doesn't really bother me. "It's okay. You don't have to tell me."

"They can be such jerks. Don't even listen to them." She picks up a piece of driftwood and tosses it in the fire. "My friend Mabel has a mad crush on one of them, so I always get dragged down here. Right, Clay?" She sticks a toe out and nudges his thigh, but he just makes a noncommittal grunt. She's got a thing for him. I can see it in the way she kind of leans toward him, but if Clay knows anything at all about it, he's good at pretending otherwise.

"How do you two know each other?" I ask.

The girl laughs and tucks her leg under her. "You get to know all the Yacht Squats after a while."

"Yacht Squats?"

"Yeah." She shakes her head. "It's a term we use…sorry, for all the folks who live down here in the summer. You know, the ones with houses and yachts." She glances at Clay, tugs at her hair.

"Ouch," I say.

Clay looks up. "I don't own a yacht."

She swats at him. "Oh please. Don't act all wounded. You call us Townies." To me, she adds, "Clay and I used to work together at Stony's, over on the pier." She gestures behind her, toward the ocean. "One summer. Until he got it out of his system."

Clay raises his eyes teasingly. "I was trying to save up for my yacht, until my dad went and ruined it and bought me an airplane instead." The girl loses it in a flurry of giggles. "No," Clay continues, "what Tammy means to say is that I had crew."

"Oh god, *crew*," she says. "Like you're already in the Ivy League." She shoves him playfully, then thrusts her hand toward me. "Like he said, I'm Tammy."

"Maureen," I say, shaking her hand. "And as you may have figured out, I work at the carnival. Ten cents for your chance to take home a five-foot frog and see if he's your prince."

Tammy laughs, but Clay scrunches his face in disgust.

"Oh god, Yacht Boy, don't tell me you're one of those." I kick sand at him. "It's an honest living, you snob."

"Not that." He frowns and brushes the sand off his legs. "I just hate carnivals. I hate the rides. They make me sick."

"He won't even go on the Ferris wheel, can you believe it?" Tammy says. "The best ride there is."

I have to agree with her there. There's nothing like the very top of the Ferris wheel, that moment just before descending, when you can see everything and nothing at all. Feet dangling below you, the world in all directions. Outside the turning twisting machinery of the wheel, you could be flying.

"I'll try not to hold it against you," I say. "In fact, I know how you can make it up to me. My stomach's growling. Let's go get pizza."

"Oh," Tammy says. "I can't leave Mabel. She's down there by the water. She wants to go roller-skating, I think."

I stand up, stretching.

"You could come with us," she says. "Skating, I mean."

"Nah, not my bag. But that's cool. Clay will take me for pizza. Won't you, Clay?"

When Clay stands up, too, Tammy's face falls. Her eyes flick from us to the water.

"Oh, well, I guess it'll be fine if we come right back…"

I can tell she's torn, but I also know her decision has already been made. She just wants to feel less bad about it.

"Let's go," I say. "I could eat a horse."

We've all had too much to drink, but Tammy and Clay are way more gone than I am. Tammy's giggling into her fist, swaying into me. I feel like she's going to pull me down, and then we'd all be for shit. But it's funny, to see her so messed up. To not care. We both surround Clay and start singing a Bee Gees song, screaming it at the top of our lungs. Someone on a dark balcony above us starts catcalling. We wave into the blackness.

"You're going to get us arrested," Clay says, which gets us both giggling again. He's still carrying the pizza.

"Clay, you're the best. Seriously," I say.

"You just met me. You have no idea."

"No, I totally know these things."

"She totally knows," Tammy agrees. "Can we just sit down here and eat that?"

"You're a genius," I say, and before Clay can protest we're both on the curb in the parking lot of a hotel, grabbing at the box.

Tammy scoots over so he can sit next to her, but he chooses the other side of me, close enough that our legs are touching. I can feel Tammy's eyes on us and I shift away from him, even though I like his warm weight, and busy myself with selecting a slice.

"God that smells good," I say, and take a large, gooey bite. It is the best thing I've ever eaten. I lick my fingers and lean back, staring up into the night sky. Even with the parking lot's glaring lights, I can see so many stars.

Tammy needs to find her friend, so we go back to the beach, where it's clear the party has died. The fire's still raging, but only a handful of people are sitting around it. Some might even be passed out. Mabel is nowhere to be found, and Barron and his dopey friends are gone, too.

"Looks like it's time to go home," Clay says. He's got his arm around me, and he's still sipping out of the bottle of brandy he bought at the liquor store.

"Shit, she's gonna be pissed." Tammy paces the beach.

"I'm sure it will be fine," I say, tired and longing for my bed.

"I have to get home now. I need to make sure Mabel's there."

"You guys go," I say. "I'll be fine. Go."

"No, we'll walk you back first," Clay says. "It's on the way."

We walk back mostly in silence. Clay's in the middle, holding hands with both of us, but he keeps sending me these sideways grins like we're in a 1950s diner sharing a milkshake. Tammy keeps tugging us ahead, clearly in a hurry to get home to Mabel. Or to get me away from Clay. I'm not sure which.

We stop at the gates of the fairgrounds, and I'm embarrassed at the thought of the two of them seeing where I live. "Well, bye," I say. "It's been fun."

"We'll see you soon, yeah?" Tammy's wide eyes are now slitted, sleepy. She kisses me on the cheek. I'm taken aback by the sweet gesture.

"I'm sure I'll see you around," I say.

"You okay?" Clay asks. His forehead is creased with concern and he's looking at me like the dads at the carnival look at their kids who just tip over the top of the You Must Be This Tall to Ride measurement stick to ride the Whipper.

"I'm fine, *Pops*." I poke him in the side. "Go home. Sleep it off."

I watch them disappear, and once they've slipped into the shadows, I turn and walk the perimeter of the fence. In the back are the trailers.

Jacqueline isn't home. Sometimes when she knows I'll be gone she hangs out in Trina's trailer, playing board games and smoking clove cigarettes. I flick on the light. Our room is a mess. Both beds unmade, clothes strewn everywhere. An empty box of pizza from the other night smells like grease, and I make a note to dump it in the big trash bin outside tomorrow morning. Oh, if someone like Clay could only see this now. The Yacht Squat.

I fish out my favorite T-shirt—a faded gray V-neck with a yellow moon man face that says Blame It On the Moon—and pull off my tank top. As I turn to put it in my drawer, I see a face peering in the window. His head dips down quickly. I throw on my T-shirt and whip outside after him.

He's walking back toward his trailer, carrying a Super 8 camera under one arm. "Desmond," I yell, and he spins around, stares at me with dead eyes. "Were you just watching me?"

"Of course not." He's wearing a Tasmanian Devil T-shirt, red and faded, the devil's face scrunched up under his belt buckle. "Just making the rounds."

"I saw you in the window." I point at his camera. "Were you *filming* me?"

"Not worth the film," he says, smirking, and all the lines in his dry, scarred face crinkle up like worn leather. "Maybe you should keep your curtains closed. People might get the impression you want them to look."

He spits a squirt of tobacco juice. His eyes flick over my breasts, and it makes my back prickle. I consider kicking him in the crotch. There was a girl I knew back in Maryland who taught me some self-defense stuff. I remember her jaw set and hard as she demonstrated. *Grab it as hard as you can and twist it. No hesitation. You've only got one chance.*

"Go back to bed, little girl," he says. Maybe it's the drinks I had, or the way Desmond's looking at me, like I'm small, like I'm nothing, but I want this fight. To punch back at him.

"You owe me money," I say, sticking my chin up.

"What money?"

"Last week's. You didn't pay in full."

"I don't owe you shit."

"You mean you think I can't prove it, right?" I walk up to him, stare him down. His eyes drop down and he spits again. This close, I can tell he's been drinking. The smell of shitty stale beer. "Is that what you're saying? How do you think Clyde would feel about this? What if Clyde found out you go around sticking your neck in all our trailer windows at night? Filming the girls getting dressed. What do you think he'd say about that?" My heart's slamming against my chest but I stand my ground, waiting.

"You think you're special, don't you?"

"I want my money."

Desmond's eyes narrow and he grabs my arm. I try to pull away and he jerks me close. I can see the tobacco juice gurgling between his teeth and it makes me gag. "I paid you what you're worth."

"Excuuuse me! Hello? Is the fair still open?"

We both jump, turn. Desmond drops my arm, and I back away from him. Clay is standing nearby with Tammy, swaying like he is extra special drunk. He keeps his eyes on Desmond. "The fair? I want to ride on the roller coaster." Clay makes this gesture with his hands, up and down imaginary

hills. Tammy dissolves into nervous giggles and falls to her
knees. How they got inside the gates is a mystery, but I am
relieved to see them.

"Who the hell are you?" Desmond advances toward them
and then stops, looking back at me and then again at them like
he's worried we're going to pounce on him from both sides.
"You kids need to get your drunk asses out of here."

"They're my friends," I say. "And they'll call the cops if you
don't leave me the hell alone."

"I have no interest in you, you little bitch," he says. "I have
no time for this bullshit." He turns and walks off toward his
trailer.

"I want my money," I call at the back of his head. "You
goddamn pervert."

We watch him until he slams the door behind him, and it's
not until then that I realize I'm holding my breath.

Clay is concerned. "Who is that guy?"

"My boss."

"Did he hurt you?"

My arm still stings from his grasp, but I shake my head.

"Shit. Why didn't you tell us?"

"I can handle him."

"We knew something was wrong and Clay said we needed
to follow you to make sure you were okay." Tammy says this
with confidence. "Clay found a part of the fence back there
that's broken, so we were able to climb through."

"Good job, Sherlock Holmes," I say.

"But we were right," Tammy says.

I can't look at Clay, but I feel his eyes on me.

"That guy's bad news. You need to quit," Clay says.

"It's my job."

"Get another one."

"Oh yeah. I'll just polish up my résumé and send it around

to a few law firms tomorrow." I glare at him. "Doesn't work like that, Clay. Different world."

"It's not that different."

I think about telling him about those times I'd come home from school to find my mom and her friend Gwen passed out on the couch or so high they were chasing imaginary paper airplanes around the room. "Miles different. Whole planet different. Trust me. You don't need to save me. I'm fine."

"Well, you can't stay here tonight at least. I'd be crazy worried," Tammy says. "I have a sleeping bag. You can crash in my room. I insist."

Tammy shouldn't be asking strangers back to her place. We could rob her, piss all over her carpet. It's been known to happen. But she links her arm through mine, like we're best friends. Like we're going to skip all the way back to her place and exchange Care Bears.

The famous Mabel sits up on the couch and glares at Tammy as we walk into the apartment. Mabel is the kind of bunny that thinks she's really hot, but she'd actually be a lot hotter if she laid off the orange makeup and thick mascara.

"Where were you?" she huffs at Tammy, all wounded eyes and pouty lips, crossing her arms at her chest. "I was worried about you."

"I'm sorry." Tammy sits down on the couch next to her and attempts to give her a hug. "I thought we were going to be right back. I didn't realize—"

Mabel cuts her off and looks at me. "Who are you?"

"Maureen," I say, giving her a cool stare back. I'm in no mood for a petty fight with this bunny after my encounter with Desmond. I feel like I can still smell him on me, and I try not to shudder.

Tammy's rattling on. "Maureen and Clay and I went to get pizza, we were hungry, and it took longer and I couldn't believe everyone had already cleared out when we got back."

Mabel peels her eyes from mine, as if not interested in the battle either. "Oh rad," she says scathingly to Tammy. "I should've known it had something to do with Prince Clay."

Tammy flushes. But to her credit, she ignores Mabel's jab. She sets her purse down and sits back. "Well, how was your night? Anything good happen?"

Her move works. Mabel drops the mean act for a moment, flinging her hair back behind her, and turns on a gushy voice. "Ted and Barron tried to throw me in the ocean."

"No!" Tammy seems to play her game.

Mabel nods. "They did." She giggles. "It was kind of cute, actually. I think Ted likes me, maybe, but I don't know. Like, after that they all wanted to go roller-skating but I was like no way because by the time we all got down there it would be like last skate and I'd be done with that."

"So you guys exchanged promise rings and he gave you his jacket and you swore on your momma's best pie pan that you'd stay true to one another forever and ever?" I can't help myself. I even manage to smile through Mabel's cold stare down.

"Who the hell *are* you? I've asked several times, but not gotten a real answer." She looks over at Tammy, who stands up, halfway between us, unsure what to do to make it all better.

"I told you—"

"No, I mean, why is she *here*, Tammy?"

Tammy sputters.

I save her. "I needed a place to stay for the night and Tammy said I could crash on her floor. No worries, I'll be gone before your pretty head gets up in the morning." I follow Tammy into her room before Mabel decides to hurl something heavy at my head.

●━━●

When I wake up the next morning, a Duran Duran poster is staring down at me, judging. My brain is pulsating in my head. It's nine o'clock. I've got an internal clock. It's my magic trick. Tell me what time you want me to wake up and I'll get it within five minutes.

Tammy's place is not a dump, but it's nothing glamorous either. She's got the bigger of the two bedrooms, given her steady job at the manufacturing plant about fifteen miles from here, and pays ten dollars more a month for that privilege. Her room is decorated in various shades of neon, and there are so many clothes and shoes spilling out of her closet it looks like she's been ransacked.

The fair opens at noon on Sundays, early bird special for the bratty kids, but I have to get back to help Clyde start his cleaning at ten.

Tammy hears me rummaging around and rolls over on her bed, props her head up with her arm. "You okay?"

"Yeah," I whisper. "Go back to sleep. I need to get going."

Tammy yawns, stretches and squints down at me. "I can see about getting you a job at my work," she says. "If you want."

"Thanks for letting me crash. I owe you one."

"I love your hair," she says. "I've always wanted long hair, but I can never seem to grow it beyond a certain length."

"It's a big pain to deal with. I often think about shaving it all off."

"No! You can't do that. It's so perfect. Here, wait." She gets out of bed, goes over to her dresser and starts rummaging around the top drawer. "I got this years ago, and it never worked." She's wearing a T-shirt and men's boxers and this all feels very intimate, like I've known her my whole life, like we are children up early after a sleepover party. I can tell Tammy's the kind of girl that has seven best friends forever and would do anything for them. They'd gun the engine and she'd get closer to the middle of the road to make sure they had better aim when they plow over her. I'm not the type to get that close to anyone, but I admire it. And maybe sometimes envy it.

She turns around, holding a piece of fabric in her hands triumphantly. "Try this."

"What is it?"

Tammy comes over, kneels down on the floor and fixes it on my head, looking serious. I stick my tongue out at her, but she ignores it, and I feel self-conscious. "Okay, check it out," she says, sitting back on her heels.

I get up, my body unhappy with me. I need to pee, my bones ache, my mouth is dry. In the dim light of morning I see myself in Tammy's mirror, her scarf cradling the top of my head like a headband, the ends of it dangling below my shoulders.

"It looks so good, doesn't it?" Tammy says. "Take it. You should have it."

"I'm not going to take your scarf." I slide it off my hair. It's silk, sort of paisley, and beautifully soft. I fold it up in my hands.

"No, please take it. It just sits in my drawer. I can't wear it. I look like I'm ready to clean my house, but on you it's… exotic. Bohemian."

I laugh. "Well, that's me, I guess. A wandering hippie."

"No, no. Oh, I'm getting everything wrong."

"Thank you," I say with a rush of gratitude. "I'll keep it forever."

"Oh, stop making fun." She blushes.

"No really. They'll have to bury me in it."

7

ALLISON

So this was how the other half lived. I felt ridiculously privileged. Even Duke's family had nothing on the wealthy families of Opal Beach. The overcast days that plagued my first week had finally moved on, and in their wake came eye-blinding sunshine. I spent my days mostly outside on the beach, enjoying the wide expanse of untouched sand.

I embraced the chill in the air, preferring it to the unbearable humidity that was the beach in high summer. My sister owned coats that weighed more than she did, but I'd rather suffer for a few minutes than be bogged down by puffy jackets, scratchy scarves, clothing that made me feel like the Stay Puft Marshmallow Man.

The ocean was alluring—those roaring waves and the salty smell that seemed to follow me everywhere. I took selfies, sending the best ones to Annie, who always responded with near glee. The beach is doing you good, she'd say, or, Save some sunshine for me, you wench! On the warmer afternoons,

I'd run to the surf, kick off my flats and let the water rush over me. I'd sink my feet into the cold sand until I couldn't bear it anymore and had to run back up to wrap my frozen ankles in a towel just so I could feel them again.

I slept late, read a lot and watched a few movies, blatantly ignoring all of John Worthington's to-do lists. Those opaque windows crusty with sea salt could wait. I'd get to the power washing. Eventually.

Late one afternoon, I changed into my sneakers and went for a run. I was celebrating two weeks at the house and, as usual, had the beach to myself. Not another jogger or dog walker in sight. It was mid-October, heading quickly into that dead of winter where everyone hunkers down, closes blinds and opens dampers for the raging fires.

I ran close to the water's edge where the sand was hard, getting into the zone, increasing my speed. The rhythm of my sneakers hitting the sand, the wind snapping at my face, felt good and right. I could feel myself beginning to relax, could feel my muscles, which had seemed to tighten in defense over the last year from stress and exhaustion, unwind. Loosen. It was possible that I could do it—get back to the old me.

I ran faster, gasping in the cold air that froze the back of my throat. It was nice to feel anonymous. To be just a person, any person, out on a jog. Duke and I had run together when we'd first started dating. He'd always hated that he couldn't keep up with me, and I'd been annoyed that I'd had to go slower to appease him. We had finally stopped trying—I'd continued solo while he'd claimed he enjoyed going to the gym more. Then after we married, he stopped doing that, too, becoming doughier with every beer he downed. Maron could have him. She could bake him in her oven and watch him rise, rise, rise.

You're still so young, my friends—the few who'd remained after the divorce—liked to say reassuringly. *You can find some-*

one else. They'd meant well, of course, but with that sentiment was an underlying assumption—that I needed someone else to be happy again.

They'd gotten it all wrong. And that was why I'd had a hard time staying in touch with anyone over the past year, why I'd politely declined the trickle of happy hour and baby shower invitations from former coworkers, silenced my Facebook friends, stopped answering text messages. It was easier to say no than to deal with the well-meaning but hurtful platitudes, those sympathetic side-glances, the earnest *are you okays*.

An endless line of monster houses dotted the coast, but I focused on the pier ahead of me. I could see the giant crab on top of my neighbors' restaurant, lit up in red, brighter as the sky dimmed. And next to that, sprawled atop the long arcade building, a giant clown lay on its side, waving red hair wild around its head. *Crab and clown*, I remembered Dolores telling me. Behind the clown, the silhouette of the mega Ferris wheel loomed like a skeleton, shut down for the season.

I must've run a few miles before I realized I should turn back. The sun hung low, an orange balloon bobbing on the horizon. It was getting chillier. The houses all looked the same. I was surprised at how dark it had gotten so quickly. I ran faster, my breath curls of mist in my face. What if I couldn't figure out where to turn up the beach, which of the many dunes would take me back? What if I got lost? I didn't bring my cell phone with me. And even if I had, who could I call?

But it turned out I didn't have anything to worry about. When I got back, although it was dusk, the house was easy to spot between the two larger homes. My calves were sore as I trudged up the dunes, out of breath. I pulled Patty's scarf out of my pocket and tied it around my head to keep my hair out of my face.

The light from the next-door neighbors' house helped guide my way in the rapidly darkening evening. I stopped as I got to the top of the dune and looked up at their house. A giant window framed the dining room table, and the family was just sitting down to eat. There were three of them—an older woman, shiny gray hair pulled into a soft bun at the nape of her neck, was helping a little girl with her food, while an older man sat at the other end of the table, sipping wine. What I could see of the house seemed elegant—modern decorating, a funky blue glass chandelier, gray slate walls.

Something inside me ached as I stood there watching them, still catching my breath from my run. The everyday way they went about their dinner—pouring their wine, cutting the little girl's meat, waving their forks to emphasize a point they were making as they talked. Everything I'd wanted for so long—a nice house, a family, something to come home to. And now? It made me feel very alone.

8

MAUREEN

"Where's Tammy?" I stare at Clay, surprised. He's all alone, his hair half-wet like he's just taken a shower. When he turns, thumbs shoved into the back pockets of his khaki shorts, I can see a few nicks on his neck where he cut his skin shaving.

The last couple of Friday and Saturday nights, ever since I ditched Barron, I've been meeting up with Clay and Tammy—a party here and there, but we've also taken to just wandering up and down the pier or scurrying out onto the beach with a six-pack of beer. I've come to look forward to it. But seeing Clay all by his lonesome tonight feels different. Not surprising, actually. Just different.

"Her mom wasn't feeling well. She told me to come anyway."

Tammy's mom gets sick sometimes. I'm not sure what's wrong with her, and she never seems to want to discuss it.

Before I can open my mouth to ask Clay more, Desmond

shows up, doing his last-round call. "Time to pack up and move on here," he growls, staring at us with disdain. "You all cashed out?" I hand over the box, and he holds it between us for a few seconds. I'm grateful Clay's standing right there. "It better be straight, kid, or I'm coming after you."

"Let's go," I say, glaring at Desmond's retreating back, and sling my small purse over my shoulder.

It's one of those unbearable summer evenings where the temperature never drops even after the sun goes down. Still, it feels a few degrees cooler as we get closer to town, away from the funnel cake fryers and neon lights of the carnival.

I turn toward the pier, where we usually walk, chat, maybe grab a piece of pizza or a beer. But Clay stops. "Uh, I was thinking," he says, tapping his sandal against the curb.

I stop and face him.

"My parents aren't home tonight if you want to go there and listen to music or whatever. They've got good liquor."

It's no secret that Clay's gone for me. It's the way he looks at me even when he thinks I don't notice. That's the key you know. If you can catch someone looking at you without them knowing it, you can tell a lot about their true feelings.

"Oh, I don't know, Clay."

"What?"

I can't help but find his flustering adorable.

"Well, a girl might think a boy inviting her to his house is an indication of something else, is all. And, well, I know how Tammy feels about you."

"About me?" His eyes get large. "Maureen, seriously."

I poke him in the side. "You're a dodo," I say. "You know very well what I'm talking about, and I have to say she's a good friend of mine. I don't want to piss her off."

"She's the one who told me to come get you!" He pulls out the rubber band that's holding back his hair and it comes loose, falling around his face. I have the urge to kiss him, so I lean up and plant one on his cheek.

"What—what the heck was that for, then?"

I smile. "You're cute when you're embarrassed."

He shakes his head and smirks. "I don't understand women."

"I'm not a woman. I'm a mermaid." I start walking in the opposite direction. "So how do we get to this fancy house of yours?"

"My car's this way," he says. "But, Maureen—"

I turn.

"I can't help who I like. Tammy's a great friend and all…"

"She's great. Pretty. Sweet. Totally righteous. I'm just a mess."

"You underestimate yourself, Maureen."

He puts his hand in mine. But already the cards have been shifting this way.

⊷

There's no yacht, but his house is breathtaking. It's right on the water, and there's a big back wooden deck right off the dunes. It must have at least six bedrooms. There's a real chandelier in the dining room, and in the living room, these awesome round orange crushed-velvet stools fresh from the days of disco. I walk around, petting things—a shaggy maroon pillow, a fancy chessboard, a heavy brass eagle statue that's tacky as Graceland but probably cost a hot sauce.

Clay switches on a tall floor lamp and slides open the deck doors. It's a beautiful night, so clear you could probably see Jupiter if you knew where to look.

"What is that?" I say, pointing at the strange tarp blowing in the breeze next to his house. It's an empty lot filled with construction, a half frame of a house in progress.

"They're building this whole place up. Drives my mom and dad mental, as you can imagine. They've had all this to themselves for years, and now they're squeezing in as many houses as they can here."

I can sympathize. The view is amazing.

Clay steps back inside and we peruse his game cabinet, whipping out a checkers board. As we lie there on the living room rug, I can hear the surf crashing even over Joe Jackson on the record player.

"So where are your parents?" I ask as he sets up the pieces.

"At some party." He squishes his nose together. It's a tic of his I've noticed that he does whenever he's disgusted with something or disagrees. "They won't be home for a while, don't worry."

"I'm not worried," I say, and leave it at that. There's lots I don't want to talk about either.

"How about your parents? They care that you're traveling with the carnival like this?"

I laugh. "No, they don't care."

He stares at me. "Where are you from?"

"Originally? I guess Maryland."

"You guess?" He peers at me with concern. He is such a superhero in training. "And are your parents still there?"

I shrug. Then I poke him with my toe. "It's your turn." I point at the board. He makes a bad move, clearly not paying attention, and on my next move I steal three of his pieces. He doesn't even seem to notice.

"Do they care that you travel around like this?"

I sigh dramatically. "You're assuming they know."

"So you ran away?"

"Clay! Is this an inquisition? I don't really want to talk about it. It's a sad story. No one wants to hear the sad stories."

"I do."

I ignore him and roll onto my back and stretch my arms above my head. Clay moves over, puts his face above mine. He kisses me, lightly, on the lips, like he's testing the water of a cold swimming pool. It's pleasant, sweet, and I find myself pulling his head down again. A deeper kiss this time.

"I like you," he says.

I smile, close my eyes. "Clay."

"I like how you say my name."

"Clay," I say. "Clay, Clay, Clay." I'm cut off by another kiss.

We get up, tumble onto the couch. Kiss some more. He hikes my shirt up and I say, "Hold up, tiger. Should we do this here?"

"We can go up to my room." But he's trailing his tongue down my neck. I look up at all the little brushed patterns on the ceiling, like someone tried to do snow angels up there. I wiggle my hand down his shorts and cup him, but instead of seeming pleased, his body immediately freezes up.

"What?" I say, sitting up.

"Nothing, sorry. It's just—this is miserable, but I don't have any…you know."

"Any what?"

I watch the blotches of red creep up his neck. "You know. Protection."

I raise one eyebrow. "Weren't you a Boy Scout?"

"Do you want me to go get some?"

I make a face.

He leaps up. "I'll go. I'll be back. Just—stay right there. Don't move."

⊷━━━━━⊶

While he's gone, I straighten up my clothes and walk around the house again. I'm not snooping, but I'm not *not* snooping either. I open a few of the cabinets. In one I find a roll of money in a drinking glass, lots of tens and twenties, and I can't help myself, I slide one of the tens into my pocket. They will never notice it's gone, but it could feed Jacqueline and me something besides pizza or microwave soup one night. Clay would give it to me if I asked him, anyway.

I end up on the back deck, wishing I had a cigarette. I think better when I'm smoking. Clay's questions got to me. Images of my mother keep flashing in my head despite my best attempts to swat them away. She's a sad sort of woman, was chronically depressed before anyone knew how to diagnose it. My grandpa managed to keep the very terrible parts of her sadness at bay. He kept us going—making sure I did my homework, had a lunch packed. Everything was fine, normal enough, until he died five years ago. Then she lost it. The "clouds," as she called them, came back, and the only way she thought she could keep them away was with pills, then other stuff, until she dumped us both into a nightmare that no one who lives in a giant beach mansion like this one would ever understand.

Sadness descends on me like a heavy wool blanket. It's suffocating, being surrounded by all this beauty, knowing I'll never be part of it. Clay's sweet. I like him, probably too much. Soon he'll tire of the prize, too. And then what?

Could I be wrong? Maybe Opal Beach isn't my destiny. I pace the deck, tracing my fingers along the wind-worn wooden railing, feeling the pricks of exposed wood splinters against my palm. It's bothering me that my intuition might be off—that I've been distracted somehow. Foolish.

I see a figure coming up the dunes. His light-colored pants billow in the wind and he carries a matching jacket over one shoulder. His tie's trying to escape from around his neck. I'm startled when he walks right up to the lawn toward the steps of the back deck. He's like Jay Gatsby, I think.

"Hello there," he says slowly, drawing it out.

"Hello."

"To what do I owe this pleasure?" he asks.

He watches me with an amused smile, a lazy cat batting halfheartedly at a mouse.

"Destiny." It's the first thing that pops into my head, and it's stupid. I blush, glad it's dark so he can't see.

He sprawls on one of the lawn chairs, legs spread, looking up at me. "Is that your name? Destiny?"

"Maybe."

"So you're one of Clay's gals, huh? He's beneath you."

My face gets even hotter.

"Where is he? If I were him, I'd not let you out of my sight for a minute."

"Oh god, you're laying it on thick, aren't you? He's out getting cigarettes." The lie comes to me quickly and I like the sound of it.

"Cigarettes? My lord." He pats his pockets, pulls out a pack and hands me one. I lean forward and he lights it. "See? A true gentleman always has cigarettes on him."

"Who are you?"

He sighs, like he's bearing the weight of the world on his shoulders. "I'm Joseph Ezekiel Bishop, but you can call me Uncle Joe."

"I like Zeke better."

"That's what most people call me. It's like you know me so well already."

"Where were you coming from?"

He flicks his thumb at the beach. "Down at the club. Poker game. I lost my shirt. Well, not literally, but might as well.

Also drank too much. Can't drink too much and expect to win at poker. My fault. Decided to walk it off on the beach."

"Poker? So you're a gambler?"

"I like to say I'm in 'risk management.'"

I roll my eyes. "So do you play regularly, then?"

"There's always a game going around here somewhere."

"You should take me sometime. I'm very good at poker."

Zeke laughs. "They would eat you alive, Destiny." He looks past me, into the house, and I turn to see Clay walk in through the front. "Looks like your boyfriend is back."

"He's not—" I stub out my cigarette on the deck railing and walk inside. The air-conditioning feels refreshing.

Clay looks like a deflated balloon.

"What's wrong?" I ask, but I figure it out when the door opens again and a middle-aged couple comes in behind him. A tall man who I guess is his father, thin like Clay with the same nose and eyes, though his hair is salt-and-pepper and cut close. Clay's mother is wearing sparkly heels and a green dress I'd knock out my molars for. It's like she just stepped out of *Dynasty*, all attitude and big gemstones and an Alexis Colby kind of danger-glam glint to her. They're chattering, but they stop when they see me.

His mom's eyes flick over me like they would over a speck of dust in the shower stall. She sets a take-out container on the dining room table and pulls off her heels. "Your father and I are quite tired, Clay," she says. "Please don't stay up too late. Remember you have practice in the morning."

"Mom, Dad, this is my friend Maureen," Clay says miserably.

As they assess me once more, Zeke slides open the deck door and steps in, his dress shoes in hand. Mrs. Bishop's face gets even harder, and her nose twitches like she's smelled something rotten. I am relieved the attention is off me.

Zeke smirks and waves. "Ah, well, it looks, Destiny, like you get to meet all the Bishops tonight." His voice fills the room. He walks over to the take-out container that Clay's mom set on the table and opens it. Selects a piece of chicken and eats it with his fingers. "You kids have fun?" he asks Clay's mom.

"Don't you have your own entrance to this house, Joseph?" she says cooly, staring him down.

Not fazed, Zeke shakes his head. He gestures at me. "It's this little lady's fault. She dragged me up from the beach." He shrugs. "Don't worry. It won't happen again."

9

ALLISON

A couple of mothers sat at a small round table near the turtle sandbox, which didn't actually have sand in it, while their two little girls played. I took a table on the opposite end of the shop, pulling out my laptop, relieved to see the strong internet signal pop up at the top of the screen. I hadn't seen that for days at the house.

Tammy came around from behind the counter, retying her apron. "Oh my god, I'm so glad you came back. I've been thinking about you." The door opened and a group of customers swarmed in. "Let me take care of them, okay? Do you want the same thing as last time?"

I logged in to my email while I waited for my drink. Annie had been nagging me to update my résumé and email her producer-patient, which required both internet and coffee. She seemed confident that her lead would work out. Vaughn is eager to see your résumé! she'd texted me the day before. But did my résumé even sound good? I'd lost all ability to judge myself. And what would I say when a potential employer asked why I'd left my last job? Once Vaughn (which sounded like the name of a villain from a 1980s movie) figured out what I'd done, would he change his mind about giving me a chance?

Still, I went through the motions like a dutiful sister, sending Vaughn a friendly but professional email and attaching my résumé as promised. I hope to hear from you soon! I wrote, then replaced the exclamation point with a period and hit Send.

Patty had written, asking how everything was going at the house. How's my Catarina? John says the basement smell might just be dampness. He says you can run the floor fan to air it out if you want. Yes, I'm so sorry, the internet is properly terrible. We've all complained. They give us a new reason every time for why it's so weak. I hope it's not too inconvenient.

I logged in to Facebook, but there wasn't much to check. Since the incident, I'd only kept the closest of friends and family in my circle and changed my privacy settings so that I wouldn't even show up if someone searched for my name. I considered posting a photo of the beach, but I was afraid that someone who shouldn't know where I was would find me.

Tammy was still busy, so I checked the television station's website and saw smug Ms. Brittany, my replacement as meteorologist, on the home page. She wore an Easter-pink sheath dress, a bright attempt to hide the fact that her forecasts were not as accurate as mine had been.

I knew I shouldn't take it out on Brittany. It wasn't her fault. I was once the Brittany. The young perky meteorologist hardly able to believe my good luck at snagging a job at a local major news station. I shouldn't take it out on Duke's mistress, Maron, either—my other replacement in life—although she was as thick as a concrete slab. She was young, too, and I'm sure Duke put on all the charm—

"How's house-sitting treating you?" Tammy stood above me. "I'm sorry. I didn't mean to scare you." She handed me a coffee with a scoop of ice cream in it.

"No, no, it's fine." I quickly closed my laptop. "It's good. The house, I mean. But the internet doesn't work so well, so I feel a little cut off. Weird to be in such a big place by yourself."

"I bet. Those houses out there are as big as city blocks. You're near the Bishops' place, aren't you?"

"Right next-door. You know them?"

"I know just about everyone around here." She smirked, then fiddled with her bangs. "Grew up here, so I've pretty much seen it all."

"I'm house-sitting for the Worthingtons."

Tammy nodded. "Dolores told me." She paused, then took a seat across from me. "I've been thinking about you. It must be lonely staying up there by yourself."

"Oh," I said. "It's okay, I guess."

"Opal Beach is not exactly a bustling metropolis, especially in the off-season." She smiled shyly. "But there are some fun things to do. Would you maybe want to hang out sometime or something?"

"Sure," I said slowly. Her eagerness was a bit unsettling— I wasn't used to people seeking me out to do things. But it was also nice to be asked. It would be good to have someone to talk to. I missed Annie's constant presence. Hanging out with a stranger could be horribly awkward, of course, but it wasn't like I had anything better to do. "I mean, my schedule is pretty free. Except for trying to find a part-time job."

Tammy's eyebrows shot up. "During the off-season?" She threw back her head, letting a peal of laughter burst from her lips. Like a little kid. It was right from the tummy.

"Okay, well, that doesn't sound very promising. So what did you have in mind?"

"I don't know…wait! Yes, I do. Well, maybe. If you're up for it. Are you up for an adventure?"

I shrugged. "It's my middle name."

She clapped her hands together and made a squeal. "Awesome. Dolores has a bout on Friday."

"Is she a boxer?" I thought of her tattooed, muscled arms.

Tammy laughed again. "Oh gosh, no. Roller Derby."

"Roller Derby. Huh. I've never seen that before. Interesting."

"It's great. You'll love it." She stood up, slapping her dishrag against the edge of the table. "Dress casually. We'll go out for drinks after. It'll be fun."

* * *

On my way out of Tammy's shop, I noticed an old man standing next to the driver's side door of my car, hunched over as if examining something in his hands. His face was anchored with a dark puffy beard and he wore a dirty, oversize navy blue sweatshirt. The knit cap perched on his head came with a tassel on top that made him look a bit silly. I hadn't seen any homeless people in Opal Beach yet, but every town must have them.

I approached cautiously to avoid startling him, but he seemed deep in concentration. I coughed, fumbled around in my purse to find a few dollar bills. In Philadelphia, the homeless often gathered in pockets near cars, hoping people would offer up some loose change.

The man finally fixed his eyes on me. He was smoking, and when I caught a whiff, my eyes raised in surprise.

"Medicinal," he said, unashamed. "Helps my joints."

He took another hit, still taking up rent in front of my car door. His sweatshirt collar was frayed, and the front had Opal

Beach Surf Shop in fading print across the chest. He seemed in no hurry to move.

"Do you know," he said, "that building right there has been flooded out and gutted no less than four times and is still standing? You can see the waterline right there from the last time." When I didn't comment, he looked over at me. "Not used to the beach in winter?"

"I'm sorry?"

He pointed at my hands. "No gloves. No hat. I'm guessing you're not from here."

I blinked, taken aback by his candid tone. "I suppose I stick out."

He gave a short cough, a puff of smoke bursting from his nostrils. "Nah. Just teasing. My daughter Dolores tells me I'm not funny at all, but I sometimes forget she's right."

"Oh," I said. I dropped the dollar bills I'd been clutching into my sweater pocket. "Dolores is your daughter? You must be Jim Gund? The artist?"

He put a dirty finger to his lips. "Shh, don't tell anyone. I'm sure I owe someone money." He offered me his joint, and I shook my head quickly, scanning the road. There was no one in sight, but smoking marijuana in public still didn't seem like the smartest thing to do. It would be just my luck to get arrested during the first month of my "new" life.

"I'm house-sitting for the Worthingtons? Up on Piper Sand Road? They have your art all over their house."

"Good people," he said. "Patty makes a mean deviled egg." He took a slow suck on his joint and exhaled it above our heads. "Yeah, they must have, what, I think five pieces of mine now."

"They are very striking. I love carnivals, Ferris wheels, all that stuff. I guess in the summer the pier really gets busy?"

"Oh, that wasn't the pier." He narrowed his eyes. Standing closer to him now, I could see the deep creases in his face, cracked like dried clay. "That was a traveling carnival that used to come through here. Back in the day."

I could sense that Jim Gund was one of those people who absorbed the history of a place, the kind of guy who, if you let him, could spend hours telling stories down to the tiniest details.

"The beach evolves. The ebbs and flows. I try to capture it all." Gund took another hit on his joint. He would've been terrible on television, a nightmare interview for the reporters. The kind of guest that prefers slow, deep thoughts over soundbites. I imagined Marty, our cameraman, sweeping his arm to signal we only had forty-five seconds before the next commercial break. "Back in the day that carnival was the thing. Came for years, as predictable as the tides. Then they had some scandal in another town—one of the owners killed a young girl. Beat the hell out of her, raped her, whatever. The works. Real scumbag. They tried to get another carnival in here, but it never caught on the same, you know?"

"That's horrible," I shivered.

"Eh, was probably good in the end. Made way for the pier folks—gave them more business." He dropped the stub of his joint on the curb and crushed it with his paint-speckled boot. "Anyway, I'm heading back in. Want to come see the gallery?"

"Oh, I'm sorry. I'd love to. I definitely want to stop by while I'm in town. But I've run out of cat food." I held up my car keys.

"Ah, yes. Can't keep those felines waiting." He smiled crookedly and pointed at his sweatshirt. "Surf shop has hats and gloves if you need 'em."

10

·———·

ALLISON

The Roller Derby "rink" was a taped-off oval in the middle of a smelly basketball court at a local rec center. Women in skates, looking like they could kick my ass in three seconds, rolled around chatting with one another, adjusting their helmets, pulling up tights and neon striped leg warmers. I spotted Dolores right off. She waved and made her way over, her bright purplish hair tumbling out of the back of her helmet. In her tank top and shorts, all her magnificent tattoos were on display.

She gave Tammy a big hug and then me, too. It was like hugging the weightlifter I'd dated briefly in college—if it hadn't been so loud in the gym, I probably could've heard my ribs crack.

"You a virgin?" she asked me, nodding at the rink.

Tammy answered for me, proudly. "First time."

"You're in for a treat, then." She adjusted her helmet strap.

"Join us after? We always go to Crenshaw's. Tammy'll fill you in." She skated away into a huddle with her teammates.

There were only a couple dozen people in the audience, but they were vocal. When Dolores's team—the Manech County Vixens—was announced, the cheers were deafening, echoing off the gymnasium walls. Derby names were a big thing—all the women had them stenciled on the back of their jerseys. Dolores was called Spine Cracker. "She has her master's in library science. Get it?" Tammy said.

Sitting in the front row of a Roller Derby bout is like standing on the fault line during an earthquake. The women rumbled past us quick and close, causing the old recreation center's wooden floor to tremble. I couldn't help but wince each time they circled, certain one was going to slam out of bounds, skates careening in the air, and end up in my lap.

Tammy tried to explain the game to me. Roller Derby was all about blocking and lapping, as I understood it. We were supposed to watch out for the skaters with the stars on their helmets. They were the ones who could score. Every time they passed a pack of blockers, they got points.

Dolores was vicious on the rink, crouching low and striking fast. I wouldn't want to meet her in a dark alley. When she tripped someone who went sprawling, knocking over three of her teammates, the crowd erupted.

"You're supposed to make yourself as small as possible when you fall," Tammy said over the referee's whistle, elaborating on the nuances of strategy and penalties and such. "So that was bad for the other team."

"She's really good," I said about Dolores, my nerves fading away as the excitement of the game took over.

"Dolores is the oldest member of the team, I think," said Tammy. "Or close to it. She keeps saying it's her last year. This might finally be it. She almost broke her wrist last month, and I think that gave her a big scare. She talks about coaching."

The pack was a blur. It was glorious to watch them, to feel that deep rumble of the gymnasium groaning under their wheels, to absorb their fast, chaotic energy, their thighs fat with muscle, their faces tense, dripping with sweat. These women were a force. The gymnasium was alive with the short bark of referee whistles, the sound of hard elbow connecting with jaw, knee, the tender part of the lower back. I could taste that metallic scent of blood as they spat into the corners of the court, could feel the bruises as though they were blossoming on my own upper arms. I still didn't completely understand the game, but I was swept up nonetheless.

"How come you aren't playing?" I asked Tammy. "You clearly love this."

"I tried out once. I was terrible. No, totally terrible," she said, glancing back and forth between me and the skaters. When the referee stopped the game, Tammy focused on me again. "I used to roller-skate when I was younger, you know? We all did. It was the thing. So I thought it would be easy. Not easy. Not for me."

"I'm definitely not tough enough," I said ruefully.

"Oh, I don't know about that," Tammy said, her face getting softer. "Remember that woman I was telling you about? My friend who disappeared? She was big into roller-skating. We used to go all the time."

"Oh my gosh, me, too," I said. "We used to skate around the rink trying to make eye contact with all the cute guys. My friend Edie and I spent most of our middle school weekends at Roller Dance."

"It was definitely the thing to do back then, wasn't it?" Tammy said, but I could tell she was still thinking about her friend.

"I'm sorry you lost touch," I tried. "But I bet if you really looked into it, you'd find her. It's hard to hide these days, with all this technology, you know?"

"You're sweet," she said. "But I won't ever find her."

"Well, that sounds ominous." I laughed, nudging her with my elbow.

But Tammy didn't smile back. In the blur of it all, in the echoing chamber of the Roller Derby bout, surrounded by all the energy, I could swear for a moment that a dark cloud of anger had crossed her face.

But then the moment passed, and Tammy turned back to the bout, cupped hands around her mouth and shouted for Dolores.

⎯●————●⎯

Crenshaw's Inn was nothing like an inn. It was small and dark, loud, stinking of smoke and filled with old men drinking beer out of frosted mugs. One of those new digital jukeboxes played Journey. Large wooden booths with high backs lined the rear of the place, and in the middle, people sat on barrels over small tables.

Dolores and her teammates arrived soon after we did, crowding up the bar. One of the skaters lifted up the back of her shirt to show off a purple bruise the size of Texas. A couple of men at the bar admired it, but when they saw Dolores glaring at them, they turned back around.

"Hey," Dolores said, giving Tammy a hug. "Thanks for coming."

The other skaters noticed us and made room in their circle. "So what did you think?" asked a small blonde who went by Flossy Fiend.

"It was great," I said. "You guys were amazing." It felt odd being up close to all the women now. I wondered if it was hard to come down after a game.

"It was too close for my tastes," said the woman with the Texas-sized bruise. Her derby name was Miss Misbehavin', but I'd heard someone else call her Mary.

"It wasn't that hard," Flossy said, her New Jersey accent shining through. "They were wobbling like wind-up Mc-Donald's Happy Meal toys." She imitated it, rocking back and forth, then giggling. "All it takes is a little shove."

I chuckled. "Well, I thought it was awesome. Really."

"So this is your first time in Opal Beach?" Flossy asked.

"We used to vacation near here. But I particularly like it during the off-season. It's lovely."

Dolores snorted. "Hardly."

"It's a shitty town," Tammy agreed. "We're allowed to say that, though, since we've been here for so long." She laughed. "My mom says I need to be more positive."

"Tammy, whatever you do, don't listen to your mother," Dolores said snidely.

A loud fight broke out on the other side of the bar. Everyone turned their heads, and the bartender had a word with the two guys who'd started it. They rolled out into the night, still drunkenly muttering to themselves. Dolores shook her head. "Tourists."

"Dumbasses," agreed Flossy.

"I can imagine that you guys are relieved after the tourists head out for the summer," I shouted over the noise.

"Most of them are stupid as hell, but they're our bread and butter," Dolores said.

"I make more in one month during the summer than I make during the entire off-season," Tammy added.

Dolores smirked. "Like we said, this town is shit."

I leaned back against the bar. It felt nice to be out, to be in the middle of something. Like I belonged. Like things were normal. "Oh come on. It's a great place."

"Slap some sand and some sun on anything and it'll look pretty, but don't venture too far off. You want to talk inequity? Let's talk inequity. Opal Beach has it all. The top 1 percent run everything, and the rest of us can just suck it up." Dolores was clearly in a groove, like these were talking points she'd been over time and again. She gestured to herself and Tammy. "And we're the lucky ones. Just once try driving past Ventura, circling through some of those neighborhoods. Then the pretty beach town won't look so pretty anymore."

"So why do you guys stay, then?" I asked, more to make a point than anything else. Everyone complained about their hometowns, but many stayed. Grass is always greener.

"My mom needs me," Tammy said, and Dolores rolled her eyes. "Otherwise, I would've gone a long time ago."

I nodded. "With your friend?"

"What friend?" Dolores piped up, and something in her tone made me pause.

Tammy stared at the ground. "No one."

"Tammy?" Dolores was focused intently on us now. "Oh lord, not this again."

"Just forget it," Tammy said, flustered.

Dolores looked at me and shook her head slowly, mouthing the word *no*. I felt my face get hot. Had I done something wrong? I scanned the room. The bar had grown more crowded, and the two guys who'd been interested in the derby women were now focused on two pretty girls at the other side of the bar. They had identical chunky highlights and long bobs and were furiously typing on their cell phones while they tried to talk to one another and sip what looked like Long Island iced teas from pink straws.

"Anyway, you need a beer." Dolores tapped one of her

teammates on the shoulder and asked her to get the bartender's attention.

We jostled around newcomers, and Tammy and I ended up on the outskirts of the group. She was going over the names of all the girls for me again when Dolores finally made her way through with three frosted mugs of beer, distributing them amongst us. Tammy held hers out for a toast, and we all clinked glasses. "To new friends and old," Tammy said. I felt a warmth go through me, even though it was cheesy.

Dolores drew in almost half of her beer. "I used to be able to do a couple of bouts in one weekend. And now I can barely move for days after one."

I laughed. "You talk about being too old for Roller Derby? Try working on television. Then you'll feel ancient."

The alcohol had settled in my head like a nice, light mist, and I felt comfortable. The pretty girls at the bar were now talking with a tall guy. He hunched over, probably to hear them better over the noise, nodding, and placed his large palm on one's back and started rubbing it.

"They only want perky blondes willing to stand out in the rain and giggle and do water balloon fights on air for charity." I drew circles with my finger in the frost on the side of my mug. "Once you turn thirty, they start watching you for wrinkles. Start telling you what to eat."

Dolores shook her head. "I could never deal with that."

"Well, we're even, then. Because I could never do what you all do out there."

"Oh, sure you could," Dolores said.

"No way. I'm not tough enough."

Mary overheard and poked me surprisingly hard in the arm. "Sure you are, honey," she said loudly. "Anyone who can tell off her husband on live TV is tough enough to push a few broads around on skates."

That drew the other girls in. "What's this?" Flossy asked.

I chuckled, an automatic response, but I felt my guard go up.

Mary pointed at me, but I stepped back so she wouldn't jab me again. "She told off her husband on-air while giving the weather."

My face burned up. How stupid of me to believe I was now somehow anonymous, fooling everyone. To think I could hide here.

"Wait, I remember this." Flossy snapped her fingers, oblivious to my discomfort. "You're the Weather Girl?" She pretended to open an umbrella. "What did you say? Something like, 'you might treat women like broken umbrellas, but you won't be using me anymore in stormy times.'"

"Disposable," I corrected.

"Okay, let's drop it, girls," Dolores said, but her voice was drowned out.

"Yeah! I remember that," one of the other girls said. "Brilliant. This girl's a hero." She held up her drink, and it sloshed out of the side of her glass.

The bar—which just moments ago had felt festive—now seemed too loud and harsh. I half expected the jukebox to come to a screeching halt, a spotlight to center on me. Here I was, congratulating myself on being "normal," all the while the entire room knew all about me.

Tammy grabbed my arm. "Come on, let's go outside."

We headed out through the back door to a small outside patio that was probably popular in the summer months but abandoned now that it was so cold. It was quiet, though, and I was relieved to be away from the crowd. Tammy led me to a small table in the corner and we sat under a heat lamp that didn't do much to stave off the October chill.

"I'm sorry. It's a small town, you know? Things get around."

"So you all knew?" I groaned, smacking my hand against

my forehead. "I should've known I wouldn't be able to be some anonymous person. Not so soon."

Tammy's red hair was glowing under the harsh neon lights on the bar's building. Above her, the remnants of the summer spiderwebs glittered. The lights cast strange shadows over her face, but her smile was warm. "I thought you were brave for doing what you did," she said.

"The thing is, I *knew*. I knew something was wrong. But every time I confronted him about it, he made me feel crazy." I felt my eyes well with tears, and I brushed them away impatiently. "I felt like no one was listening to me."

"I know exactly what that feels like, Allison," Tammy said quietly. "I'm sorry you had to deal with it. All of it. He deserves everything he gets."

"Well, he got to keep his insurance job, keep his girlfriend and move on. I got fired and lost everything. Talk about justice."

"Why am I not surprised?" Tammy asked. "Men are mostly scum, aren't they?"

I was taken aback by her tone. "You sound like you know."

She shrugged. "I've never been married, but I know what it's like to be burned, let's just say that."

"I'm sorry," I said.

She waved her hand at me. "I didn't mean to start in on me. This is about you. I'm just saying I know how you feel. And it sucks."

Behind us, the bar door swung open violently, and the tall guy and one of the girls I'd noticed earlier stumbled out. Their voices stabbed the night, interrupting the intimacy of my conversation with Tammy. They didn't even notice us in the corner, too concerned with slamming up against the back wall and kissing fiercely. I looked at Tammy and rolled my eyes, and she giggled into her fist. I coughed loudly to announce our presence, but the couple seemed to be in their own little world.

Then something changed between them, and the girl tried to shove the guy back. The tall guy snickered and pushed her back against the wall. "Come on, don't be a bitch."

The girl's face was obscured in shadow, and I couldn't help but think of Kristen Gernstein, the sophomore who'd gone missing my senior year of college, last seen late night at a bar. Her friends had left her flirting up a guy, and every weekend night afterward that year, we were bombarded with warnings to arrive in groups and leave in groups.

"Excuse me," I called, standing at the same time. "Do you two need anything over there?"

The guy glanced at us with irritation. He flicked his eyes up and down, assessing me first, then Tammy. "It's okay, honey. Have a good night," he said, and turned back to the girl.

I heard Tammy say something behind me, but I didn't catch it. In the harsh light I focused on the guy's checkered dress shirt, half untucked from the back of his jeans. Something about that sloppy detail made me act.

I moved closer. "You guys, okay?" I asked innocently, but with a little more edge. "It's cold out. Wanna come back in?"

The guy rotated his head. "You my mother?"

The girl took that moment to squeeze her body from between him and the brick wall, stumbling on remarkably high heels, sweeping her highlighted bangs from her face. "Asshole," she blurted at him, stomping past us. I caught a glimpse of her face up close, the smeared mascara and the rosy red cheeks.

The tall guy glared at us. "Mind your own fucking business, bitches." He hocked and spit into the gravel, then followed the girl inside.

"Well, that was pleasant." I wrapped my scarf around my face and breathed in through the wool.

"Shit like that happens all the time around here."

"Happens all the time everywhere." I thought about Kristen, all those grainy photos of her in the newspapers. And the one night a few months after she'd disappeared, when my friend had torn me away from a soccer player I'd been dancing with at a club. She'd wanted to leave, and I hadn't. We'd fought in the parking lot and all the way home. I'd been convinced she'd made me miss out on the love of my life. The police had found Kristen's body a week later, in a ditch about a mile from our campus.

I was shivering now, more so from my interaction with the couple than from the weather. Everything seemed so fragile, as if tragedy was just snaking around us, ready to strike.

"Hey, look, it is freezing out here. Would you want to come to my apartment?" Tammy pulled her keys out of her bag. "It's just a few blocks away from here. I can make us some coffee."

11

·———·

MAUREEN

July 1985

It's Tammy's birthday, and Clay's promised us a big night out in Jasper: it's a neighboring beach that skews a little younger, a little cooler, than Opal Beach, with bars that sell sweet frozen drinks in big plastic fruit-shaped containers and offer up glow-in-the-dark body paint so you can draw butterflies on your chest that will flutter in the black lights of the dance floor.

Clay's been away for a few days at a crew tournament and then Clyde had me on double shift at the carnival, so I haven't seen Clay or Tammy in nearly a week. We've become quite the threesome, and it's rare we go this long without hanging out. It's a Monday night, so all of the best places will be closed, but none of us care. Clay knows of a band playing and says we can take his daddy's convertible, open beach air, top down, driving fast over the bay bridge. We just need to do his daddy a small favor for the privilege.

Bishop's Seafood is the most famous local chain in these

parts, and the original restaurant is near all of Opal Beach's family hotels and the Jolly Timber miniature golf course, overshadowing a small enclave of insurance companies and real estate agents. There's a giant crab statue near the front entrance, which I make Tammy pose with me in front of while Clay reluctantly takes a picture. He's clearly unhappy to be here, in the kingdom that is his family's biscuits and butter, and I slide my hand in his and rub his palm with my thumb.

"So do they crown you immediately upon entering and kneel down to praise your name?" I whisper in his ear, trying to lighten his mood as we walk into the over–air-conditioned building. But he shrugs me off.

Clay leads us inside, past the hostess stand where a young girl with crimped hair and big yellow hoop earrings chews on a long fingernail. It's early evening, before the dinner rush, but a few families are already there for the early bird special. Wide walkways and plenty of booths attract families with tiny, sticky children pegged up in wooden high chairs with flimsy plastic shark bibs. It smells like fish and saltines. Over the speakers, jaunty pirate music plays, and the waitstaff balances large black trays filled with steaming crabs, clams and oysters.

Clay settles us at a small booth near the kitchen doors. There are newspapers scattered on the table and an open paperback romance novel flipped upside-down to save a page. The hostess walks over, snatches it off the table, and carries it back to her stand.

"She's pleasant," I say. "We should get her to sing 'Happy Birthday.'"

Clay slings a heavy arm around my neck and squeezes lightly, but I can tell he's still on edge. "We won't be here long," he tells us, surveying the place. "I need to get the menus from my dad and we'll be on our way."

They've just redesigned the menus, and Clay's dad has dangled the convertible car keys in Clay's face in exchange for us driving out to the Jasper branch of the restaurant chain to drop off a couple boxes there.

"I'll go see if he's in the back." He gets up, pushes through the swinging doors and disappears.

Tammy picks up a crossword puzzle, studying the clues. With a pencil from her purse, she starts filling in the grid, twirling a lock of curly hair, and I briefly wonder if maybe she doesn't want to be spending her birthday, of all days, here with us, a third wheel. How much happier would she be if it were her shoulders that Clay had been rubbing? But then Tammy looks up, catches me staring at her. "You okay? No sadness on my birthday, lady. Got it?" I snap out of it and toss a paper straw wrapper at her.

Clay's dad takes that moment to wander by from another part of the restaurant, his light blue dress shirt rolled at the sleeves and unbuttoned enough at the top that I can see a few dark chest hairs poking through. He whistles as he walks past us, then stops. He points a finger at us. "Are you two here with Clay?"

I nod, point at the kitchen doors. "He's looking for you."

Mr. Bishop flashes a million-dollar smile. "Wonderful timing. Dean just needs to box them up and you'll be on your way."

He stands behind Tammy and watches her work the puzzle for a moment. Then he bends down, pointing at one of the clues, and murmurs something I can't make out. Tammy laughs. From across the table, I can smell his cologne, something woodsy and strong. It reminds me of my grandfather, his head stooped over the low-hanging light at our old kitchen table, tinkering with some broken appliance, his hands dotted with grease. I shake the image loose.

"Think about it like in Ancient Greek terms," he says to

Tammy, his head bent so low I can see my reflection in the lenses of the sunglasses perched on top of his head.

"Oh! Vessel," Tammy says, scribbling. Mr. Bishop pats her on the back. He's still resting it there when Clay comes back.

"She's a smarty," Mr. Bishop says by way of greeting his son. He straightens up, cracks his knuckles and points at Clay. "Puzzles are good for the brain. She's got the right idea, son."

"Stop hitting on my friends, Dad."

I laugh. Mr. Bishop shakes his head at me. "This is what I put up with all the time. Can you believe it?"

"It's an utter shame," I say.

"He and his mother gang up on me all the time. I'm lucky I have a thick skin." His smile dims again when he meets Clay's eyes, and he holds up his hands in surrender. "Okay, okay. I'll go check on Dean."

Clay flops down next to me with that deflated look he seems to get whenever he's around his parents. "Sorry. He's the worst."

"He's not that bad," I say.

"You don't have to live with him."

"I could work with him, though." I spread my arms across the back of the booth. "I could be a waitress. Be on your payroll."

"Oh yeah, there's something to aspire to," Clay says with a sneer.

I raise an eyebrow. "Oh, so sorry. I forgot that service jobs were beneath you."

"Oh god, Maureen. Don't turn everything into a social statement. I just meant you'd always smell like fried shrimp. And I'm the one who'd have to smell you." He sticks his nose in my neck, sniffing my hair, all over my face, and I squeal, shove him away.

"Stop it, you fiend." I smack at him playfully. "You should

be more grateful for all this. It's what gets you your fancy shoes and your convertible night out and your ocean view."

"Okay, *Mom*," Clay says, trying to stick his face in my neck again, and this time when I shove him he nearly falls out of the booth.

"Come on, guys." Tammy frowns at us, tapping her pencil against the edge of the table. "No picking fights. It's my birthday. And this place is lovely. Maureen, you're lovely. Everything is lovely. It's a great honor to own your own business. Be your own boss. That's the way—" She stops midsentence, her face draining of color as her eyes gaze behind me.

"What?" I say. I check behind me, but all I see is the hostess greeting an older woman who just walked in. I turn back. "What's wrong?"

Tammy is clawing her way over Clay and out of the booth. She rushes toward the hostess stand. The woman has shifted a bit, and now I can see that she's wearing pajama pants and carrying a large plastic bag.

"Who's that?" I ask Clay.

He shrugs. "Her mom."

"Tammy's mom? Do we need to help her?"

"She always looks like that." Clay picks up the newspaper and starts reading.

"Wow, you're just full of compassion."

"What?"

"Get out of my way. Now. Get up." He stands, newspaper all aflutter, muttering to himself like an old man. I ignore it and push by him.

Tammy's mom has thin arms and a mop of curly gray hair that's greasy and tired. Up close, she seems fragile, almost transparent, like a hearty gust of wind would send her off to Kansas. "I just wanted some food," she says to Tammy in a small voice, and I realize she seems scared.

"Tammy? Can I help?" I ask.

"No, you can't help," Tammy nearly shouts, then catches herself. "I'm sorry, Maureen. Everything's fine. I can handle this."

"Are you Tammy's friend, dear?" She smiles weakly but warmly.

"I am," I say. "It's so nice to meet you Mrs. Quinn."

Tammy is about to melt. "And we could all sit down and have tea and cookies, except that Mom's supposed to be across town at her therapy group in forty minutes."

"I guess I got confused," Mrs. Quinn says.

"Well, I can't drive you," Tammy says, her voice getting higher by the minute. She's drawing attention from some of the other patrons. "I don't have my car here."

"It's okay, Tam, sweetie. You go enjoy your birthday. Don't let me ruin it. I'll just go next week."

"You can't, Mom. It took me forever to get you in there. You need to go. And there's no way you'll be able to get back on the bus in time."

"Tammy, we can just drop her off when we leave," I say.

"We can't. It's in the complete opposite direction. Besides, we won't all fit in the convertible. Shit," she says, fists bunched together in frustration. "Shit, shit."

"Tammy, I don't mean to be a burden on you," her mom begins in a watery voice. She reminds me of my mom then, those birdlike eyes, the shifting fragility, and I feel something shatter inside me. I just want to make it all right, for Tammy's mom, but also for Tammy, who I can see is about ready to burst into tears. The panic wells inside me—I know that feeling, the helplessness. Wanting to do something but not being able to, not knowing what's right. And the anger. The anger, that *I shouldn't have to take care of you* feeling. *You should be taking care of me.*

"We can call a taxi," I say gently. "There's still time."

"The group meets in Enidville," Tammy says. "It would cost, like, a fortune. I don't get paid until Friday."

"I got it," I say, waving my hand. "Mrs. Quinn, what did you want to eat?"

"Hush puppies. They have the most delightful hush puppies here. And the butter sauce is just wonderful."

"Maureen—" Tammy pleads, but I ignore her.

I ask the hostess to put in an order for hush puppies to go and call a taxi for us. To her credit, she doesn't give me any lip or even ask any questions. So there are perks to walking in with the boss's son.

"Maureen, I can't let you do this," Tammy says, her face red with embarrassment. "It's like your whole pay."

"It's no problem, Tammy. Please. Let me." I usher them outside into the sun. The brightness reminds me of Mr. Bishop's easy confidence, and I try to tap into that. "It's all going to be grand."

But Tammy's fretful, her face pinched with worry. "No, no. Absolutely not. I'm paying you back."

We wait, Tammy's mom sitting on a bench, Tammy pacing, checking her watch every five seconds. Even I worry the taxi isn't going to get here in time for Mrs. Quinn to make her meeting, which would be a total waste of everything. But then just as Clay brings out the hush puppies, all packed up, the taxi arrives. As Tammy helps her mom inside, I explain the situation to the driver.

"That'll cost you about thirty-five dollars." He sizes me up. "Plus tip," he adds a little desperately.

"No problem," I say, and open my purse. I have four tens, my entire budget for the rest of the week. I fold them in half and hand them to the driver. "Here you go. She needs to make it there by six thirty."

Clay comes over. "Do you need money?"

"I got it."

"You sure?"

I touch his cheek. My irritation with him has melted away in all the nervous energy of helping Tammy. "You're sweet. Thank you. But I'm good."

Just as Tammy closes the back door of the taxi and steps to the sidewalk, Mr. Bishop pushes open the restaurant doors with his shoulder, carrying two boxes of menus. "Everyone ready?" He spots the taxi driving away. "Did you call that?"

"My mom needed a ride to a...doctor's appointment," Tammy says quickly, her face scarlet.

"You should've told me," he says. "I could've put it on the restaurant's tab."

"Oh, that's very nice of you," Tammy stammers, "but we're fine. Thank you."

Clay takes one of the boxes and follows his dad to the convertible. When they are out of earshot, I frown and say to Tammy, "I guess it's easy to be generous when you're rich."

But Tammy's eyes are misty and she tackles me with a hug that nearly knocks me over. "Oh, Maureen. Thank you. You didn't—" She stops, choked up.

"Oh, come off it," I say. "You would've done the same."

"That was the nicest thing anyone's ever done for me," she says. "Honest to god. I'll never forget it."

12

ALLISON

Tammy's place was small, one-half of a duplex, but cozy. While Tammy busied herself in the kitchen with the coffee, I sat on a maroon couch that had seen better days and set my purse down beside a scarred coffee table piled with magazines and books. She'd lit a Duraflame in the fireplace, which felt toasty after the cold, windy night, and I got up to stand closer to it, warming my hands.

"I like your place," I called to her, studying the framed pictures on the mantel. Tammy with Dolores and the Roller Derby team. Tammy in front of the Statue of Liberty. Several photos of Tammy and an older woman with Tammy's same tight curls but a dull grayish white. She seemed pale, ghostly, compared to Tammy, thin and fragile, her hand always resting on Tammy's shoulder as if for support.

Tammy came back to the living room with two large mugs. I made a mental note not to drink the whole thing or I'd be up all night. "You look just like your mom," I told her.

She picked up a photo of them in front of a Christmas tree. "You think? I can never see it."

"Totally. You have the same eyes." I walked back to the couch and noticed a small card table in the other corner of the room with a half-worked jigsaw puzzle. "Oh wow, you like puzzles? My mom loves them."

"Yeah, it's a hobby." Tammy made her way over, studied the pieces for a moment, then selected one and placed it with a snap into the puzzle frame. "I've done them ever since I was a kid. I like the really hard ones, too." She pointed at a framed painting of a lighthouse on the wall behind me. "That one took weeks."

"That's a puzzle?" I stepped over to the wall so I could see the tiny lines of interlocking pieces. "It's huge. Must've been a thousand pieces."

"More like two thousand, I think. My friend Maureen and I did that one. That summer." Tammy sipped her coffee. "Sorry, she's just been on my mind. Ever since you walked into the shop, actually. Something about you…" She trailed off.

I snorted. "I have that generic television personality kind of face."

Tammy got pink. "No, I wasn't saying that! I just meant that— Oh, I'm always getting things wrong."

"I was just joking, Tammy." I nudged her playfully with my elbow. "Seriously, thank you. I loved going out tonight. It was nice, really nice. Thank you for asking me. You're a good person."

"I don't much feel like one," Tammy said in a resigned tone, looking down at her toes. She said the next thing so quietly I almost missed it. "If I was, I would've been able to save her."

"Save who? Your friend?"

"Yeah. Maureen."

"Save her from what?"

Tammy reached out, laid her hand on my shoulder just as her mom had in the photo on the mantel. Her eyes glittered in the firelight. I couldn't tell if she was tearing, or just tired. "You know how you were saying you just knew? With Duke? That something was wrong? That he was cheating on you? It's the same with me. I know. I know something bad happened to Maureen. I just *know* it."

"Oh, Tammy, I—"

"She never made it out of Opal Beach, Allison. I can feel it."

The mood had shifted in the room. The warmth of the fire felt more suffocating, the walls felt closer in. The hairs on my arm prickled, and I shifted away. Tammy's hand fell back to her side and she turned from me, sunk into in a small leather chair. I went over to the couch and set my mug down on her coffee table. I was fumbling for what to say.

"Did you—did you talk to the police?"

It took her a moment to answer. "I tried to get them to do something when she disappeared. But they said they see this stuff all the time. They said she probably ripped someone off and left town fast. They told me I was lucky it wasn't me."

"But you didn't believe that?"

"Never. Allison…" Tammy took a deep breath and looked me dead in the eye. "I think she was murdered."

The word echoed in the apartment.

"Oh god, you must think I sound crazy, going on like this." Tammy tried to laugh, but it came out wrong, sounded more like she was trying to dislodge a cough drop from her throat. "I'm sorry. I didn't mean to lay it on you like this." She pulled at her curls.

"No, it's just—I guess I'm just…shocked," I said. Murder in Opal Beach? I couldn't imagine it.

"We had become really good friends. She wouldn't have just left. Without telling me. Without saying goodbye. I filed a missing person's report when she didn't come back to the apartment, but everyone kept telling me she— Oh, I'm getting ahead of myself, aren't I?" Tammy picked at a chip in her mug. "Maureen was—well, I met her one summer when she was working one of those traveling fairs. You know, the kind that come in for a few months in the summer and then leave to go on to another place?"

I recalled Gund's story about the traveling carnival. *The dead girl.* "Dolores's dad was telling me about that carnival," I said carefully. "He said there was...trouble?"

"Trouble?"

"Yeah. Something sketchy with the managers or something? Is that what you meant?"

"No. No. If there was trouble, it was with the people who live *here*," she said bitterly. "Everyone in town was glad when that fair stopped coming, said it was better for the pier. They called them 'carnies,' like they were some kind of circus freaks." Her eyes flashed with anger. "It was just a job, like everything else."

"Yeah, but you know, a job like that, it's easy to go off the radar," I said delicately. "Could be she went on to another town and something... Maybe she got married and changed her name?"

"I guess it's possible. But Maureen wasn't exactly the type to settle down, at least, it didn't seem like she was. I mean, we had a blast. She and our friend Clay and I hung out all the time that summer. And she lived with me and my roommate, Mabel, for a while." Tammy paused. "Wait, I have a photo of her."

Tammy ran upstairs. When she came back, she thrust an eight-by-ten photo in my hands. "Dolores found this photo in her father's stash. He took a million photos of Opal Beach back in the day. That's us."

Two teenage girls, angled so you could see them posing for a boy with a different camera. Behind them a sign proclaimed, Mermaids for Sale. Tammy was easy to spot—those same curls, the freckles prominent even at a distance, those large doe-like eyes. Maureen was taller, her long dirty-blonde hair tied up in a scarf similar to the one I'd found under Patty's bed, though a different color.

"She—well, she's very beautiful."

Tammy rubbed a finger across Maureen's image. "After that night, there's no trace of her. She just…vanished. I asked Dolores to look into it." I remembered—the Spine Cracker. Dolores would have the library skills to research Maureen, at least. "Nothing in real estate, no phone number or address or Facebook page or anything like that. That's not normal, is it? But Dolores just blew it off."

Dolores *had* acted strange at the bar when I'd mentioned the friend. That exaggerated *no*, her eyes wide. Like she was trying to warn me off.

"I guess some people like their privacy? Not everyone is a viral video star," I said, my sarcasm coming off weaker than I'd hoped.

"She'd had a bad life. She came from nothing—like me." Tammy pushed her hair back from her face, and I could see her hands trembling. "She never told me what it was, but she was running away from something and trying to make the best of it, and when shit like that happens to you, well, you don't always make the best choices. But that doesn't mean she's not worth anything. That no one should care."

Of course. *Disposable.* I felt that familiar anger bubbling up. It was true what I'd said on-air about Duke—the world treated women as if we were umbrellas. Pretty and useful for a time, but once we started showing our age or became cumbersome, it was time to toss us aside and move on.

"I'm so glad you came here, Allison. It's—nice to be able to talk to someone who's outside of it all, you know?"

I knew exactly what she meant. Annie, Duke, my parents. The only people I'd had to talk to over the last year were people who were intensely immersed in my problems. "Yeah," I said. "It's almost a relief."

Tammy's eyes welled up. "I haven't been able to talk about any of it for so long. No one understands. But I can't shake the feeling that something… Maureen was so vibrant and funny and good-natured." Her voice caught. "She had her whole life in front of her. And then—" She broke off. "It's just so strange how quickly things can change, isn't it?"

13

———————

ALLISON

"So how did it go?" Annie asked, her voice too chipper for so early in the morning. "Did you have fun?"

"Yeah," I said carefully. "Yeah, I did."

"You must've. You were out late enough."

I'd texted Annie when I'd gotten home from Tammy's apartment. I'd had a hard time sleeping, though it had been so late. The caffeine, for one, but also everything Tammy had told me. Carnivals. Small town secrets. Murder. In the early morning light, with the distant soothing sound of the waves coming through the walls of the house, it all felt like some weird nightmare. But the purple stamp with the inexplicable word *XTRAMP* was smudged in the middle of my left hand, my proof of purchase at the Roller Derby bout, and my hair smelled of the wood smoke from Tammy's fire.

"I wasn't out all that time. We went back to her house to chat."

"On the first date? You slut."

I laughed, rolling over in bed, appreciating the luxury of having nowhere to go, nothing to do. "I feel bad for her, Annie. She seems sad. She started telling me this story—"

"Oh no," Annie interrupted. "No, no, no. You have no time for sad right now, Mongoose. You need to think positive. Prep for your big interview this week."

"I know—it's just—"

"You've got this, sis. Trust me. You just have to focus. Remember, this is your chance. I can feel it."

So I did focus, as best I could. Over the next few days, I researched Vaughn's station, wrote down some potential questions and practiced my answers. I prepped forecasts in case he asked, taking care to check current Philly conditions against the models. As I worked, my brain fell back into that mode. It was like doing a cartwheel, jumping rope, driving a stick shift—once you learned, your brain never forgot, it settled back into that comfortable groove, the satisfying buzz of working, executing. I went to Tammy's shop when I needed a good connection, tapping into whatever models I could—the ECMWF, the Global Forecast System, the NAM. I didn't have access to all the models that WDLT had, but I could find enough data on my own to feel confident that if Vaughn asked, I'd be able to hand him a forecast I could stand behind.

Tammy didn't bother me much, except to refill my coffee, but I could sense her hovering, waiting, could see the way her mouth parted slightly when I looked up, like she was about to say something but stopped herself. Or the way her sneakers would squeak on the freshly mopped floor as she passed by my table, the stop and stutter, but then she'd continue on to wipe down a table or straighten the pile of brochures of Opal Bay attractions stacked near the window.

I was wrapped up in low-pressure system changes, precipitation levels, downdrafts. I'd forgotten how much I loved studying the more primitive satellite models, the way they reminded me of a child's color-by-number book, splotches of dark green, light green, small swaths of blue, dots of red and yellow. It was *my* jigsaw puzzle—a pattern to fit together, to figure out, and the more precise you were, the better your results. It was amazing how messed up a winter forecast could get just by forgetting a surface northerly wind in a valley.

The morning of the interview, I took half a Xanax to calm my nerves and gave Catarina some catnip so she wouldn't start howling in the middle of my call. Then I settled in the sunroom, dragging a chair as close to the window as I could afford. It was the place in the house that seemed to get the best reception, if the wind was blowing in the right direction.

Vaughn Winters had that producer voice. Even over the phone it was big, booming, confident. It immediately took me back to my news days, the early morning caffeine hits, the yelling, the rushing—the bustle of a newsroom where everything was always on fire.

"So tell me about yourself," he said by way of opening, and already I was fumbling for words. *Well, sir, what would you like to know about? My husband's affair? My on-air rant that was both unprofessional and insane? Or maybe you want to hear about the way the basement in this house I'm staying in smells like mold?*

"I was the morning meteorologist for WDLT in Annapolis for five years," I told him instead.

"Oh yeah. Wonderful," Vaughn said.

"Yes. I really enjoyed it. I love being able to translate science to the general public, you know? It's nice to be that face on the television that's useful."

"Well, about that," he said, and for the first time I sensed hesitation in his voice. "I have to be up-front with you. I'm not looking for an on-camera person. This would be more behind-the-scenes. Research, forecasts, the like."

"Oh." My immediate reaction was disappointment. Part of me had imagined getting back on-air, proving to everyone (Duke and his family) that I wasn't ruined. That I was back and better than ever. But I tried to swallow it. *Give him a chance, Allison.* Besides, there were pros to being off camera, too, weren't there? Easier to stay under the radar. And I could focus on the job, not the performance.

"That's actually perfect," I said, hoping I seemed upbeat. "I've been doing some forecasting this week, getting back into it, you know? And it's been—well, at the risk of sounding like a geek—really fun."

"Great. I'll have you send those to our meteorologists if you don't mind. So tell me more about yourself. How has this beach vacation been treating you?"

I paused. The word *vacation* tripped me up. Was that what Annie had told him I was doing? The word *vacation* felt trivial, light. Was he trying to be polite by calling it that? Or did he not know I'd been fired from my last job? I'd been going back and forth for days about what to tell him about my past. If to tell him at all. *Breathe, Allison.* "It's nice. Feels good to be here. To recharge," I said.

"I can imagine."

Did his voice have a hint of sarcasm to it? Or was I overthinking it? I was tired of hiding, exhausted from worrying about who knew what about everything that had happened and what they thought of me. I might ruin everything, but it was time to face it.

"Look, I need to be up-front with you, too, Mr. Winters," I said, drawing in a breath. "There's a—well, I should let you know why I'm no longer working at WDLT."

"Okay?"

"I—well, it was a poor decision on my part. I take full responsibility for it. I was going through a tough time person-ally and I said some things on-air that I shouldn't have."

Down here in South Annapolis, you'll be seeing some rain this weekend. So if my husband, Duke, is watching, you should know, honey, to bring your umbrella this weekend when you and your little girlfriend go off to your beach house weekend getaway.

My face was getting red, and I was grateful this was a phone call. I fully expected Vaughn to hang up on me at any mo-ment.

Instead, I heard him chuckle. "Disposable umbrellas?"

And a tip to all you adulterers out there—If you like treating your umbrellas like you treat women, then you can toss out your old one and head over to Macy's this weekend where they're having a sale.

"It wasn't my finest moment," I said, remembering my final closing line before the cameras had cut off and they'd gone to commercial break.

Women aren't disposable, Duke.

I let my breath out in a rush. So Vaughn knew. *And he still called.*

"I do my homework, Ms. Simpson. Plus, there's not much else to do in this depressing rehab place."

"Oh," I said. Then realization flooded over me. "Oh! Right, I understand now why you emphasized the off-camera part of this."

"No, not at all. I'm telling you that because you were a damn fine on-air forecaster and I didn't want you to be dis-appointed."

I didn't believe him, but I was so unused to hearing any sort of compliment that I thought I was going to cry. I bit the inside of my lip. "Well, tha-thank you. I mean that."

Vaughn started going into more detail about the station, about how many news anchors they had, how many on-air weather forecasters they rotated. The research position he wanted me for was a new role. I tried to focus on his words, to think about what questions I should ask to sound smart. It had been so long since I'd had a job interview. And like when Annie had first told me about the Worthington house, I felt a glimmer of light opening up inside of me. The promise of hope.

Vaughn's voice was getting a little crackly, so I stood up and shifted even closer to the window, praying the connection wouldn't break. He was talking about the demographics of the station's audience, but his words kept fading in and out. "Cable news station…need people for that…early mornings."

"We had a sister cable channel in Annapolis." My own voice echoed strangely back at me. I moved across the room, trying to get back a good connection.

"…so if you're interested, I was thinking maybe we could set up a time for you to come into the station, maybe in a few weeks when I'm discharged…"

Vaughn's voice cut out completely then. There was an odd metallic buzzing sound, and then I heard faint music. An old '80s pop tune. *Girls just wanna have fu-un.*

"—meet the crew, talk more about your qualifications "

"Hello, Vaughn? Can you hear me?"

A woman's voice cut in, low, confessional. *Lobster,* she said. I tensed up.

Then the buzzing again, and the woman, breezier this time. *Yeah, I got the recipe from a* Southern Living *issue.*

"Vaughn? Are you there?"

Vaughn came back faintly. "—Annie speaks very highly of you—" But then he cut out again.

The woman's voice. It was stranger, louder than before. *I never left.* The call disconnected.

"Goddammit," I said aloud, dropping the phone on the couch and rubbing my sweaty palms on my pants. I took a few deep breaths and then picked up the phone to try to call him back. When the phone rang again in my hands, I jumped, startled.

"Allison? You okay over there?" There was concern in Vaughn's voice.

"Yes, why? I think we just got cut off?"

"I thought something happened," he said, hesitantly. "It's just—it sounded there for a minute like you were screaming."

⊷

After I hung up with Vaughn, I dragged one of Patty's crocheted blankets out onto the deck and curled up in it, listening to the ocean. It had been strange talking to him about what had happened and not having him hang up on me. For so long, I'd been worried, hiding from it all. Or at least trying to.

The day my video had gone viral on social media, I hadn't been able to sleep. In fact, I'd believed I might never be able to sleep again. There had been thousands of emails from people who'd seen what I'd done. Many from scorned women. To them, I was a hero. Men are scum, some of them wrote, sending me pages and pages on their own exes, torrid stories about dirty motels, secret cameras, stuffed animal fetishes, online hookers. Some of them were armchair therapists, offering up unsolicited advice on what I should've done, what I should do now. You had it all, said another. Don't throw it away because of a man. Still others were my greatest cheerleaders: You'll get back on your feet! We so loved you on the morning news. It's just not the same without you!

They were feminists, housewives, reporters, academics, other television news weathercasters. My lawyer told me to delete them without reading them, that I was just upsetting myself, but it was fascinating. Fascinating to see myself go viral.

For a while—maybe two or three days—it was even kind of fun, therapeutic, the delight of so many people agreeing that my husband was little more than pond scum.

And then it hadn't been fun anymore. Somewhere between that initial weird high and the days, months, following, I'd changed. Become anxious, unsure of myself, unsure of others.

But now? Now maybe my confidence was coming back. Maybe it *could* be okay after all. Maybe this wasn't the end of my career. Of my life.

I could feel a warmth growing inside me. I just had a *job interview*—something I'd thought would never happen after my old producer had locked the studio door behind me for the last time. I was making new friends. Sure, I hadn't yet made it to page two of the Google search results, but it was going to be okay. I could feel it. This wasn't my *forever*, but it was my *for now*. And I was going to make it work.

14

· ———— ·

ALLISON

With a plan ahead of me, I felt energized and renewed. I started a more regular exercise routine, running on the beach in the mornings. When it got too bitter outside, I used some of Patty's old aerobics DVDs. Even Catarina and I seemed to be getting along well. She'd warmed to me, waking me each morning with a pitiful, sweet mew, nudging her wet little nose in my wrist looking for love.

After the interview, Vaughn Winters had emailed about visiting the station and meeting the rest of the team, and Tammy had sent over a box of pastries to celebrate. A few days after the Roller Derby game, Dolores had even called to apologize for telling her teammates about my rant. "Come down to the gallery whenever. See Dad's stuff. I'll take you out to lunch."

I finally turned to my neglected house chores, dusting bookshelves and cleaning the stove according to John's extensive instructions. When the inside was clean, I went outside for the power washer. I wheeled the thing out of the garage and stared at it. It looked like a miniature lawn mower. It couldn't be that hard, right? I unwound the hose and remembered John had told me to fill up the tank with the water and mixture. Once I got it all set, I turned the machine on and almost fell over. The water pressure was high, no doubt. I felt like I was maneuvering a jackhammer.

Once I got the hang of the machine, the job was actually therapeutic. As I moved from the back of the house to the side, I was even feeling a little proud of myself. Wouldn't Duke be surprised? He'd always made fun of my yard-work skills, or lack thereof.

As I forced off the grime, I imagined it was his face I was hosing down, blasting off that smug smile he liked to use on me. Like the time we'd gotten into a fight on a motorboat with his parents and their friends. About what—I couldn't even remember. But I did remember him leaning against the gunwale, holding a glass of wine and shaking his head while tears streamed down my face. *Don't make a scene, Allison. You'll just embarrass yourself.*

"Whoa, you don't want to do that." A man's voice behind me jolted me out of the memory.

I lost my grip on the wand, and the water went spurting all over my feet and his. I bent down to grab for it, but he managed to get there first and switched off the power.

"Oh my gosh, I'm so sorry. You scared me."

"You shouldn't point the water upward under the siding like that. It could rip the whole panel off."

His salt-and-pepper hair was cut short and traditional. I placed him about early seventies, but he was handsome and fit, with a good tan that hadn't faded yet from the summer.

"This is my first time doing this."

"I can tell." He smiled. "John teach you how to use this? He never could get it quite right."

"No, he—showed me, but it's been a while."

"Here, let me help." I watched as he angled the water above the siding panels, moving in wide arcs. He was in command. The type that intervened and helped out when he was needed. The water drizzled down on both of us and the drops colored rainbow haze in the bright autumn sun. "It's a good day to do this," he shouted at me over the motor. "Right after the rain."

I nodded and caught movement in a window next door. A woman peering out at us. The curtain shifted and she quickly disappeared from view.

The machine spurted and whirred, and he bent down to shut it off. "Ran out of solution. You need to reload it." He pulled the bottle off the side and showed me. Empty.

"Oh no," I said. "I still have more than half the house to go."

He smirked. "You can always try again tomorrow. The house isn't going anywhere."

I laughed. "Yes. Yes, I agree." I'd been smart enough to wear a raincoat, but my jeans were drenched, and even though the sun was warm, the cool air made the denim feel like ice against my thighs. "I'm so sorry I got us so wet."

"Oh, it was my pleasure. Anytime." He winked, and I felt myself blush. "I'm Phillip Bishop," he said, holding out a hand.

"Allison," I said.

"Ah, yes, the house sitter. Patty told us you'd be here, but she didn't tell us how lovely you'd be." He reached out and plucked a leaf out of my hair. "Nice scarf," he said, tugging on one end, his knuckles brushing against my shoulder.

I tried to ignore the warmth that came through my body at his touch. "So how often are you here?"

To my relief, he grew more serious. "Not as often as we'd like, I'm afraid. We're in the restaurant business—" At this I nodded, and he continued, unfazed. "Of course, I sometimes forget it's a small town. Well, we're opening a new place in Ocean City, so I'm up there quite a bit these days. Lorelei, my wife, is here more often, and my brother comes down, though less than he used to. And then, of course, we always try to get my son to join us when he can." He moved closer and held his hand to his mouth, whispering, "Mostly for time with the granddaughter, though. Don't tell him."

I gestured toward the ocean. "This view is a good bargaining chip, right?"

He sighed. "Yes, but Clay is stubborn. Always busy at the college. I suppose I raised him that way. It's like that song, you know? 'Cat's in the Cradle'? Oh, I'm just being depressing now, aren't I?"

Clay? Where had I heard that name? But before I could figure it out, a woman rounded the corner, a drink in her hand.

"Depressing *now*, honey? Or always depressing?" She was smiling, but I felt the tension in the air. "What is he going on about now?"

I wasn't sure how to respond. I didn't want to be caught awkwardly in the middle of a marital spat.

"Lord, Phil, you've rendered the poor woman speechless." She still had a half smile, and a voice that seemed slightly condescending, like the joke was on me.

"Not at all. I'm teaching our lovely neighbor here how to clean the house."

"Ah, yes." She paused, assessing me. "You're a weather person, is that right?" She said it in the same tone she would use to point out a pile of dog shit on the sidewalk.

"I'm a meteorologist, yes," I stammered, startled.

"On television." It was a statement, but I nodded anyway. "Good. You should replace the young woman on our NBC station. She is, frankly, a nitwit." She extended her hand. "I'm Lorelei Bishop."

At that moment a little girl, bundled up in a thick hooded sweatshirt, came running around the corner of the house, clutching a doll in her hand like she was trying to make it fly. She stopped short, stared up at me with beady eyes. "Are you a zombie?"

"Letty," Lorelei said, rubbing the child's arms briskly through her sweatshirt. Mrs. Bishop had high cheekbones and perfectly sculpted eyebrows, but her face was angular. Her steel blue eyes looked warily at me, but her large mouth curled up in amusement at the little girl. "We don't talk about zombies. Now please get inside. It's getting chilly."

"Brains," the little girl said, twisting her mouth in a ridiculous grimace. "They eat brains." She picked up her doll and marched into the garage.

"Her mother lets her watch these awful movies," Lorelei said. "I think they're perfectly horrid."

"I think they're character-building," Phillip said, winking at me. A fierce gust of wind swept up between the houses. "This weather's been terrible," he added. "I'm missing all my complaints about the humidity."

"This is actually a nice calm before the storm," I said. "There's been a strange cold front in the north, closer to Canada, and it's been fighting with the warmer air for a while. But it will move here soon, do its griping here for a few days."

Lorelei studied me. "Well, you would know."

"Beautiful and smart. What a combination. Lorelei's right. You should replace the local weather girl."

Was this his regular MO? His harmless flirtation earlier now seemed almost malicious in front of his wife. I thought of Duke again, at his boring company picnic when he'd insisted on having Maron as his teammate during horseshoes. Watching him "coach" her on the proper way to throw the horseshoe, while I stood off to the side with some of the other wives, sipping warm Coke out of a plastic cup and trying to think of nice things to say. How pathetic I'd been, dismissing my jealousy even as the prickling beneath my skin had told me that things weren't right...

"Allison?"

Lorelei and Phillip were looking at me funny.

"Sorry, what?"

"I was saying you should come with us to the club," Phillip said slowly. "The Autumn Harvest is coming up. It's next Thursday evening."

"Oh my, that's so nice. But I couldn't—"

"It's the final party before the club closes for the winter," he interrupted. "The food is good. It's our treat."

I took a step back, nearly tripping over the power washer. "Thanks, but I've been kind of a homebody here. Trying to get things done. Taking advantage of the peace and quiet, you know?"

"Have you been downtown yet?" Lorelei asked, taking a sip of her drink, though it appeared to be nearly gone.

"I have."

"You need to go to The Sweet Spot."

"Actually I have. Several times. The internet here at the house is so spotty."

"Oh really?" Lorelei's eyes lifted. "What did you think?"

"Good coffee."

"The best," she said, her voice growing warmer, like I'd finally said something she thought wasn't idiotic. "She's got the best coffee around here. And you're right—a good internet connection. I'm sure you'll find it a favorite place of yours."

The little girl came running out of the garage, trailing a homemade kite behind her. She ran between the houses, out toward the beach.

Phillip called after her. "Letty! Don't go too far. It's getting dark." Then to me, "You really must come to the Autumn Harvest dinner with us. The whole family will be there."

I looked to Lorelei. She was also nodding. "You can meet some other people in town, too. I'm sure they'd love to meet you."

I opened my mouth to decline politely, but then something made me stop. *You can't hide forever, Allison. This is your start-over. Your new life.*

"Yeah. Sure. Okay," I said. "I'd love to meet the family. You said everyone?"

"The whole lot of us," Lorelei said, her eyes glistening, and I realized that the drink in her hand wasn't her first of the evening. "Think you can handle it?"

15

• — •

MAUREEN

This is my new life, walking arm in arm with Clay Bishop to a house party at the beach. It's one of those houses with a mile-long driveway, and as we approach we're greeted by a giant metal sculpture, hideous but probably as expensive as a car. Its long sticks of metal protrude upward like fingers, and I have this weirdly satisfying image of drunk kids falling out of the second-story window and impaling themselves on it.

"I'm glad you're here. With me," Clay says, brushing back my hair from my shoulder to kiss it. He's been extra sweet these past few weeks, after having apologized for the way he'd acted at the restaurant, whipping out all the fancy things he'd learned in his psychology class about his "repressed resentment" of his father. I'd wanted to tell him he can't even begin to know what real problems are, but that would've meant telling him the Sad Story, and I'm not ready to let Clay peek behind that curtain.

It's a perfect summer night and we're heading up this crazy

perfect lawn with tropical-looking flowers and plants, and the thumping bass of the music seems to match my heartbeat. When we get inside, the party is already in full mode, people in clusters along the walls, talking and holding beers in red Solo cups, laughing.

"How are we going to find Tammy?" I ask Clay, but he's already pushing through like he's been to this house millions of times and who knows, maybe he has. I follow him through a living room, snake around into a smaller den-like area in the back, where a bunch of people are playing with expensive-looking sailboat replicas, their beer bottles leaving sweat rings of condensation on the wood end tables. Clay leads me through double doors to a deck out back where I immediately spot Mabel, her sometimes-boyfriend, Ted, Barron and a few others. Tammy's there, too, off to the side, talking close with a shorter boy wearing one of those glow bracelets around his wrist.

Clay heads over to Barron and his other toady friends, but I hang back behind him. Barron isn't exactly happy that I dumped him for Clay. They all nod at each other, and even though I know Clay doesn't really like them—even though he's mocked them several times to me—there he is, completing the circle, all of them with their expensive watches, Coppertone tans and turned-up collars. But just as I'm growing resentful, he turns, winks and gestures for me. I reach out and squeeze his arm. "I'm going to say hi to Tammy, be right back," I say, and he whispers hot in my ear, slow, suggestive.

"Don't be too long."

And just like that the world's righted itself again for a moment.

I come up behind Tammy and tweak her side. She jumps, then hugs me, drips a little of her drink down my back. "You made it," she says, then pulls me over to the boy. "This is my friend Luke."

He's smiling at me, but it's not real *real*, and he keeps glancing at Tammy in a way that makes me think I've interrupted his moves. I make a note to yell at her later for not noticing he's into her.

"I'll be right back," I say to them. "I'm going to find a bathroom."

I push back inside, wandering through the house. I follow a winding staircase up, where the music grows fainter and the air cooler. The bathroom door is closed, and when I knock someone inside yells, "Busy!" I step across the hall into an expansive bedroom with a fireplace. Above the bed is a painting of a naked lady lying under a tree, her curves exaggerated, hair tumbling behind her.

On the mantel opposite, I spot a small mermaid statue. She's sitting on a ceramic rock pedestal, waving at me with a delicate hand. I pick her up. Her wavy blond hair feels like corn silk, her scales glittery, painted metallic. *I have a secret for you, baby*, my mom used to whisper to me, back when things were okay. When she still tucked me in. *I'm not really your mom. Your real mom is a mermaid*, she'd say, knowing I'd dream about it that night, the soft coolness of deep water, the castles under the sea.

I set the statue carefully in my purse and zip it shut.

Downstairs in the kitchen, there's a huge spread of food worthy of a wedding—a cheese plate, piles of fruit, crackers, fancy cured meats. It looks so untouched, and for a moment I imagine it's mine, all of it. The mermaid queen in her castle. I select several pieces of cheese and some meat, taking a handful with me.

I continue to wander through the house, but the other two bathrooms I find are also occupied. As a last resort I try the basement. The music's originating from here, and I feel like I've entered one of those dance clubs that start going at midnight. Now I know where Luke got his glow bracelet from,

because everyone down here is wearing them, dark silhou-
etted bodies wrapped in rings of neon pink, yellow, orange,
dancing under black lights. I slide around them, toward a back
room that looks lit by a normal light, which I hope is a bathroom. But it's a utility room with a sink and a beer keg. On
the other side of the room, three boys sit at a card table and a
bunch of people circle them. They get quiet, then shout, then
get quiet again. I peer over a girl's shoulder and see they are
tossing dice. There's a pile of money on the table that seems
dangerous to just leave out in the open.

The girl in front throws some money in the ring and then
centers herself, putting the two dice in the cup. She tosses it,
and her boyfriend groans.

"Lost again. That's it, Bernadette."

One of the guys sitting down catches my gaze. "Wanna
play?"

I shake my head.

"Come on. You're feeling lucky, aren't you?" He cocks an
eyebrow. "Follow your destiny."

Destiny. The word slides over me, inviting, like the guy has
put his arm around me, drawing me close. The boy with Bernadette nods, waves me in. "Come on, go for it."

Bernadette agrees. "Yeah," she says. "Maybe you can take
some of Mike Ryan's money from him." Their confidence in
me pushes me forward, settles between my shoulders.

"Roll anything higher than eight and you get your money
back," says Mike Ryan, his hat on backward. "Pairs wins two-
to-one." I can't figure out the odds quickly enough, though
I suspect they aren't very good.

Still I hear myself saying, "Okay," and the crowd cheers,
egging me on. They shuffle out of the way and I find myself at the head of the table. I fish out a dollar from my purse.

"Five's the minimum," Mike says when I try to hand it to

him. I flush, embarrassed, but now everyone's waiting, and I can feel their energy. It's like being at an outdoor concert, pressing your way to the front, feeling the driving beat of the music and the vibe of the crowd and feeling alive, ready to tackle anything, so I get caught up in it, reach back in my wallet and pull out a five.

One of the other guys hands over the cup, and I close my eyes and shake it, think about all the times I played Yahtzee with my grandfather, the way the rattling dice always seemed so satisfying. I throw them. *Destiny*.

I hear a quick intake of breath from someone, and then I open my eyes. I've rolled two ones. I breathe out. From what they said, I doubled my money.

"Snake eyes," Mike says, slapping his hand on the table. The people around me start shouting. Bernadette throws me a high five and kisses her boyfriend.

"Well, hot damn. You are lucky," someone behind me says.

"What's snake eyes?" I ask, but to my surprise Mike is already counting out from the pile of cash.

Bernadette squeezes my arm. "Snake eyes is ten-to-one. You're wiping him out. It's about time."

Mike hands me a bunch of bills, which I gather clumsily. Bernadette and her boyfriend are bumping me with their hips in a drunken dance. I throw my head back and laugh, swept away by the giddy feeling.

But Mike's all business. "Wanna try again?"

"No," I shout. "No. I think I'll quit while I'm ahead."

• ⎯⎯⎯ •

Clay and his friends are still where I left them, at the edge of the deck. "Clay, you'll never guess." I open my palm to show him the money. Everyone else stops talking and stares at it.

"I won, can you believe it? Snake eyes." He's peering down at me, his eyes a bit glassy, and I wonder if he's been getting high while I'm gone. Is Barron acting fishy? Palming something behind his back? But I'm too excited to care. "Fifty dollars," I say. "One roll. *It was so easy*."

"Oh shit, snake eyes?" Ted asks admiringly. "I've never rolled that. Thought Mike Ryan rigged those dice, to be honest."

Mabel glares at Ted and moves closer to him. But Barron nods, catching my eye, and now I can see he's got a joint cupped in his palm. A mossy sweet smell hovers in the air. "How cute," he says slowly, taking a hit. "Maybe you can treat the sword-swallower to dinner one night. Or I know—the tattooed man? All your carnival freaks—I mean, friends."

Mabel cackles, and the blood rushes to my ears. I think of something Jacqueline told me, our first week in Opal Beach. *Don't let the sunshine fool you into thinking you belong here.*

I open my mouth to say something, but I'm drowned out by a yell from inside. There are murmurs and shouts, a tidal wave building, and then I hear it more clearly. "Cops!"

"Let's go," Clay says, grabbing my arm and pulling me forward.

Barron smashes his joint on the edge of the railing and flicks it into the night sky, where the embers sputter like dud fireworks.

Everyone's rushing off the deck, pushing and shoving their way out of the house. Clay's found Tammy, and he's guiding us like we're his toddlers at a busy amusement park. As we head down the deck stairs I can see the blue and red dancing off Mabel's hair like Christmas lights.

"Jesus, Clay, chill out," I say, shaking him off as we get down to the yard. A plastic cup falls from the balcony above, just missing us, splattering warm beer on the deck.

"You don't understand," he says. "They're looking for someone to—" He stops, his face changing, and I turn and see a police officer standing there, hands on hips, his radio crackling. Clay steps in front of me and Tammy like a shield.

"Can I see some ID, son?"

"Certainly, Officer." Clay takes his wallet out of his back pocket and slides out his license smoothly. Beside me, Tammy's frozen.

The policeman uses his flashlight to check it. "Bishop?" he says, looking up at him. "Related to Phillip?"

"Yes, sir. He's my father."

The policeman taps the ID on his fingers, then hands it back to Clay. "What about you two?" he asks, nodding at Tammy and me.

"They're with me, sir. We were just leaving."

He nods again. I can see him thinking, wrestling with something. I realize I'm holding my breath. "Okay, get out of here."

"Thank you, sir," Clay says, turns, grabs my arm again and propels us out toward the bay.

"Hold up," the officer calls. We stop. I feel my heart flutter. "Tell your dad we say thank you for his donation to the Police Support Fund."

"Of course," Clay says carefully. "He'll be happy to hear it."

16

ALLISON

November 2015

I've always loved the idea of a country club. The comforting sense of community, a way for adults to gather and eat or go to events, to learn or play, something like a church without the religion. When Duke and I had been married, his parents had belonged to a lovely country club on Martha's Vineyard that I'd always felt like royalty stepping into. Crushed velvet drapes, oil paintings of important-looking people, a ballroom where they sometimes screened classic movies on weeknights. Duke's parents were chairs of the International Club, which as far as I know meant that every month or so someone went to World Market and bought snack foods from England or Italy or Mexico and ate them while discussing what language expert they might bring in someday. Country clubs felt like a cross between a nice wedding reception, college club activities and vacation resorts. The bonus for me was getting to dip into that lifestyle every now and then without having to pay for it.

But the Opal Beach Country Club lacked that pizazz I'd

come to expect from these kinds of places. The building was low and long, and faded flags flanked the entrance, flitting about in the wind as if bored. Inside, the coral carpets had seen better days, their threads worn bare in well-trodden spots. Painted metal seahorses decorated the chandeliers, which gave them a sort of antique-store feel. Round tables filled the ballroom, all draped in that same coral color.

As I walked in, waiters whisked by with steaming silver trays, still setting up the buffet. I felt self-conscious arriving alone, but I hadn't wanted to travel with the Bishops either. I'd forced myself to put on a black dress and sparkly heels and toss back a shot of vodka. Now I felt a little wobbly and a lot nervous.

Lorelei spotted me, stepped out from a group she was talking with, and waved. She greeted me with a hug and a kiss on the cheek, told me to put my purse on a round table in the corner. "Hands free for drinking!" she chimed, and I wondered if her over-cheery demeanor was because she'd already had a few.

Phillip, who was talking with a woman I'd never seen before, took a quick moment to shoot me a wink. Next to him stood a tall, rounded man in a burgundy jacket with the same salt-and-pepper hair and thin nose as Phillip. I guessed he was Phillip's brother. He glanced at me, his hands shoved into the pockets of his crisp dress pants. He might have once been handsome, like his brother, but unlike Phillip, he hadn't aged well. He was paunchy, and his skin was plagued with age spots. He'd lost much of his hair, combing over the few strands that remained. But his eyes were small and shrewd, flicking quickly from one person to another, surveying the crowd, judging, dismissing and sizing up.

"Oh my word. Sugar." The loud voice behind me tore my attention away. I turned, but I already knew who was giving

Lorelei a flurry of hugs. Mabel Halberlin. She was wearing a deep purple floor-length gown and silver ballet flats. She noticed me and reached over with her painted claws to shake my hand. "Hello, dear. Have we met?"

"I believe we did, at the coffee shop downtown," I said, forcing a smile. "I'm Allison."

"That's right," she said with a snap of her fingers. "Lorelei was just telling me about you. You're house-sitting for Patty and John."

"That's me," I said, weakly.

"And this is my son, Clay," Lorelei said, introducing a professorial-looking man with small round glasses who had just come off the dance floor with his daughter, Letty. Clay shook my hand politely, his blue eyes barely meeting mine. He was not unattractive, but certainly hadn't inherited the same natural charisma that his father had. It was as if Phillip Bishop had sucked all the charming good looks out of the family and saved them only for himself.

And then it clicked. *Clay.* The name of the boy Tammy said she and Maureen had hung out with all those years ago. Could this man be Tammy's old friend? It was hard to imagine Tammy hanging out with a Bishop. And Maureen? I couldn't imagine what Lorelei would think of her.

"Okay, Allison." Mabel moved closer. "So Lorelei here was saying that you are a television personality." She tapped my shoulder with her fingernail. "And I just got the most smashing idea. I need a host for my real estate association's holiday party."

"Host?"

Mabel nodded. "And wouldn't you be perfect? We have an emcee every year. Just to welcome everyone, do the raffles. Oh, usually it's someone so boring, like the mayor—don't tell him—but this year, well, I want to do something different."

I'd done my share of those kinds of events—usually charity dinners or university fund-raisers. It was easy, and even could be fun. Wear a brightly colored cocktail dress, toss around a few jokes, pose for some photos. I was good at them. I *had* been good at them. But that seemed far away, another lifetime ago. "I'm not exactly a— I'll think about it," I said. I found a waitress and waved her over.

"Okay, but don't think too long. I'll need to nail someone down before Thanksgiving."

Phillip sidled over, tipping his drink in my direction. "So, Allison, how are you finding Opal Beach so far?"

"Oh, it's great," I said.

"Yes, yes. This really is a special place," Mabel piped up again, her eyes gleaming. "Shame to see it going downhill."

Lorelei gave me a knowing look. "They're building another *public* beach farther down, where Mabel lives." She said *public* like it was a dirty word.

Mercifully, it was time to be seated, and Mabel went off to find her table in a flutter of hand waves, air kisses and "sugars." I followed Lorelei and Phillip to the table, and after a scramble in which Letty insisted on sitting next to me, I found myself next to her and Phillip, with Clay on the other side of Letty, next to his mother. Phillip's brother was across the table from me and extended a hand across to introduce himself as Zeke. "Pleasure," he said in a tone that implied the exact opposite, and then proceeded to snap at a food server for a fresh glass of wine.

Clay busied himself breaking the hard bread crust off Letty's slices while she told me in great detail about every second of her day. "And the sand crabs make little bubbles, that's how you know they're there. They won't drown, though. But you're not supposed to dig them up..." Thankfully, the waitress brought my glass of punch swiftly.

"So you're from Annapolis?" Phillip asked when Letty took a break. "We know that area well. Big sailing community."

Lorelei chimed in. "Clay was on the crew team in high school and college. Then it was sailing."

"My ex-husband's family was very into that," I said automatically, and then wanted to kick myself for mentioning them.

"Oh yes? And who's that?" Phillip asked with interest.

"Their last name was Shetland," I said.

"Dennis and June?" He lit up and nodded and pointed at Clay. "Clay used to sail with their daughter."

"Jenny?" I picked up my punch and downed the rest of it. Opal Beach was a small town, but it seemed to get smaller and smaller every time I turned around.

"Oh right, I remember her. Weren't they the ones who did the duck boat races every year for charity?" Clay asked. He told Letty to stop hanging off her chair and, to his mother's dismay, shoved a large piece of cantaloupe in his daughter's mouth.

"I'd forgotten about that. Lorelei, you remember those?" Phillip said.

"Mmm-hmm." Lorelei reached across Clay with a napkin to let Letty spit out the rest of the fruit.

"Jenny was great fun," Clay said.

I bet she was. Jenny had a Vineyard Vines kind of look about her, almost-white shoulder-length hair and an eternal tan. But Duke had told me that in high school she'd been treated for gonorrhea, and once Duke and I had to drive out in the middle of the night to pick her up after she'd been in a bar fight with another girl about a drummer in some terrible cover band.

"Did you go out sailing with them a lot?" Phillip asked.

"Oh no." I shook my head, smiling. "I get terrible seasickness." The first time I'd gone out on a sailboat with Duke's family, back when we were dating, I'd spent most of the time hanging on to the side of the boat, turning green. They'd given me ginger ale to sip, and after I vomited that all over the side of their boat, I'd wanted to die. But they stayed on the water for another hour or two, claiming the weather was simply too perfect to turn around yet. *You'll be fine*, they'd kept telling me while they drank chardonnay and sang along to music. *Just keep looking at the horizon.* Even later, after I'd learned to take Dramamine and wear the pressure point bracelets, I never forgave them for that day.

"Lovely family," Phillip said. "Haven't seen them in years."

"A pity," Lorelei said. She caught my eye and I saw a hint of something there. Distaste, whether for me or for the Shetlands I wasn't sure.

The Bishops navigated to other topics—the new manager at the club, a friend of theirs who was supposed to be there tonight but skipped out because she was sick, food shipment troubles at their restaurant. I was still mad at myself for bringing up Duke. Or maybe they already knew the whole story, I thought with bitterness. Maybe they'd all gathered around for a family viewing of my *weather report*.

I played "I spy" with Letty during the meal, but she grew antsy and started wandering around the ballroom. Clay watched her go, weary. With the empty seat between us, we found ourselves chatting.

"That punch is good, but watch out, it's a killer," he said.

"I know," I said. "It's so easy to keep drinking it. What are you having?"

"A salty dog. Ever have one? It's my favorite beach drink."

"What's in it?" I asked, but Clay was not paying attention. He was swiveling his head back and forth to try to catch a glimpse of the trouble his daughter might be getting in. Earlier, Phillip had mentioned that Clay was a math professor, and I could believe it. He wore a tweed jacket complete with leather elbow patches and didn't seem to fit in with this crowd, growing bored each time anyone brought up gossip about another local, taking quick glances at his phone where someone—I'd guessed his wife—kept texting him. He seemed like he would rather be anywhere else than sitting at a country club dinner and would be more at home up on the band's stage with a PowerPoint presentation, lecturing on something brilliant. Perhaps Mabel should be asking *him* to host her dinner.

Growing bored myself, I tried to imagine him as a teenager, hanging out with Tammy, drinking on the beach, not a care in the world. What had it been like growing up as a Bishop? Having access to a beach—to anything, really—whenever he wanted? I had only had one childhood friend who was rich—Edie Almar. Her parents were both doctors, and going to their house had felt like going to an amusement park—a built-in pool, an ice cream bar, a pool table in the basement. They even had a fish tank built into the wall of their dining room, and I had been mesmerized by the giant orange fins of the goldfish, undulating like tiny billowing wind socks around and around. But whenever I'd hung out with her, somewhere below the surface I'd always been aware of my generic-brand jeans, frayed at the hem. The embarrassing inflatable kiddie pool in our backyard that my father refused to throw out, that he'd sometimes, to our horror, go and sit in when it really got hot, his bare chest white like a ghost. The fish tank on the kitchen counter, its glass always a filmy green, the small neon tetras dying out regularly. I knew, no matter how close Edie and I got as friends, that we'd always be different. Was that how it had been with Clay and Tammy?

"Hey, so were you friends with my friend Tammy years ago?" I asked when he'd finally caught sight of Letty dancing and relaxed.

"Tammy? Quinn? Oh yes, we go way back. She's got the best coffee around here." His phone buzzed again on the table between us, and he grabbed it and stuck it in his pocket, but not before I caught the words, Ha ha. You poor thing! From a glowing text box. "Tammy's great," he said again, clearly flustered.

"She is. And you're right about the coffee."

We both watched as Letty whirled by with an older gentleman who was carrying her on his back. She waved enthusiastically to us as the man reminded her to hold on with both hands. "She's always the charmer," he muttered. "It's one of those things where you never know if you should let them go off, be independent, or stay close to protect them."

"I can imagine. I'm sure it only gets harder as they get older. Especially for girls."

Clay took his glasses off, blew on them and put them back on. "Her mother's in Spain this semester working on a research project. She calls us every night. The separation's been difficult."

"But I bet it's nice to spend more one-on-one time with her, right? Show her this lovely beach town you grew up in?"

He considered that. "Sure, we don't get down as much as we'd like, though."

"You used to spend your whole summer here, right?"

"Long time ago." He sighed. "Different times. We did all kinds of stupid stuff. Tammy and I have some crazy stories from those days."

"Like what?" I said in a teasing voice, sipping on my punch. I could feel it blurring my head, but I also felt good. Comfortable.

"Oh, I'd have to have more of these to spill those secrets," he said, rattling the ice in his drink.

"Come on," I said. "Besides, Tammy's already spilled some

of the best ones, I think. Like the time you and her and her friend Maureen put sand crabs in some guy's sleeping bag?"

"Barron." A sneaky smile spread on Clay's face. "God, he was pissed. Never did get the smell—" He stopped. Tilted his drink my way. "Did you say Maureen?"

"Yeah. That girl who went missing?"

"Missing?" For the first time, I felt him focus in on me, really look at me, and I got goose bumps on my arms. "I don't remember that," he said slowly.

"Oh really? I'm sorry. She made it sound like you guys were close."

Zeke's head turned toward me. But when I glanced his way, he shifted again and nodded at something Lorelei was saying.

Clay paused, took a drink, and then his voice got more casual. "Oh, Maureen. Yes, my god. I'd forgotten about her."

"So what did happen to her? She just vanished?"

"Nah, she was a Summer Girl—that's what we called them." *Summer Girl.* I found the term interesting—wasn't Clay technically a summer boy? But I kept my mouth shut, let him continue. "I haven't thought about her in ages, honestly. There were a lot of girls." He chuckled, and I recognized the innuendo beneath his words.

"So you two dated?" I said, surprised.

"I'm not sure I'd really call it that. I mean, nothing serious. Like I said, there were a lot of girls." He broke off, waved his hand. "That sounds awful, maybe, and I don't mean it that way."

I forced myself to laugh with him. *So many girls. Who can tell one from the other? Ha-ha.* I swallowed my anger and tried to stay breezy. "Did you ever hear from her after that summer?"

He looked down at the table. "Nope. She left. Just like everyone else did."

"She worked for the traveling carnival, right?"

Clay relaxed a bit now that my questions moved off him. He nodded. "Yeah. That was all bad news, wasn't it? Hey, you need another drink?" He gestured toward my glass.

"So you didn't stay in touch, I presume?"

He picked up a fork on the table and twirled it in his fingers. "What? Like pen pals? Nah." He put the fork down and pushed his chair back to get up.

"What is this you're going on about over here?"

I jumped, turned to find Zeke standing over our chairs, one hand on the back of each, a grin on his face. He kneeled down, smirking, and I felt my skin crawl. "Didn't mean to scare. It's just the conversation on the other side of the table is dreary."

Clay pointed at me, and I got the sense he was relieved for the interruption. "She was just talking about an old friend of mine. The gal who runs the coffee shop downtown?"

Zeke held his palms up. "I don't do caffeine." His face was so close, I could smell the wine on his breath. He grinned, showing his teeth. "You're not interrogating my nephew here, are you?"

"Of course not." I shifted in my chair, putting more space between us. "I was just...curious."

"Well, you know what happened to the curious cat." He chuckled. "I'm just joking, of course. My nephew here is full of great stories. Can I get you another glass of punch?"

● ─────── ●

When I stood up, the room started spinning. I took a few seconds to hate myself. Whenever I got nervous, I needed to have something to hold in my hand. I'd refilled how many times?

I excused myself and walked slowly to the ladies' room. The bathroom was large and spacious, with four shower stalls and dressing rooms for the summer pool. I took my time, not too eager to get back to the Bishops' table. I wasn't sure how much more small talk I could muster. My energy levels were sapping, like they'd used to after a long shift at the station. I could only be "on" for so long, and then I felt like an egg, my shell forming small cracks. My face hurt from smiling.

I felt untethered. Was it being around someone else's big happy family that made me feel this way? Or just the alcohol? I wanted to go home. And not just back to the beach house. A real home. Not Annie's apartment, which had never really been mine, even though she'd made me feel as comfortable as she could. Not my parents' house. Not the home I'd shared with Duke, which was tainted and tarnished by all that had happened. I wanted to go home. But I had no home. I had nothing.

I splashed some cold water on my face and reapplied my lipstick, trying to shrug off the blanket of loneliness I'd wrapped around myself. *Get it together, Allison.* I straightened my bra straps and took my shoes off one by one to rub my toes in the bathroom rug. Next to the sink, a pile of wrapped French-milled soaps sat daintily in a bowl. Like everything else, they looked expensive. But they did look attainable. I plucked two and shoved them into my purse.

●————————●

On the way back to the ballroom, I went the wrong direction and ended up on the other side of the club. I opened another door but it led to a smaller, empty dining area overlooking the ocean that I imagined was a more casual place for lunch or drinks.

Turning back, I nearly bumped into Phillip. "Oh sorry," I said. Behind him, a waitress was walking quickly the other way, smoothing down her hair.

"Allison." He beamed, putting an arm around me. "Did you get lost? I can show you the way back."

I pretended I had something in my shoe and bent down to get his heavy hand off my back. That charm I'd felt outside with the power washer—I recognized it now. So Phillip was carrying on with a waitress? Or what, harassing her? I felt a raw anger working up inside me, scratching at old wounds. Like the time Duke had come home late, drunk, supposedly at some work event. How he'd laid down next to me in bed and, in the dark, half-asleep, had muttered, *I'm a bad, bad man, Ally.*

I straightened up. Phillip did not touch me again, but he did walk me back to the ballroom. "The beach in the winter is such a special thing," he murmured. He seemed thoughtful, content, not at all like a man who'd just been caught with a woman who was not his wife. "Have you ever seen the ocean glaze over with ice sheets? It's quite stunning. It's always been my favorite time of the year."

"I'm sure," I said.

"Most of the major decisions of my life have been made walking on the beach, staring out at the ocean. It really clears your head."

Before we hit the table, I excused myself and told Phillip I needed fresh air. I headed away and pushed past the heavy doors before he could invite himself to join me. It was freezing outside, but a relief to be alone.

I stepped onto the patio, which led out to a small field of beach grass that eventually trailed into the golf course. At the edge of the patio, I propped myself against the concrete wall, a little woozy, willing myself not to throw up.

I turned to observe the people inside, most still chatting at their tables with drinks. A few couples danced at the center of the room. They thought they'd conquered life. But right outside their windows, just beyond, it was still wild. That vast, secretive ocean. Just beyond, nature was the true queen. She could decide at any moment to whip through, rip the roof off all this Pottery Barn decor, fancy coral jewelry, delicate starfish centerpieces.

The door swooshed open and Lorelei stepped out.

"Hi," I said. "I just needed some fresh air."

"That punch will get you every time."

She stared out past the golf course toward the ocean, her gray hair tossing in the wind. She reminded me of an old movie star from the silent era, beautiful and haughty, cold and delightful. Had she seen me walking back with Phillip? Had she thought *I* was the reason he'd disappeared during dinner?

"Hard to believe it's almost the holidays," she said finally, though she didn't seem like the type of woman to want to make small talk.

"Do you normally spend them here?" I asked.

"*We* will be here for Thanksgiving," she said with a scowl, "but Clay's wife will be home from Spain, so he and Letty will be spending Thanksgiving at her parents' house. I'm not sure about Christmas."

The wind shifted, and I could smell the cloying mustiness of her perfume. She lifted her arm to put a hair back in place and her bracelets jangled. "Duke deserved everything you did to him…and more."

I opened my mouth to respond but came up empty. Had I heard her right?

"Not all men get what they deserve," she said calmly. "You're better off without him."

"I—well—thanks," I said. "So you know."

Her eyes stared fiercely at me. "You deserved to get fired, but I'm glad you did what you did." She handed me a glass of water. "Drink this. It will help hydrate you."

"Thanks."

She turned to leave, then stepped back. "Just one thing," she said. "Did you feel any better? After?"

I looked her in the eye. "I did. Yeah."

She nodded and vanished as quickly as she'd come. Only a trace of her perfume remained.

17

·———·

MAUREEN

Clyde seems happy about how good Opal Beach has been treating us. He says we've already surpassed last year's sales and went out and bought a case of sparkling wine to celebrate. After closing we have a little party in front of the giant slide, lounging on all the burlap sacks like they are sleeping bags. Jacqueline, I notice, is sitting close to one of the new boys that works the Tilt-A-Whirl. Clyde and some of the other guys are making a night of it, but I am tired and bail early.

I wander back to the trailers, wrapped up in my thoughts. Why am I feeling so lonely? The square peg, that's why. My mom used to tell me all the time, *Maureen, you're a square peg on a grid with round holes.* She'd meant it as a compliment—you stand out, you're different, but I'd always taken it as, *you don't belong.* Never had any friends in high school—how could I when I was always taking care of my mother? Not really part of the C&D crew. And besides Tammy and Clay, I don't really have any friends in Opal Beach. After Barron's comment at the party—well, I feel like I'll always be the outsider here. And once the summer is over, Clay and his friends will be heading off to their Ivy League campuses, burning through bunnies there like blunts on the beach.

No, I am alone. Usually I'm okay with this. Tonight, though, for some reason I'm letting it get to me, mess with my head.

I'm almost to my trailer when I spot Desmond. I hide behind one of the trailers and squat down, watching him. He's walking slow, swaying a bit. Probably downed one of Clyde's bottles all on his own. He's got a sloppy grin and looks loose like Jell-O. That's when I notice he's got his camera in his hand.

I hold tight, watching as he stops at each window, peers in. Looking for something to film. He finally enters his trailer, but in a minute he's out again, tucking a baseball hat in his back pocket and walking off toward the grounds.

No camera.

I wait until he's out of sight and then head quickly to his trailer. He didn't lock his door, which means he won't be gone long.

I've never been inside here before. It's dark and smells bad. In one corner sits a cheap desk, messy with newspapers and empty potato chip bags. On the walls above the bed are pictures of nude women ripped from magazines. I stare at them for a few seconds, but tacked above his unmade bed they make my stomach turn, and I force myself to keep moving.

Where to look for the camera? I don't see it, but he couldn't have had time to hide it that well.

I hear a crunch of gravel outside and pull the blinds out, but it's just one of the cooks stumbling back to his trailer. Still, Desmond could be back at any moment.

I try the top drawer of Desmond's nightstand. It sticks and

fights me but then it gives away with a groan. Inside are more porn magazines, a deck of cards with an Atlantic City hotel on them, a package of condoms (unopened, I note with satisfaction) and a fat wad of bills. No time to count if they're all ones or not, I slide them into my bag. They're slick, a bit greasy, but they also feel substantial.

Outside, I hear a bark of laughter and a few voices. The party's breaking up. I need to get out of here. Halfheartedly, I open the other nightstand drawer.

Bingo.

The Super 8 camera is sitting on top, and there are several small boxes of film. I don't have time to read the labels. I slip everything into my bag.

The door opens. I'm too late. I crumple to the floor. It's a ridiculous move, because if Desmond even looks in my direction he'll spot me. But it takes a few seconds for his eyes to adjust to the dim room. Lucky for me he heads straight to his desk, stumbling slightly, singing under his breath all merry-like.

I'm a panicked deer, all limbs and no brains. I stand and lunge for the door. Too late, I realize he could be one of those people who carries a gun on him, and if so I'm about to get whatever brains I've got in my head splattered all over the wall.

Desmond turns, making a surprised noise in his throat. He sees me. "What the—" His eyes narrow, and he grabs me before I can even start to pull the door open. Throws me on the bed. I try to get up and he slaps me. I scream. He shoves his dirty hand over my mouth and pins my arm down, laying his weight over me. "You dirty bitch. What are you doing in here?"

I try to roll away. Kick my legs up. It's no good. I can smell the wine on him. And something else. Something dark and potent.

"I said, what are you doing in here?" He takes his hand away. There's a speck of food at the corner of his mouth that I fixate on. What if it's the last thing I ever see?

I spit in his face. He curses and moves his hand to wipe it off, and I use that opportunity to push him to the side. I shove my knee in his stomach. He falls off me. "Get off me, you dick," I say, standing up.

But he's already recovered. He goes for my bag but I yank it away, clutching it to my chest like a baby. He's breathing hard. I shift my body and get the side of his face with my elbow. Then I've got the door open and I'm running.

Desmond doesn't follow.

I head away from the carnival, out into the street toward town and the pier. I know this is it. Another turn of fate's Ferris wheel, another step through a door in the Hall of Mirrors from which I can never turn back.

C&D Amusements is behind me.

I stop running after a few minutes, collapse into a grove of trees at the edge of a park. My breath is ragged, each one coming before the other is finished, wave upon wave.

I pull the boxes from my bag and unravel the film, crushing it under my fingers, tearing and twisting the reels into a heap of shiny, shimmering trash that I gather up in my arms and dump into the nearest trash bin.

"Go to hell, Desmond," I mutter. I bend over, feel something drip from my lip, and when I touch my face, I realize my nose is bleeding.

Good. I wipe it slightly, leaving a smear, and keep going. Tammy's house is past the pier, on the other side of town. I could take the bus, but the walk doesn't bother me. I'll figure it out. I might be a damaged mermaid, but a mermaid for sure. Sprouting my tail. Claiming the ocean. Saving myself. My hair trailing out behind me, dancing in the salty air.

Tammy opens the door in jogging shorts and a white T-shirt, her hair pulled back in a ponytail. I'm so happy to see her I nearly burst into tears. Her face changes from questioning to recognition to concern in about two seconds flat. "Maureen? Oh my god, are you okay?"

So the blood's still there.

I nod.

"Come in. My god. What happened? You look terrible."

I step inside, and because destiny has to throw you a few curveballs here and there, Mabel stands behind Tammy with a blank expression on her face.

"I'm fine," I say. "I just had a… I caught Desmond filming in the windows…and I just…"

"Did he hurt you?" Tammy drags me into the light of the kitchen. She wets a paper towel and hands it to me. "Do we need to call the cops?"

"Oh, Jesus Christ," Mabel says in irritation.

"No, it's fine," I say, dabbing off the blood. "I'm done with him. I quit."

"Good." Tammy squints over me like a nurse examining her patient. She seems satisfied. "We've been wanting you to do that for a while now. I can help you find a job or whatever. I know you were worried about that."

"Actually, could I ask a favor?" I glance over at Mabel quickly. "Could I just…maybe…crash here for a few days while I get things sorted out?"

"Absolutely not," Mabel says, just like I knew she would.

I flinch. I don't like asking for help just as much as Mabel doesn't like giving it.

"Mabel." Tammy's voice is low and chastising.

"She steals your guy? And you offer her a place to stay?"

Mabel crosses her arms in front of her chest and glares at both of us.

"She didn't steal him, Mabel." Tammy takes the bloody paper towel from my hand and tosses it in the trash. Then she offers me an aspirin and a small glass of water. "She can't help it if he likes her."

I swallow the pill. "Forget it, it's okay, Tammy. I can find another solution." I stand, place the glass in the sink, and move toward the door.

Tammy holds her hand out. "No, no wait. Maureen, it's fine." She turns to Mabel. "She can stay in my room. We won't bother you."

"Tammy, are you serious? She's a—"

"How many times has Ted stayed over?" Tammy interrupts, hands on her hips. "And have I ever said one word about it?" I haven't seen Tammy get angry very often, but when she does it's something.

Mabel backs down. She sighs dramatically and flicks her hair back. "Fine. Whatever. Ruin your life. Just don't eat any of my food."

"I wouldn't touch a raisin of yours." To Tammy: "This will only be for a night or two, I swear."

"Take as much time as you need," she says. "Really. It's fine."

"There's just one thing," I say carefully. "My stuff—I need my stuff. Do you think you could drive me over there so I can pack my suitcase? Before… Desmond gets to it?"

"Tonight? Is it— Do you think it's safe?"

I think about Desmond's eyes when he saw me in his trailer, the feeling of his arm across my chest. Already, though, that feels like another lifetime. I flap my mermaid tail under the kitchen stool and smile tentatively at Tammy, trying to sound braver than I feel. "It'll be fine. He won't do anything tonight. I can sneak in and pack my bag quickly while you wait with the car."

"You should *not* do that, Tammy. Absolutely not. Do you want to get in the same kind of trouble she's in?" Mabel cocks her head in an am-I-the-only-one-who's-sane-around-here kind of way.

"I promise, if it looks like any sort of trouble, we'll turn back," I say. "It's just—well, I don't have many things, but the things I have I don't want to lose. Like my clothes. My journal. You know?"

Tammy nods, stands up. Decision made. She heads to her room to get her car keys, leaving Mabel and me alone. "I can see right through you," Mabel says. "Tammy's always been too nice. Easily manipulated by people."

"You mean people like *you*? If you expect me to believe you've got Tammy's best interests at heart, then you are even dumber than I thought."

Mabel steps closer. Her voice lowers almost to a hiss. "You think I'm afraid of you and your tough act? You better be gone by the end of the week, Maureen. Or I'll make sure you are. Got it?"

Before I can respond, Tammy comes back, car keys in hand. "Let's go," she says.

Mabel gives me one last pointed look and then flounces back on the couch. "Just remember what I said," she calls as Tammy closes the door behind us.

18

ALLISON

The morning after dinner at the country club, as I nursed a slight hangover from all that punch, the doorbell rang. By the time I lumbered over to the door, no one was there.

But there was a package.

It was about the size of a cell phone, wrapped in plain brown paper and addressed to me in block letters with black ink. I picked it up and scanned my surroundings, but I didn't see anyone. Had a mail carrier come and gone that quickly?

I brought the package inside and put on Patty's yellow gardening gloves. Once at the news station, a "fan" of one of the evening anchors had sent her an envelope filled with a white substance. It turned out to be just talcum powder—the man had been upset that she'd ignored his emails asking her out and wanted to "teach her a lesson." In the weeks after, however, our executives had given us training on being vigilant about opening unexpected mail. The memory of the panic that ensued, the police officers and ambulances, stuck in my mind, and I always heeded that advice.

I cut into the paper with kitchen scissors. It was slow going, but I finally got through. Inside was a white box.

I removed the lid to find a necklace tucked in a plastic sandwich bag. I opened it and shook the charm out onto the counter. It was one-half of a best friend charm, a heart with its inner edge cut into a zigzag. On the back were the initials TQ. A note on a simple index card read: "Was SHE Disposable?"

I pressed the heart in my palm. The months after my on-air rant was posted to YouTube came flooding back as I read the words on the note over and over again. I got up from the kitchen table and walked hurriedly through the house, making sure all the doors and windows were locked. I peered out from all sides of the house, but I didn't see anyone. No prowlers in the bushes. No cars in the driveway. No one clambering over the dunes or in the backyard.

I opened my palm. The zigzag part of the charm had left red marks where I'd squeezed too hard.

Had someone found me here?

It had been months since I'd had to worry about the trolls, the ones who had appeared like maggots, who had twisted my story into something ugly after all the feminists moved on.

Had made *me* into someone ugly.

The crude jokes. The threats. A photo of a dumpster with a woman's legs hanging out of it. My face as a bloody tampon. The person on Reddit who'd published my parents' names, address and phone number. Those faceless enemies who for a time, it seemed, just wanted to tear me apart.

I'd thought it was over, but now... I looked at the half heart in my hand. Who were they talking about? Who was the "she"? Maron? Annie? Was it a threat? A prank of some kind? But aside from family and a few close friends, no one outside Opal Beach knew I was here. So why—

I traced the initials—TQ—with my finger. And then it hit me.

Tammy Quinn.

19

·——·

MAUREEN

"Hey!" Tammy advances toward me, waving one hand while the other steadies her purse strap. It's the second half of July, height of the season, and the pier is packed with tourists. Some kid nearly runs Tammy over on a skateboard. "How's the job search going?"

"Predictably shitty," I say.

"Yeah. Well. Sorry." She sighs. "It is midseason. Every-body's got their crew at this point."

"It's okay. I'll find something," I say, but I'm more worried than I let on. I tried a few of the upscale restaurants, but when they found out I worked at the carnival, their faces curled up like they smelled weeks-old garbage. At one souvenir shop I got a ten-minute rant from a lady about how she'd hired too many employees and none of them wanted to work Saturdays. I got halfway up the pier and gave up. Most managers wouldn't even give me a job application to fill out, and the ones that did handed it to me with a sort of sad pitied face that said unless a sea monster washes ashore and eats all of their employees, I ain't got a chance until next May.

"Well, you can stay with me as long as you need to," Tammy says.

"I'm sure Mabel will love that."

"It's fine." She flutters a hand in dismissal. "Come on. Let's go in Mason's. I need a new belt."

We wander around Mason's. I check out the accessories, gliding my fingers along earrings, necklaces. Everything's either red, white, and blue clearance or lace, lace, lace. I slide on a mesh glove and practice my Material Girl moves in the mirror. Tammy's still browsing the belts when I grow bored.

"Just wait outside for me," she says. "I'll be right out."

Tammy's taking forever, so I walk down the pier. On the beach, a group of kids howl as they shoot off bottle rockets, blues and greens and purples. I stand near the railing and stare down into the waves. Squint my eyes, try to spot a shimmery tail just beneath the surface. A tousle of hair clipped back by a seashell pin. But all I see is ragged seaweed, drifting in muddy clumps.

I could leave Opal Beach, but the thought of starting over again is overwhelming. Where would I go? I can't go back home.

I breathe in the hot, humid air and lean against the railing, fishing out Desmond's Super 8 camera from my bag. I've thought about selling the camera—the pawn shop would probably give me at least a week's worth of pay for it. But I like it. I've never had anything as expensive as this before. And it's dumb, but part of me feels like I could use it for good, to make up for all the images that Desmond filmed through it.

It's dinnertime and people are milling about. A little boy makes his way like a bullet through the crowds, nearly colliding with two women in intense conversation. I film as one woman squeals with surprise, then glares at the mother chasing after him. Above, on a balcony, a group of teenagers balance beer bottles on a thin railing, Van Halen blaring. I lower my camera and see one of the boys wink at me and beckon me to come on up, his finger curling like a New Year's paper noisemaker.

I shake my head, smirking inside—*you wish*, I think, shoving the camera back inside my bag—and it's then that I spot a tall, loping figure sauntering past, taking his time. Clay's uncle. Zeke. He carries himself different from everyone else—it's the suit, I think, which really does make him look like a transplant from the 1920s. He stops at Shark Shack, opens the heavy doors and disappears inside. The kernel of an idea starts to blossom inside me.

"Okay, sorry." Tammy's standing in front of me, clutching a paper bag.

I blink and then focus on her, still thinking about Zeke. "What?"

"I said I bought you a present. Well, us," she says. Her cheeks are slightly flushed, like she's just come back from a run. She rummages around inside the bag, finally removing two small blue boxes. She hands me one, and I open it at the same time she opens hers. "Best friend necklaces," she chirps, her flush deepening.

"They're so cute," I say, plucking both charms from the satin nests inside the boxes and cupping them in my palm. Two puzzle piece halves of a heart, zigzagged down the middle, each with its own chain. A best-friend-necklace kind of girl is about as far from me as one can get, but I won't hurt her feelings. "Tammy, that's so sweet."

"And look, they're engraved." She turns mine over. "You get the TQ one, for me," she says. "And I get the MH. They were running a special. No extra charge for the engraving."

I clasp it around my neck. "What do you think?" I twirl.

"One thing. Mabel would kill me. You can't tell her."

"Tell her? Won't she see it?"

Tammy stops. Her eyes widen a bit as she ponders. "We just—we won't wear them around her. Okay?"

"It's hard to keep anything from that girl, but I'll try. But hey, don't they have three-way best friend necklaces? I feel like she and I have become really close in the last few weeks."

Tammy frowns. "Maureen, don't joke. Seriously. She'd spaz. I mean, we're not close. Not like that, but she wouldn't like it all the same. I just don't want to hear all about her opinions on it and everything, it's just easier—"

I kiss her on the cheek. I have this sudden surge of affection for her. This sudden wish for everything to work out. For there to be this forever friend-ness that her necklaces suggest, anniversaries and birthdays and weddings and old ladies locking hands over brunch. For a second, I allow myself to believe it's possible. Me. Tammy. Clay. Opal Beach.

"Cross my heart, hope to die," I say. "It's our secret."

Later that night, Tammy and I are making dinner—a casserole, for god's sake, like an old married couple—when there's a knock on the door. I'm in the middle of chopping broccoli, so Tammy wipes her hands on a dish towel and goes to answer it. She returns seconds later, jerking a thumb back. "It's for you." I raise my eyebrows. "It's Clay," she says, and I can't help but sense a weird kind of disappointment in her tone.

At the door, he stands tall and awkward. "Can I borrow you for a minute?" he asks earnestly. "I won't take you away from your girls' night, promise."

I tell Tammy I'll be back before the oven timer goes off and follow Clay down the hall and out the glass double doors of the apartment building. He's parked in one of the visitor spots, clearly the fanciest car in the lot, and I imagine the goons who hang out by the dumpsters smoking weed will be circling it soon if he leaves it too long.

"What's up?"

He leads me across the street to the beach access bridge. We walk up halfway where we can see the ocean.

"I just wanted to see you. I keep thinking about going to this tournament, and I hate leaving you again, Maureen," Clay murmurs in my hair, kissing the top of my head.

I envy him, and Tammy, for their eternal optimism. I want to lean into it, get caught up in it, but I can't.

"But you're not leaving for a few weeks," I say. "It's going to be fine."

"But summer will practically be over by the time I'm back."

"I know, Clay. I've been thinking about that." I take his hand and wait for him to look at me. "Summer has to end at some point. You know that."

"Ouch," he says, clutching his heart. "You're a cruel woman."

"We have to be realistic, don't we?"

"*We* don't have to end, though." He brushes back my hair with his hand. "Right?"

"How? You'll be going off to college. You'll forget all about me."

"It's not that far. I'll come back on the weekends."

"That's sweet, but I know how these things go, Clay."

"I won't forget about you, Maureen. And you'll find something here, I know you will," he says, as though it's a given, as though I haven't been song-and-dancing at every business in Opal Beach for the last week or so, kissing ass, spinning lies about my experience, all for nothing except the one asshole at the surf 'n' turf grill who suggested with a wink that I might have luck pole dancing at the strip club in Jasper.

"Look, just think about it," Clay adds. "Come on, I'll walk you back."

We hold hands as we start walking. "I saw your uncle earlier today at the pier, by the way," I say.

Clay's frown deepens. "At Shark Shack? Yeah. No surprise. That's where he goes to get drunk and hit on the waitresses."

"At your house, he told me he plays poker. Maybe he'll let me play. I can earn some money…you know, until I find a job."

Saying it aloud seems to make it more real, like I've cemented it in the sidewalk we're walking on.

But Clay shakes his head. "That's a terrible idea. My uncle's an asshole."

"That's perfect, then. I'll be able to take his money."

"I know you think everything is a joke, Maureen. But this is not. My uncle Joe is lazy. Everyone hates him. Worse than Barron. Worse than that creep boss of yours from the carnival."

"I'm not joking! Is that what you think? This is my chance, Clay." I stop in front of Tammy's building. Try to calm down. Maybe Clay doesn't understand after all. He sees the world in black and white, right and wrong. I try again. "Don't you see? It's the way I can *stay*. Here."

He softens. "I just don't want you to get hurt. We'll figure it out, okay? Together." He tilts my chin up. "Hey," he whispers. "This isn't why I came tonight. I have something for you." He reaches into his pocket and pulls out a small box, the kind you see in Valentine's commercials where the girl gets all emotional. My heart stops.

"Clay—"

"Look." He opens it, and I see a small ring with a red heart in the middle. "It's a promise ring." He adds sheepishly, "So you won't forget me while I'm gone."

"Oh, Clay, it's…" I trail off. Pick it up, slide it on. It fits perfectly, and yet it seems wrong. Too good to be true. "I can't take this…"

He leans in and kisses me. "Of course you can. Just promise me you'll be here when I get back."

I know I can't promise that. Everything's shifting, ending, beginning. I don't know where I'll be tomorrow, or the next day, let alone two weeks. I want to tell Clay that I'm scared. I want to tell him about my mom. I want to tell him how, when I'm with him, it almost—almost—feels like everything could be okay. Almost.

"Promise," I say. "The moon."

20

ALLISON

Her face went white. I know people say that all the time, white as a ghost, a sheet of paper, snow. Tammy's face was usually a tad red and ruddy, a natural complexion that came with her fair skin and freckles, I imagined. But when she took a look at the necklace, her freckles turned into black polka dots on her drained skin.

"Where did you get this?" she whispered.

"So it is yours?" I asked.

"I haven't seen it in thirty years." Tammy was in her own world, murmuring to herself. "Why would she do this?"

"Who?" I asked.

Tammy looked up. Her eyes were shiny. "Maureen. Why would she leave this behind?"

"This was Maureen's?"

"I have the other half. With her initials on the back. It was a gift—I—" She thrust the necklace back at me, and in the process, it fell to the floor. She stared at it like it was a live snake ready to strike. "I'm sorry. I can't—I have to wait on my customers. Put it away, please, Allison."

So Maureen was the "she" in the note. The disposable one. "But why would someone leave it with *me*?"

Tammy walked over to a young guy standing at the register. I was dumbfounded. The necklace was meant for me. It couldn't have been a mistake. They used that word from my video—*disposable*. But why? I never knew Maureen.

The customer left, and Tammy came back to me. "Allison, I can't do this right now—"

"I know she and Clay were dating," I said gently.

She jumped as though I'd bit her. "Clay? He has nothing to do with this."

"But why didn't you tell me? That night in your apartment. You knew I was his family's neighbor."

"Not here, Allison," she said angrily, as the bell above the door announced another customer. "Come to my house tonight. We can talk then."

●━━━●

"I remember the day I bought these," Tammy said later that evening in her apartment. She seemed calmer now. I was pacing back and forth in her living room. I'd brought pizza, but it was sitting on Tammy's coffee table getting cold. Neither of us felt like eating.

Tammy slouched on the couch, fingering the necklace again. She'd turned the note upside down, as if she couldn't stand to look at those words anymore. *Was SHE Disposable?* "I thought everything was going to be so great."

I sat down next to her, trying to bring her back to the present. "Tammy, you have to think. If not Clay, who else was there that summer that could have had this?" *And that knows about me?* I thought.

There was Lorelei—she clearly knew about my past. But then again, half the town had probably seen my video by now. Yes, her son had dated Maureen, but I couldn't see that woman giving Maureen the time of day, let alone keeping a necklace of hers for decades.

There was Dolores and her teammates—could any of them have known Maureen? They all seemed too young.

My intuition was still pointing to Clay. I remembered his casual reaction at dinner. *There were lots of girls.* Had it been so casual after all? Or had he loved her? Could he have hung on to her necklace all these years? Did he know something, something he couldn't tell me at the club?

I sat back, ruffled my hair.

But Tammy still seemed to be slipping back to the past. "It was great, for a while. If only she'd listened to me. Things could've been so different."

"It didn't sound so great."

Tammy stood up. "It was! Here, wait. I'll show you. I mean... I was at my mom's house last weekend. After we talked, I...went and found some stuff I had in her attic."

While Tammy was gone, I tried to clear my head. On the television, Dilly—the Opal Beach weather forecaster I'd grown fond of—was predicting snow and ice for the next couple of days, frantically gesturing in front of the green screen about air patterns. Her graphics guy was a little off on his timing, so she kept having to change her report to keep up with him. She looked nervous, and I didn't envy her at the moment. People were going to be planning their lives around her weather report—and in a beach area especially, bad weather hitting was big news. Panic-inducing, sell-out-the-bottles-of-water, cancel-plans kind of big news. If she got it wrong, people would be writing hate mail for weeks.

Yes, it wouldn't be terrible to have a behind-the-scenes job. A nag of worry crept into my chest. Vaughn. Shit. I'd forgotten to email him back about the station visit. I needed to get in touch before he forgot all about me.

Tammy came back lugging a giant backpack and a few boxes, and that nag twisted, became something else as Tammy unloaded a wrinkled, faded yellow neon tank top and a few summer dresses, which she refolded and tucked beside her. "These were some clothes of hers that she left in my apartment," Tammy said. "I never could bring myself to get rid of them."

She also showed me a notebook, which she flipped through casually. "She never would've left this behind."

The journal was mostly blank, except for the last few pages, on which were scrawled random quotes in pink ink. "Life is what happens to you when you're making other plans," read one. Another: "I must be a mermaid. I have no fear of depth and a great fear of shallow living." The quotes were surrounded by sketches that Maureen had doodled, mermaid tails and hearts and music notes. It was like a precursor to those memes that people shared all over the internet.

The largest, in the center of one of the pages, surrounded by arrows: "It's not what you are, it's what you don't become that hurts." I ran my fingers over the page and felt the indentations where Maureen had pressed hard with her pen. I liked her and her earnest quotes, her loopy teenage handwriting. And indeed, she was right: what you didn't become did hurt. A lot.

"I also—Mr. Gund gave me more photos the other day," she said shyly, in a way that made me think that Dolores didn't know about it. "They're from his archives."

Some were in black and white, but most were in that faded Technicolor hazy rainbow that I recognized from my parents' old photographs of my sister and me as kids. Gund had an eye for finding the right moment. He liked to capture the rides, it seemed, legs dangling from Ferris wheel cars, geometric close-ups of mechanisms and machinery, the rounded dip of the roller coaster against a cloudless sky. But there were images of people as well, teenagers and young kids, couples holding hands.

Tammy stopped me at a smaller print. I recognized Maureen, standing alone inside one of the carnival game booths, gazing off into the distance. Behind her was a pillar of cheap stuffed animals—prizes for whatever game she was manning— and the whole booth was covered in a floral print wallpaper. She looked introspective, maybe even sad, and I wondered if that's why Gund had been compelled to snap the photo, one moment of solitude in an otherwise chaotic world.

Behind that was a photo of Tammy posing with another girl with dark hair and a crop top while they waited in a line.

"Mabel," Tammy murmured.

I took a closer look, but I would've never placed the girl in the photo as the overbearing real estate agent with teased hair. The only similarity was the slightly haughty expression.

"Wait, Mabel lived with you and Maureen, right? Could *she* have had the necklace? I wouldn't put it past her to know about my…past. She seemed to be the center of town gossip."

"Oh god no," Tammy said. "Mabel hated Maureen. No way she would want to bring her up again after all these years."

My frustration was building. Nothing made sense. Every trail I tried to follow just dead-ended or circled back.

"And look here," Tammy was saying, still flipping through the photos. At the end of the stack was another photo of Maureen, piggyback on a handsome, lanky guy with long light hair. "That's Clay," Tammy said, her voice full of affection. The young Clay was smiling, joyful, boyish, his hair half in his face.

He and Maureen were standing next to one of those strongman games where you smashed a large padded hammer down on a pad to see how far up the scale you could move the bar. Behind them, someone was in midswing, but Gund had clearly been photographing Maureen and Clay, two young people in love. For they did look in love, happy, adoring. "Wow. He was really into her, wasn't he?"

"He did like her, yes. A lot. He—" She stopped. "This is what I mean. He would never have done anything to hurt her."

But maybe he knows someone who did. I narrowed my eyes in concentration.

Another photo of Clay and Maureen caught my eye. I picked it up and realized there was another photo stuck underneath it. I pulled it off and part of the photo underneath tore. "Shit, I'm sorry," I said, and Tammy snatched it from me and tucked it in her backpack, but not before I could see it was a photo of her and a man sitting on a couch.

"It's fine," she said.

"Was that your boyfriend?" I teased her, but her face grew dark, and I regretted it.

"No," she said quietly. She put the photos away in the box and shoved it under her coffee table.

"Allison, there's something else. I don't have any proof of this, but I think Maureen was involved with someone else that summer. I got the impression he was older, and Clay didn't know about it. She wouldn't give any details." Tammy squeezed her eyes shut, then opened them. "She'd go with him to these games—gambling, I think—I felt like he might've been taking advantage of her—I don't know. I didn't like it, and I told her so."

Another guy. Maybe that was the thread that came loose, then. If Clay and Maureen had been an item, and she started dating someone else, well…the rich boy could've gotten angry. Ran her out of town. Or worse. Maybe that's what whoever dropped off the charm had been trying to tell me with their note.

"Tammy, did you tell the police any of this?"

"They wouldn't listen!" She stopped, as if shocked at how she'd raised her own voice. "Allison, I'm so sorry you got involved. I didn't mean—" She broke off. Blotches of red started to creep into her cheeks, under all the freckles. "Remember what we talked about the other night? About no one listening?"

I nodded.

"Well, if some older man was involved… You can't exactly go accusing powerful people in Opal Beach, right?" She chewed on her fingernail. "That's why Dolores backed away. That's why everyone backs away."

So that was it.

"And what? You think I'm different?"

"You *are* different. What you did, Allison? It was so brave. You're so much braver than I am. You stood up to your husband, despite all that it cost you."

"Tammy," I said. "It didn't end so well for me, remember?"

"People will listen to you. You can ask the questions that I can't. Look how much you've already done." She held up the charm, her eyes filling with tears. "This was *hers*. Someone sent it to you. We're close, Allison. I can feel it."

I remembered the way Duke's mother had stood in the middle of the living room the day I'd moved out of our house.

Their house, really, since his parents had bought it for us. She hadn't spoken a word, just watched as I moved box after box, as though I might steal something that belonged to her. She made me feel like I was scum—yes, *disposable*—like she couldn't wait to get me out of her life. The satisfaction that I'd humiliated her son—and by extension her—publicly for his sins was the only thing I'd had to grasp on to those first few weeks. When it came to the wealthy, reputations were everything.

"Will you help me, Allison? Please? We can go to the police. I have a friend there—"

"I don't know, Tammy." Thanksgiving was only a couple of weeks away. I'd be out of Opal Beach soon and back in Philadelphia in time for the new year. There was a promise of a new job. New beginnings were ahead.

And yet, Tammy had been kind to me here. She reminded me of me—trapped, anxious, feeling helpless. I couldn't just let that go. Surely it wouldn't hurt to just investigate. And possibly help her. Or at least get to the bottom of who had sent the necklace. Why they had sent it to me.

"I can't promise anything," I said.

Tammy's face melted in relief. "Thank you. Oh, Allison—"

"And no police yet."

"But—"

"No, wait. You have to understand, I'm trying to—rebuild my reputation. So if it's at all possible to resolve this without the police, I'd prefer that. If anything else happens, anything at all shady, we'll go."

"Okay," Tammy said. "Whatever you think. Oh wait, I almost forgot." Tammy reached into a box beside her and pulled out a reel of film. "I just found this. I'd forgotten about it completely, but Maureen had a Super 8 camera. She used it all the time that summer, just messing around, you know?

I don't even know where you find them anymore, or how to play this. I called around to a couple of places, but no one seems to have a player."

I twisted the reel in my hand. It felt heavy. "My parents used to have a projector. They used to take films of our vacations and Christmases. If they still have it, I could borrow it?"

21

ALLISON

It was the middle of the night, dark and hot. I was sweating, radiating an earthy, mildew smell like the basement. Had I forgotten to turn down the heat? My head felt drained, dried out, my skin taut. I was thirsty—when was the last time I'd had any water? I turned on the bathroom light, fumbling for the sink handles.

It wasn't my reflection in the bathroom mirror. It was Maureen. Maureen, with a long, braided scarf trailing down her back. Her hair was in motion, like she was underwater, like she was swimming in my bathroom mirror, and as I watched, her mouth opened and out came thousands of tiny bubbles.

Mermaids for sale. She giggled.

She lifted an arm and removed her scarf. As it came off the top of her head, so did her hair and her scalp. *Oops,* she said, as the mirror got redder and redder.

I woke up, gasping. My legs kicked out under the blankets

and Catarina leaped off the bed, annoyed at being disturbed. "I'm sorry." I pressed my hand to my heart.

The bathroom door was cracked, the nightlight inside creating a soft glow along its edges. No way was I going in there now, not after that dream.

In the hallway, Catarina let out a loud howl. I called for her, but she howled again, a strange, terrible sound that forced me out of bed. When she saw me, she jumped again and ran down the stairs.

"Catarina? Come back, you daft cat. What's wrong?" I followed her downstairs, worried that she'd hurt herself. Or maybe something had gotten into the house. Oh god, I thought. What if a mouse was in here? How the hell would I deal with that?

I heard her again down in the basement. A low growling, and then a mewing cry. Something was freaking her out. "Kitty?" I stepped down the basement stairs carefully, my heart pounding. If it was a mouse, I might just sleep in the car until morning.

The smell felt all the stronger in the darkness of the basement. I could see the cat digging furiously at the carpet in the corner. I turned on the light, hoping to startle whatever it was she was after, but nothing moved. Catarina kept kneading at the carpet, making an odd mewing sound, rubbing her head against the floor like she'd just found an amazing pile of catnip.

"What are you doing, you silly cat?" As I got closer, she stopped and walked off. I knelt down where she'd been. There was nothing there.

I stood up too fast, and my balance shifted. Everything in the room was spinning like I'd had too many rum and Cokes. I focused on the Ferris wheel painting in front of me. The Ferris wheel turned, like the carnival had opened up for the evening. The words behind the wheel were moving, too—

not shifting around but pulsating in and out. I could hear the roar of the crowd. Smell popcorn, the spun sugar of cotton candy. I closed my eyes hard, blinked a few times, resisted the urge to shake my head fast. Holy god, I was losing it. Letting Tammy's photos from the night before get to me. "Get a grip, Allison."

I stepped toward it, pressed my palm against the cold wall. The pages were shellacked, and they weren't whole pages of text but layers of text, arranged like elaborate random notes. Most of them were unreadable script or in some other language like Latin. I ran my hands across the painting, felt the ridges of layers. Tucked under one Ferris wheel cart was a newspaper clipping for movie times at a local theater—*Back to the Future*, playing on Friday at 7:20 p.m.

My fingers brushed against a word—*Lobster*—and pulled back as if stung. Not so far away from it was the word *baby*.

I stared at them like the words might morph into something else right before my eyes, but that was silly. The text was under a glaze, permanent, set right under the bottommost cart of the Ferris wheel. I sobered for a moment. That's where I'd seen it, then. That first day, I'd seen those words in the painting. *Lobster baby*.

I'd nearly forgotten about Catarina when I heard a loud cry, so odd it almost sounded human, like someone was right behind me. I turned, too quickly again, but there was no one there. It was just an empty room. So why had it felt, for just a moment, like someone had breathed down my neck?

●━━━━━●

In the kitchen, looking sleepy, Catarina sat, calm, staring up at me. Her tail flicked once. I sat down next to her and opened a jar of treats. She purred and crunched on a pile of them.

My heart was still pounding. I pressed my hand against my chest and saw the time on the microwave clock. It was 2:45 a.m.

The same time, about six months ago, that I'd called Duke and threatened to kill myself.

I hugged my knees on the kitchen floor, taking deep breaths, trying to block it out. But the memories came like a whoosh, the smell of that sweet, sickening liquor bottle. My hand gripping the cell phone, dialing Duke over and over again, tears clouding my vision, until he finally answered. Angry. Barking. And me, my senses dulled beyond the point of reality. *It'll be done before the ambulance can get here, Duke.*

Threatened. That was the key word. I hadn't really wanted to kill myself. I'd tried to tell everyone that, but no one had believed me. I still hated myself for letting Duke see me so vulnerable.

I got up, grabbed a blanket, and took it to the large wooden rocking chair in the window of the top deck. Catarina hopped up and curled in my lap. Her gentle purrs calmed me down. I felt a bit majestic framed in the large window in the dark, staring out at the ocean, the rumbling waves, the massive, eclipsing dark sky. I felt like a ghost myself. I could be the vanishing figure glimpsed in the upstairs window, no more significant than a trick of the eye. I could disappear, remembered only in fiery flickers, behind the rustle of a curtain. A local legend whispered about by kids on the beach as they tried to scare each other, their eyes dancing with the glitter of the flames.

I tried to drown out that horrible dream, my wooziness in the basement, but my mind kept flooding with images of Maureen. She'd been a kid, one young girl with so much ahead of her. And in just one night, had gone. Vanished into the summer. *And no one cared.*

I clasped the chain around my neck where I'd strung the charm, squeezing the half heart to make sure it was still there.

22

• • • • • • •

MAUREEN

There are parts of the ocean that no human has ever explored. Parts that remain so deep they are colorless, perhaps dense instead of fluid, a state of matter out of our reach and beyond our imagination. There are species of fish and mammals that we've never seen, living things that have learned to survive amidst so much pressure and weight, animals with no need for eyes.

Why can't there be mermaids who live there, who skim the surface every now and then, somewhere far off at the edge of the horizon, breaking the surface only to gaze at the unending blue waves for a time? These mermaids flick their tails at the stars and wonder about the life and loves on other planets, in worlds beyond what *they* can imagine. They aren't afraid to take risks to get what they want, what they need. They aren't afraid to enter the castle under the sea, to play their magical harps for the kings and the princes, to let those mermen watch as they dance, as their hair sways back and forth into curls and question marks, soothing and calming. And when the mermen's eyes roll back and they fall into deep dreams of glittering scales and fluttery goldfish-fin-kisses, the mermaids strike. They find the golden necklaces. They nestle the small jewels in their cheeks. They unravel the roped keys from the mermen's necks and unlock all their secrets and take them with them, to a better place. To a happily-ever-after.

Those mermaids are not the mermaids of fairy tales. They don't cut out their tongues or hack off their hair. They are smarter. They make the right choices. They swim back to the cities, the shores, when they are ready, and they claim their daughters.

Their daughters are always, always waiting for them.

23

ALLISON

There was something about Opal Beach. The strange sense of both having nowhere to hide and feeling insignificant. The lack of trees, which gave the feeling of being more open, exposed. The small streets, with buildings that seemed to lean, squared up with one another in a defensive way, as if to say to outsiders, *You don't belong here*. And yet—from the neatly trimmed bushes lining the edges of the streets, those immaculate golf courses everyone fawned over, and even the light music pumping from the gift store next door—so much of it seemed so *perfect*. Maybe Dolores had been right when she'd been so disdainful of the place. I couldn't help but wonder what was underneath the surface. What the locals said and did to one another behind closed doors. What happened to the teenagers late at night, under the boardwalks.

I stood at the door to the Gund art gallery, unsure whether I should knock or just walk in. I'd told Dolores I was going to drop by to finally see the gallery, but I had other motives in mind as well. I couldn't help but wonder if Dolores sent me Maureen's necklace or knew who had. I kept focusing on that word *disposable* in the note—and Dolores was the one who'd told her entire team about my video. Had her dad somehow found the charm in his archives?

The tiny dollhouse gallery stood right across the street from Tammy's coffee shop, its blue paint, no doubt once vibrant, faded and flecked from the salty surf air, giving the building a shabby look. A crooked sign on the front door listed the hours, with a handwritten addition in purple Magic Marker: "May change abruptly in the off-season."

I wondered if Tammy could see me through the window of her shop. I hadn't told her I was going to see Dolores. I didn't want Tammy to get excited, to think that I could help her. I was still holding on to any semblance of peace I could muster, even if the arrival of the necklace had thrown me off.

A gust of wind kicked up, convincing me to try the door. It opened easily, and immediately a dry wave of heat from the radiators welcomed me. The dark wooden floor creaked beneath my feet as I entered a small, stark gallery. A few beach scenes hung on the walls—abstract oceans, collages of the pier, crabs stranded on the sand.

In the back of the room, Dolores sat behind a desk, scooping French fries out of a grease-stained paper bag and watching something on her laptop. When she saw me, she waved one hand in greeting and shut the laptop with the other.

"Is it lunchtime already?" I asked, glancing at my watch. My belly protested at the scent of fried food, and I realized I hadn't eaten anything yet.

"All the good places downtown close in the off-season, so I'm forced into fast food," she said, pushing aside the bag and standing up. "Did you want to see Dad's art?" She was in salesperson mode now, her tone measured and hushed, like she might wake up the artwork if she spoke too loudly. "He's got the collages up now, as you can see. He's been big into those lately. Different from what Patty and John have at the house?"

I peered at an image of a crab made up of bottle caps. "I like how three-dimensional they are."

Dolores rolled her eyes, but I could see the affection in them. "He's been experimenting with trash. He uses all kinds of stuff, old book pages, scraps he finds on the beach. I call them his trash collages. It riles him up."

"It's cool. And are these photographs underneath?"

"Oh yeah, all photographs. He's been digging up the archives. Come on, I'll show you his library."

She pushed aside a black curtain I hadn't even noticed. Behind was a large room lined with metal shelves on both sides, with worktables, supplies and canvases in various states of completion. Directly in front of me was a large painting of a lounging woman, half in the surf, her long, wavy hair crafted from what looked like pieces of tire. Beyond her, on an old table, sat stacks of newspapers, tubes of paints and inks, and a banker's lamp that looked like it had seen better days. There were more crabs, a series of them in different positions, some colored in with bright reddish-pink paint, others sketched in haste in dark pencil. The room felt crowded, but still pleasant, with an underlying creative energy.

"And so we meet again." Jim Gund hunched over a small wooden table, half-hidden by a rickety, paint-speckled metal shelving unit. I was surprised he'd remembered me, but then I recalled the mantra: small town. He had a red bandanna tied around his head, and he was using some sort of knife tool to cut a piece of thick canvas.

"Yes, and I'm afraid I still haven't gotten used to bringing a hat and gloves around with me," I said.

He nodded, wiped his hands on his apron and went over to a shelf that had dozens more plastic bottles of paint.

"He doesn't like to be disturbed when he's at work. Interrupting the genius," Dolores said playfully.

Gund grunted, a noise that could've meant agreement or dismissal, I wasn't sure. When he moved back to his work, I noticed a large table behind him with several boxes of photographs. On each box were dates labeled in black Magic Marker. So this is where Tammy's photos had come from. "Wow."

Dolores caught me looking. "Yeah, so this is what I call 'the library.' He's basically got an archive of Opal Beach. The actual library's been trying to get their hands on it for years."

Gund piped up, "And if they knew how to store and organize anything, we could talk."

"This is amazing," I said, wandering over to a box labeled 1995. I flipped through the photos, many of them of the pier, of tourists with souvenirs, musicians playing in the bars, their saxophones and guitars glinting like Christmas trees in the stage lights. I looked around for the 1985 box, but it was nowhere to be seen.

"This isn't even half of it," Dolores said. "Every year, my dad goes back ten, twenty, thirty years to his photos. He does a special series of paintings based on a few of them." She tapped me on the arm. "Let's go back up front so I can finish my food while we talk."

We ducked back through the curtain. Dolores motioned to an empty chair across the desk, and I sat obediently. She took a bite of a sandwich and wiped her mouth with her napkin. "So whatcha been up to all this time?"

"Oh, you know, a little bit of everything," I said. "I was at the fall festival dinner at the club last week with the Bishops. How come you weren't there?" I asked, half teasing.

Dolores raised her eyebrows. "Me? Lord no. A team of derby girls couldn't drag me to one of those things. Besides," she said, cracking her knuckles, "I was up in Philly visiting Sharon. Just got back last night, actually."

If that was true, then Dolores couldn't have been the one to drop the necklace on the porch. But that didn't mean she didn't know who did.

"So what's the deal with Tammy and that friend of hers who went missing?" I said. "Why'd you wave me off the subject that night at the bar?"

Dolores rolled her eyes. "Oh man, I knew it. I knew she was trying to rope you into it, too."

"So you don't believe her?"

Dolores put down her sandwich and took a sip of her soda. She sat back, unzipped her fleece jacket. Underneath, I could see part of a tattoo peeking out of the collar of her shirt. I imagined what it must've felt like to have needles and ink drilling into skin so close to your neck. "It's not so much that I don't believe her as I can't really help her."

She handed me a French fry over the desk. I waved it at her reproachfully before I ate it. "Really? It didn't seem that way at the bar."

"Eh, it's just that I didn't want it all to come bubbling back up again, you know? Tammy's been through a rough time lately."

"Oh," I said, surprised. "What happened?"

Dolores shrugged. "No idea. She was fine—and then all of a sudden a few months ago it was 'Dolores, you have to help me find out what happened to this random friend I had years ago.' It was right around the time her mom got *sick* again." Dolores made quote signs with her fingers. "This one seemed particularly bad, though, and her mom had to go to a hospital for treatment."

"Is she an alcoholic?"

"Nah, I don't think so. More like depression. Helpless-ness. Frankly, I think she just likes someone to wait on her. Tammy doesn't like to talk about it." Dolores's voice thick-ened with conviction. "I know that sounds harsh to you, but trust me, I've seen it in action. Tammy's always trying to save people. She's been in this town her whole life, always helping her mother out with whatever new *affliction* she gets. Tammy hasn't had much of a life of her own."

"So is that what is going on with this friend of hers? Some kind of savior complex?" I asked.

"Something like that. I mean, I tried to help. I did a good job, too. But I didn't find much." She opened a desk drawer. "I still have it all here. I should be a private eye."

I stared at the thick folder. It certainly looked like Dolores had found more than she'd implied. She flipped through. "This was like three months ago? Tammy came in, asking about old photos. Like I said, Dad keeps everything. So she wanted to look through ones from thirty years ago. First she said it was some project she was doing, and I thought she meant like a scrapbook or something. Then I find out it's about this friend of hers. She said she thought something bad happened to her."

I nodded. "That's what she told me, too." I didn't say the word *murder*, but Tammy's words still echoed in my ear.

"Well, honestly, something probably did," Dolores said. "But not here in Opal Beach. Maybe after, and that's what I told Tammy. She had no proof the girl died here or anything. Just a *hunch*."

"Tammy thinks Maureen might've been involved with an older guy," I said, not wanting to mention Clay Bishop quite yet. "That he had something to do with it."

"Yeah, she told me that, too. Some mysterious married guy or something. It seemed like she was just grasping at straws, though. To me this is more of a classic case of teenage run-away."

I raised an eyebrow. "So you think she just left town? Without telling her best friend?"

Dolores ignored that. "Did you know that Maureen's not even her real name?" She smirked with pride. "Well, not her first name anyway. I had to widen my search terms to find her at all." I suspected that even though Dolores hadn't gone into library science, she was feeding her habit in another way—as a hacker in her spare time. "Her full name is…" She stopped and rummaged through the papers. "Here it is. Her driver's license. Janet Maureen Haddaway." She slid the printout of the license over to me. Maureen had shorter hair than in the pictures I'd seen, but it was definitely her. "Haddaway," Dolores was saying. "I remember that because it sounds so much like 'hideaway,' doesn't it? And that's kind of what she was doing."

"Hiding?" I said. "From what?"

"Whatever runaways hide from. In her case, sounds like her mom. Her mom was a druggie. Overdosed in 1989. No father on the birth certificate. Sad story."

She opened her folder and started ticking things off. "Our Janet went to high school in Maryland, but she never finished. I couldn't find any evidence that she worked at the carnival, like Tammy said, but I don't think they kept any real employee records. Paid off-the-books."

"Wow, you found a lot," I said.

Dolores closed her folder. "I mean, none of this solves anything about where she went when she left here."

My fingers flew to the necklace tucked under my shirt, and I had to stop myself from pulling it out. I didn't think Dolores knew anything about it. She was blunt, and I couldn't see her sending something anonymously—she'd want the credit. And I didn't want to show it to her. I was afraid of how she'd react—that she'd laugh in my face or tell half of Opal Beach about it before I even stepped off the gallery's front porch.

"What about Clay Bishop? Did Tammy tell you he was dating Maureen?"

Dolores's face changed. "Every time I bring up the Bishops, Tammy gets all weird. I think she had some kind of thing for that guy, to be honest, but she won't talk about it."

"Really?" I frowned. I never got that vibe from her. Friendly affection, sure, but I'd never gotten the impression there were romantic feelings there.

"Hey look, I'm not saying that family's full of Mother Teresas or anything. Who the hell knows? But, dude—I wouldn't touch that with a one-hundred-foot pole. When I told her that, she got really mad, told me to forget she'd ever even said anything. I feel bad, but I can't really help." She lowered her voice. "Listen, for whatever reason, this whole thing's stirred up a bee's nest in Tammy. She's—she's grasping at straws. This isn't about this girl. It's about Tammy. It's about her feeling guilty about anyone and everyone in her life that she can't save. If she starts going around accusing random people of stuff here…well, let's just say it's not good. You want to be her friend? Just drop it. For her own good."

24

·————·

MAUREEN

The mass of people. Older than me, but still young. To them, I am just a child. I get elbows and disdainful looks and occasionally a few spilled drops of cosmos on my shoulder because I shouldn't be here. I am one-too-many in an already packed bar in a tourist town where happy hour is almost ending. I despise this place, which is how I know Zeke will be here, how I know, almost like he's a doll I've placed in my Barbie mansion, that he will be positioned at the very end of the bar, against the wall, the best seat in the house.

I see him, flicking a toothpick between his teeth, murmuring to a blonde fox in a halter top next to him. She shakes her head, sips her drink and moves away, rolling her eyes at her friend, then melting into the crowd. As his eyes transition from her, he catches mine. Spots me before I want him to, and I'm surprised when he smiles. Surprised but not surprised because I am just another girl in the bar, another prize to try to win—a trade up or a trade down? Remains to be seen.

"Destiny," he calls as I approach, sliding out the bar stool next to him. He's wearing another one of those linen suits, a skinny tie, a man with a mission and nowhere to go.

I slide in. "How lucky for me, a seat," I say. Up close I can smell his cologne and the gin burning off his breath.

"How lucky for *me*," he says, staring at me like he's not sure I'm real. Like if he blinks, I might disappear. "What brings you here?"

"You," I say simply, crossing my legs and getting comfortable.

The bartender comes over. Zeke orders another martini "and whatever the lady's having." The bartender surveys me, and I know I can't hesitate.

"What kind of vodka do you have?"

He lists off some, his eyes already shifting to another customer leaning in with bills in his fist.

"Hmm," I say, trying to sound unimpressed. "Do you have sambuca?"

"Fresh out."

I frown. "Okay, a Bloody Mary, then. Hold the garden," I say and turn back to Zeke.

"Well, well. An expert." He takes a sip of his drink. "You keep surprising me, Destiny."

I shrug. The music's loud, and we have to talk in each other's ears to hear. "So, about that poker game."

"I knew you had an ulterior motive," he shouts. "No real love for Old Joe. Just take, take, take."

"Not true. Nothing *but* love for you." I touch his arm. "Just try me out one time."

"Oh, I'd like to."

I roll my eyes. "Seriously, Zeke. It'll be worth your while. I'm good. I'm really good. Poker's my thing."

"Does my nephew know you're here? Seems like he wouldn't approve of all this."

If Clay knew, he would be crushed. But I had to think for myself. I was hot out of cash. "I don't care who approves of what I do."

The bartender comes back, interrupting us. He hands me the drink. "You got ID?" he asks, hesitantly, but before I can answer Zeke holds up his hand.

"She's cool, she's with me."

I grin at the bartender, and he shakes his head and walks away.

"Just one game."

"Destiny—"

"My father was a blackjack dealer," I lie. "I grew up in casinos, practically. I won't embarrass you."

"It's not about that." He leans back against the wall, surveying me. One eye narrows. "How did you know I'd be here, anyway?"

I dodge that question with another. "Why *are* you here? I thought you'd be a regular at your family's restaurant."

Zeke snorts, takes a sip of his drink, pinkie out. "Oh sure. I'll hang out there. Put on my plastic bib and sip the OJ with all the kiddies." His face darkens. "The good ole family business. I don't think they'd want me there, soiling their wholesome image, do you?"

I think about the way Clay's mom looked at him when he walked in from the beach that night, and I understand what Zeke means. He doesn't fit in either. We have that in common, anyway.

He gestures with his hand. "Besides, I believe this is a slightly more interesting place."

"A little young for you, maybe."

"Ouch. Be careful, little one. Uncle Joe is buying the

drinks, remember? Now…you were telling me how you knew to find me here."

"Clay said you hang out here." I don't mention that I saw Zeke walking on the boardwalk.

"So he does know you're here?"

I don't answer. Zeke chuckles, fingers the bottom of my chin. I draw back.

"Don't patronize me."

"Oh, I'm not. I just like the idea that you and I have a secret."

"We can have plenty of secrets," I say, meeting his eyes.

We stare at one another for what seems like hours. Then he breaks the gaze and sighs deeply. "You drive a hard bargain, Destiny."

"So yeah?"

"I'll see what I can do."

I jump up, hug him, nearly knock his drink over.

"But don't go blabbing it around to your girlfriends. This is all hush-hush."

"To my girlfriends? Honestly, Zeke? Who do you think I am?" I slip off the stool, get my purse. "So when will you pick me up?"

"Leaving already?"

"I got what I wanted."

"I didn't."

"Good things come to those who wait."

Zeke smirks, drains his martini. "Friday. Wear something nice."

———●────────●———

Outside Shark Shack I stop at a pay phone. I'm not expecting her to answer, so when she does, I nearly hang up in surprise.

"Mom?" I finally say hesitantly.

"Baby? Where are you?" Her voice sounds dry, cracked. But not terrible.

"I'm fine, Mom. I wanted to let you know I'm okay."

"Come home," she says. I can hear the soft gasping, and I feel a sharp pain in my chest. It takes a moment for me to recognize it as guilt. "I need you, baby. Mr. Frank has been calling 'round again, on me about the rent again. I keep telling him—it's hard, you know."

I close my eyes, feeling her need, like a giant wrecking ball. Everything I'd run away from. Each time the "clouds" came— doing the laundry. Cooking meals. All my paychecks from the grocery store going to pay the electric bills. And after she'd lost our house—Grandpa's house—all the apartments, each one worse than the last, each one with the everyday dread of the landlord coming knocking, peering in the windows, *Shh, Reen, just duck down, he'll be gone soon.* I'd tried and tried and then I'd left. Headed into the sun. Toward my destiny. But the shadows followed me here.

"Has Gwen been to see you lately?" I ask.

"She was just here the other day… Wednesday? Asking about you. But we didn't do anything. We didn't." Which means they got high as kites, I know. I bite my lip.

"Mom?"

Silence on the other end of the phone, and I'm imagining my mother in her dark bedroom, cold compress over her face, empty Jack Daniel's bottles on the nightstand. I feel a surge of panic and force myself to turn, to look at the hot street, the tourists on their way to fun. To remember the ocean air.

"I'm here, Reen baby. It's so good to hear your voice." Is she slurring? I can't tell.

"Mom, just please. Hold tight, okay? I'm going to fix everything. I swear it. I've got a plan, okay? I'm going to get some money. And then I'll be back and I'll help you."

I am your mermaid.

I hang up. The heat of the evening feels heavy, harsh. I try to regain the light, airy feeling I had leaving Zeke in the bar, but it's too far away.

Tammy and Mabel are supposed to be roller-skating, so I'm surprised to find them at home. They're seated around the kitchen table, busy at work. Mabel's got a make-up bin splayed open, and it looks like a crime scene, with red-stained cotton balls and piles of fingernails all over the table.

"What did you guys do, kill a gang of Barbies?" I ask.

Tammy smiles, but Mabel doesn't even look up. She's pressing a large, fake white fingernail on Tammy's ring finger. "I'm getting a manicure," Tammy says. "Want one?"

"No, thanks." I open the refrigerator. "Did you gals have fun at the roller rink? Did Big Bird come to give you balloons?"

"Oh, I wish you wouldn't make fun," Tammy says. "You should try it sometime. You'd like it."

"She's way too cool and hip for that," Mabel says, shaking a bottle of neon pink nail polish.

"No, I'd just fall and break my ankle," I say from the refrigerator. "It's not my thing. We've all got our things, right? Tammy likes roller-skating, Mabel likes polishing her pitchfork."

Tammy laughs, then covers it with a cough when Mabel glares at her.

"Out with your boyfriend, Clay, again?" Mabel asks. She

starts painting Tammy's new nails with the pink polish, careful, shiny strokes, like a professional.

"No." I'm still thinking about my mother and don't feel much like talking. I sit down at the table with cheese and crackers. It's the last of the food I bought myself, and though Tammy's been sweet about "accidentally" making too much dinner and sharing with me, I know I've got to do something soon. I'm grateful for her kindness, but the last thing I want to be is someone's charity case.

Tammy gives Mabel her other hand. "Isn't he at his tournament?"

"He's leaving on Saturday."

"Oh boo-hoo," Mabel says. "Then who will you sponge off? Oh right. Tammy."

Tammy and I ignore her. "Did something happen with Clay?" Tammy asks me quietly.

"No, why?"

"No reason," Tammy says. "I was just wondering."

Mabel and I both give her looks.

"Really. What? You guys, I am so not into him anymore. I've moved on." She says this last part mysteriously.

"Seriously?" I push my problems aside for the moment. "Who's the guy?"

"Here's my thing." Tammy says in a way that makes me think she's been dying to tell us this. She's blushing furiously, so I know it's going to be good. "I can't tell—well, I don't know how to say this without sounding stupid."

I try to help. "When will you know if you should sleep with him?"

Tammy shakes her head. "No, we've already done *that*," she says, and laughs at our expressions. "You guys think I'm such a virgin or something. Stop it. No, I'm just wondering about orgasms. Just…how will I know? It never feels…right."

Normally I'd lie, tell her some elaborate thing just to get in her goat. But Tammy's looking a bit misty, so I reach over and pat her arm, careful not to smudge her polish. "No worries, gal. It never feels very good."

"Never?"

"Like 99.9 percent of the time," I say.

"But how will I know when it's that 0.1 percent?"

"Oh, you'll know," Mabel declares, and I resist the urge to roll my eyes. "Trust me, it'll happen, don't worry. When Ted and I—"

Tammy starts humming loudly. "No way. I don't want to hear about you and Ted, Mabel. For cripes' sake, he's like my brother."

Mabel looks wounded, and I smile into my hand. "I wasn't going to give you details, Tam. Jeez. I'm just saying—it can happen."

"Yeah, yeah. And it's beautiful. One-in-a-million-lifetimes amazing. But who is this guy?" I ask again, leaning across the table and pinching her. She pulls away, still deep in thought.

"I can't tell you that," she says. "It's complicated… He doesn't want anyone to know about us yet."

"Oh jeez, Tammy. He's not taken, is he?"

"No," she says instantly, in a way that makes me think he's most definitely married.

"Tammy, you don't want to go there."

"He's not married," she says again. "He's just—it's a delicate situation, that's all."

"Do you work with him?" Mabel asks. A smart conclusion, I'll give her that.

"Your boss?"

"You guys, please stop. Just stop asking questions, okay. I'm sorry I brought it up. I just thought…" She stops, waves her fingers in the air as if to dry them. "Never mind."

"No, it's good," I say. "I'm glad for you. Just be careful, okay?"

She looks at me, and in her eyes I see a shine of panic before she blinks. "Of course."

25

● · · · · · ●

ALLISON

Drop it. I kept hearing Dolores's voice in my head over the next few days. And yet I couldn't. Someone had sent the necklace, with a note just for me. Someone was trying to tell me something. Maybe even warn me. And I needed to know who.

I tried a few Google searches, but I was no match for the Spine Cracker and came up with a bunch of Janet Haddaways on Facebook who were nowhere near the right age, and one Maureen Haddaway who had died at home in Lincoln, Nebraska, with her pet parrot at the age of eighty-nine. Searches on the traveling carnival turned up little more information than Jim Gund had shared, but the girl who'd been killed was definitely not Maureen.

Even Clay Bishop was hard to find online, except for a few research papers he'd coauthored about something called "diophantine approximation" and a professor bio from his college that made him sound smart if also dull.

Clay. Tammy was adamant that he wasn't involved. Yet while Clay had acted so flippant about Maureen at dinner, Tammy's pictures showed them together so often. They had clearly been an item—Tammy had all but admitted that.

I kept thinking about Maureen, on her own, her mother abandoning her, or at least not being able to take care of her. How had she ended up in Opal Beach, with no one to protect her or watch out for her? Everyone seemed so convinced she had just wandered off at the end of summer. But had she? Maureen had been straddling two worlds—working for a traveling carnival on the one hand and dating one of the richest boys in Opal Beach on the other. So which one had gotten her in trouble? Because if her trail stopped at Opal Beach—and even Dolores had said so much—then chances are so had Maureen.

I was messing around with a genealogy website, trying to decide if I should pay the fifty-dollar annual fee to find out more about Maureen's family, when the doorbell rang. The sound was majestic, church-like bells that echoed through the house. I'd only heard it a few times: when the mail carrier had delivered packages from my parents and when someone had dropped the necklace on my porch.

From the upstairs window I was stunned to see my sister's truck in the driveway. What day was it? Had I really lost that much track of time? But no, the day on my laptop screen clearly said Saturday. And Annie had told me she was coming to visit on Monday, her day off. So why was she early?

"Surprise," Annie said, sheepishly, when I opened the door to find her and her boyfriend, Mike, standing there. She held up a large plastic bag. "Looks like the early turkey dinner we'd planned on is happening even earlier. I hope we're not intruding?"

"No, come on in," I lied, doing a quick panicked survey of the house to see if it was a disaster. Luckily the big mess was upstairs, in my room, where dirty laundry was scattered in the corners.

"Don't be mad," she said as she slipped by me. "One of the girls had to switch shifts with me because of relatives coming in for the holiday, so Mike and I thought it would be fun to surprise you, you know?" She trailed off and turned to face me, and I could almost hear the rest of her thoughts. *And we wanted to make sure you were alright.*

Mike was already wandering the house. His wowing was amusing at first, but then started to get on my nerves. He was a pharmacist at Annie's hospital—how they'd met—and a good-looking athletic type, affable, with a generous mop of brown curly hair. I liked him, but he always brought out a conflict in me. Part of me wished he had more snark in his bones and part of me wished that *I* had found someone so easygoing.

But it wasn't just that. After living alone for so many weeks, I didn't *want* the company. An overnight stay—an early Thanksgiving, Annie had called it cheerfully. But everything seemed to grate on my nerves. The fact that they'd invaded my space with food and drink, shoving it into my refrigerator and knocking over my pitcher of Kool-Aid. And they talked too loud, settled into my space, dropped their duffel bags in the hallway. But the worst was my creeping suspicion that Annie had come to check on me.

"This house is amazing," Mike said again, for maybe the tenth time, sitting back on the low couch and balancing a glass of the Thanksgiving punch Annie had made from our mother's recipe. She was trying hard to make it all seem festive and normal. It was a sweet gesture, and I found myself feeling guilty for being annoyed with her. I missed our nights together in her apartment. Even if many of those nights had been rough, with me going through my many stages of grief, it had been comforting to have my sister so close.

"So do you absolutely love it here?" Mike asked.

"Sure," I said, trying to sound upbeat, though it fell flat. My mind kept drifting to Annie's motives, then to the necklace, to Maureen.

"Are you sure you don't want to come back with us for the holiday?" Annie asked. "Mom and Dad would love it."

"I can't. The cat." Which was true, but not the only reason. It was my first Thanksgiving since Duke and I had split up, and I wasn't sure I was up for a big happy family gathering.

Annie nodded, but frowned. "I just hate to think of you here all alone on Thanksgiving. And the weather..."

As if on cue, the wind picked up and howled outside, and we all turned and watched the waves spiraling and crashing in the misty air. Dilly the weather forecaster had been predicting more snow and ice over the Thanksgiving weekend.

"I'll be fine," I said. "I'm actually looking forward to it. No traffic and all. It'll be nice. Peaceful."

Mike chuckled. "You mean 'quiet,' right? Without the likes of us dropping in?" He put his hand on Annie's knee and squeezed. I imagined him at my parents' house, helping our mom cut the turkey, fussing over her green bean casserole. Duke never had. Duke always seemed too big for anywhere— the bull in the china shop—shifting in his seat, pacing the outside of the house for a smoke break, finding some reason to run an errand. He didn't like my parents' house, with its fading wallpaper, overstuffed sofas, mismatched scrap-yarn afghans draped over all the furniture.

In the beginning, I didn't blame him. I wanted something different, too, lured in by his parents' immaculately landscaped home, tucked between two small hills down a mile-long driveway. I lusted after their two-story-tall Christmas tree, decorated with matching colored ornaments and lights, delicate ceramic doves and gold-coated trumpets that were the complete opposite of the mash-up, chaotic tree my mother put up each year with homemade ornaments from when Annie and I were kids.

When I'd married Duke, I'd thought I'd have a life of perfect family photos, elegant champagne cocktail parties, spacious rooms and long vacations. How wrong I'd been.

"Have you talked to Vaughn lately?" Annie asked, taking a pinch of the banana bread from a napkin on her lap. Her voice was measured. Was this it, then? She'd come here because of the job?

"We're talking about scheduling a time for me to go to the station," I said.

"He said he tried to set a time, but you canceled?"

"I didn't cancel. I just—postponed. It was a bad time…" It had been right after I'd gotten the package, the necklace, and I'd been too distracted to think about an in-person job interview. I wasn't even sure I had a clean suit.

"He said you didn't send over some reports you were supposed to do?" Annie's voice was still calm, but I could sense what was underneath. I felt myself flush with embarrassment. I'd done all those reports to prepare for the interview and then forgot to send them over. Shit.

"Look, it's just been—I got wrapped up in helping a friend out and I forgot. Don't worry, I'll blame it on the bad reception," I tried to joke, but Annie was having none of it.

"Allison, I just don't want you to miss out on this opportunity," she said. "I spent so much time—"

"I'm not going to mess it up. Or embarrass you," I said, too loudly.

"I just hope it still works out," Annie said quietly. "It's perfect."

I bit back the words I wanted to say, *You can't fix me. Not like you want to.*

"Dinner smells great, babe," Mike jumped in, as if Annie had been slaving away for hours in the kitchen instead of just reheating the turkey and sides from Popeyes that she'd picked up on her way down. She had, however, pulled down all of Patty's china and glassware, cleaned it and set the table. "I've been eager to get down here ever since Annie told me about the place," Mike was saying. "And it's better than our apartment, where the water takes about twenty minutes to get hot."

I watched Annie's face turn scarlet. *Our* apartment?

"Yeah, so, Mike moved in," Annie said, uncomfortable, glancing at Mike. "Didn't I tell you that?"

"Oh. No, I don't think so." I forced a smile to cover up my surprise. "Well, congrats," I said brightly, holding up my punch glass. I hadn't really expected to move back in with my sister when I was done with the housesitting job, but I guess I also had always considered it a possibility. A safety net. I was hurt. She could've at least told me.

"I mean, if you need to come back...after..." Annie hesitated, waving her hands like she was trying to grasp something out of the air. "We can figure it out. I just thought..."

"No, no." I took a drink to recover, dabbing the side of my mouth with my napkin. "Oh gosh, of course not. Don't be silly. I've got plans for after I leave here. This is great. Really."

Annie nodded slowly, but she didn't look at me. I didn't want to be someone they had to worry about. I felt hot.

Mike stood up, jingling the ice in his glass. "Time for a refill. Can I get anyone anything?"

———

"Are you and your sister fighting?" my mother asked when I answered her call.

"Now there's a greeting," I said, plopping down on my

bed. I'd gone back to the bedroom for a quiet moment, but I should've known she'd call. My mother always had an uncanny way of sensing when Annie and I were anxious or angry. "You know we never fight. We always agree on everything."

"Well, now I know you're lying."

"No, it's fine. I just found out—I didn't know Mike was living with her."

There was a slight pause. I pictured my mother, hair askew around her head, reading glasses perched at the end of her nose, rummaging around in one junk drawer or another. I settled farther into the pillow, enjoying the comfort of her voice. "He's good for her, I think."

"Oh, he is," I said quickly to reassure her I wasn't implying anything bad about Mike. "I just didn't know. It caught me by surprise."

"What about you?" she asked.

"I definitely am not shacking up with any dudes, Mom."

"Not that, Ally." She grew quiet. "I did a reading last night."

My mom was famous for her tarot readings. For a long time when Annie and I were kids, she'd done them—or astrology readings—for the neighborhood moms as a way to make a little bit of money while she stayed home with us. She'd wanted to put a sign in our living room window—a palm with a giant eye in the middle of it that creeped me out—but thankfully Dad wouldn't allow it. I can still remember that soft rap on the back door, which meant some friend of hers was hovering outside, waiting to be let inside for her appointment. Sometimes I'd sit near the kitchen door, pressing my ear against the wall to listen as my mom discussed the Sagittarius sun conjoining Jupiter or reassured someone that the Death card was nothing to fear. In college, I was exhilarated to take courses on actual scientific phenomena—weather—rather than worrying if a certain planet's moon shift might bring me a setback or cause havoc on my love life. But that had been a long time ago, and now my mom only read for herself or close friends and family.

"Are you going to win the lottery?" I joked. I got up from the bed and peered behind the drapes. Snowflakes swirled around on the beach.

"Are you having any trouble there?"

"Trouble?" I paused, felt the familiar tension grow between my shoulder blades. "No. I'm fine, Mom."

"Just something in the cards." She sighed. "Probably nothing. I'm getting rusty in my old age. I just—wanted to make sure. You're sure?"

"Yeah, Mom, everything's fine. Pinky-swear promise."

There was a knock on the door, and Annie peeked her head in and slid around my bedroom door, closing it behind her.

"I've got to go, Mom. We're about to eat." I hung up.

Annie stood, hands in her pockets, in front of the door. "Did she have an intuition?"

I nodded. "It was your aura," I said, but it was more of an autoresponse than anything else, and neither of us laughed. "She seemed worried. Did she send you down here to check on me?"

Annie did that frowny face she turned on whenever she was chiding me. "We just miss you."

"Seems like you're doing fine without me." It slipped out before I could think better of it. When she flinched, I realized how it had sounded. "I'm sorry. That wasn't fair."

"I suppose I deserve it. I wanted to tell you, I just never seemed to find a good time to bring it up."

"No, that was unfair of me. Your life. You don't have to brief me on everything you do. And you don't have to drive down to check on me either."

"Ally, are you okay?"

"Look, about Vaughn—"

She held up her hand. "I'm over it, okay. I didn't mean to be pushy." Annie perched on the edge of the bed and folded her hands in her lap. "Mom said you had a project you're working on?" She was looking at me curiously, and I wondered what my face betrayed. "Is this related to the friends you told me about?"

I nodded. "I just—"

There was a loud tap on the door. Mike called from the other side tentatively. "Ladies? Sorry to interrupt, but something smells like it's burning?"

Annie looked at me, stifled a laugh. We were sisters again, coconspirators, giggling together in the dark.

⁃———⁃

The next morning, we were all hungover, and I knew that Mike and Annie were going to have a long drive home. Dilly, in her perky but stern way, was predicting the weather to arrive even earlier than expected. I knew what was ahead of her—having to camp out in a nearby hotel or perhaps in the studio itself so she could go on-air nonstop to report on all the twists and turns of the storm. I didn't miss that part of the job.

We did a flurry of awkward hugs, and I waved goodbye from the icy front porch as they pulled out of the driveway and disappeared. Their company, it turned out, had actually been nice. Had I made a mistake in staying behind? I thought about calling Tammy, but she was busy with her mother.

I walked back into the house and noticed the clunky projector sitting against the living room wall. Annie had brought it from our parents' house, and I'd forgotten about it in the whirlwind of their visit.

I lugged it upstairs to Patty and John's bedroom—the darkest room in the house besides the basement—removed a Jim

Gund painting from the wall and pointed the projector at the now-blank space. The machine started to whir, the tape made a sputtering sound, and for one panicked moment I thought I'd broken it. Then the movie started.

It was a flickering image, old and blurry in parts. Immediately I felt immersed into the world. The first clip was of a summer day. The camera scanned the beach, showing mostly families sunning or playing with their kids in the water. It was a woman filming, Maureen, I assumed—I watched as she focused on her own feet, tanned, speckled with white sand, toenails painted bright red. Then the beach again, zooming in on the ocean, the waves.

A teenage boy appeared, his long wavy hair pulled back into a ponytail. Clay. I recognized him from Tammy's photo. Sitting on a towel, he stared out at the ocean. Navy blue bathing trunks and a necklace that looked like a shark's tooth. He turned and jokingly pushed the camera away when he saw it trained on him. But Maureen was persistent, zooming in on his face. I saw few traces of this boy in the adult Clay Bishop. This Clay seemed a little awkward, sure, but he was handsome and lively. Young. Innocent.

The camera cut for a moment but came back to Clay, walking down the beach with a plastic bag in his hand. He stopped, towering above the camera, sticking his tongue out as he reached into the bag for a Miller Lite, pausing to flex his muscles before cracking it open and taking a sip. Cut again.

Now we were on the pier. It looked much the same, that tacky painted clown sign above the arcade, vendor signs for French fries and cotton candy. The camera glossed past the mobs of people walking like zombies up and down the pier. Tired parents pushed strollers, groups of teenagers sat on the wooden poles watching people stroll by. The girls were all in bikinis or short shorts, teased-up hair, fringe neon shirts and skates, the boys in awkwardly short swim trunks and muscle shirts, the height of the Jersey shore in the mideighties.

My cell phone buzzed in my pocket, and I paused the film when I saw my mother's name on the screen again. My thumb hovered over the answer call button, but then I put the phone down. I didn't want to deal with her predictions, her dire warnings.

I pulled Catarina into my lap and started the film again. Maureen focused on a young boy trying to eat a tower of melting ice cream that was about to fall off the cone. She stopped occasionally to zoom in on people, at one point following a teenager as he passed, training the camera as if it was checking him out.

What had happened to this playful, silly teenager? Where had she disappeared to? I wished I could protect her, tell her to watch her back. To not be so trusting. I was so caught up in my thoughts that it startled me when the pier footage cut off. And there was Maureen—the Maureen I'd been chasing for so long, the camera finally turned on her. She was on the beach, wearing a bright orange-and-white-striped bikini, her hands on her hips. Her dirty-blonde hair was down, but wrapped in the silk scarf I'd seen in Tammy's photo, just like the one I'd found under the bed, the one, I realized, I was still wearing now. I touched it and jerked my hand down when I saw Maureen on screen also touch hers, adjusting it. She looked self-conscious, smiling, but her eyes flickered away from the lens of the camera. The watcher being watched. Then she opened her mouth, and although there was no sound, I could make out her saying, "Ready?" She paused, then did a perfect cartwheel on the sand, ending with her arms thrust up in the air, demanding applause. She rushed over to the camera, tried to pry it away, but whoever was filming her—Clay?—

wouldn't let her and so she squatted in front of it, her mouth close-up, blurred.

I stood up, walked over to the wall. "Maureen," I said quietly, and as if she heard me, she threw back her head and laughed. She and I looked nothing alike. She put her finger to her lips and shook her head. The film cut away.

I lunged back to the machine and rewound it, playing the Maureen footage again. I wanted to go inside the film and ask her what happened. But there was something more. At the end of the footage, right before she put her finger to her lips, you could see it in her eyes. Something haunted. It was brief, a look off to the side, when her face fell a bit. That quote from her notebook: "It's not what you are, it's what you don't become that hurts." But then she forced a bright smile and shook her head as if to say, *Nope. You'll never figure out my secrets.*

I let it play farther, eager to see if she showed up again. But the next clip was dark. At first I thought it was just the blank, undeveloped film at the end of the reel, but no, it was nighttime. The camera focused on a house, several windows lit up from inside. The Bishops' house, I recognized with a start. The shrubbery wasn't there, and the dunes behind were smaller, but there was no mistaking the rest of it.

Was it Maureen, spying on Clay? But why? The footage lasted for about three minutes, but nothing happened. No one even walked by the windows. Then it cut, and when it came back the camera was still aimed at the house, but from a different angle. You could see a movement in the downstairs window, a flash of a person's silhouette passing. Maureen tried to zoom in, but the camera couldn't get very far. The lights in the house went out. And the camera cut to black.

26

ALLISON

The Keurig was still broken, but Annie had brought my old coffeepot, so I got in my car and drove to the Parkins Plaza grocery store for coffee beans. As I drove, I replayed the film in my mind. Who had Maureen—if it was her—been spying on at the Bishops' house? Was this just another of her pranks or experiments, messing around with her camera? Or was this proof that something was off between her and Clay?

I wished I'd pushed Clay further at the club, but that would've been awkward. And of course he wouldn't have told me if they'd had a fight. Men liked to avoid anything that showed their darker side—they pointed fingers at everyone else first. Like Duke accusing *me* of being too friendly with our neighbor at a Christmas party, acting all fiery jealous and wounded when he, indeed, was the guilty one.

That thought stopped me. Maybe it wasn't that Clay was upset Maureen had another guy. Maybe Maureen had suspected *him* of being with someone else. And she was spying on him to try to prove it. My mind raced with that new possibility. If Maureen thought Clay was cheating on her, and then she confronted him about it—well, that could've gotten heated fast. And something terrible could've happened.

Everyone in Opal Beach was at the grocery store, it seemed, picking up Thanksgiving ingredients or stocking up for the storm. As I waited in line, my head was still full of Maureen, the necklace, the way this town seemed to hold so many secrets. Someone knew what happened that summer—the truth. And they wanted *me* to know. But who? And why wouldn't they reveal themselves?

In the parking lot, I heard my name being shouted. "Yoo-hoo! Over here."

Between two SUVs, a figure waved, bundled head to toe, bunches of bright gold hair peeking out from under her hat. Mabel Halberlin.

"I just wanted you to know I found someone else to host my event," Mabel said as I got nearer, a fake smile to match the fake fluttering eyelashes.

"Oh, I'm sorry I never—"

"It probably wouldn't have worked out anyway." Mabel put her weight on a large shopping cart, and the thick peacoat she wore made her look like a giant tree stump. "Now that I know why you're *really* here." Her words felt like an unexpected attack. What did she mean? Was she talking about my weather report? Did she think I was here to hide out?

"I knew her, you know," she continued. "But Tammy probably already told you all that. And I can see the resemblance, even though it's been, what, thirty-some years?" Hunched over the cart, she studied me, like if I made the wrong move, she'd charge me with it like a bull.

I stepped back. "What are you talking about?"

"Why, *Maureen*, of course," Mabel said, spitting out her

name like it was a small bone in a piece of chicken. "Don't look so shocked. I told you Opal Beach was a small town. I was in Jim's gallery the other day, and he told me all about it, how you were in there asking about this girl who'd disappeared all these years ago." She smiled cruelly.

"Did you send me the—" I broke off, feeling light-headed. I must've still looked stunned, because Mabel rattled on, pushing her cart even closer to me, so close I could touch it now, its cold metal between us like a cage.

"I wish I could help you, I do, but honestly I'm not surprised she ran off. No offense, sugar, but, well, I'm a straight shooter, you know. I tell it like it is. And I feel like you should know the truth about your cousin. She was a little…trashy."

My cousin? But beyond her association that I was somehow related to Maureen, something in her tone made me pause. Was this how it had been for Maureen? The constant reminders you don't belong, that you aren't good enough? I knew a little something about that. A slow angry burn began to build in my chest.

"I knew who it was Jim was talking about, of course, but I asked Tammy just to be sure. And then when she told me you were a relative, well, I just—" She adjusted her bulky coat and grinned at me. "I just want to know why you never asked me about it."

"I didn't—you just said yourself how much you hated her," I sputtered. My mind was going in a million directions, but I tried to keep calm. Mabel had called me over for a reason. Because she was *wounded* that I didn't ask her about Maureen? Or was there something she had to offer? Something she wanted to tell me?

The necklace.

Mabel's eyes were twinkling. She was enjoying herself now. "Well, sure, but that doesn't mean I don't know anything.

I make it my business to know things around here, after all."
She made a *tsk tsk* sound in her throat.

It took all I had not to tell her off and walk away, but I
knew what game I had to play. If she was the one who sent
me the necklace, then I needed to hear her out.

"You're right. I should've asked for your help," I said. "I
should've gotten your…signal. Do you know what happened
to her?"

Mabel pushed the cart closer, wheeling it beside me so she
could lower her voice for once. "Did Tammy tell you she stole
my suitcase?"

I shook my head slowly.

"Yes," Mabel said triumphantly. "The night she left town.
Maybe to pawn it? For money? There were always these gangster thugs hanging around, looking for her. Maybe she got in
bad with one of them. Or married one of them," she scoffed,
as if unable to help herself.

"She had people looking for her?" I asked, more to myself
than to Mabel. *I got the impression Maureen was involved with someone else that summer,* Tammy had said. "Was she dating someone
else besides Clay? Someone forbidden? A boss? An older man—"

Mabel sniffed. "Yeah, for *Tammy.* She's always liked the
older men."

"No," I said, disappointed. "That's not…" I trailed off. My
mind was going in circles. I couldn't keep anything straight.
What did Mabel want from me? "So, wait. Why did you have
the necklace for so long?"

"Necklace?" Now it was Mabel's turned to be baffled.
"What necklace?"

I'd gotten it wrong. I could tell immediately by the blank look
in Mabel's eyes. No way was she that good of an actor. I'd read
it all wrong—she wasn't trying to tell me she'd sent the package.
She was trying to get in on town gossip. And I'd fallen for it.

"Oh gosh, sorry," I said. "I meant suitcase. I mean, I'm getting myself all turned around."

Mabel chuckled. "Sounds like you need a vacation. I'd love to stay and chat, but I've got to go. I'll try to think of anything else, though. If you need me." She tapped my arm. "And I'm sorry about your cousin, but if I can give you some advice? Just leave it alone. You keep drilling down this rabbit hole? You'll find nothing but trouble at the bottom."

"You told Mabel I was *related* to Maureen?" I clutched the steering wheel with my one hand, the other pressing my cell phone to my ear to hear Tammy better.

"Don't be mad, Allison. I was going to tell you, but it's just—"

"Why in the world would you…"

"Mabel came in to the shop. She was really overbearing, asking me about it. Who are you, how do I know you, why are you asking about Maureen…"

"And?" I said slowly, dread creeping up inside my chest.

"And, well, I just freaked out. I didn't know what to say—and you hadn't told me you went to Dolores—so I was caught off guard, and it just…came out. I told her you were a distant cousin," Tammy mumbled.

"So much for keeping this discreet," I moaned. "The whole town knows by now, doesn't it?"

As I pulled into the driveway, still reeling from my conversations with Mabel and Tammy, I saw a figure disappear around the back of the house. I pressed the brake quickly, too hard, and jolted forward.

Why would someone be lurking around my house? It was too far off the path to the dunes. And the wind was too bitter to walk on the beach.

I parked, shut off the car. *It's just someone cutting through to take a quick look at the ocean. Stop being paranoid.* I got out of the car, grabbed my bag of coffee and headed up the porch steps.

Then I froze. Sitting right in front of the front door, on the woven mermaid welcome mat, was a small white box.

I dropped my coffee, bolted around the side of the house to the back. Suddenly determined. No more games. No more warnings, gossip, second-guessing. I was going to find out who was behind all of this once and for all.

I stumbled over the dunes, sand squishing in the bottom of my sneakers. But at the top, I could see the beach was deserted.

There was no one there.

How could someone disappear so quickly? I checked the back of the house, peered around the other side, even opened the plastic bin where the garden hose was coiled. No trace of anyone. I thought about the box on the porch. *Someone had been here.* It wasn't my imagination.

Or was it? I shoved my hands in my pockets, hurrying back to the front of the house. What if there was no box? What if there had been no person in the back? What if I was just imagining things? Letting Maureen—that film—get in my head?

I was so wrapped up in my thoughts that I didn't hear or see the person coming around the corner.

Until I smashed into him.

He let out a groan and fell into the lemongrass. I registered his face, and the anger boiled inside. "Just what the *hell* are you doing in my bushes?"

27

ALLISON

Duke stood up, brushing himself off. He looked surly in his stupid windbreaker, a pair of sunglasses tucked on top of his thick head. "I believe you pushed me in the bushes, Allison. I wasn't spying, for Christ's sake. I was just coming around to see if you were out back."

"So after you left me your little package, you decided to make a house call?" I was practically spitting my words at him. Of all the people to have turned up, he was the last one I'd have suspected.

"Package?" Duke picked a piece of bark out of his jacket hood and tossed it down. "I just wanted to talk to you for a minute. Can I come in?"

"Absolutely not. What are you doing here anyway?" *Had he been taunting me this whole time? Leaving me messages just to mess with my head a bit further? Everything that had happened hadn't already been enough?*

"Allison, what the hell are you talking about? I just wanted to talk for a minute and here you are tackling me and accusing me of threatening you? Jesus, this is worse than I thought." It was that condescending tone I remembered all too well. When he'd wanted me to seem crazy, irrational, after all his disgusting lies.

"Then why are you here? Don't tell me you drove all the way up here to check on my mental health in a bout of holiday generosity."

"Maron's family lives a few miles—"

"You know what, just go away." I pushed past him to the front of the house. Sure enough, the white box was still there on the mat. My heart leaped. I wasn't crazy.

"Jesus Christ, Allison. You asked."

I stepped onto the porch, grabbed the bag of coffee and slid the white box in my coat pocket. I tried to unlock the door quickly, but Duke followed, stuck his big arm in the way. I glared at him. "Get out of here. Now."

"Allison. It's like two degrees outside."

"It's actually nineteen degrees, with a windchill of ten."

"Please. I just want to talk for a minute."

"I'll call the cops. I swear I will call the cops." I circled to the back of the kitchen counter because I liked having that barrier between us.

Duke appeared unfazed, which made me even more irate. If the house impressed him at all, he didn't say it. He shook his head. "Ally, they already think you're loony."

That stopped me. "Who?"

"My dad was at the boating association this weekend and he ran into Phillip Bishop."

I crossed my arms in front of my chest to keep them from shaking. "So he's been saying what? Or, should I ask, *you've* been saying what?"

"They say you're going on about a woman who's been missing? Some runaway from thirty years ago? Allison, it sounds crazy." What was he talking about? Was that how I was coming off to people?

He started to walk toward me, and I pulled a knife out of the knife block. "Stay away from me."

"You said you're related to her? Do you realize how it sounds, Allison? Haven't you done enough damage to yourself? I feel like I need to talk to Annie, or your parents, but I wanted to—"

"Don't you dare."

"I don't *want* to," he stressed, like I was a five-year-old he was trying to reason with. "I'm just worried about you."

"You're worried about me? Ha." I stared at him with suspicion. "Since when have you worried about me? So kind of you to suddenly care after you went ahead and stuck your dick in another woman."

He kept his cool. It was like shooting at a bulletproof vest. "Haven't you already covered that territory on-air?"

"Not enough to keep you away from me, apparently."

"You've ruined your life and my family's reputation. Don't go ruining other people's lives, too."

"Funny, your lives don't look ruined at all to me. In fact, I'd say you're doing just peachy. Maybe that's how it goes for those who are willing to treat people like they are disposable?" I was shaking with anger now. "Like you thought our marriage—I—was disposable, right? And this girl, too? No one gives a shit what happened to her either, Duke." I walked over to the door, opened it. "Now get out. Or I'll call the police."

"Allison—"

"Don't Allison me. Get out, Duke. If I find you creeping around the bushes again, I'll shoot you."

He rushed past me, and I shifted so we wouldn't touch. I waited until his car pulled away before breathing again.

I poured bourbon in a juice glass and sat down at the kitchen table until I stopped shaking. I set the box on the table.

Inside, cushioned on a bed of white fluff like it was an expensive piece of jewelry, was a dark brown chess piece.

A bishop.

A tiny folded piece of white paper was under it. I opened it to find a new message: "He killed her."

My whole body tensed. Why would Duke—

But it couldn't have been Duke, I realized. His car had been *behind* mine in the driveway. I'd watched him leave. He had arrived after I'd gotten back from the grocery store. No way he could've dropped that box, slipped around the house, gotten to his car parked somewhere else and driven up behind me that quickly.

No, this was someone else. The same person who'd sent me the necklace. Someone who wanted to make sure I knew that I was on the right track about Clay Bishop.

He killed her. A tremor went through me.

I called Tammy, but there was no answer. When her voice mail kicked in, I left her a short, quavering message. "I think it's time we talk to your cop friend."

28

· ——— ·

MAUREEN

August 1985

Zeke's got another white suit on, maybe he has a whole closet full of them. He's handsome in a villainous sort of way. In my white dress I bought for four bucks at the Beach Town Thrift Store I feel like we are going to the Mad Hatter's tea party. He whistles low, looks me up and down. "Hot stuff, Destiny."

The evening's got a pulse about it. Like something magic's going to happen. I'm all about business, though. Zeke is the gateway to my new plan. If I can win enough money, I can find a place of my own. Maybe here in Opal Beach. Maybe somewhere with Clay. It won't matter, as long as I don't have to rely on anyone else. I'll take care of myself—take charge of my own destiny. And then I can save my mom, too. Go back, get her out of there, take care of her. If Tammy can do it, so can I. All I need is a little magic and a little luck.

We drive away from the coast. Zeke's very quiet, contemplative. I wonder if he's nervous, wonder if this is how he al-

ways gets before games or if this night is different because
I'm with him.

"So how many people usually play at these things?" I, too,
am nervous. I keep rubbing my palms against my dress to
dry them.

"Don't worry yourself about the details. Your job is to be
pretty." He looks over and smirks at me. "Which you've already succeeded at, so it's all a wash from here."

"Just wait," I say. "I'm going to wipe the table with these
guys."

* * *

The group is smaller than I expected. Just five guys, including Zeke, and a ferrety-looking airhead who's throwing me
daggers as she wraps herself around one of them like a pret-
zel. Her boy is eating from a bowl of peanuts. He's younger,
probably only a few years older than me, and he's got his serious face on, a Slim Jim fuzz stripe of a mustache and glower-
ing eyes. Boy thinks he's a gangster in a black button-down
shirt and tight black jeans. His gaze settles on me, and I feel
a pinprick of unpleasantness behind my neck.

They're all smoking the room into a haze that makes my
head light. Someone adjusts the record player and we get
treated to the Rolling Stones. The edge of the table is padded in black leather and has occasional holes for drinks and
ashtrays. I notice the numbers: five guys, five seats.

"This here is Destiny," Zeke says finally, patting my shoulder and pulling me close. "And this is Bob and Doug." They
nod at me distractedly. "And Jake the Snake." Dark-haired,
mustache the size of a giant caterpillar.

"Your good luck charms are getting bigger and bigger,"
Jake says. I watch his mustache wiggle as he speaks.

"He needs it," says Doug, rubbing his finger along the edge of the table. When he catches my eye, he looks away.

Jake angles his head toward the bar, at the younger guy eating peanuts. "That's my cousin Benny."

"Is he a troublemaker?" I ask.

Jake laughs. "I don't know. Are you a troublemaker, Benny?"

Benny looks like he's not happy about being talked to. He takes his time, cracking open a shell and digging out the nut with his teeth. The woman gives me her best pouty glare, and I want to tell her I have no designs on her Scarface-wannabe boy, who stands a little too straight, arms across his chest. I begin to think he's just not going to answer. Then he wipes his hands together and says, "Let's play some poker."

I start to pull out a chair, but Zeke grabs my arm. "Destiny's going to watch and learn tonight, boys. Watch how I take all your money and run."

"Yeah, like last time." A chorus of snickers.

"Actually," I say, hoisting a hand on my hip to feel more confident than I am, "I was thinking I could play with you all."

Zeke flashes me a nervous, irritated look. "Oh, Destiny, my dear. Maybe another time. Not tonight."

"Why not?" I ask.

There's an uncomfortable silence. Zeke says, "We need a bartender, baby. Remember?" He pulls my arm and drags me outside the room into the stairwell. He's mad, and in his anger he looks like a little boy, a toddler. "What are you playing at, Maureen?" It's the first time he's used my name—I am surprised he even knows it. "I thought I told you—"

"You told me shit," I say. "You know why I came tonight."

"It's not like that," he hisses. He straightens his collar. "You can't just waltz into these games. Do you even have any money?"

"Fifty dollars," I lie.

He shakes his head. "Minimum bet to even start these games is ten dollars. You'd be cleaned out after the first round. Leave the games to the adults. Watch and learn. You be a good bartender, they'll tip you. If they're winning, they'll tip you good."

"I'm not a goddamn bartender," I hiss.

"They'll love you. All your 'hold the garden' talk. The boys will eat that up. This is the big leagues, baby."

"Big leagues? Really, Zeke? It's five guys in a basement."

"Don't embarrass me, Maureen. I mean it. I'm doing you a favor here." He puts his palm on my cheek, caresses it. I can see the flecks of anger in those blue eyes of his. He and I are alike that way. Always a live wire underneath us, snapping, threatening to strike. "It's an easy gig. Trust me, okay?"

When he's gone, I sulk in the dark hall by myself. Was this my plan? The reality of it hits me—how stupid I am to think I'd be able to get rich quick in this damn town. To save anyone, when I can't even help myself. Across from me on the wall is a framed portrait of a family—a mom, dad with bad toupee, and a girl who's not smiling. I wonder where the girl is now, if she's still that age or long grown up and fighting off her own group of assholes. *I hope you keep on not smiling*, I say in my head to her, and bite my lip real hard.

I consider my options. Leave now, find my way home somehow. Keep trying to get some shitty job in Opal Beach that won't get me somewhere fast enough. Or stay, eat crow, walk back in there with all those dickweeds waiting to pat my ass and look down my dress. And hope that maybe they'll get sick of each other and let me play.

When I go back in, they're all at the table, smokes in hand. The girl who was fusing herself into Benny's side has disappeared. I size them up. They've all got their tics. Bob flips his chips through his fingers. Jake's all talk, trying to distract the crew with bad jokes. Doug constantly smooths out his plaid jacket and blows smoke into the air with a hissing sound. Benny, who brought his peanuts with him to the table, makes a steady, neat pile of dusty shells next to him, careful to keep them in line with the side of his pinkie. He's at least a decade younger than these jokers, but he seems older. Meticulous. He's the one to watch.

Zeke looks up and winks at me. He's a showman, and I suspect there's not much substance under it. I can already tell he's bad at poker. Everything's written all over his face. It's only luck on his side, and you can't win poker based only on luck.

I take a deep breath and play their game. "You boys need something to drink?"

●━━━━━━●

When he starts losing, Zeke gets mean.

"Come here, Destiny," he says, wrapping his arm around my waist. I see Benny watching us.

"Not now, Zeke," I say, trying to spin away.

"No, come here. I'm going to show you how to really play poker." His breath is hot on my cheek.

I cross my arms over my chest. "Oh, so now you're going to start playing well?"

Jake snorts at that, which doesn't make Zeke happy. He reaches for my purse on the side table. "Where's that money you say you brought? Want to loan old Uncle Joe some funds?"

Before I can grab it from him, he opens it, dumps it out on the table. My lipstick, Zeke's car keys, the mermaid statue I'd swiped from the party house, and my three ten-dollar bills fall out pathetically.

"Thirty dollars? Thirty dollars?" He holds up the statue. "And what's this? Aren't you too old for dolls?"

I grab it all, press it back into my purse. He's doubled over laughing, and I want to slam my fist into the back of his neck.

"You think it's funny?" I say. I get up, but Zeke grabs at my hand. I try to pull away and my wrist twists. The pain is sudden, fierce, and I fight the tears back. "You're a bastard."

"Let her play," Benny says.

We all stop. Look at him. It's the first words he's spoken that confirm he's actually noticed my presence in the room.

Zeke's eyes narrow. "What?"

"I said give her your chair. You're out of money anyway. Go home and sleep it off."

"You've got to be kidding me?" Zeke's met with silence. "This is a goddamn joke." He gets up, knocking his chair over, and stomps off.

Benny leans over and rights the chair, motions for me to sit. "Dealer's choice," he says. "I'll cover you. Fifty-fifty split on whatever you win, though."

"That's—" I begin.

He holds up a hand. "Fifty-fifty, or nothing."

It's like I've slipped into the devil's embrace. But I go willingly.

●━━━━━━━━●

While the boys take a piss break, Benny offers me a highball, but I ask for a can of soda. He raises his eyebrows but doesn't comment. I don't want to drink tonight. I need my head.

Then everyone shuffles back in. "Okay, boys, let's do this," I say, smiling, willing my hands not to shake as I deal out the cards. I rub Clay's promise ring for good luck and here we go.

I deal myself a low pair. Stay in, but decide to play conservative. Jack and Bob fold on the first go. I get a king and realize I've got four spades. Benny raises, and I meet it, staying in. When I get my fifth spade, I do a small raise. Doug raises me again. My heart's racing but I can't show it. I meet his bet. Flip my cards over. He's got a pair of sevens.

Benny pats me on the shoulder. I jump. I'm wound tight. "Sure you don't need something, princess?" *Princess?* I raise one eyebrow at him, but he's too busy gesturing at the side table, where, I realize with a start, he's put out an impressive array of drugs. Jack is snorting coke through a cocktail straw. Benny gives me that curled smile. "Go ahead. Take the edge off."

The image comes quickly, before I can bat it away. My mother's hand, limp across the couch in a darkened room. The smell of stale beer, rotten food. The endless looping flashes of television light casting everything in a greenish hue. The hand, waving a one-dollar bill. *Go get yourself some dinner, baby.*

"No, thanks," I say, turning back to the table. "I don't touch that stuff."

I hear Benny chuckle. He leans in as the next guy deals, and I smell cigarette smoke and something sharp and medicinal on his neck. "Never say never," he says.

———•———•———

Someone is pulling at me, calling my name. I lift my head. It's dark. "Come on, Maureen. Get up."

It's Clay. Why is he here? He wasn't at the game—the game, oh Christ, the game. I hadn't even lasted an hour. I look up at him. I'm sitting on a curb somewhere in beach town suburbia. Clay's car is parked in the middle of the street, his headlights like a knife twisting in my head. "Why are you here?" He's hauled me to my feet now, but I'm so tired. I just want to sag against him.

"Here," he says, and shoves a cup under my nose. The steam feels good and the smell—coffee. "Drink it," he says. "We gotta get out of here."

"How did you know where to find me?" I ask again, in the

car. Clay's driving too fast, but I ignore it, trying to piece together the evening, cringing with each memory like a blow to my chin. It started out great. I was up, I was doing well. Could feel the respect of the guys in the room. And then luck took a turn, not a big deal. I went under. But got too confident. I always get too confident. I was sure my straight had it, had all of them—

"You called me, Maureen. Do you not remember? Jesus Christ. I just can't believe you would do this. Didn't I tell you not to get involved with my uncle?"

"Well, you were right," I say. My head is roaring. Each bump in the road jostles my brain, sending shoots of pain behind my eyes. "He's a dick."

Clay takes me to his house. I consider asking him to drop me off at Tammy's, but she's been gone a lot of nights lately and the last thing I want is to bump into Mabel when I'm feeling like this. We go up to his bedroom, where his suitcase is packed and ready to go by the door. Of course: he's leaving for his tournament tomorrow. No wonder he's mad. I take off my dress, pull on one of his T-shirts and crawl into his bed. He shuts off the light and lies next to me, not touching me.

"Clay? I'm sorry. Please don't be mad." My brain feels like it wants to pulse out of my head. I want an aspirin, but I'm afraid to ask for any more favors.

For a long time, he doesn't say anything. Then I hear him talk into his pillow. "You lied to me. Straight to my face."

I close my eyes tight and take a deep breath. "I had to try. Don't you understand? And it wasn't my fault. I was winning. I think they drugged me."

He rolls over, and I can see his face dimly in the moonlight. "Yeah, sure they did. Do you ever take responsibility for yourself, Maureen? For your bad choices?"

I feel his words go through me like a sword. I sit up, even though it makes the room spin. "My bad choices? What is this, a lecture?"

"I can see what's in front of me, Maureen."

"Oh yeah? And what's that? A *carnival* girl?"

Heavy sigh. "You have a chip on your shoulder, Maureen. You're afraid of letting anyone get too close and slip past the bitchy I-don't-care attitude."

I laugh bitterly. "So you think because we've slept together a few times, went out to some dinners, hung out with your friends, that you *know* me? You don't know shit, Clay."

"Maureen—just come back to bed. I need to get up early." Clay's voice is tired, resigned, like he doesn't have the energy for me anymore.

I get up, looking for my dress. I can't bear to put it back on, it reminds me of everything that's gone wrong. I pull on a pair of Clay's boxers instead. So this is how it ends. I bite my lip to keep from crying.

Clay mutters from the bed, "You just need to sleep it off."

"No, I don't. What I *need* is someone who's not always trying to tell me what to do and what not to do." I'm hysterical, but I can't stop. I'm so mad—at him, but mostly at myself. I want to tear it all down, burn it, but I don't know how, and he's my closest target. "What I *need*, Clay, is someone besides you."

"Fine. Go. You don't listen to me anyway. I don't know why I bother." He waves an arm in the air and then pulls his covers over his head. I consider for a moment jumping back on the bed, ripping them off him, but my body feels too weak, too tired. So I listen to him, one last time.

I go.

29

• ———— •

ALLISON

Tammy said Sheriff Horace Clapper usually wandered into the shop around 9 a.m., before his shift. I was there at eight, sitting at the window table with my laptop and my mocha, two scoops of vanilla gelato erupting over the edges like white lava. It had become my regular thing, without my even having to ask Tammy, though I'd switched from plain coffee to mocha because the chocolate seemed to go better with the ice cream.

The necklace and the chess piece were tucked in my pocket. I could feel the soft lump against my thigh, but that didn't keep me from touching it every so often to make sure they hadn't disappeared.

I spent an hour worrying that Clapper wouldn't show up and worrying what to do if he did. My stomach felt like I'd eaten a pile of spicy sausage—it was churning, stabbing, the stress working overtime. Tammy was mopping the floors, polishing the coffeepots, rearranging the syrups. We barely spoke to one another.

Then, like clockwork, the police car pulled up in front of the store at exactly 9 a.m. Clapper did a pretty terrible parallel parking job. The familiar bell above the door clanged as he sauntered in. He took off his sunglasses, surveyed the room briefly, and headed to the counter. He was about my age, with a thick mustache that he petted as he waited, and I remembered that first day in the shop, when he'd been chatting with Mabel. What if Mabel had said something to him about who she thinks I really am? I hadn't thought about that. Maybe I should've had Tammy do this on her own.

"How's it going, Tammy? All ready for Thanksgiving?" he said. I couldn't make out Tammy's answer. He ordered "the usual," and when he walked over to the bulletin board to wait, Tammy wiped her brow. She looked pained, and I had a vision of her dropping the coffeepot and running out the door, forever, leaving only her apron behind. No, there was no way Tammy would be able to do this by herself. I had to stay.

She came around the counter and handed Clapper his coffee. Her hands were shaking, and when I looked down, I noticed mine were, too.

"Ah, thanks so much." He took a sip. The steam wetted his mustache.

"This one's on the house," Tammy said, "but I need to ask you something. Do you...have a minute?"

"Sounds serious." He smirked, but then when she didn't respond, he sobered up. "You okay, Tammy?"

Tammy led Clapper awkwardly to my table. I closed my laptop and stood up, nearly knocking over the table.

"This is my friend Allison," Tammy said.

Clapper nodded at me cautiously. "I think we've seen each

other around," he said. I could tell his guard was up. This wasn't going to be as casual as Tammy had imagined.

Tammy's voice was shaky. "I—we have a question. We need some help, some advice, I guess."

She sat down, and after a slight pause, Clapper followed suit. With all three of us around the table, it felt more like we were playing tea at a children's birthday party. Clapper's knees kept bumping the bottom of the table, sloshing our drinks. I braced it with one foot to keep it steady.

Tammy took a deep breath. "I had a friend, from a long time ago. She disappeared—we all thought she ran away." She paused, stared down at her hands. "I was telling Allison about this recently, you know, just reminiscing, I guess. Hadn't thought about this woman in years." That was a lie, but I knew why Tammy had to lie. "Anyway, we may have mentioned it to a few people—"

"Because I thought it was an interesting story, you know?" I interjected. "I mean, I find it fascinating that anyone could just disappear these days, with everything being online." I shrugged. Trying to be casual.

Clapper's eyes narrowed. He reminded me of my high school principal with that naturally suspicious guard—*why are you in the halls between classes, Ms. Simpson?* I wondered if he knew the story already, pictured a tiny, winged version of Mabel hovering near his ear, whispering, *She's a fraud, sugar. Just trying to stir up trouble. I know these people when I see 'em.* He turned to Tammy. "So you haven't heard from this person in how long?"

"Thirty years." Tammy flushed.

"Okay." Clapper folded his hands in his lap, patient.

"Tammy filed a police report about it back then," I added. "But they said that this woman had probably just run away. So no one ever investigated further."

"It sounds like she was a Summer Girl," Clapper said, rubbing that mustache again. And that term—*Summer Girl*. The same one Clay had used. The same dismissive tone that Mabel had used, too. As though because she worked at a carnival, she wasn't as important. I was beginning to understand why Tammy had kept her mouth shut for so long.

"It sounds like something terrible might have happened to her," I said, maybe a little too harshly.

Clapper took a long sip of his coffee before he answered. "And you ladies are going to fix it, right?"

"I'm not sure *fix* is the right term," I said, feeling my guard go up. This had been a mistake.

"What would be the right term?" he asked coldly. "*Meddle?*"

He'd poked my hornet's nest, and I felt the anger fly out, buzz around me, looking for a victim to sting. "So does that mean you don't want to hear about the package I received?"

"A package?" His eyes flicked in annoyance, but he sat up straight again. "Well, of course. I wasn't aware there was any evidence."

Of course you weren't. Because you didn't want to listen. As I reached into my pocket to show him, a customer walked through the door, a man in a brown fleece jacket and jeans, staring at his phone. Tammy jumped up like she'd been waiting for an excuse to leave, glancing over at us nervously from behind the counter.

Clapper leaned over the table toward me. "What was in this package?"

I could feel Tammy's stress radiating off her. I didn't want to give him any details without her there with me. "It was a necklace," I said low.

"Do you have it? Here?"

"I think Tammy should explain…"

Clapper made a noise in his throat. But to his credit he

nodded, sat back in his chair and sipped his coffee. His radio squawked, but he ignored it. Tammy came back over to us, rubbing her palms against her apron. "Did you show him?"

"She wanted to wait for you," Clapper said.

I put the necklace on the table between us. He examined it but didn't touch it.

"It was her half of a best friend necklace," Tammy said.

"Best friend what?"

Tammy explained what that meant. "So she took my half, the half with my initials, and I took hers." She sighed, and then pulled out something from her apron. "Here's my half. You can see, they're the same. But the one Allison got had my initials on the back." Tammy told him the abbreviated version of the story she'd told me that night in her apartment, plus some of the details that Dolores had uncovered. While she talked, I picked up the two charms, fit their zigzags together to form a complete heart. BEST FRIENDS.

When I looked up again, Clapper was fixated on Tammy, his jaw tight. "Maureen Haddaway, you say? I'm not familiar with that case."

Tammy fiddled with the edge of her apron, picking at a loose thread. "Well, like I said, Horace, it was a long time ago."

"So someone just randomly sent you jewelry from a thirty-year-old case?" His eyebrows raised. "It sounds like someone's playing a pretty mean prank on you, Ms...."

"Simpson," I said sharply.

"Ms. Simpson," he said. Then, to Tammy, "And you. I thought you had better judgment than this, Tam."

Her eyes welled up. "No, Horace. Really, this is not—"

"Tammy, think about it. You go around, talking about this woman from thirty-some years ago, acting like Cagney and

Lacey, and so of course someone's going to fool around with you. You know the folks around here…"

Clapper was watching us with an amused look on his face. So sure of himself. I felt foolish, having pushed Tammy to set this meeting up.

"The person who sent me this necklace also sent me a message," I said evenly, trying to control my anger. I pulled out the notes, and once he read them, I slid the chess piece in front of him. "A bishop," I said. "Maureen was dating Clay Bishop the summer she went missing."

Tammy glared at me at the mention of Clay. Clapper's mouth rounded in astonishment. "You're accusing the Bishops of killing some teenage runaway?"

"No," I stammered. "I just thought maybe you could talk to him, see if he remembers anything."

"You want me to waltz over to the Bishops' home and ask them about a girl who disappeared thirty years ago?" He sighed. "Clearly you aren't from this town."

"Clearly you aren't taking this seriously, Sheriff," I said, feeling my fire return. I stood up. Tammy stood up, too, motioning for me to calm down. But I was sick of being told I was stupid. Something was going on, and no one wanted to figure it out. "I have lots of friends who are television reporters who would be very interested in this story."

"Are you threatening an officer of the law, Ms. Simpson?" Clapper's eyes flashed, angry now.

"Absolutely not," I said with a bright smile. "But if you need further information to investigate, I was just offering that I have a way to engage the public in inquiry—"

"That won't be necessary, Ms. Simpson."

"I hope not, Sheriff Clapper." I had the urge to take back the necklace, the notes and the chess piece. But I was too afraid. "I think I'll be going now. Thank you, Tammy, for the coffee." And with my knees shaking and my dignity spilling all over the floor, I walked out.

•————•

After I left the coffee shop I turned off my cell phone and drove around Opal Beach for a long time. I wanted to be alone, to sort through my thoughts. No, I wanted to go back to Philly, to curl up on my sister's couch and forget about all this. Forget about Maureen and Tammy and the Bishops. But something wouldn't let me. No, *someone*. Maureen. She'd gotten under my skin. She didn't deserve this.

But how muddy it had all become. Nothing made sense. There was no evidence—except for the mysterious packages—that any harm had come to Maureen here in Opal Beach. So the only other possibility was that she had run away—or been run out of town.

But someone was trying to make sure I kept looking into it. Who sent those things? And why? How had they gotten Maureen's necklace? And why nudge me toward the Bishops—was it to make them seem guilty, to throw me off the track of someone else? Or was it all just an elaborate prank, like Clapper had said? One of the trolls who'd made death threats—had they followed me here to mock me? But how had they known where to find me?

I wanted to call Tammy to see what happened after I left her and Clapper in the shop, but I was feeling strange about her. She kept insisting Clay was innocent but couldn't give me a good reason why. And then there was her lie about me being related to Maureen—and to Mabel, of all people. I had told Tammy that there were few people who could've had access to that necklace—Clay and Mabel, for example—but Tammy could've, too. What if she had been the one to leave me those packages—as a way of keeping me interested?

I pulled over to the side of the road and put my head in my hands. What was going on? I couldn't shake the idea that I was missing something, like I was driving in circles in a heavy fog but didn't know where because I couldn't see past the small swath of headlights.

Look at you. You're a mess, Duke had said to me on one occasion when he'd come home late, missing a play he'd bought tickets for as a late birthday present to me. He'd been with Maron then, had completely forgotten about our plans. He'd lied straight to my face about some work meeting, blaming me for getting so hysterical. On some level I'd known he was lying, but I'd been too afraid to dig too deep. So I'd believed him.

Gaslighting was the word for it. I'd suspected it, had known it in the farthest edges of my mind, had felt it in my fingertips and toenails, had grasped it in the moments just before sleep, but he'd done a great job of keeping it all smudged. When I'd become suspicious of his behavior, when I'd grown sullen and angry at all the dinners gone cold, he started telling me I needed to go on meds. When I refused to have sex with him, he'd tell me that I was taking out my unhappiness with myself on him. That I should find a hobby. My husband had delightfully, unabashedly, been sticking his dick into another woman for six months, had been hiding hotel and dinner receipts, and had still had the nerve to tell me I should take up gardening.

Who was lying to me now? I sat up straight, stared at the barren beach road ahead of me, the sides of the pavement encrusted with white road salt. Here in the dimming light, that salt looked like ancient crumbling rock, like the ground beneath me was going to dissolve, suck me and everything else inside. I recognized immediately what was happening. Panic attacks, my doctor had called them. I'd gotten them regularly after I'd found out about Duke. They would come on unexpectedly, before I'd learned to control them. Cardboard walls, pushing inward, boxing me inside until I couldn't focus on anything, until I forgot where I was or what I'd been doing. I'd come to, panting, my skin cold and clammy, clawing at the air like an animal. But I'd plowed through it myself, with Annie's help. And some Xanax.

Here in the car, though, I didn't try to prevent it. I embraced it. The box walls came, closing in, pressing from all sides. My skin was clammy. I tried to catch my breath, but I could only gasp, shallow and fast, like all the oxygen had gone out of the car.

I was the fool. Once again. Always.

Everyone was lying to me.

"Well, screw Horace." Tammy pushed past me into the house. "He was such a jerk to you, Allison. I'm sorry."

I followed her into the living room where she made herself at home. I realized that this was the first time Tammy had ever come to my house. We always met at hers.

"Are you okay? I've been trying to call you all day," she said from the couch. I'd forgotten to turn my cell phone back on. After I'd calmed down, I'd driven some more, enjoying the speed of the highway, the miles ticking by, nowhere to go, until I'd finally headed back, stopping only once to fill up my gas tank and buy a cherry slushy and large weekender-sized bag of tortilla chips, which I put an embarrassingly large dent in on the drive home. I took a long, warm bath, taking care to wash my face and hair. But my nerves were still frayed.

"Yeah, I'm fine," I said, though I wasn't sure it was true. I'd made a mess of everything. Why hadn't I listened to Dolores when she'd told me to drop it?

"He kept the necklace. And the bishop. All of it," Tammy continued.

"I figured he would." I sat tentatively across from her. "Even though he didn't believe us."

"Oh, he believed us. He was just pissed that we didn't come to him earlier." She was still spitting mad. "He has that whole manly cop shtick down. After you left, he gave me the whole lecture about not being amateur detectives. About leaving that to the 'professionals.'"

Outside, the skies were black, even though it was only 5 p.m. I hated this time of the year, that veil of darkness that came so early, that made you want to retreat into yourself.

"You sure you're okay?"

"Yeah." I smiled weakly. "I just need a long nap."

Tammy stood up, pulled out a ring of keys from her pocket. "I should let you rest. I came because I want you to have this. It's to my place. In case—in case you ever need it."

I frowned. "What would I need it for?"

"Just in case anything ever happens." Her eyes were shiny. "If you feel unsafe, or…scared. If you need to. That's all. I'd feel better if you had it."

"Thanks, Tam. That's really sweet."

"Everything you've done for me—Allison, I want you to know I appreciate it. You're a good friend."

As Tammy was getting ready to leave, I noticed headlights sweeping over the driveway. "You might want to wait—looks like one of the Bishops is coming home," I said. But as we peeked through the kitchen blinds, we saw it was a police car. As it passed and went over to the Bishops' house, Tammy and I stared at each other.

"Oh no," she whispered.

"It's going to be okay," I said. "If Clay really has nothing to do with this, then he'll be fine. And maybe he'll be able to help."

After all that, I felt my excitement slowly building again—just a small stirring. It was possible, maybe, we'd get some answers now. Horace Clapper put on a good tough-guy show, making me and Tammy feel like idiots, but it seemed he acted pretty fast.

30

MAUREEN

I'm surprised to find myself crying as I make my way downstairs. At least I'd waited until I'd left Clay's room. Hadn't I? I still feel blurry inside, as though someone has taken my memories and shaken them like a snow globe. I pass the Bishops' grand living room, where Clay and I had spent that first night here playing games. A lifetime ago, it feels like, and sadness overcomes me. Stop. You knew it was going to end this way. Why would you expect any different?

In the quiet and darkness, I'm aware of the sleeping bodies upstairs. I find my purse and shoes next to the couch where I'd dropped them when we'd come in. I open my purse to look for aspirin. It's much lighter than usual, and I immediately know why. My mermaid statue. I've lost her. I frantically check each pocket, even though I already know she's gone.

And then I find a business card sticking out of one of the side pockets. "Benny," it says in black permanent marker. Followed by a phone number.

I hold on to the couch for support. Shit. How much did I owe him? I try again to remember how it all went down, but I can't pull anything new from my mind.

Across the room, the bar glows with a soft light, the bottles of alcohol lined up on the shelf like jewels. I walk over, pick one up, test its weight, wonder if I could sell it to the guys at the carnival who like good liquor. Cash is cash, at this point.

I take off my ring and set it on the bar in exchange for the bottle. I can hear the weary creaking of the house as it settles, bracing itself against the unending wind outside. I know I should go. But once I leave, it's really over. Once I'm out there, I have no idea what will happen to me. Will the wind wreck me? Blow me right back to where I started, everything I've tried to escape?

When the light goes on, it's like an explosion. I jump, nearly dropping the bottle in my hand. I turn, half-hoping it's Clay, that's he's come to make things right.

"Pardon," Mr. Bishop says, like we are meeting in a hotel lobby instead of in his house in the middle of the night. He's wearing striped pajamas and dark slippers. The smell of woodsy cologne fills the space between us.

"I woke very hungry."

I hesitate, confused by his lack of alarm. "I am—I was—just couldn't sleep," I settle on, placing the bottle awkwardly back on the bar.

"You, too?" He walks past me into the kitchen, and I follow him. He opens cabinets, pulls out a plate and then unloads a bunch of food from the refrigerator. "I'm making a sandwich. You want one?"

I shake my head. We don't say anything at all while he makes his sandwich. Like that night we saw him at the restaurant in Jasper—carrying boxes and taking care of business—everything he does seems effortless, delivered with a confidence I envy. I wonder if I should just leave, but it's like I'm glued to the chair. Everything I think to say seems immature, so I just sit and watch.

Finally he turns, glances over his shoulder. "I need to be the responsible adult and ask why you're here."

"I needed a ride home." I blush, knowing that's not much of an answer. I retie my scarf in my hair nervously, trying to think how to explain. "I was…out…and my ride left, and so Clay came to get me…"

He interrupts. "What is your name again?"

He thinks I'm a bunny, I realize. A hair-twirling twit. As if this night couldn't get any worse.

I tell him, my name sounding immature to my own ears. "I'm sorry. I shouldn't have come here." I stand to leave, but he motions for me to stay.

"It's okay. Can you grab that bottle you were holding before?"

I flinch, but I obey. Mr. Bishop doesn't seem like the type of person who people disobey. I leave it next to him on the counter and stand awkwardly in the doorway.

He licks a bit of mustard off his fingers and leans against the counter, taking a bite from the middle of his sandwich. He washes it down with the scotch.

"So it was a rough night?" Mr. Bishop asks.

"I've had worse." I look up at him and then away, too embarrassed to make eye contact. He's handsome, intimidating in a way that Clay is not. Solid. A square jaw, with just a hint of stubble. And twinkling eyes, like he's always in on a joke that you definitely want to be part of. Not many men—for Mr. Bishop was definitely a man—could look good in pajamas. Zeke would never have pajamas like that. He'd probably make fun of them.

Mr. Bishop washes down the rest of his sandwich with the

scotch. He sets the glass down with a satisfying clack on the counter and places his plate into the sink. "You should be careful. There are, if you'll excuse my language, a bunch of assholes out there."

I laugh, can't help myself, but it makes my head ache. I am very tired.

"Am I right?" His eyes are a blue like the ocean is supposed to be. Everyone talks about the ocean being this beautiful blue, but in truth, if you really look at it, it's more of a dark gray. Mr. Bishop's eyes are the kind of blue people want the ocean to be.

"I need to get back to sleep, Maureen. Thanks for the drink and the chat." The way he says my name startles me. Intimate, comforting. I realize that I don't want him to go.

I think, desperately trying to prolong the moment, but my brain is a snow globe again, and I'm unable to concentrate. I feel my eyes tear up, and I brush the wet away impatiently.

"Maureen, remember. It's never too late," he says earnestly. "Believe that. There's always a way through something. Always a solution to a problem. Remember that."

I nod. He claps his big hand across my back, the same awkward paternal kind of gesture I'd seen him do with Tammy that day in the restaurant.

"Thank you," I manage to say.

"Things always look better in the morning. You'll see."

Mr. Bishop is right. Everything seems brighter in the morning light. I managed to make it back to Tammy's apartment, sleep off whatever awful thing Benny had given me and slip away while Tammy was still in the shower.

It's going to be a beautiful day. There are no shadows, no

places for anything dark to hide. Just the hot sun, glinting off metal, boiling the black pavement so that I feel like my flip-flops might sink into the tar like it's water-clogged sand.

I still feel groggy, but it's okay because I also feel the destiny again. The magic dances through me. I can shoot it out the tips of my fingers. *Go, go, go.* Everything as bright, as twinkling, as Mr. Bishop's eyes. I walk along the shops and the bakery's got smells of yeast, hot fresh bread in the window. Somewhere a radio faintly, ironically, bleats *vid-eo killed the rad-io star.* A woman washes down the sidewalk with a hose, the water sizzling in the heat.

Mr. Bishop. In his matching pajamas. He's right. There's always a way through. I can fix this.

I pull out the business card and call Benny from a pay phone. It's even hotter inside the box, so I keep the door propped open with my foot, dodging the crumpled newspaper slick with some liquid I don't want to identify. It rings and rings. I wrap my finger inside the curled cord, watching as the tip turns red. Someone's written Mandy Sucks Dick above a postcard for a pizza delivery place that's taped to the wall.

Benny finally answers. "Well, well," he says after I say my name. "I figured I wouldn't hear from you for a while."

"I'll pay you back. How much?"

"Princess can't remember?"

"Just tell me how much." I turn to use my other foot to hold open the door. There's a strong smell of urine on this side, but I have a view of the street, where the town's just starting to wake up.

"Twenty-five hundred. I need half of it by Wednesday." I can hear the cruel curl of a smile in his voice.

I close my eyes, will myself to stay calm. The magic's still there; he won't suck it out of me. He can't. "I don't have that kind of money."

"Half, princess. That was our deal."

"We had no deal. You drugged me."

His laugh sounds like a bullet, sharp and sudden. Dangerous. "You wish. You're not as good as you think you are."

His words sting. Isn't that what everyone's been telling me since I got here? *You're not as good.* Zeke. Barron. Mabel. All barking at the edges, reminding me of my place. I wrap my finger tighter around the cord. The pain from the numbness is satisfying.

"But hey, I know a way you can pay me back quicker. I have parties, you could join us. My guys would like you." He chuckles, and even in the glow of the sun, my skin ices over.

"Uh, no."

"You wanted to play in the big leagues, remember?"

I try to keep the desperation out of my voice. "So give me another chance to pay it all back. Let me into another game."

"No way. You had your chance. Half. I'll tell you what. Since it's such a lovely day out there, I'll give you till next Sunday. Either in cash or, like I said, more…creatively. You'll have fun. You should think about it."

"I'd rather eat a bag of glass."

"You may have to." He pauses. "And don't think about skipping town either. I mean, if you care about your friends. I know where you and your little girlfriends live. And if you skip out, well, they might find themselves at a party…unwillingly."

I drop the phone cord. "Stay away from them."

He chuckles again. "We'll see."

31

• —————— •

ALLISON

The Pilot gas station at Parkins Plaza was all decked out and ready for Thanksgiving. The front of the store was plastered with paper turkey signs offering Gobble It Up Deals on Coke and cigarettes, and while the attendant was filling up my tank with gas, I went inside to grab some snacks.

It was snowing something fierce. The storm that had been predicted was coming on strong, and I was excited about staying in Opal Beach to witness it. Snow at the beach is something to behold. I've always loved the randomness of weather—the heat wave in the middle of January, the snow squall in early June. Or the hailstorms where drops froze during the updraft and bounced around like popcorn, growing to the size of acorns before plummeting to the ground to dent car hoods or smash gutters. But squalls at sea were particularly special. When frenzied, airy large snowflakes mixed in with the cold coastal wind, it made you realize you were part of something larger and more mysterious than you. The sand

and the snow became one, a virtual whiteout of whistling air currents and bitter ice crystals. If you stood out in the middle of it, you'd feel like a thousand tiny little knives were stabbing your face. It was absolutely brilliant.

But my opinion must not have been very popular, for the town seemed even more deserted than usual. The cashier behind the counter barely looked up from the magazine she was flipping through. I thought I had the place to myself, but as I rounded the corner, I nearly ran into a girl standing next to a display of candy bars, her back to me. Her long, wavy, dirty-blonde hair swayed down her back. She seemed lost, carrying a woven droopy bag whose bottom dragged on the floor as she moved, worn silver-and-pink high-top sneakers squeaking softly on the worn tile floor. Her thin legs were clad in leggings, and she wore a coat much too light for the weather.

Maureen.

My heart stampeded like a herd of buffalo. The girl stopped again in the middle of the aisle, slightly hunched. I saw the lift and fall of her breath, saw a small circular burn hole, the size of a cigarette, on the back upper arm of her coat. Before I could catch myself, I reached a hand out. I was close enough now to smell her, a light floral scent that reminded me of something—of somewhere—though I couldn't quite place it. I tapped her on the shoulder, amazed when it was solid, when my hand didn't just pass through her, icy cold. When she didn't disappear.

"Maureen," I said, almost whispering it, the name curling over my tongue like a secret.

When she turned, I immediately realized my mistake. Her face was small, overwhelmed by large round glasses, the kind that had been nerdy when I was in middle school but were back in style now. Bright blue earbuds trailed down to a battered cell phone cradled in her hand, and I could hear the tinny sounds of a rock song vibrating through them.

"Well, look who it is. Opal Beach's most famous resident."

I jumped, whirling around to find Dolores, holding a giant bag of Doritos and a bottle of medicine. She was looking at me funny, and out of the corner of my eye I noticed the young girl wander away, the echoes of her music following her.

Dolores held up the bottle, rolling her eyes. "Dad caught a cold, of course. Right before I'm leaving, too. I think it's his passive-aggressive way of saying I shouldn't go visit my mother."

"I'm sorry," I said, trying to shake the image of Maureen out of my head. What was wrong with me? I was seeing ghosts now.

Dolores jabbed a finger in my shoulder. "Dude! You are, like, literally the talk of the town right now. I mean, for someone who wanted to be all anonymous and get away from things, you're, like, right in the middle of it."

"In the middle of what?" I asked, inwardly cringing at her comment.

"Do you know how many people are talking about this? I was on Reddit last night, and there's a whole thread of people speculating about what's going on. Wacky shit, too. Drug raid. Financial ruin. One person did chime in, though, and mentioned the girl..."

"Mabel," I groaned.

Dolores made a face. "Yeah, right. As if Mabel even knows what Reddit is. I don't even think she uses Facebook except to post the houses she's sold. And even that she screws up." Dolores shook her head. "No, not Mabel. But don't worry, she's got everything else covered. You're like her favorite new topic."

"Great," I said. "Just what I need." The clerk was watching us now, her magazine forgotten.

"Holy crow, though." Dolores's voice lowered. "But seriously, are you guys nuts? Taking on the Bishops?"

"I'm not really taking on... I mean, it's just—I think it's fine."

"Yeah, fine. That's what Tammy said, too." Dolores shifted her groceries in her arms, her scarf slipping off one shoulder to reveal those tattoos, and I was reminded of the way she used her whole body to slam the derby girls to the floor. "She won't tell me anything. I think she's mad because I wouldn't help her. But I'm worried about her. She's not been the same since…well, I told you this kind of thing gets her worked up."

I glanced over at the clerk, who had moved from her station behind the counter closer to us to straighten a rack of sunglasses. Dolores sensed what was going on. She strode to the counter and paid for her stuff while I waited by the door. If the clerk wanted to ask us anything—and I was sure she did—to her credit she kept her mouth shut. But I felt her eyes on us as we left.

"Look," I said. "I can fill you in sometime, okay? It's just—complicated right now, I guess. And you know, with the way word spreads around here, we have to keep stuff close."

Dolores's eyes widened. "Well, I wouldn't say anything to anyone, you know."

"Of course you wouldn't." I remembered the entire derby team winking and nudging me. *The Weather Girl*. Dolores, I suspected, was even worse than Mabel when it came to gossip. She'd have the whole story spread around by sunrise. "I'll stop by the gallery after the holiday. Sound good?"

Just then the headlights of a car blinded us as it pulled in by one of the gas station pumps. From the side, I could see clearly who was in the driver's seat. Clay Bishop. He looked over, and for a moment I thought he might get out to confront us, but instead he just drove away from the pump, disappearing toward downtown.

Dolores turned to me, awe spreading over her face. "You see?" she said. "You've really started something."

32

◦━━━━━◦

MAUREEN

The winding down of summer is sad. The air loses its heaviness, the hint of chill sneaks in at night. People start to get serious, drift away. The sense of fun, the possibility of magic wanes. August puffs up mightily, brutal and steamy, and then explodes, blowing us all away into the fall. I've always hated fall. Things dying, withering, growing old.

Maybe it's Benny's deadline rapidly approaching. Or maybe it's just the general mood of Opal Beach, like everyone's had enough. Even the sun seems tired. Clyde's fair is petering out, and Jacqueline says they're all getting restless, releasing the last of the hermit crabs into the ocean, handing the kiddos stuffed monkeys on the sly, even if they don't win the games. The surf shop is already advertising its summer clearance blowout sale, marking down its bodyboards 60 percent. The beach parties have started to die down, too, and Tammy and I spend a lot of our nights listening to the local late-night love show on the radio and putting together old jigsaw puzzles she found in her mother's attic.

The latest one is a painting of a mansion on a hill, surrounded by an immaculate garden of lilacs. An estate for a king, unlike anything either of us has ever seen in real life. There are several different patches of lilacs, which makes it hard to find the right pieces. All that purple everywhere. Tammy's singing along to Linda Ronstadt and munching on popcorn. I stop and watch her for a moment. She's wearing a bright pink tank top with flamingos on it, concentrating hard on the puzzle while she sings. Happy.

"Tammy?"

She looks up, grins. "Is my singing that bad?"

The nice girl. How did I manage to stumble upon such a nice girl?

"Maureen, really. My voice isn't *that* bad, is it?" Tammy's smirking, waving her hand in front of my face. "Back to Earth?"

"Sorry," I say, clutching the half heart charm at my neck. "I just—well, thanks."

"For what?"

"For...well, for being you. And inviting me to live here."

"My pleasure," she says, but then she frowns. "You okay, Maureen?"

I nod, but I sense she knows I'm lying. My increasing dread about the money I owe Benny and what he might do if I don't pay. Everything—even this safe, simple moment—is colored by it like a cancer. I have nightmares about Benny ambushing Tammy on a dark street corner, shoving her into a dark car. I wake up and feel a slicing pain in my chest. I can't bear it. The person in Opal Beach who's been the most kind, most generous to me when she had no reason to be? Benny's not going to touch a hair on her head if I can help it.

I've asked around, but I can't get any leads on other games, not anything beyond a bunch of boys playing for quarters and bragging rights, anyway. I even briefly considered sucking it up and asking for my job back at C&D, but one look at Desmond huffing through the carnival grounds, his hands shoved in his dirty jean shorts, changed my mind quickly.

"I just wanted you to know that I appreciate everything you've done for me," I say.

"Well, gee, that sounds like you're leaving or something." She reaches over, and I think she's going to take my hand in hers, but instead she snags a piece of puzzle and presses it into place. Then she sticks out her tongue. "Lighten up, lady. Everything's going to be just peachy. Pinkie swear it."

Finally luck shows up long enough to grant me a measly job handing out daily special flyers for one of the crab shacks. It's not a bad job, and it's better than scraping seagull shit off the pier benches, but it pays next to nothing and requires so little thought that a surfboard could do it. The manager is a nice, stocky lady with good teeth, and on Mondays she closes the shack so that she and her husband can sing Irish folk songs at a pub in the next town over. She's taken me under her wing, she thinks, always asking if I'm okay, talking about the benefits of owning your own business, spouting off all the daily vitamins I should use. She promises she'll bring me on as a food server as soon as one of the summer kids quit, although I know at this point we've only really got Labor Day weekend to look forward to, and then her business is just going to keep slowing down as the tourists leave.

It would be too easy to swipe cash from the register at the end of the night—she's a terrible bookkeeper. But each time

I think about it, she says something nice, or pushes through the kitchen doors with her wide hips, whistling "Danny Boy," and hands me a plastic bag stacked with leftover food to take home—"fill yer fridge"—and I can't bring myself to pocket even one penny.

• • •

It's Saturday. Six o'clock. I'm nearly done with my shift, but I don't have it in me to approach more strangers with the buy-one entrée, get-one-free coupons. I feel bad dumping half of my pile into the trash can at the end of the pier. But there's only so much smiling one girl can do each night. I lean against the railing. Clay told me once that his father wants to build a restaurant here at the edge, but I think it would be a shame to ruin the peaceful quiet.

My feet are killing me—I shouldn't have worn new sandals with tiny straps. My right ankle's rubbed raw, and I prop it on one of the benches that the seagulls shit all over.

A few couples stroll, holding hands. I bend over to scratch my ankle again and realize I smell like fried dough. Which Clay would still say is better than fried shrimp. I miss Clay. Thinking of him makes me sad, makes me realize how badly I've screwed everything up.

Benny's going to want his money tomorrow, and I don't have it. I should just leave, catch a ride to the next town. Start over. But if there's any chance that I've put Tammy in danger, I can't risk it.

I pull out the Super 8 camera. But there's nothing much to film out here, so I start walking. It gets hotter as I reach the busier part of the pier. Other girls are passing out dinner flyers, but the crowds have already thinned, most everyone having already made their food choices for the evening. I stand on the side and film a group of boys shopping for surfboards, waiting until 6:30 p.m. so I can head back to the restaurant for my pay.

I like looking through a lens. How glamorous it must be to be a filmmaker, to get to set the world as you think it should be. How powerful it must be to replay life, to rewind and fast-forward, to edit out what you don't like. Change things. To control your own destiny.

I notice a man taking photographs on the other side of the pier. He's got a thick brown beard and the kind of tan that lifeguards get. I think I've seen him before, at the Opal Beach events, the Fourth of July parade and summer art festivals. I train my camera on him, zoom in, watch him watch a gaggle of bunnies giggling next to a sweets shop. He looks over at me and snaps a photo. In return, I lift my camera and point it his way. I film him until he finally wanders away, his camera down at his side, and he disappears into the night.

33

·————·

ALLISON

The ice storm hit the entire East Coast. I turned up the heat in the house and cooked myself a small pile of turkey breast and potatoes left over from Annie's dinner the week before and opened the last bottle of wine. I sipped a glass alone while halfheartedly flipping through the various weather-casters. Anchors were telling us all to settle in and save our Thanksgiving leftovers, chuckling in their holiday sweaters, while Dilly stood out in the cold with a fashionable orange hat and gloves, using a shovel to show us all how hard the ice was. "Just throw some of that in a bucket and we'll make mar-garitas when we get back," said the male anchor, smirking.

By Friday, the major highways were closed. A state of emer-gency was declared. Part of me hoped that Duke was sitting in his frozen-over car somewhere on the highway dying of exposure. But I'd never been that lucky.

Restless, I tried to put a puzzle together that Tammy had given me, but I'd never had the patience for such things and ended up sweeping the pieces back in the box before I even got the border together. The television stations only seemed to be playing heartwarming holiday movies filled with families and love, so I rifled through Patty and John's DVD collection and found an old Vincent Price horror flick. It seemed to fit my mood, but was hokey enough not to terrify me.

I fell asleep on the living room couch and woke past midnight. The DVD player had shut itself off, and the cable channel was on again, Dilly still giving her updates like a trooper. Outside the wind howled. I went upstairs to take a shower, and as I passed Patty and John's bedroom, I realized the projector was still set up. When I tried to rewind the reel, I noticed there was film left. I played it, fast-forwarding through the blackness. Just when I thought it was all blank undeveloped film at the end, a new scene emerged. A slight gap between shootings. I stopped, my heart pounding, and rewound.

The footage was of the inside of a house. The camera turned the corner to show a kitchen. An older man stood at the stove, cooking breakfast in a pan. He wore jeans and a T-shirt and was barefoot. He spun, spatula in hand, and saw the camera. The surprise on his face quickly melted into anger, and he struck out a hefty arm and pushed the camera down. There were a series of blurred images, a leg, a green linoleum floor, those painted red toes again, before the footage cut out.

I stopped the projector for a moment. What had I just seen?

I turned the film on again, dread pitting my stomach. There was only a bit left. It was darker, and now we were inside a bedroom. The same man, sleeping, one leg draped over crumpled covers. His chest was bare, his face half pressed into the pillow. The camera zoomed in, defiant. A statement. *I will record you when I want to.* I felt a chill go down my back that had nothing to do with the bad heat in the house. It wasn't Clay, but in the close-up on his face I saw the resemblance.

I'd had the wrong Bishop.

———•———•———

"Tammy, it was Phillip," I hissed into the phone, like I had a chance of being overheard by my neighbors.

"What?" Her voice was groggy. It was late. I'd woken her up.

"Phillip," I said again, impatient, eager for her to catch up. "The guy Maureen was involved with. It was Phillip Bishop." I paced as I told her what I'd seen on the film. Each time I walked in front of the projector, Phillip's face, frozen, sleepy on the wall, slid across my body.

"Of course," Tammy said, an odd tone to her voice. I could hear some rustling, like she was on the move, and pictured her flipping over the covers on her bed and rising, squinting at the clock, scrambling for her glasses.

My heart raced. I thought of Phillip Bishop flirting with me in the wet patch of grass between our homes, and then later, turning quickly, decisively, from the waitress at the country club when I'd accidentally interrupted them. A wandering eye, a hopeless flirt at best, or a man with a long history of cheating at worst. A man who'd been carrying on with a girl half his age. A teenage runaway, at that.

There was a loud crash on the other end of the phone, and I heard Tammy cuss. "You okay?" I asked.

"Yes, yes. Just trying to move in the dark."

"Tammy, I know you think Clay didn't know anything, but what if he did? What if he sent me the necklace?"

Clay. The mathematician. Good at detail. It might be just his style to send me an anonymous message. Maybe he knew his father had been involved with Maureen. Maybe he knew something terrible had happened, and he'd lived with the burden of it for so long. If he'd had the necklace for all those years, it was because he'd truly been in love with Maureen.

And now, maybe, he saw his chance to give her justice, even if it meant revealing her relationship with his father.

"Maybe we should just go to the police. Let them sort it out." I recognized fear in Tammy's voice.

"I think we should talk to Clay."

"No." Tammy was vehement. "No, Allison. We're done. Do you hear me? Done. This is enough. We'll turn this over to the police and let them handle it all. Right? Okay? Promise me you won't try to talk to anyone else."

I touched the projector, running my finger along the edge. I had evidence. The film. It had to mean something. I wasn't crazy.

"Allison, this isn't a game anymore. You're in danger."

I laughed. It was an automatic response, but my pulse increased at that word. "What kind of danger? I never said it was a game, Tammy. What the hell are you talking about?"

"I'll handle it from here." And she hung up.

I sat, stunned. Was she overreacting? Scared again? I grew angry at her hot-and-cold attitude. She wanted me to help her. Then she didn't. Why had I been wasting my time? She told me to stop acting like it was a game, but Tammy was the one who was playing around.

I tried to call her back a few times, finally leaving a voice mail. "We need to talk. I'm not sure what's going on, Tammy, but we need to sort this out. We can go to the police together, with the film. Whatever you're worried about, just let me know. Please."

But when I peered out the window, listening to the howling wind, I knew I wasn't going *anywhere* for a few days. And as I tried to sleep that night, thinking about the Bishops, about Phillip, all I heard was *You're in danger.*

34

MAUREEN

On Sunday, Marta, my boss, hands me a package instead of the stack of daily deals. She's looking at me oddly. "Some young man dropped this off for you," she says.

I expect her to walk off, but she stands there like she's waiting for me to open it.

"He did not look like a nice young man," she says, hands on her hips.

I open the package, hands shaking, wondering what horrible thing it could hold. A seagull's head? My mother's pinkie finger?

Marta chuckles when she realizes what it is. "What is that? A clock? Strange present." She takes it from me before I can register what it means, which gives me the chance to read the note without her seeing.

Time's up, princess. Tomorrow the interest goes up.

I sneak around to the back of the Bishop house, past the looming construction site to Zeke's basement door. I knock, wait.

A small beetle crawls out of a crack at my feet, starts working its way across the hot tile, then changes its mind and wiggles back into the hole it came from. What are the chances Zeke will be home? And if he is, what are the chances he'll actually loan me some money?

Can't be any worse than your odds of winning poker, Maureen.

There's no answer. I knock again, biting my fingernails. I know this is a bad idea, but as my mom says, desperation makes you do stupid things.

The door swings open. But it's not Zeke. It's Clay's dad standing there with a half smile.

"Oh hello, Mr. Bishop," I say, taking a step back. "I thought—I was looking for—"

"You sound disappointed," he says in a strangely playful tone.

"Oh no," I say. "I just—I needed to talk to Zeke—your brother. About something."

"As long as it's not disappointment." He opens the door wider. "And please, call me Phillip. I hear Mr. Bishop, and I look around for my dad."

I walk inside Zeke's place. I've never been down here, but it feels familiar somehow. Wood paneling, leather chairs, a huge record player console against one wall. It smells like cigars, but there's no sign of Zeke.

"This is about his poker games, isn't it?" Mr. Bishop—I mean, Phillip—asks. "I should've known when you said last week that you'd had a bad night, that it involved good ole Zeke."

"Well, I—"

Phillip holds out a hand. "No, no. No need to explain it to me. But it is a shame. Zeke had a sudden work emergency at one of our sister restaurants. I thought about going myself, but really, it's his turn. The lazy bum has been here, hardly working most of the summer and I've barely had any time to myself. Do you think that's fair?"

I shake my head, but Phillip isn't really waiting for an answer.

"My brother, as I'm sure you can tell, is not the most responsible soul out there. He's been that way since he was a child. Our parents coddled him, and he learned early on how to do the least amount possible to get by. What he doesn't understand, of course, is that the money doesn't just come from anywhere. I don't make it in the back room and toss it around like confetti. You have to work for it. Like everything good in life."

I stand still, unsure how to respond to this fatherly lecture.

"Anyway, I'm sure you didn't come to hear me rattle on. I'll be talking to Clay and his mom tonight. I'll make sure to let him know you said hello."

I flush. "Oh, that's okay. We aren't really—" I break off, unsure what to say.

Phillip lifts an eye. "Oh? Don't tell me my son has hurt you, too."

My eyes brim with tears before I can help myself.

"Maureen, Maureen," Phillip says softly, holding out his arms. "If I'm not being too presumptuous, it seems like you could use a hug."

He folds me into him, and I find myself resting my head against his chest. That smell again, the deep forest of his cologne and a sweeter, cleaner laundry scent. He's a sturdy tree, and I lean against him. All this time, all this running around. Trying to fix it all myself. And here he is. I'm tired— exhausted—and it all comes out of me. I let myself cry like I haven't in a very long time.

●━━━━●

Upstairs, while I clean my face, he makes me a sandwich. I pour him a drink without him asking. We take the food in the living room and sit at a small table near the window with a nice-looking chessboard on it, heavy, not the flimsy kinds that fold in the middle. Mr. Bishop picks up the board and moves it to the coffee table. "You play?" he asks.

"No."

"Too bad," he murmurs. "No one in this house does, except for me."

"I'd love to learn," I say. "My grandfather loved chess. He used to say, 'Chess is like life. You don't have to be the best to win, you just have to play better than the other guy.'"

"Your grandpa sounds like a smart man." His eyes meet mine, and they've got that twinkling again. I feel something shift, the air changes, like destiny turning another key. A jumble of images fly through my mind like Tammy's puzzle pieces—flashing red and blue lights, the officer's piercing stare, Clay's casual confidence, *Yes, sir. Phillip Bishop is my father.* Phillip's power, his influence, washes over me. Here I am, on the inside.

We finish our food, and Phillip pours us another drink. "Care to go for a walk on the beach? It's a nice night."

I follow him, stumbling through the dunes to where the beach begins to flatten. It is a nice night. The humidity is low and it's even a bit cool when the wind blows. I rub my arms and feel goose bumps. Phillip sits in the sand far enough from the ocean that it won't wet us, and I sit next to him. "Cold?" he asks, and scoots closer to me, putting his arm around me.

"I've always liked the beach at night," I say.

"It's my favorite time," he murmurs.

"It's when the mermaids come, you know," I say. "My mom used to say that. She used to tell me this story before bed, about this mermaid family that dropped me off when I was a baby, before I had a chance to grow my tail." I break off. "Anyway, it was a kid's story, you know? But I always sort of believed it a little. Just a tiny sliver, anyway. That if I just did everything right, my mermaid family would come back for me."

He cocks his head. "You're an enigma, Maureen. You're like a lobster, you know that? Hard on the outside, but soft on the inside." He's rubbing my arm now, and I settle into him. The alarm bells are going off, but I silence them.

He takes another sip of his drink, stretches his feet out in the sand. "Clay and his mother will be back on Saturday. And then I won't be alone any longer."

"Oh good," I say. The mention of Clay's mom as Phillip caresses the inside of my arm gives me a guilty kind of pleasure. I think of her in the green dress, flicking her eyes over me, and I push farther into him. *Take that.* "Look, I'm sorry. About before. I shouldn't have gotten so upset. Clay and I—well, he's a good person. It just—didn't work out."

"You don't have to apologize." He sits up, takes his arm off me. I immediately feel cold again. He's staring at the ocean, deep in thought. "Have you ever been just completely overcome by the beauty of the ocean? It's like nothing else, is it? Once you've seen it, you just have to have it. Again and again."

I stay silent, feeling like Phillip wants to say more. Feeling like he's not really talking about what he's talking about. I hold my breath.

"I think you're beautiful, Maureen. But I wonder, what do you think we're doing here?"

"I don't—I'm not sure," I say quietly.

"But yet you're still here."

I feel something inside my belly shift. "Because I want to be."

I can't see his face in the darkness, but he doesn't seem to react for a long time. Then I hear him say, without looking at me. "That's a very dangerous thing, isn't it?"

35

● —————— ●

Maureen

As soon as I enter the kitchen and see Tammy and Mabel, I know something's up. It's the energy in the air, that feeling when you walk in the room, in the middle of two people whispering, and you know it's about you and you know it's not good. That's what it is, crackling above them, their guilty, hushed faces. Mabel's standing next to the card table we use as a dining room table, orange juice sloshing back and forth in her glass like she's just been twirling it around. Tammy's sitting, and she doesn't look up at me as I enter.

"Good morning," I say cheerfully.

They don't answer me.

"Is everything okay?"

"Where have you been?" Mabel asks, surveying me with those beady bug eyes of hers. "It's been days."

"I've been busy."

Tammy doesn't look at me. What would she think if I told her about Phillip? I am suddenly embarrassed by the weight of it all, the secret I hold between us. *But it's all for her*, I tell myself.

"Besides, it's none of your business," I say to Mabel.

"It most certainly is." Mabel slams her glass down on the counter and glares at me. She's puffy this morning, her eyes round, with dark circles under them. She's got on one of her boyfriend's T-shirts, and as she crosses her hands across her chest the football logo smashes between her breasts. "Tammy, if you're not going to do something about this, I am."

"What happened, Mabel?" I sit down next to Tammy and unwrap a Pop-Tart. "Did you mistake your hemorrhoid cream for toothpaste again?"

Tammy remains motionless. It's like someone's just said her dog's missing. I'm worried something bad really did happen to her—her mother, maybe? Or had Benny bothered her?

"You're a *thief*," Mabel says dramatically. "Try and lie your way out of it this time. I've caught you now."

I poke Tammy. "Hey, what's with all this?"

She looks at me then, and there's a hatred in her eyes that I've never seen. It throws me. Through all of Mabel's bullshit I always had Tammy on my side at least. I feel heat coming to my cheeks.

"Where's my rent money, Maureen? I want it back." Mabel's eyes are flashing. It's a good performance—she could rival Bette Midler—but it's not a joking moment. Something's wrong. Really wrong.

"I don't know what you're talking about. Like you said, I haven't been around. I didn't touch your rent money, you twit."

She recoils, but I can see the triumphant glare in her face. She knows she's won this one. "It was here, on the table. I left it for Tammy. And now it's gone. So who would've taken it?"

"Maybe you were drunk and you spent it on Doritos and don't remember."

"Oh, that's just great. Yeah, great. Do you hear this, Tammy? Do you hear her?"

"Tammy?" I ask. "Is everything okay? You don't believe I'd—"

"I want you out," Tammy says in a low, determined voice. "Get out."

"What?"

"Out!" She screams it, standing up from the table and slapping her hands on it. She tips the chair over and runs out of the kitchen. Even Mabel seems surprised.

Tammy heads to the living room, where she curls up in a ball on the couch, sobbing, while Mabel looks on from the doorway.

"My god, Tammy. I didn't. You listen to her?" I go close to the couch, staring down at her in disbelief. Mabel huffs and rolls her eyes. "You really think, after everything, that I would take a few lousy dollars off the table?"

"It's not about that," Tammy says, her words clipped. I've never seen her so angry.

Mabel steps forward now. "We don't want you around anymore. Ever."

"Tammy? She's setting me up—"

"Just get out," Tammy says.

Someone raps on the front door. I'm closest, so I throw it open. My heart's beating and I'm ready to rail at whoever's there. It's a guy, not much taller than I am, with a white-brimmed Dick Tracy-style hat hiding a bunch of bushy brown hair. He's wearing a short-sleeved shirt and a skinny tie. He's a dweeb, twitching like a nervous boy ready to ask someone to the prom. Only missing the wrist corsage.

"Can I help you?" I bark at him, no interest in patience.

"Are you Maureen."

I feel my stomach twist at the way he says my name, and

the fact that it's not really a question, not at all; this boy knows I'm Maureen. And I know who sent him here.

"I gave him money yesterday," I say, low, my voice catching in the back of my throat. I can feel Tammy and Mabel behind me, aware they are listening to every word. I try to move out into the hallway, but the goon won't budge so I'm stuck here in the doorway. He twitches again, sniffs, rubs his nose, and I realize that the twitchiness isn't nerves. He's high as a skyscraper.

"Who is that?" I hear Mabel hiss.

The goon sniffles at this and wipes his nose again. "I've brought you a present." He thrusts a box at me. It's wrapped in red paper with a black bow. It's about the size of a tissue box. I stare at it warily. "Go ahead."

I open it, half expecting to find a mound of earthworms inside. But it's not worms or insects. It's a slinky black garment that glides across my hand, too thin to be a dress. Some sort of negligee. I hold it with the tips of my fingers, then let it quickly fall back into the box like it's going to bite me. There's a card, too, in Benny's handwriting that reads: "Saturday, 6 p.m.," along with an address.

The goon smiles, twitches his head to the side like a puppeteer above him just had a sudden itch to scratch and lost the tautness of the line. "Benny said to tell you it's worth one grand."

I throw it back at him, and it hits his shirt and falls to the floor across his feet. "Keep it," I say. "I'll have his money for him soon. You tell him that."

The goon kicks the lingerie to the side. He leans in the apartment and looks Tammy and Mabel up and down, rubs a hairy hand across the edge of the door and shakes his head. "Ladies," he says, clucking his tongue. "My dad's a locksmith, you know. I could get him to come by and put something heavier on these doors. If you'd like." He turns to me. "He charges a lot, though."

"I think we'll be fine," I say.

He shrugs, winks, points at the dress. "I'll leave it there in case you change your mind."

I shut the door.

"Will someone tell me who the hell that was?" Mabel's angry, her voice rising an octave. She's loud but she's scared, too.

"Don't worry about it."

"Don't worry about it? You have the goddamn mafia coming to our door!" Mabel advances toward me. I think she's going to strike me, but she shoves me aside, throws the dead bolt on the door and slumps down on the couch next to Tammy. "I mean, what the Christ?"

For a second, I see a flicker of the old Tammy. The one who gave me her scarf. Who drove me to the carnival in the middle of the night to get my suitcase. The one who thought Mabel was over-dramatic. But then her face hardens again into its new mask. And the thought knocks me off my feet like an unexpected tidal wave: no one's coming to save us. This is up to me.

I push past Mabel and into Tammy's room. My tears keep getting in the way as I throw random clothes in a bag, grab my purse, and go back into the living room. "Don't worry about it. I'm gone. I'll be back for the rest of my stuff once I'm settled. You don't have to worry about me anymore. I'm going to fix all this. Tammy— listen, I'm going to fix it. No one's going to bother you."

"You don't fix anything," Mabel says. "You make things worse."

I close the door behind me.

As far as I can tell, Tammy never once looked up.

36

———•———

MAUREEN

The sheet slides off my face and Phillip's above me, grinning.

"Morning, sleepyhead." He kisses my forehead. I twirl around, wrap the bedsheet around me and sit up.

"What time is it?"

"Just after nine." He's already dressed in khaki shorts and a polo shirt. "You need to get going. I need to get going." He slips his wedding ring on, and I pretend I don't notice. His hair is still a bit damp from the shower and in the bright morning sun he looks very real. He clasps on an expensive wristwatch that probably costs what I'd make the entire year at the carnival.

"You should come back to bed," I say, wiping the dry crusts out of the corners of my eyes. As my vision adjusts, I see the arm of a pink silk blouse poking out of the half-closed closet door across the room, and I think of the awful black negligee that Benny sent me, the way Tammy looked at me last night.

What am I doing here? I think again, the same thought I have each time I stay here with Phillip. I don't like the sweet smell of Mrs. Bishop's perfume, the half-filled water glass on the far nightstand. I don't like thinking of Clay's room just down the hall, and the last time I saw him there. I shudder and curl into a ball. In the dark of the night it's easy to forget everything, to give into the comfort of Phillip, but here in the no-hide light of day, there is evidence everywhere I turn that I am an intruder and a liability.

He comes over, pulls down the sheet and cups one of my breasts, kissing me deeply. I feel a mix of emotions, slightly cheap and used but also aroused and happy. "You're special, my lobster baby," he says. "Don't forget that."

I push myself out of bed and find my clothes on the floor, slip them on. He's already skipping down the stairs, whistling to himself, and I take the moment to stare at myself in Mrs. Bishop's vanity mirror. Dark circles under my eyes, dry lips. My long hair trails down my shoulders, *dirty-blonde,* my mom calls it, which I've always hated. Nothing about my hair is dirty. I look away quickly, like the mirror is a camera that Mrs. Bishop will be able to rewind and review. There is the bench on which she sits each morning to get ready, to roll on lipstick and comb her hair. There is an array of nail polish, a dozen shades of pink and red, all nearly indistinguishable from the other. I pocket one of them, a dark pink named First Love. I feel it rest against my hip as I follow Phillip's trail down to the kitchen where he is pouring coffee into heavy black mugs, still whistling, always whistling, and I remember that someone had once told me that to whistle was to call the devil.

"I need to drive to Shetland this morning and meet the HVAC guy. There's a problem with the heating unit and they won't be able to open for dinner tonight if we don't fix it. But I was thinking," he says with raised eyebrows as he bites into a piece of toast, "that perhaps I can take you out to dinner tonight?"

Phillip pours me some orange juice. It seems like we are always pouring each other drinks of some kind or another.

"Sure," I say, mustering a smile. "That would be great."

I'm feeling something I can't quite put my finger on. A sense of dread. But that's dumb. It's something about the house, I think. Everything screams domestic. The smell of soap on Phillip's hair. The pulp on the side of my juice glass. The sound of water dripping in the kitchen sink. Each tiny detail amplified, overbearing. I twitch in my seat and think of the goon in the hat kicking the negligee in the hall. *I'll leave it here. In case you change your mind.*

"Phillip?"

"Yes, my love?"

"I need to ask a favor. I need—I need some money."

He looks up from his toast, concern in his eyes. "Money?"

"Remember the poker?"

"Not you, too, Maureen." He rolls his eyes. "Didn't I tell you not to get involved?"

"You did, and I am stopping. I really am. But I need—I'm in trouble. I need to pay them back. Quickly. And then I'll pay you back, too. I promise."

"Do you know how many times I hear that from my brother?" He takes a knife and slits his egg down the middle and the yellow yolk bubbles over and leaks like pus. I look away.

"It's just this one time. I swear."

"I can't, my love. I'm sorry." I feel the panic bubbling up inside me as Phillip gets up, leans down and kisses my neck. "I can't do that, my love. If anyone found out… It's a family business. Money like that—it would be noticed." He nibbles on my ear and I break away.

"But—"

The doorbell rings. Phillip's face shifts. His voice is tight. "Go downstairs," he says. It's a hiss. An order.

"Downstairs?"

But he's already moving, opening the basement door. "Go," he whispers. "I don't know who it is. I'll get rid of them."

I obey, and he shuts the door behind me. I hear him slide the lock. I sit on the top step, hugging my legs to my chest, my ear pressed up against the door. But it's too heavy, and I can't hear anything through it. Instead I listen to my own breathing. I pick at flakes of wood breaking off the bottom of the door. I contemplate heading down into Zeke's place and leaving out the back door, slipping away. But I can't leave. I have to stay, if not for me then for Tammy. For her safety.

I hear footsteps and I stand up, like a prisoner waiting to be freed. Phillip opens the door and seems all businesslike, formal all of a sudden. "I'm so sorry," he says. "One of my wife's friends."

"I should've left," I say. "I almost did."

"I'm glad you didn't." He kisses my head. "I'll make it up to you tonight. Promise."

I go to work and hand out flyers, but I barely make eye contact with people and hardly anyone takes one. I don't have it in me. Marta takes pity and hands me the full payment anyway, even though I have half my stack left. In the restaurant's bathroom, I change into the random bits of clothing I'd swiped from the floor of Tammy's room in my distress and try to freshen up.

Phillip picks me up in a side alley like Dick Tracy, his tinted windows rolled up tight. He seems tense, gripping the steering wheel and constantly checking his rearview mirror as though

he expects we're being followed. We drive for a long time.
I'm not even sure where we're going. Phillip holds my hand
as he drives. I want to ask him again about the money, but I
need him to be in the right mood.

We get farther away from the ocean. The towns larger, the
houses closer together and taller. Finally we stop at a strip mall
in the middle of nowhere. There is a restaurant, a tiny Italian
place. It's dark and there are only families inside, moms and
dads with their kids in booster seats and high chairs. It feels like
everyone is watching us. Phillip requests a booth in the back.

"Do you want me to wear sunglasses?" I joke.

"No, it's fine. I'm sorry. I just have to be cautious. Surely
you understand that?"

"We shouldn't be doing this," I say. "It's wrong and I'm
sorry. We should probably just stop."

Phillip takes my hand and forces me to look at him. He's
all teddy bear again. "Do you really think I could stop seeing you?"

"I don't know," I say quietly.

"Well, then, you don't know me."

"Well, and then what? What happens in a couple of days
when your wife comes back? When Clay comes back?" I fid-
dle with my fork, frustrated. "I'm not an idiot, Phillip. I know
how these things go."

"You're too good for me. You should just leave, go live
your life."

I glare at him. "I thought you just said you couldn't stop
seeing me now?"

He rubs his hand through his hair. "What we have here,
this is real, Maureen. I've never felt like this about anyone."

I didn't just fall off the turnip truck. If he's bullshitting me,
it's because he's bullshitting himself. Still I can't help it. Underneath it all I feel special. There's something about Phillip

that gets to me—the way he can make you feel like the rest of the world has dropped away and it's just you and him. I'm a sucker and I know it and still I find myself beaming inside and nodding. Beaming inside and flicking my mermaid tail under the table as he orders us a bottle of wine. The waitress brings over appetizers and pasta and another bottle of wine, nestled in its own bucket of ice, and Phillip and I talk, like real people, about books and art. He tells me about the times the carnival came when he was a kid and all the things he used to do at the beach.

"What do you want to do with your life, Maureen?"

I am full of wine and pasta and I smile sleepily. "I don't know," I say. "But I want to be free. I don't want to owe anyone anything."

"You'll always owe someone something. It's just the way of existence." He reaches across and squeezes my hand. "Every time you interact with someone, you form a connection. Every choice you make affects someone, somehow. You take a job? Someone else doesn't get it. You fall in love with someone, there's someone else you're hurting."

"I don't want to hurt anyone. I've hurt too many people. I'm trying to make things right." I frown. Phillip and I seem to be talking past each other. He's rolling and unrolling the paper straw wrapper in his fingers, twisting it up into a tight snake and then letting it loose, slack. I feel like I can't get my mind straight, like each time he unrolls the paper, my thought unravels with it, and I lose it.

"You worry too much, don't you? Remember what I said. Things have a way of working out. You just have to be patient."

I shake my head. "No, that's just it. I don't have time to be patient. I can't wait around." I take a deep breath, wish I hadn't had so much wine. "There's no magic. I've figured that out. No mermaid family's coming to get me. There's not even destiny, Phillip. It's just me. And I have to fix it. *Me*." I take a deep breath. "But you can help me. Fix it. I need your help. Just this once."

His face darkens, and I know I've ruined my chance again. "I thought we already discussed this, Maureen."

"I'm sorry, I just—" I pause, reach my hand out to him. "You mean a lot to me—"

"As a bank?" he asks, taking a sip of his wine.

"No," I say, wounded.

He relents, shakes his head. "Oh, Lobster Baby, I'm sorry. I don't mean to hurt you. It's just…complicated. I'll think about it, okay?"

"Okay," I say, but I'm dissolving.

He reaches over the table and refills my wine glass. "But I do think you're on the right track. Taking the reins. Making your own fate. That's how my family's been so successful. Did you know my father grew up dirt poor? Fought for everything. He earned it. Anyone can, if they have initiative." He leans back with a lofty air, and I can see for the first time how he must be as a manager, a touch of egotism with the doling out of unrequested platitudes, advice. I can see for the first time why Clay rolls his eyes when he talks about him. "You can do this."

"You make it sound so easy," I say. "I believe that where we end up is who we become. I need to end up somewhere better than I've been, Phillip. Surely you can understand that? I've been—well, I've seen people I care about mess up. Badly. And I can't make that same mistake."

"You're so softhearted. Who would've thought," he says, and I feel his foot graze against mine under the table. "My sweet lobster baby."

37

•———•

ALLISON

The weather, as if conjured up by Tammy's deepest desires, kept me from doing much of anything for the rest of the holiday weekend. I paced, all day and all night. I watched the film again, and then again. I tried to called Tammy back, but she wouldn't answer, and when I got sick of trying, I left a message for Dolores at the art gallery, which was of course closed for the holiday.

It felt as if Maureen had completely taken me over, like she'd seeped into the very walls of the house. I could hear her whispers in the wind gusts. When I closed my eyes, I saw her face flickering from the grainy film, a haunted, hollow laugh.

She'd had three months, too. Three months of an endless-seeming summer to figure it all out. To hold her life in the palm of her hand. And instead, she'd opened her hand too soon, scattered it all to the ocean breeze. Three months in Opal Beach, and then she'd vanished. How easy it had been for someone to get rid of her without a second thought. How easy for her to just disappear.

The sadness settled over me. I felt trapped, like everyone here in Opal Beach. And it wasn't just the weather. Tammy, with an eternally sick mother, stuck in a small town that she thought had only one place for her, still wrapped up in the events of thirty years before. Dolores, caring for her artist father, spending day after day in that small art gallery, eating greasy fast food, while families like the Bishops carried on at their fancy cocktail parties and people like Mabel tried to flit between the two castes, selling her real estate and wearing fake gemstones on her fingers.

And what would become of me?

Right next door to Phillip Bishop. The adulterer. And maybe more? What did Phillip know? And Clay? If only Tammy would answer my calls.

Desperate to do something, I finally dialed the Opal Beach police station, but the dispatcher said that Horace Clapper was taking time off. "Can I patch you through to someone else?" she asked, half-bored, but I declined. No way I was telling the whole story again to someone new.

I thought I might drive myself mad. On Sunday morning, I spent hours outside trying to chip away the ice on the front porch steps. I made progress, but my arms and legs and back ached. Next door, the Bishops' house was quiet. Eerily so. I kept glancing over, wondering if anyone was home. I didn't like the idea that we were all in such proximity with no way to escape.

On Monday, I was about to go completely insane when my cell phone rang. I picked it up, fumbling, and managed to click the green answer button.

"Ms. Simpson? This is Horace Clapper. You called?"

Even with his usual brisk tone, I was relieved to hear from

him. So I wasn't in a movie where everyone had disappeared off the planet.

"Yes, thank you... I thought... The dispatcher said you weren't available."

"They let me know about your call." I waited to see if he'd say more, but he was, as usual, not very forthcoming. I longed for warmth, something to show I wasn't nuts, but he was stoic. I wondered if it was a police tactic or just his personality.

"Well, I... I'm sorry to bother you on your day off. It's just..." I had new evidence? Everything running through my head suddenly seemed ridiculous and childish. "I just wondered...if you'd heard from Tammy at all?"

"Tammy? No...should I have?"

"Oh, I don't know. No, I guess not. I mean, we were going to contact you anyway, but I thought... I've been trying to call her and she hasn't returned my calls and I just wanted to see...to make sure she's okay."

"Are you okay, Ms. Simpson?"

"Yes." I picked at the bedspread, nervously. "Yes, I'm fine." There was a long pause, and in my nervousness I needed to fill it up. "We found a film. An old film of Maureen's."

"And what was on the film?"

"Well, we were...going to bring it in to you. To see. For yourself. But with the storm and all. And now I can't find Tammy...and..."

"Well, that's the strange thing," Clapper said. For the first time, I could hear hesitation in his voice. "She hasn't returned my calls either."

"Your calls?" I was startled. "Did you find out something?"

"No, not exactly." He paused again, and I could picture him petting his mustache. "It's odd—"

"What?" I asked impatiently.

"Well, you know I thought she told me that she reported

that woman as missing all those years ago—foul play suspected. But when I looked up the report, there was a note in it."

"A note?"

"Taken from the dispatcher. Tammy called in a week later, said she was dropping her report."

"Dropping it?"

"Yeah. That she was sorry for the trouble but her friend wasn't missing anymore. She said she'd heard from her and everything was fine."

"Heard from her?" I couldn't stop repeating his words. "After the night she went missing? Are you sure?"

Clapper sighed. "Of course I wasn't here then, but that's what it says. Noted and dated. Exactly one week after the initial report."

"But why would she—if she heard from Maureen a week after that, why would she…?" None of it made any sense. Tammy had been insistent that Maureen was murdered.

"Well," Clapper said quietly. "That's what I wanted to ask her."

"Do you think she was lying?"

"Could be," he said. "Could be that she felt like she was in danger, talking to the police. Maybe someone threatened her to drop it, or she was worried about something happening to her, too."

It made sense. It would also explain why Tammy had been so jumpy about the necklace and the film. Even all these years later she felt threatened.

"If that's true, then we need to find her," I said. "She could be in danger."

"Now, I don't think we need to get that dramatic, Miss Simpson," Clapper said in his condescending tone. "With this storm, you never know. Her power could be out. Phone dead.

It's the holiday season—people are traveling, things come up…
I'm sure Tammy is just fine."

But after he hung up, I wondered if he was more worried
than he was letting on.

———•———•———

The house was closing in on me. I kept walking from room
to room, the walls pressing me closer and closer inside. I'd
shut the basement door, but a chilly draft billowed in through
the crack at the bottom, and if I pressed my ear to the door it
sounded like a chorus of voices whispering. My mother had
always believed that houses contained spirits, that their energy
could infect the people who lived there, in good ways and bad.

What if she was right?

I considered for a moment all the crazy things I could do.
Hold a séance in the house. Dig out the tarot cards my mother
had given me when I'd turned thirteen—they were currently
in a box in the garage that I'd never bothered to unpack. Test
out a strange purple thing that looked like a genie lamp on
the bookshelf. I walked over to it, reached up to pull it down
and accidentally spilled a bowl of seashells all over the carpet.

I knelt down beside the shells and started putting them back
into the bowl. There were all sorts—the white rippled shells
my mother called angel wings, long curly pointed ones that
reminded me of pasta, smaller iridescent slivers that were pol-
ished and smooth as marble—and I wondered if they'd been
collected from the beach or bought at one of the tourist shops
along the pier. There were several perfectly intact starfish and
a delicate sand dollar that had broken in half.

The last shell I picked up was a hefty conch, dotted tan and
white, with an inner pale shiny pink like an ear. I placed it to
my own ear, like Annie and I had done when we were kids,

plucking the largest ones from the giant bins in the board-walk stores. *Listen to the ocean*, eager shop owners would urge, hoping our parents would buy them for us. I remembered one year our mother had caved and bought us two orange conches. I'd wrapped mine carefully in a T-shirt and tucked it into my suitcase to bring home, certain it wouldn't work once I took it away from the beach. And when I'd unwrapped it on the floor of my bedroom and found I could still hear that lull-ing roar hundreds of miles from the ocean, it felt like magic.

I heard it again now as I pressed the shell to my ear. I closed my eyes, feeling a bit silly, but also mesmerized. The trick never got old, the dull whoosh, but now I realized it didn't sound so much like the ocean as it did Duke's white noise ma-chine. An air conditioner, or the hum of an airplane's engine, or a chorus of whispers and murmurs.

Get him.

I dropped the shell, startled. My ear rung and itched, and I rubbed it. The voice—it had been sharp and sudden.

I felt prickles of fear dotting my back, something inside my belly unwinding. I'd heard it. Clear as if someone was stand-ing right next to me. But there was no one there.

It wasn't until Wednesday that the road salt had done enough work to make the streets passable. It was raining by then, but if the temperatures dipped again it could turn to sleet, and I knew I needed to get out, see Tammy before I was shut in for longer.

The rain tapped against the windshield as I drove past the quiet, closed downtown. Tammy's store was dark and locked up. The beach felt sleepy, abandoned. I turned off the main strip onto Tammy's street, but her apartment duplex was dark,

too. Her car nowhere in sight. She was probably still visiting
her mother. But part of me also worried she might be avoid-
ing me. Had my phone calls scared her away?

I looked down at my ring of keys, at the one Tammy had
given me *just in case you need it*. I could go in. Wait for her.
Force her to talk to me. But somehow it all seemed fruitless.
How long would I have to wait for her to get back? If she'd
been able to get to her mom's house for the holiday, chances
were she'd stay there for a few days extra and wait out the
weather. And I couldn't afford to get stuck at her house with
Catarina back home needing to be fed.

I took the long way on the highway rather than cutting
through the tall grass in the weather and was relieved to pull
into the shared driveway, ready to put on my pajamas and
watch Dilly fight the winds in her peacoat—until I saw them.
Phillip and Zeke. Standing between their cars. I hadn't seen
them together since the country club dinner. They stared as
I passed by and veered off to my driveway. Dark winter caps
pulled over their heads. Long, black overcoats. I drove into
the garage, breathing heavily.

You're being ridiculous, Allison, I tried to tell myself.

I pressed my hands together. It was cold in the garage and
my breath puffed out in white gusts. I thought about the
vicious trolls on social media, all those anonymous posters
wishing me harm. It felt like nowhere was safe. I felt myself
crumble, felt that old familiar longing to just hide, sleep, forget.

Leave them alone, Allison. My brain alarm went off. Duke
might not have left the chess piece for me, but he could still
have been warning me off.

I moved. I got out of the car and unlocked the door leading
into the house. The basement was dark, and I forced myself
up the stairs, a child afraid of the boogeyman. The main floor

was better lit because of the windows, but they didn't make me feel any better. Anyone could be looking in.

I kept moving to the top floor. Pushed open the door to the top deck and stepped out. Icy snow hit my face. In the swirling wind, the ocean seemed dangerous and angry. Far off, the pier lights danced, but all the rides and stores loomed against an upset sky.

I peered over the railing. I could see one light on in the Bishops' house.

Why did it seem like they'd been waiting for me?

38

●━━━━━●

MAUREEN

"Tammy?"

As I enter the apartment slowly, I feel like the thief Mabel accused me of being. The place is quiet, empty. Relief washes over me. I don't want to run into anyone right now.

In Tammy's room, the familiar smell of her shampoo, the sight of her neon bedspread and the silly rock posters, feels like a museum shrine to a time past, of a friendship now gone. I can't get emotional now, though. That's what bunnies do. I am on a mission. I need to make sure she's safe. I owe her that at least.

I was half-expecting my suitcase to be packed and ready for me at the door. But my clothes are still spilling out of the side of the closet I'd claimed, my journal is still tucked under my sleeping bag next to my copy of *The Great Gatsby*, which still has the bookmark inside it. Tammy's makeup is scattered all over her dresser. Lipstick and concealer. Mascara wand unscrewed. I close it for her so it doesn't dry out. She always leaves it uncapped when we get dressed to go out. All those times we got dressed to go out, blasting Duran Duran, singing into our hair brushes… And then I remember there's a party tonight. Barron's party. Everyone's going. The final party of the summer, before all the rich kiddos go back to their winter mansions, back to their Ivy League schools or cushy jobs at the family company. The final party. So Tammy had been getting ready to go out—just not with me.

My suitcase is still in the closet. I consider packing it, but no. Not yet. I open the bottom drawer of Tammy's dresser, which Tammy designated for me. I need clean clothes. The ones I've been carrying around with me for days are dirty.

Inside the drawer, on top of my clothes, is a piece of paper. A note, my name at the top. I turn on Tammy's desk lamp to read it.

> *Dear Maureen—*
> *I'm sorry. By the time you read this, I'll be gone. I need to leave town for a while, for reasons you will understand. I've been angry with you, as you know. I'm sorry.*
> *I thought you betrayed me, but it's not your fault. It's his. I know that now. Please don't judge me too harshly. I love you.*
> *Your BFF,*
> *Tam*

I read it several times, puzzled. Leave town? A bad feeling wells up inside me. It's *his* fault, she says. Clay. I trace my finger over the ink. I remember all her cheerful insistence that she was fine with us together. That she was over him. That she'd moved on. Did she invent this new mystery guy she talked about? Pretended to be happy when really all this time she was stewing inside?

And all for nothing. I haven't seen Clay since our fight, and he hasn't contacted me since he got back a few days ago. Not that we can ever go back to what we were, anyway, not after what I've done with Phillip.

"We're not even together anymore," I say stupidly to the paper. "You can have him."

But of course. That's the whole point, dummy. Clay doesn't want Tammy.

I leave the note on the dresser and get ready, hurriedly. There is no way Tammy will miss the last party of the summer. Which means there is still time to find her.

●━━━━●

I half run to the bus stop, but the bus is late and, as I wait, a big guy with a baseball cap saunters over. I don't like the way he glances at me, so I stand on the other side of the bus stop and pace nervously, watching him out of the corner of my eye. He sits down on the bench, staring at his hands, and I try to ignore him. I'm thinking about Tammy, if I can catch her and explain things. I realize I've left my half of the best friend necklace back at the apartment, and it seems like some kind of bad omen. But I can't go back now, or I'll miss the bus and possibly miss Tammy.

"Ever hear that song 'Bennie and the Jets'?"

He says it so low that at first I think I imagined it.

"Bennie!" He sings in a false high voice. "Bennie!"

Where the hell is the bus? I contemplate running. I think I could outrun him—he's big, but I'm fast.

Luckily an older woman walks up and stands between us. She checks the printed schedule, then her watch, and sighs dramatically. Baseball Cap stops his singing as the woman rifles through her large purse and pulls out a slice of bread and starts chewing on it.

The bus rolls up then, all gasoline smelly and hissing, and I am relieved that it's packed. I let the bread lady choose her seat, and then I find an empty place next to a woman with a young boy in her lap. The large dude sits sideways on a seat in front, facing me but not looking right at me. He's whistling under his breath, and I bet I know what song. I wait, my nerves razor sharp. If I get off at the stop for the party, it will be quiet and fairly deserted, and I'm not sure I want a confrontation. Plus I'd be leading him straight to Tammy and putting her in more danger. So when the bus stops downtown near the carnival, I wait until the last possible second and jump up, heading out the back doors.

Baseball Cap follows, surprisingly fast for his size. I might not be able to outrun him after all. Thankfully there are still people milling about. The carnival's closing soon, but Clyde's still got the gates open and the ticket takers are gone, so I run through, risking a quick glance behind me. The man's still there, though following at a slower pace now as to not attract attention.

I take advantage of his lag-behind to run, darting around a few carnival game booths. In front of me is the Hall of Mirrors, its twinkling lights framing the sign that dares you to "Come on in, if you can risk NEVER leaving." Jacqueline is managing the ticket booth for the night, and when she sees me, her face lights up. "Maureen," she says with her thick Southern drawl. "Oh my god. How are you?"

I'd love to stay and catch up, but I can't. "Some creep is following me," I say instead. "Can I go in?"

Jacqueline waves me forward. She's not one to surprise easily or to ask many questions, and I'm relieved for that right now.

"I owe you one," I call as I open the imposing black door.

"Just be out in ten minutes," she says. "We're closing up."

●────●

The Hall of Mirrors smells the same, that combination of mold and paint and grease from all the droppings of food the kiddos spill, despite the warning to leave your edibles at the door. I move fast, confident now, hoping to cut through to the back exit and shake Benny's toad quickly. But as I slide through the first doorway, I realize they've changed it up since I've been gone. I stop, disoriented. Instead of the high room with the ornate mirrors, this is a low-ceilinged hallway with mirrors on each side. The effect is dizzying—endless rows of Maureens, like a robust army, everywhere I turn. I lift my arm, and a thousand Maureens do, too. I step cautiously, focusing on my feet instead of my infinite reflections.

The next room I recognize, though it's also slightly changed up. The vampire is hanging above the door instead of in the corner, and as I move through I trigger something that causes a nest of plastic spiders to come spilling into my hair. I scream, immediately angry for falling for the dumb gag, and rotate the big mirror on the far wall, where thankfully, there's still a door and a shortcut to end the nightmare.

But even the shortcut leads me somewhere different. A room filled with clowns, their bright-colored outfits nauseating. Their bulbous noses pulsate as I pivot, looking for the way through. I'm turned around. I grasp near my neck, looking for the necklace, my lucky charm, and curse again for forgetting it. Tammy. I need to get to Tammy.

I stumble through several other rooms—the crooked room, where one end feels shorter than the other; a room with a suspension bridge in the middle; the room that Jacqueline always called the Banana Room because of its bright yellow tarps and crescent-shaped mirrors. Each escape brings more and more obstacles—when did this place get so big?

Finally I find myself in the last room with the distorted mirrors. In front of me is the giant mirror that makes you seem stretched like taffy, but I'm looking at the two doors on either side of it. Trying to remember. One of them is the exit. And one of them takes you back into the house again. But which one? My brain is all screwy, disoriented.

Get a grip, you dumb bunny. I take a deep breath and throw myself at the door on the right. The humid summer air greets me, and I start to skip, heading quickly down the exit ramp toward the gates. I feel giddy. I've done it. Of course I've done it.

"Well, look who it is."

Benny stands calmly at the edge of the trailer exit, tossing a handful of peanuts into his mouth. "Maureen, Maureen," he says, clucking his tongue. "So predictable."

"Oh Jesus Christ," I say, barely audible. I am mad, a ball of angry energy ready to strike. I want to claw off Benny's sharp, smarmy face with my fingernails. In the distance, someone bursts into loud laughter, reminding me there are other nights, other fates, happening right now where things are good. "So you sent that piece of shit after me?"

Benny shrugs. "Just making sure you don't skip town on us."

"If I was going to leave, I would've already been gone."

He considers that with another handful of peanuts. Does he have a goddamn vending machine in his pants? "You seem to attract trouble, princess."

"I can take care of myself." I look down, smooth out my shirt. "Don't you have anything better to do?"

He smiles. "It's like a fly. I had a fly stuck in my car the other day. That ever happen to you? The damn thing kept bouncing off window to window, so goddamn hopeful that it was going to break through. Escape. Sweet to see. And sad, too. So very sad." He holds out his hand, offers me peanuts from his pocket. When I don't respond, he shrugs again and pops them in his mouth. "It's not so much that, actually. You're growing on me. You remind me of me."

"We are nothing alike."

He points a finger. "See? That's something I'd say."

"I need to be somewhere, Benny."

He ignores me. He's gazing at the dark sky thoughtfully. "It's not so much the money, you see. I think I want you."

"Don't make me puke."

"Oh, princess. You break my heart." He hugs himself, frowns dramatically. "I think we'd be good together."

"I don't work with snakes."

"Not with. For."

I glare at him. "And just when I thought you were getting soft on me," I say. "Don't worry. You'll get your money. I'm taking care of all of this tonight."

He takes a slow, deep sigh. "What a shame."

39

ALLISON

I woke up to my phone ringing. The sleeping pill I'd taken before bed made me feel like I was cutting through a thick fog. I fumbled, searching for my phone in the dark. I found it wrapped up in the sheets, near my feet.

My brain was flickering with images of the night before. The Bishop brothers. Their thick black coats.

"Allison? It's Dolores."

I sat up and checked the bedside clock. It was 5:33 a.m. Why on earth would Dolores be calling me this early?

"Allison? I'm so sorry to wake you, but I needed to tell you—to tell someone." Her voice caught. She'd been crying. It wasn't hesitation in her voice, but grief.

"Dolores? What's wrong? What's happened?" I rushed out of bed, opened the blinds and surveyed the beach, half expecting to see a mob of people with torches and pitchforks. Instead it was empty, just the stormy ocean churning, beating against the sand.

"It's Tammy," she said. "Tammy—they found her." She took a deep watery breath. "They found her last night at the pier. A terrible accident. She must've fallen in."

"Fallen in?" My heartbeat was pulsing between my ears, a loud thudding sound.

"She drowned. She's dead, Allison. Oh my god." She burst into sobs.

"No." My voice was hollow. "No, no, no. It must be a mistake."

"It's not a mistake," Dolores said between sobs. "I wish it was. I do."

I paced the room frantically. "Dolores. I need you to come over right away. Here to the house."

"I can't, Allison. I'm still in New York. I'm taking the train tonight, but I felt like you needed to know. Can I come tomorrow? Allison?"

"Yes. Come. Soon."

I went back to the window. Below me, a figure slipped out onto the Bishops' deck. The man walked to the bannister, stared at the ocean, his gray hair whipping in the wind. He turned and looked up in my direction. Icicles shot through me. I stayed frozen in place, my head light as a helium balloon. A dull noise at the edge of my mind turned sharper. The roaring in my head, louder. Maureen's voice, screaming now. *What will you do with me?*

40

·•——————•·

MAUREEN

Barron's house is packed, hot with bodies despite the blasting air-conditioning. I am apparently the only one who forgot about this party. I push through the mob of drinkers.

The music is loud and pulsing, all *come on and get me now darling*, and I find my head pounding painfully to the beat as I search for Tammy's red curls. I move to the back of the house, where Barron's built-in pool is filling quickly with tan girls and dudes trying not to spill their beer in the water. I'm so busy pushing through the bodies, trying not to trip on any empty cans, that I almost run into the person in front of me.

"Sorry," I shout, and then stop. Clay is staring at me. He's wearing bright red, short swim trunks and is shirtless, showing off his crew tan, his long hair pulled back into a ponytail. I feel like I've been hit by a bag of bricks.

"What are you doing here?" He tips his red Solo cup my way and takes a swig of it. I can smell the cheap whiskey on his breath.

I can't meet his eyes, afraid if I do he'll see right through me. Being with him again makes me sad, after all that has passed and all that can never now be, and I need to get away before I say something stupid. But as I try to go around him, he steps in my way and blocks it.

"I didn't know you were invited."

"Is there a guest list?"

On the other side of the pool, Barron and a few of his dumbass friends are chanting, parade-like, "Drown the witches, drown the witches," and shoving squealing bunnies in the pool one by one. We watch them grab one tiny pixie by the ankles and swing her three times before tossing her in the deep end with her friends.

"Classy," I say to Clay, who ignores the comment.

He studies me, cocking his head and closing one eye. "I had you all wrong, didn't I?"

I take a sharp breath in. Does he know? But no, he's just drunk. "Clay, I'd love to sit down and talk about everyone's relationship issues, but I've already been through hell tonight, and I'm not in the mood."

"Hell?" He raises his eyebrows. He looks me up and down and his attitude shifts slightly. His eyes relax into that super-hero gaze. "You okay, Maureen?"

"I'm fine," I say, irritated. "I'm looking for Tammy."

"Haven't seen her." He reaches out like he's going to touch me, and then changes his mind. "I still think that we could've been something." He's definitely drunk.

"I'm not sure about that, Clay," I say sadly. Dodging Baseball Cap drained all my energy, and I just want to sit down.

Just then a girl walks up behind him, puts her arm in his and gives me a jealous pout. So she's the replacement. It's not so hard for guys like Clay to find a replacement. I think of Tammy's note. *It's not your fault. It's* his.

I smile brightly at his new bunny, but she scowls and then looks up all innocently at Clay. "Baby, why don't you come over here with us?"

"The world's a shitty place, Clay," I say pointedly to him, ignoring her. "But remember that I tried, okay? I really am trying to fix it all." I tilt forward and give him a kiss, right on the lips, right in front of his bunny.

I hear her gasp, "What the hell, what are you getting at." She echoes in my ear like a dim gnat as she shakes Clay's arm hard.

He turns. "It's fine, babe," but she's already gone through the crowd, working her sad face, and Clay turns back to me. "Why did you have to do that?"

"You should be with Tammy, Clay."

He narrows his eyes. Barron and the parade are making their way toward us again with their stupid chant. "Life isn't a game, Maureen. You can't just move people around like pawns however you see fit."

"Oh, please."

He lifts a finger. "You know, you're right. Didn't you tell me once that summer has to end at some point? That we can't just go on forever?" He moves toward me like he's going to kiss me and puts his lips close to my ear. "Goodbye, Maureen," he whispers. I feel his hands at my stomach, but it's not a hug. A hard shove, just as Barron and his parade are passing. I scream as I hit the pool and water goes up my nose and down my throat, the chlorine burning. My stomach muscles twist, like a knife burrowing in my ribs, and for a second I think I cannot swim, cannot propel myself up. But then I surface, sputtering, splashing, raw. I see Clay's ponytail cut through the crowd toward his new girl. Barron cheers, dancing in a circle. "Clay," I call, but he's gone, and all I'm left with is a bunch of jerks laughing, turning their backs, already forgetting me.

I rush into Tammy's room, flicking on the light. I'm wet and cold and I'm so mad at myself that it takes me a moment to process that Mabel's standing there.

She gasps, presses her hands to her cheeks, but not before I notice they were buried in the top drawer of Tammy's dresser, which is still half-open. She looks at me with intense hatred, but I start laughing. I can't help myself, enjoying how her face changes from hatred to confusion to annoyance all in a flash.

"So, you're the thief!" I finally say, shaking my head. "I should've known."

"I am not," Mabel says hotly, managing to look huffy. "Why are you wet?" she asks with disgust, eyeing me up and down.

I have no time for this. For her. All I want to do is burrow under Tammy's neon comforter and sleep for a week. But I don't have that luxury. I start rummaging through my suitcase for a change of clothes. Still, I can't help a little jab. "I told Tammy she should hide her money someplace decent."

"I. Wasn't. Stealing. It's just—I'm worried about Tammy," Mabel says.

I snort. "Tammy will figure you out eventually." I find a new bra and underwear and, buried under everything, my hair brush.

"Like she figured you out?" That makes me stop. I look up. Mabel's got a nasty glint in her eyes that I don't like.

Her words are like daggers. "What's that supposed to mean?" I ask, hating that my voice wavers. I think of the way Tammy looked that day she told me to leave. Of Benny, his goons. That awful black nightgown thing. *Why wasn't Tammy at the party tonight?* Fear floods through me. "Did someone else come here? Tell me, Mabel."

"She thought you were such a good friend. Even though I *told* her what you are."

"Mabel, where is Tammy? You have to tell me," I say grabbing her. Shaking her shoulders. "Is she okay?"

"Don't touch me," she shouts. "You psycho. Didn't we tell you to get out? Everything's better without you." She stalks out, slamming the door behind her.

I take a moment to catch my breath.

She thought you were such a good friend.

You can't just move people around like pawns, Maureen.

"I need to fix this," I say to myself, determined now. I strip off my wet dress from the pool and find my red dress, the one that Phillip said he liked. I comb out my hair and tie Tammy's scarf in it.

On the top of Tammy's dresser, I spot an orange envelope of developed photos. I flip through and take one of Tammy and me, standing on the pier in front of the Mermaids for sale sign we liked.

Life isn't a game. I know that. I don't want to be the person Clay thinks I am. I don't want to be who Mabel thinks I am, or even Phillip. I want to be the person Tammy thinks I am. Tammy, the only person here in Opal Beach who cares about me—or did care, anyway. Maybe the only real friend I've ever had.

But I have to play. One last time. For Tammy.

On my way out I see my half of the best friend necklace and hook it around my neck, hoping it'll bring good luck.

41

ALLISON

I had to leave. *Go. Go.* My brain, my body, was screaming. *Get out of here.* Tammy was dead. Was I next? I needed to go to the police station, find Clapper. It wasn't an accident. There was no way Tammy would've gone wandering on the pier at night in that kind of weather. He'd believe that. He had to.

I headed downstairs. Opened the front door and felt the chill. There was a thickness to the air, a wet winter cold. I closed the door, threw the dead bolt and rushed downstairs to the garage, my purse bouncing behind me.

The car started. I don't know why I'd thought it wouldn't. I clicked the button for the garage door and angled my neck as I slowly began to back up.

I screamed and slammed the brake.

Zeke was standing in the middle of the driveway, same black overcoat, black knit cap smashed onto his head, waving his hands. In the dim light of the storm, his coat flapping around him, he looked like a specter, something I'd conjured out of the horror movie I'd watched days ago.

He gestured wildly for me to roll down my window, shouting something I couldn't hear.

I cracked the window, my arms poised to steer away. "I have to go," I yelled. "Family emergency."

He was still shouting, but the wind kept thrusting the sound away. I watched him wrestle with his scarf. Finally I caught a word. "Letty…"

"What?"

Zeke came closer, breathing heavy. "Have you seen her?" His bright blue eyes blinked rapidly, like a nervous animal, and he rested a hand on the hood of my car. "My grandniece? She ran out here somewhere and I can't find her. Have you seen her?"

I shook my head. *Go, go, go,* my brain was still saying. But Zeke was in the way. I thought I caught a flash of movement between the houses. Letty? Or someone else? I couldn't think straight. How had they allowed Letty to go out in this kind of weather?

"Can you help?" he called. "I'm afraid, with the weather, that she might…"

I poked my head out of the window. "I can't. I'm sorry."

He nodded slowly and lifted his weight from my hood. "It's okay." He waved, turning. "I'll do what I can." He was frailer than I remembered. Hunched over, moving slow. Was I being ridiculous?

No.

I put the car in Drive. Zeke shifted out of the way, and just as the car started to roll, I saw Zeke in the rearview mirror, heard him shout as he fell on the ice at the edge of my driveway. He went down hard. And wasn't moving.

"Shit," I said, putting the car in park and getting out. The ice cracked beneath my boots. I hadn't grabbed my coat, and even as I pulled my sweater across my body, the wind whipped right through to my skin. I hurried over, bent down. "Mr. Bishop, are you okay?"

He was making some sort of noise, his coat billowed out around him. "That would be…" I thought I heard him say. And then he was up, quick and light, standing there with an odd smile on his face. "Your concern is so delightful, Allison," he said. Then I looked down to see the gun pointed at me. "But perhaps we can chat first."

42

MAUREEN

The ocean air dries my hair as I walk, sandals in hand, through the sand up to Phillip's house. I know Clay won't be there at least, and Phillip said his wife was leaving again. Summer is almost over. It might be my last time with him, and I plan to use it well. I *need* to use it well. It's my last chance to make everything right again.

I approach the Bishop house from the back as always, slipping up the dunes to the deck. The curtains are drawn, the way he usually does when we are together. Maybe he's expecting me. I decide to go around to the front door. Like a normal person, not some mistress to hide. If his wife is still there, I can pretend I'm looking for Clay and no harm done. Just a silly bunny looking for her beau.

I knock and press my ear against the door and hear a woman's voice, then footsteps heading toward the door. I prepare my wonder eyes—*oh, Clay's not here?*—as the person fumbles with the door lock, taking a while, but it's Phillip who answers, Phillip who eyes me suspiciously. Do I see a hint of nervousness in him?

"Mr. Bishop?" I ask innocently, smiling brightly at him. "Oh, I'm sorry, am I disturbing you? I'm looking for Clay."

He breaks into a smile, looks back into the room briefly and opens the door wide. "Come in, quickly," he says, "before the neighbors see."

"You're alone?" The air smells sweet, a scent I recognize from somewhere, but I can't place it. Had I just interrupted something?

"Yes, I told you Lorelei was leaving this weekend." He's slurring, a large goblet of wine in his hand.

"I thought I heard voices."

"Paranoid, my love?" He leans in and kisses me sloppily. He's unattractive in his current state, but I have to play my part.

"Just want you all to myself, is all."

As we move to the kitchen, I still can't shake the feeling that someone's here. Phillip fumbles in the refrigerator, and I walk around the island, trying to figure out what's different. I notice a dirty wine glass in the sink. When he turns around I'm waiting for him. "Throwing a party for yourself?" I ask, holding up the dirty wineglass.

He chuckles. "You know what a snob I am. When I change wines, I change glasses, my dear."

"Do you also change lipsticks?" It's clear now, the tray of cheese and crackers on the counter, the crumpled blanket on the couch, the closed-up blinds. Does he think I'm that clueless?

"Oh, Maureen, my lobster." He turns his palms out. My god, he's drunk. "You caught me. I had a friend over earlier. She's an old friend from my high school days, and Lorelei is jealous of her. Hates her, in fact. For some reason, I thought it best not to tell you about it either. I guess it's just a habit of mine."

"To lie?" I say coolly. I realize I can't get mad at him, not yet. I need him. I soften my face. "It's okay. You can tell me these things." I step close and cup his cheek.

"What do you see in me, anyway?" he asks. "I'm old and wrinkled and pale compared to Clay. You think that, don't you?"

"Gosh, no," I say, kissing him. "Why would you say such a thing?"

"When you're with me, you think about him. I know it." He walks into the den, slumping into a chair.

I go over, try to pull him up. "Actually, I want you to go outside with me. On the beach."

"Oh no, Maureen. I'm much too tired for that."

"Please? It will cheer you up. I promise. There's a meteor shower tonight. I want you to watch it with me." I come close, hold his hand. "I want to share everything with you. This is our last night together. Let's make it special."

43

• ┅┅ •

ALLISON

Zeke had a surprisingly strong grip on my arm as he marched me to the Bishop house. It wasn't until he shut the door behind me that I started to register what was happening. I was so mad at myself. I should've run the son of a bitch over. Too late, Allison. You got fooled. *You were so easy.*

Inside, Phillip Bishop was pacing the living room. When he saw me he groaned, then resumed his stride. Zeke ignored him and shoved me with his gun.

"We're just here to chat a little, aren't we? Maybe we can all come to some mutual agreement," Zeke said as he pushed me down on the couch. He sat across from me in a leather chair, the gun trained on my heart.

"You killed Tammy," I said softly. "And Maureen. Didn't you?"

Zeke sniffed a little at that, but he didn't take his eyes off me. They were the same bright blue as his brother's. Blue-eyed devils. "It was old news. Buried history. You should've left it alone."

"She was a person. A human being. How can you even live with yourself?"

"She was a whore," Zeke spat out bitterly. He twirled the gun in small circles. "She worked her way through our family, trying to get our money. We tried to get her to leave, but she wouldn't listen."

"Now, Zeke," Phillip interjected, but Zeke waved him off.

My mind was racing in desperation. I needed to calm down. *Think, Allison. You are smarter than them.* "The police are on their way here," I said, trying to sound brave. "They know what you did."

"Yeah, sure they are. So's Santa Claus." Zeke sighed. "You talk too much. If you'd just shut up, minded your own business, none of this would've happened. But you didn't."

My bottom lip trembled. *It's going to be fine,* I tried to reassure myself. *You called the police. People are discussing them on message boards. They won't get away with this.*

"It'll really be quite tragic," he said. "A young fragile woman, depressed. Unable to handle the divorce and shaming, unable to handle the deep isolation out here at the beach in the off-season. Decides to walk into the ocean. Like Virginia Woolf. Stones in her pockets...or something less dramatic. Maybe just a shot to the head and a nice suicide note written in your hand."

Dismay washed over me. Had Duke been inane enough to tell them about my call? I imagined him shaking his head slowly. *She's not well. She tried to kill herself over me.*

Phillip seemed just as stunned. He walked over between us and looked at Zeke. "That's not what we talked about."

"Just let me handle this," Zeke said. "Like I handle everything else."

Phillip flinched, and for a second I thought he might do something. Save me. But then he simply slumped back to the bar. I grew sick, thinking about that day outside with the power washer. That I'd actually fallen, briefly, for his charm. How many other women had done that very thing?

"I won't do it." I glanced around, but the only immediate way out was a door leading downstairs. If I had the chance. Why hadn't I taken my lawyer's advice and signed up for a self-defense class?

Zeke narrowed his eyes at me. "You can stop looking around. There's no one else here. No one to save you."

My heart was slowing down. The initial shock settling, and the real fear moving in.

Phillip brought me a piece of paper on a clipboard and a pen. His hands were shaking. All the flirtation, that charm I'd seen ooze out of him, was sapped now. He didn't want to do this.

He was my chance.

I felt that steel trapdoor shut down inside my belly. The one that had given me the courage to plot my on-air rant. *Compartmentalizing*, Annie had told me. *You were able to compartmentalize your shock about Duke, turn it on itself and use it.* That's why I hadn't freaked out, set his car on fire, boiled his cat. I stayed calm.

"You killed Maureen, Phillip," I said to his back. "You used her, and then you killed her because she was going to tell your wife about the affair. And then you killed Tammy because she was getting too close to the truth. And now you're going to kill me. When's it going to stop?"

Phillip turned, walked over to me. Stopped halfway, confused. "I wouldn't hurt Tammy." He stared past me. "I didn't want to hurt Maureen. It was all just a big mistake. An accident."

"An accident?" I sneered, my voice cooler.

Zeke shook the gun, impatient. "Sit back, sister. Enough with the chitter chatter. Start writing. Start with how sorry you are. That should get things going."

As I wrote Annie's name at the top, my panic threatened to bubble back to the surface. Imagining her, hearing the news, finding the note, never knowing the truth. *No, Allison. You won't let that happen.* "This will never work, you know. The proof is already out there. It's just a matter of time." I pressed the pen into the paper. Wrote Maureen's name. "I know everything. I know about Maureen, the affair. The police know, too. They have her necklace, the one you ripped off her neck the night you killed her."

"You know nothing. Shut up," Zeke said, jerking the gun again. "Keep writing."

"What did you do with her? Where's her body, Phillip?" I asked his back. But he wouldn't turn around.

Zeke sighed. "Leave my brother alone. He's sensitive. He can't handle these…situations…like I can. I'm the cleanup crew." He put one arm across the back of the chair, like we were discussing interior design.

"So *you* killed her?"

"No, no, no, smarty-pants. It was an accident. I just helped get rid of the evidence, I guess you could say. Anything to save the precious family biz."

"Where's her body?"

His brow furrowed. "Don't you know?" He touched the side of his head. "You disappoint me. I thought you knew."

Phillip let out another noise. Zeke ignored him, leaned forward, grinning. "Let's just say you've both stomped on common ground."

I felt a chill go down my arms and settle in my heart. Before I could say anything else, Zeke stood up. "Now get writing. Or I'll break one of your fingers."

"You can end this now," I said to Phillip again as he walked over to the bar. My voice was wavering, but I forced myself to continue. "Go to the police. Confess. You can do her that justice at least."

"Finish the note," Zeke threatened.

"I know what she meant to you, Phillip." I touched my hair and thought of a lie. "This is her scarf. She used to come to this house, didn't she? She's here, Phillip. You feel her, too, don't you? She's here, and she's going to get you."

A crash. Phillip had dropped a bottle of whiskey. "How did you know—" But I didn't wait. I lunged forward, swinging my arm wide into Zeke's arm. It hurt like hell, but the gun flew out of his hand, away. I heard him curse as I ran. Into the basement, slamming the door behind me. I ran down the stairs. It was still dark outside, and it took my eyes a moment to adjust.

I stopped to look for an exit. At the back of the room were two French doors leading to the beach. Mercifully they opened just as I heard Zeke's shoes on the stairs.

Out. Outside. The air was freezing, but it felt like freedom. The sand. My shoes sunk low. Like I was running through water. Up the dunes. He was behind me, but he was older, and I had the advantage. I ran over the top, too late remembering the gun, dived, ducked for cover. My breath was hard and fast. The adrenaline was pure and pumping. I stole a glance back, but I didn't see either of the men any longer. I stayed bent low, walked quickly toward the Worthington house. If I could just get to my car. If the keys were still in it.

Around the corner of the house, Phillip appeared. His eyes were wild, his hair twisting in the wind. I screamed and lunged at his knees. We both went down. He seized a chunk of my hair. I dug into his leg with my nails.

I rolled over, grabbing fistfuls of sand, and threw them in Phillip's eyes. He cried out, scratching at his face. I got up to run. Made it to the driveway. My car was off. Keys gone. I ran around the side of my house, back toward the Bishop place.

Then I saw Zeke standing in his driveway. His hands up in the air. And a woman, steady. Pointing a gun at his heart. Lorelei. She nodded at me but didn't take her eyes off Zeke.

"Move. Here," she said, calm. I ran to her.

Phillip stumbled over from between the houses, still wiping the sand from his eyes. He stopped when he saw Lorelei.

Zeke sneered at her. "You bitch. You're going to ruin us over a stupid girl?"

"We're all stupid girls to you, Joseph." Lorelei reminded me of Cruella De Vil, standing at the top of the driveway, wrapped in a tremendous gray fur coat. Her hands encased in slick, tight-fitting black gloves that I suspected went up to her elbows.

"Lorelei," Phillip called. He sounded pathetic. His arms at his sides. "Honey, this isn't—"

"What it looks like?" she said, her voice smooth. Her lips curled up, exposing white teeth. I wouldn't have been shocked if she attacked and bit him like a wild animal. She was moving the gun back and forth between Phillip and Zeke. "It's exactly what it looks like. Get inside so we can wait for the police."

"Just put it down. We can work something out."

Lorelei shook her head. "Get over there," she shouted to Phillip, but he stayed put. Frozen. She opened her mouth to say something, but before she could I saw Zeke lunge.

"Watch out," I yelled.

Lorelei whipped back. The gun went off. Zeke fell, slumped. Phillip made a low growl in his throat, not threatening, but defeated.

"It's over," she said to both of us, and pulled the trigger again.

44

MAUREEN

I drag Phillip out to the beach. I want to be outside, under the stars, like the first time we were together. Out there, it might be easier to convince him to help me. To believe.

I have to hold his hand as we walk, keep him upright, and halfway there I almost give up. He brought the bottle of wine with him, despite my protests, and when he's not swigging freely he's singing some old folk song.

He finally collapses right after the dunes, closer to the house than I would've liked, but it will do. I sit next to him, help him roll up his khakis.

"There, this is nice," I say. "Just like that first night, yes?"

"Just like it," he slurs.

"I like full circles, you know? End where you start."

"So this is the end?"

I stare at him, surprised. "Of course. Isn't that what you said? Our last night together?"

He sighs, leans back on his elbows and pushes his toes

through the sand. He seems too big, too burly for the sand, like a tiger trying to use a litterbox. "I suppose so. All good things must come to an end."

"So we have to say goodbye, for this summer," I sing quietly, and he laughs, tells me I've messed up the lyrics. But he wants me to keep singing, says he loves my voice. I do, and then nuzzle against his shoulder. I'm afraid he's going to fall asleep on me.

"Phillip?"

He makes a gurgling sound. I shake him a bit.

"Phillip? Don't go to sleep on me. I need a favor. I need to tell you something."

"What's that?" He's drifting. This isn't how I wanted things to go.

"Phillip, I need help."

He shakes his head and sits up, wiping sand from his hands. "Not the poker thing again, Maureen."

"No, no. Look at me. Look. Here. See? Me?" I take a deep breath. "I'm pregnant."

That gets his attention. "You're what?"

"I'm having a baby. Your baby, Phillip."

He stares at me for a second through drunken eyes, and I think I see them tear up. I imagine if all this were true, what might actually happen, where we might end up. And then he shifts in the moonlight. Still woozy, drunk. But his face is hard. "My baby?" he growls dismissively. "Yeah, right."

"It's yours, Phillip. It can't be anyone else's."

"Oh, I'll believe that when you can sell me a flying pig." He knocks my hand off his arm. "Don't go trying to pin this one on me."

I blink. It's as if he's taken off a mask, allowing me to see the ugliness inside, what he really thinks of me. My eyes are pricking with tears, but I push through it all. "It's okay. I'm not trying to pin anything on you, Phillip. I love you, but I can't have a baby. We can't have a baby. Not now." I bite the inside of my lip, taste the metallic spurt of blood. "I just need—I need some money. That's all. And I'll take care of it. No one will ever know."

He tries to get up, but he's so drunk he just falls over in the sand and snorts. I am grateful that there is no child in my womb that might one day have to see this display. "Yeah, you'll take care of it. Go ask some of the other men you're with, won't you? Go see if they'll help you. How about my son?" he asks, rolling over, his eyes narrowed into slits. "Or my brother? Huh?"

"You know I never—"

"Or who else? I know your type, Maureen. Look, this was fun, but…" He rubs his eyes. "Just leave me alone. Just…go." He lays back, rolls over. Doesn't move.

"Get up," I say. I shake him, but he's gone, a slight snore coming from his lips. I push harder, yank on his shirt, but he's out. I stand, about to turn to leave, but then kneel down, find his wallet in his pocket. Count it quickly—$207. I shove the bills in my purse and throw the empty wallet on top of him. My parting gift. I stomp up the dunes, blinded by tears of frustration.

I don't get even halfway up the first dune when my knees buckle out from under me. I'm falling, and it's then that I register something has hit me, hard, on the back of my head. I reach up, my arms flailing as I go down. Where my hair should be, I feel only wet, sticky. I cry out, horrified, when I feel another blow on the side of my head. The sand is in my mouth, my hair, gritting into the tears on my face.

I roll over. There's a shadow. It's Phillip, then Zeke, then Benny, then Desmond. All leering at me. Laughing. *Help*, I try to say. I feel nothing now, but I know the pain is coming.

The shadow moves away, and all I see is the black sky. The beautiful sky. It's like that first night here in Opal Beach. Destiny. My destiny. Then the streaks begin. The meteor shower. Millions of stars, exploding, dancing, their light so very far away. It's beautiful. Phillip, do you see it? Just beautiful. Just—

45

• —— •

ALLISON

She'd shot Phillip in the arm, it looked like. He was clutching it right above his elbow, moaning in the driveway like a goose. Zeke wasn't moving or making any sound at all.

"Do you want to be next, Phillip?" Lorelei walked closer to him, her fur coat trailing behind her.

He was babbling. "My god. I wasn't—you wouldn't—I'm your husband."

She snorted. "And how many women have you slept with over the years? Do you think I'm brainless, Phillip?"

"I haven't—"

"Don't patronize me," she said, and I heard the click of the hammer.

Phillip heard it, too, and started crying. He raised his good arm, and I could see the blood smeared on his palm. "Lor, please, I need to get to a doctor."

"Oh, fucking ice it down," she snarled. "There's plenty of it around you." She kicked a pile of snow, and it burst into little puffs in the sky. "I know all about them, Phillip. Every single one. You think you're smart, right? Lying, sneaking around. You underestimate me. You underestimate all of us, Phillip. Women. That's your downfall."

"Zeke will die, Lor. We need to call—"

"Zeke is not my concern. Your scheming brother gets what he deserves, too, helping you all these years." She sighed, like this was all a bother to her, and turned to me. "But I suppose that we should call the police, yes, Allison?"

The cold wind had numbed my cheeks. I nodded, afraid to speak. Did she want me to call? My cell phone was still in my car, and I was afraid to leave them alone. Afraid to move.

Lorelei pulled her phone from her pocket, held it to her ear with the gun still trained on Phillip. But he'd already given up, his shoulders sagged. His goal now seemed to be not getting shot again.

She repeated the address twice, then hung up.

"Where were we? Oh yes, you were going to tell us how you murdered your little girlfriend Maureen." It was like she was on stage, her greatest performance yet. Years in the making.

Phillip's face crumpled. "I didn't—it was an accident. I swear. I don't even remember. I just woke up—and she was—dead. I must've—" He put his hands to his face. "I dream about it all the time. You don't know the nightmares."

"The nightmares?" Lorelei cackled. "Oh, I feel so bad for you. Don't you?" she asked me. I shook my head slowly.

"So," she coaxed. "You *accidentally* killed her?"

"We were on the beach. And she was—she had asked for money and I told her no, and then the next thing I knew Zeke was shaking me awake. It was still dark on the beach. And she was dead. I don't remember hurting her, but I had blood all over—" He broke off again, and Lorelei actually rolled her eyes. I thought she was going to shoot him just to keep him on task.

"So your brother helped you get rid of the body?" She looked over at me, to make sure I was taking it all in. As if I should have been taking notes. "Where is she?"

I could see the pain weighing him down, and I almost felt bad for him. I had to remind myself there was a monster inside that man. "It was the only way," he said quietly. "I swear."

"What was?" I asked.

"The construction next door," he said. "We just—they were putting in the foundation and…"

Oh god. "Built in 1986," the ad had said. Tammy had been right—Maureen had never left Opal Beach. I shuddered.

We could hear the whine of a police car in the distance, followed by the more urgent tone of an ambulance. But Lorelei wasn't done. "I knew you did something to her that night. I didn't know how disgusting, but I was there. I was upstairs when you were talking about it, trying to wash up," she hissed. "To clean the unclean. And your brother with all his tricks. Taking that girl's clothes, to make it look like she ran out of town. Clever, but not clever enough."

Phillip's mouth opened, closed, opened again.

"Spit it out, Phillip," Lorelei said impatiently.

"We had to go find—to see if there was any evidence of me…so Zeke said he'd do it."

"Because you're too damn spineless," Lorelei said. "But I found something your *dear brother* missed."

The police cruiser pulled into the driveway, sirens blaring. The lights reflected off Lorelei's face, an eerie glow. She stood, cold and haughty, an old statue whose day for commemoration had finally arrived.

46

ALLISON

December 2015

Maureen was a mermaid again, large and beautiful with green, blue and purple iridescent scales on her tail. Her hair flowed around her head like a jellyfish, undulating as she flapped. She came toward me, to hug me. She was wearing her friendship necklace. But just as she got close, she smacked into an invisible barrier. She seemed confused and started hitting her wrists against the glass. Shouting to me, but I couldn't hear what she was saying. She shook her head, wildly, bashing her wrists harder.

I jolted up. I'd fallen asleep on the couch, exhausted. The last few days had been a nightmare. The testimony. The phone calls. Dolores had been spending time at the beach house with me until Annie and my parents could come help me move out. But she'd gone to take her dad to a doctor's appointment, and I'd laid down for a minute in the silence and fallen asleep.

My phone rang. Sheriff Clapper sounded weary. This was probably the most action he'd gotten in Opal Beach in years. The good news was all the skepticism in his voice was gone. Or at least, it was no longer directed my way, which I took as a win.

"I wanted to tell you I'm sorry I can't give you back the necklace," he said. "I know that you asked for it, but it's got to be entered into evidence for the trial."

"I figured that," I said. "But I appreciate you trying."

"I can see what I can do…after," he said. "But no promises."

"Tammy's half, too?" I asked.

"Yes, though that technically belongs to her family."

Tammy's mom. What she must be going through… And Tammy had always been the one taking care of her, despite her crazy schedule at the coffee shop.

"Does this mean The Sweet Spot will close down?"

"Not sure about that. I guess it depends on what Mrs. Bishop decides."

"Mrs. Bishop?"

"Yeah, funny thing there. Turns out she owns the business. She's the one who put up the money all those years ago when Tammy first opened." He chuckled. "I always wondered why she nudged me to go there for coffee." He cleared his throat. "But anyway, there's another reason I called you."

"Okay?"

"We checked on Phillip's and Zeke's alibis for the night Tammy died. They check out."

"How could that be?"

"They were at a holiday party in Millstone. From about 7 p.m. to after midnight. Phillip even did a toast at around 9 p.m. There's no way they could've been in Opal Beach the night she drowned."

I felt like I'd been run over. I sat down on the couch before my knees gave out.

"I mean, we still have plenty to charge them on, don't you worry. But it looks like Tammy's death was what we thought originally. An accident."

"That doesn't make sense. Why would she be out there? So late? In that weather?" I asked.

"We'll never know," Clapper said in as gentle a voice as he could muster. "It could be that she was wrapped up in this whole Maureen thing, went for a walk, and—" He let his voice trail off.

"In an ice storm? Right near the Bishops' restaurant?"

"I'm sorry, Allison. There's no evidence of foul play here."

I closed my eyes. Tried to picture Tammy wandering along the pier at night.

Something wasn't right.

47

●━━━●

ALLISON

I wasn't sure if I'd be able to get into Tammy's house, but I needed to try. Clapper's call had concerned me. He was missing something about the night she died. I still didn't understand why Tammy would go out to the pier. How they'd lured her there. What was I overlooking?

When I arrived, the house was dark and quiet. Was it considered a crime scene? There was no police tape. I called Dolores to see what she thought, but she didn't answer, so I left a message. I drove around the block twice, but there was no squad car. I finally parked in front. Palmed the key Tammy had given me in case I'd wanted to stay at her place the night I'd been scared. The memory made my heart hurt. It was hard to believe she was gone.

I hadn't been at Tammy's place much, but the smell brought her back. I half expected her to pop out around a corner and wave. *Hey! Want some coffee?*

Her mother, or her mother's friends, at least, were supposed to come down this weekend to sort through her belongings. I headed to Tammy's bedroom and flicked on the light. I'd never been in there. The bed was unmade and a pile of crumpled clothes sat in front of the closet waiting to be washed. It was horrible to see Tammy's pillow, still crunched up like she'd woken just minutes before. A jewelry box sat open on the dresser, various necklaces and earrings spilling out. As I leaned over another pile of clothes to look inside, my leg brushed up against something hard. One of Tammy's shirts had slid off and exposed the corner of a piece of machinery. I pulled the rest away and found a film projector buried beneath.

Tammy had said she didn't have a projector, that she couldn't watch Maureen's film. I ran my hands through the other clothes on the floor, looking for the film to go with it, but it was just the projector. Then I spotted a notebook buried under the pile of clothes. On the top page, Tammy had started a note.

Dear Allison,

That was it. I stared at the words. Picked up the notebook and flipped through the rest. It was blank except for those two formidable words: Dear Allison.

Next to the notepad was a small digital recorder. I turned it on. There were four files. I pressed Play on the first, dated the day I moved to Opal Beach.

"Hello?" It was Tammy's voice.

Then another, a woman, her voice muffled, like she wasn't quite holding the phone up to her mouth. "How are you doing, Tammy? How's your mom?"

Tammy talked about her mom's health and the woman murmured in sympathy. I fast-forwarded, about to put the recorder down and get out of there, when I heard my name.

"The Simpson woman is here. Are you ready?"

Startled, I dropped the recorder and it fell. I fished it out of Tammy's laundry, sinking to the floor. There was a pause, then Tammy's voice, softer. "Are you sure?"

"Of course. You can't back out now."

"I won't."

"Good. Just remember what we talked about."

"Yes."

"Am I on speakerphone? Take me off speakerphone."

"I'm sorry." Tammy's voice. A clatter and then Tammy answered from farther away. "I was making dinner." And the tape cut off.

I stared at the recorder like it was a live snake. What was she talking about? And to whom?

I pressed the forward arrow to the next recording and hit Play. It was from November 8. Right after the Autumn Harvest dinner at the country club. It, too, started in the middle of a conversation. "—need to calm down. Everything's still on track. This is just speeding things up."

The woman's voice was clearer now, and it struck me like a sharp knife.

Lorelei.

"I just didn't know you were going to send it like that," Tammy said. "That you had it. How do you have it?"

"I didn't tell you on purpose, Tammy. We needed the surprise element, so your shock was genuine."

The necklace. I closed my eyes, remembering how Tammy's face had lost color when I'd shown it to her. So it had been Lorelei who sent it. *I found something your dear brother had missed.* I had been so quick to dismiss the possibility.

"I'm just—not sure about all this now. It's just all getting too much."

"Tammy, you can't back out now. Remember what's at stake. Your mother."

There was a pause. A sniffle, like Tammy was crying.

"It's all going to be fine. I'm handling it. Just keep doing what you're doing. We need to get the police involved and this will move more quickly. And don't call me back on this phone. It's a disposable."

The next file was my voice.

"You okay?" I asked, tinny, excited.

Tammy answered, "Yes, yes. Just trying to move in the dark."

My call to Tammy after Thanksgiving. I sounded over-excited, raving on. And then Tammy, warning me I was in danger. Hanging up on me.

The last recording. From the night of Tammy's death. The hair on my arms stood up as I listened:

"Tammy, I need you to meet me tonight."

"Tonight? But the snow."

"At the pier. It's about Phillip. It can't wait."

"The pier? Phillip? What's happened?"

"Nine o'clock." Click.

I dropped the recorder. That's why Tammy had been at the pier that night. But what had been so urgent?

I played the last recording again. *It's about Phillip.*

"I'm sorry it had to happen this way."

It took me a second to realize what was wrong. The voice wasn't coming from the recorder. It came from behind me.

I turned, and the recorder fell out of my hand and under the dresser. Lorelei was standing before me. She looked tired, dark circles under her eyes, her hair pushed back into a severe bun. She was wearing a small fur coat now, cropped at the waist, and those same black gloves.

"Oh my goodness," I said, standing. "You scared me!" I

slung my purse strap around my shoulder. "I was just leaving. I had to come get something of Tammy's…"

Lorelei stared at me, calm but resigned. "I kind of figured you wouldn't give up," she said, sighing. "I hoped you would. It really was a great plan."

"Plan?" I smiled. "I don't know about that." I tried to shove past her. But Lorelei didn't budge from the doorway. "I'll just get out of your way."

"Allison."

Her voice made me stop.

"Please, don't make me pull out the gun. You know I know how to use it."

My body went cold.

Lorelei shook her head. "Tammy was a sweet girl, she was. But she could never just let it go. I really wanted her to just let it go."

"You…killed Tammy?" I could barely get the words out. I felt the fear flood through me again. No one knew I was here. And now I was facing a killer, one much smarter than Zeke or Phillip.

"Come on, put it together. You're a bright girl. That's why I picked you."

"Picked me?"

"Get over there. On the bed. Please. I can't have you standing here."

I went over and sat down slowly. "We can go now, to Sheriff Clapper," I said desperately. "He'd understand, I'm sure—the way that Phillip treated you…anyone would understand."

Lorelei laughed sharply. "Another man? Really, Allison? You think he would understand what we women have gone through? I thought you were smarter than that."

She leaned against the doorway, and I remembered how she'd stood at the top of the driveway, that superior look in her eye as her husband, her cheating lying husband, had crumpled before her. And now, me. The final nail to be hammered down.

"Do you think the Worthingtons would really just leave some troubled nutcase in charge of their home for all that time?" She smiled. "I *groomed* them for you. Told them how I knew you and Duke, what a cad he was, how you needed something like this. Patty's very susceptible to sad-sack stories like yours. Women done wrong."

I stared at her, stunned.

"I knew you wouldn't go for it if you knew I was involved. I couldn't risk that you might remember me from the sailing club or make the connection through your husband's family. I did some research—I'm very good at research—and I discovered that your sister and Dolores Gund's sister worked together. I asked Patty to keep me out of it, given the sensitive nature of the situation. It was lovely, really. I have to tell you, I loved your outburst on-air. I have a recording of it at home. I watch it sometimes. I knew that you'd take interest in poor little Maureen."

I flushed, thinking of how easily I'd been played. Lorelei's reaction the first time I'd met her—a meteorologist, that's right. *On television.* Her insistence that I go to Tammy's for coffee. *I'm sure you'll find it a favorite place of yours.* I'd been so focused on Clay, the scorned boyfriend, so sure he was involved. Had Duke and his lying, cheating ways blinded me to the truth?

"Why? I don't—why not just go to the police?"

"I wanted my husband to go to jail." She rolled her eyes. "It's so boring to just tell you, Allison. Surely you can figure it out."

My mind was racing. "You had me chase around clues?"

"Good, good. You're getting better."

"But... Tammy...?"

Lorelei's face changed, a pitied look, like I was a child whose dead fish she'd just flushed down the toilet. As she started to speak, I realized I wasn't going to like what I was about to hear.

"Oh, she knew the whole time. Helped me plant the clues, gave you a little nudge."

"Why didn't *she* just go to the police?"

"Because she loved Phillip, Tammy did."

"Tammy and Phillip?" And then I remembered what Mabel had said that afternoon in the parking lot of the grocery store. *Tammy always liked the older men.* And Tammy—I'd felt sorry for her that night at the bar, when we'd sat out back and she'd told me she'd been in love once and been burned. She'd played me then, I now knew, but what she'd said, at its core, had been the truth. In love—with Phillip Bishop? I felt like I'd been hit by a sixteen-wheeler. I couldn't imagine it.

Lorelei clasped her hands together, giddy now. "This is so fun. It's just like the movies, isn't it?"

I shifted on the bed, analyzing her. She'd threatened a gun, but did she have one? Had the police taken the one she'd used to kill Zeke and shoot Phillip? Was she bluffing?

"That's right. Tammy had fallen in love. And when she found out Phillip was sleeping with the little carnival girl, I proposed a plan. To kill him. We'd be in it together. Two scorned women. I didn't care that she'd slept with him, too. I knew she was vulnerable. I knew how much her mother meant to her," she sputtered, narrowing her eyes. "All Tammy had to do was drug Phillip. I would take care of the rest. She was so angry and heartbroken she agreed. Of course, my plan was never to kill Phillip. I wanted him to suffer *a long time*. So I followed him and his little tramp down to the beach that night, and when he passed out, I killed her. And left them both there to be discovered by a passerby. Only his idiot brother found him first, and they decided to cover it up."

"*You* killed Maureen?" My breathing was shallow now. A panic attack? Couldn't afford to lose control. I needed to think before it all caved in on me.

Lorelei shot me a disgusted look. She was growing tired of me, and I didn't want to think about what would happen when she lost her patience. "She wouldn't have lasted very long, anyway. Girls like that—well, you know."

"But Phillip—he doesn't know. He thinks he *did* kill her." I breathed in. Imagined Phillip walking around for thirty years believing he'd killed someone, and Lorelei letting him bear that burden.

"Which would've been perfect, of course, because Phillip was so guilt-ridden he actually kept his cock out of other women for a long time."

I was beginning to understand. A terrible revenge plot that went wrong. "Except Tammy didn't see it that way."

"Oh yes. Tammy. She, of course, was appalled that her drugging Phillip had led to her friend's death. She was about to go to the police and confess, until I pointed out that we'd both be in prison. I provided a much better alternative—money. Money to help out her sick mother and to open that coffee shop she always wanted. I was her benefactor."

"To keep her quiet."

"Exactly. Of course she never knew I was the one who killed Maureen. And it would've all been fine. Unfortunately, Phillip fell in love with a waitress down at the club months ago. Oh, and this time it was *true love*," she said, her voice bubbling over with poison. "He was getting ready to leave me. I couldn't let that happen. I couldn't let him take this lifestyle away from me."

"So you decided to remind him of Maureen."

"That's right. See? You are smart. I wanted to make him pay. But I couldn't very well bring it up after all these years. I would be an accomplice. It had to be someone else. We tried Dolores Gund, but she's...too close to everything. She didn't bite. That's when I knew I had to get someone from the outside to do it. And who better but an isolated divorcée with a history of being betrayed and an axe to grind?"

I closed my eyes. Her words cut into me, but I knew I had to keep her talking to stay alive. "Yes, I see. I was perfect. I fell right into it, didn't I?"

"Well, Tammy helped with that. I laid out the plan to her. It was our chance to finally bring justice to her friend, without incriminating her or me."

"So what went wrong?"

"Tammy got scared. She started—to like you." Lorelei paused, lifted her nose as though she'd just caught wind of rotting garbage. "She thought Phillip and Zeke would come after you if you continued to dredge up more. They didn't like the town talking. Then, when the police came to the house, everyone got spooked—including Tammy. I thought she was going to expose our game, just when the truth was about to come out. We were so close. So..." She smiled cheerfully. "Women are disposable, right? Isn't that what we've learned?"

"Don't twist my words," I said, amazed at my own bravery. "You don't care about anything. You—you just played all of us. Like a game." The thought of Lorelei plotting. Picking me out. Watching me, all this time. With a sinking gut, I remembered Tammy's voice on the phone, the fear real. *You're in danger, Allison.* Tammy had tried to save me. And Lorelei had killed her for it. *Anyone* who got in Lorelei's way was disposable.

"Get up," she said. "You're coming with me."

She pulled a pistol from her coat pocket. So she hadn't

been bluffing. My heart sank. "You're just going to shoot me? Here?"

She shrugged. "Let that police detective sort it out. It'll be the case of his lifetime." But I could see the uncertainty in her eyes. She hadn't plotted this far. She thought I'd swallow the whole story like a gullible fish.

I caught a flash of something behind her. Just a slight movement. Had I been imagining it? I kept babbling. "Let's talk this out. Please? I can keep a secret."

She laughed coldly. "That's a lovely sentiment, my dear, but no thank you. You're a liability and a pressure cooker. No, you served your purpose—"

We heard a crash at the back of the house. Lorelei whirled around. "Who's there?" she cried, then swung back to me. "Don't move, Allison, or I'll shoot you. You know I will." She backed out of the room slowly, craning her neck.

There was another loud crash.

In a second, Lorelei had dropped. She was on the floor, twisting in agony, screeching through clenched teeth. There was a woman on top of her—a tattooed forearm around Lorelei's neck like she was bringing in the win at Roller Derby.

"Dolores!" I cried in relief.

She looked up grimly. "This bitch isn't going anywhere. Call the police, Allison. We're done here."

48

ALLISON

The basement still smelled like mold. I walked carefully across the carpet to the back corner where Catarina had pawed most often. I knelt down and unfolded the paper that my mother had sent, smoothing it out on the rug so I could read it.

A ritual to elevate the troubled dead.

I checked my watch. The Worthingtons were in midflight. After the police had arrested Lorelei and contacted them last week, the Worthingtons had been able to arrange an early departure from Patty's assignment.

My belongings were packed in the U-Haul outside in the driveway. My plant Linus was tucked into the passenger side of the front seat. The night before, Dolores had stopped by and given me a present—an honorary derby team shirt with The Weather Girl stenciled across the back. "Come back and see us sometime. Don't be a stranger, okay?" she'd said, but we both knew better. I wouldn't be back.

I spread a small white cloth out on the carpet and placed the photo of Maureen sitting on the beach in the middle. I added the bunch of heather I'd gotten from the front yard and a clean bowl of water. Then I unwrapped the four pillar candles my mom had given me.

When you are ready to begin, light a candle at each of the four corners of the altar, offering a prayer that will consecrate the space.

I sat cross-legged in front of the cloth and closed my eyes. I imagined Maureen's face on the video. Laughing, her hair whipping in the beach air. Alive, hopeful. She hadn't deserved her fate. Hadn't deserved the awful grave she'd gotten, right here under my feet. I took a deep breath.

"Hello, Maureen," I spoke into the empty room. I felt vaguely ridiculous and was glad that I'd declined my mom and Annie's offer to join. Because this was between Maureen and me. We'd both been drawn here to Opal Beach, hadn't we? Outsiders, finding our way to this place, to this house. I'd been lucky enough to survive, but Maureen—well, she'd been trapped for too long. Silenced. *It's not what you are, it's what you don't become that hurts.* She'd never had her chance to become who she wanted to be. And now finally that justice was served, that someone knew what happened to her, she could, maybe, get that freedom and independence she always wanted.

I cleared my throat and forced myself to continue. "I'm sorry for what happened to you. I hear your story. And you can go now. In peace. You're free."

I waited for something to happen. A crash. A noise. A feeling on the back of my neck. But nothing came. I opened my eyes and watched the candle flames flicker in the silence. Their cedarwood scent filled the air. I waited a few minutes before blowing them out. "Goodbye, Maureen," I whispered. But there was no answer.

EPILOGUE

October 2016

As soon as I got back to the dressing room, my cell phone buzzed.

"Hey, sis," I answered as I kicked off my heels and settled into one of the station's cozy armchairs.

"Mongoose! You were fantastic."

I smiled, warmed by her compliment. I wiped my palms on my pencil skirt and let out a deep breath. I hadn't realized how nervous I'd been until that very moment.

"No, seriously. You were great. I've missed seeing you on television."

"It was okay. I messed up during that one cut to break, and I feel like the interview with the sheriff could've been edited more—"

"Stop, silly. You were amazing."

A knock on the door. "Hold on one sec," I said to Annie.

Vaughn was standing in the doorway. "Ratings out the roof, Allison. Wonderful, wonderful job," he boomed, then lowered his voice slightly when he saw I was on the phone. "Come out when you're ready. We'll be celebrating."

I felt jazzed. I'd done it. Hard to believe I'd almost missed out on the opportunity altogether. After I'd come back to Philadelphia, Vaughn had told me the bad news—he'd found another meteorologist to take that position. But then he told me the better news—he had other plans. He said he wanted to create a compelling news series that would air just after the local news. Focusing on true crime. And he wanted me to host it.

At first, I'd laughed. Me? A television host? I had no experience, for one. Not in that way. And did I really want to put myself back out there again? After everything that had happened?

But Vaughn—and Annie—had been persistent. They'd had answers to all my doubts. *Of course you have experience*, Vaughn had said. *A meteorologist's job is to tell stories, to make things compelling for the viewer.* And Annie was her usual cheerful glass-half-full nurse, which didn't convince me until she'd pointed out the revenge angle. *Stick your chin out, show them you're not afraid. Duke will cream his pants when he finds out you're back on TV.*

So here I was. We'd been working on it for almost a year. The idea was that I would discuss cold cases in and around Philadelphia. With a focus on women. The title had been my idea: *One Night Gone*. Vaughn had wanted to premiere with my own story about Maureen, and after Lorelei had been convicted, I was free to talk about it.

Not that that made it easy.

"It was really brave of you," Annie said, reading my mind as usual.

"Thanks. That means a lot." But something was snagging on my happiness. I focused on it, trying to pull it loose—there it was. The betrayal. The fact that I'd been gaslighted. Again. Played like a fool by Duke, then Lorelei. Even Tammy. It still bothered me even now, even here in the humming, buzzing news station, where everyone treated me well, where I was respected. It still bothered me that, even in moments of great success and triumph, I found myself backing up, analyzing, wondering whom I could trust, if I wasn't truly *seeing* people. Maybe I'd be that way from here on. Maybe that's what made me good at this new job.

Annie broke into my thoughts. "Well, hey, I won't get in the way of celebrating."

"Whoa, wait a minute," I said, shaking off my gloom. "You think I forgot? You're not going anywhere without telling me about the tasting." I settled back into the armchair.

Annie's voice quickened in excitement. "Oh, it was excellent. Everything was good. We had a hard time choosing. Mike liked the raspberry filling the best, and I have to say, it was probably up there for me, too, but we were like, raspberry. Not everyone likes fruit filling, you know? So we went with vanilla cake, chocolate icing and filling, and a raspberry drizzle. That way, you know, best of all worlds."

"Sounds divine," I said.

"And you'll be able to make it for the fitting? Even though you're a big fat TV star now?"

"Annie!"

"Okay, because Sharon has to work that night, so that's really the best time for everyone." Annie sighed in delight. I could picture her smiling. "It's so hard to believe…everything's coming together."

"Yes. It is," I said, meaning more than Annie's wedding. For the first time in a long time, I felt like I could really breathe. "How's my kitty?" I asked. "Were you able to stop over and feed her today?"

Annie made an annoyed sound. "Of course. She's a little wench. Coming around to me, though. Rubs against the back of my hand. Curls up in a little ball. She meows like a beast, though. Always complaining. Like you."

I hadn't been looking for a pet, but one morning I'd heard

scratching at the back door of my new apartment in downtown Philly. When I opened it, a small black-and-white kitten had stalked in, confident, like she'd been there millions of times before. Walked right into my living room and jumped up on the end table where I'd framed the photo of Tammy and Maureen on the beach.

"Maureen?" I'd asked, and the kitten's ears had perked up a bit. I swear she smiled.

I printed up Cat-Found posters and hung them around my neighborhood, but no one claimed Maureen, and so Maureen was mine. She seemed pleased by the name and had no desire to leave my apartment. She also seemed to love the jangle of the two best friend necklace charms I hooked to her collar.

"Thanks for doing that. I owe you one."

"I've got to run, though," Annie said. "I'm due at work in an hour, and I haven't even gotten in the shower yet. Don't have too much fun."

We hung up. I still felt "on," but I wanted to sit for a moment by myself before joining the others. I went into my office and Googled my name. For the first time in a long, long time, I wasn't fearful of the results.

There were articles about Maureen's case:

Former Weatherperson Solves Cold Case in Opal Beach

Bishop Seafood Restaurant Maven Arrested for Thirty-Year-Old Murder

And about the sale of the Bishop's restaurant chain:

Something Smells Fishy: The Fall of the Bishop Seafood Empire

Captain Crackers Franshise Acquires Seafood Restaurants in Wake of Murder Scandal

Clay Bishop seemed to be trying to stay out of the media frenzy as much as possible—and I could relate to that, of course. From what Dolores had told me, his university had been supportive of him, but he had apparently cut all ties with Opal Beach. I wondered if it was because of the media circus or because it reminded him too much of painful things. Tammy and Maureen had been his friends, after all. Did it keep him up at night, knowing what his own parents had been capable of?

But my favorite search results, the ones that proved things were truly turning around for me, were all about my new career:

From Storm Tracker to Crime Stalker: An Interview with Allison Simpson

"Weather Girl" Follows New Storms with One Night Gone True Crime Show

No more terrible memes. No more awful emails. But best of all? I'd embraced it—my past, the on-air rant. I'd even addressed it, frankly, at the beginning of the show. What had been done to me—though unfair and heart crushing—was nothing compared to what was done to women every single day in Philadelphia and beyond. It was time to stop treating women as if they were disposable. It was time to tell their stories.

I closed my laptop and sat back in my chair, examining the strewn piles of folders and research across my desk. Photos of women from police files—Kim Amari, reported missing on Christmas Eve 2014. Elizabeth Hatton, who filed a restraining order on her ex-husband for stalking and then disappeared a week later. Shantee Wilson, found dead in an alley in West Kensington. *There's no lack of material*, Vaughn had said to me, trying to convince me of the show's potential for success. What echoed in the silence between us was how terrible that fact was.

I didn't think I was going to solve the world's problems. I wasn't even sure any of us would ever crack another case again, though Vaughn certainly hoped so. What I wanted to do was keep telling the stories. Keep them from falling through the cracks that Maureen's had fallen through. That Tammy's had fallen through. My friend—for I still considered her that, even after everything she'd done—had made mistakes. But she hadn't deserved to pay for those mistakes with her life. None of these women had.

There was a quick rap at my office door, and Lucy, one of our writers, poked her head in. "Did you fall asleep in here?" she asked playfully. "Vaughn's dying to open the champagne, but he won't do it without you."

I smiled. "I'll be right there."

I flipped to the last page of my Opal Beach folder, a photo of Maureen on the beach. She sat in the sand, clutching her knees, staring out into the deep gray ocean, that paisley scarf tied in her hair, its ends dangling over her tanned shoulders. She looked not sad exactly, but contemplative. As if she wanted to dive into that ocean and discover all its secrets, bring them to the surface and sift them through her fingers.

"I'm sorry, Maureen," I whispered to the picture. "I wish you could've done that."

I pulled the photo from the page, where it had been taped, and pressed it up at the center of the bulletin board above my desk. Then I went to join the others.

As I walked into the crowd of production assistants and writers, their voices rose in a chorus. I could swear it sounded just like the roar of the ocean.

★ ★ ★ ★ ★

ACKNOWLEDGMENTS

I'm embarrassed to admit I started writing these acknowledgments before the book had even found a publisher. This stemmed less from any confidence that it would sell and more from the anxiety that I would forget to thank all the people who helped me during this book's long journey.

First kudos goes to the kind and thoughtful Erin Fitzgerald, with whom I talked through my initial crazy idea for the book and who told me, "Go for it."

Thank you to my spooky sister-in-spirit Sheri Sorvillo for all the writing lunches and writing coffees—this book would never have been written without all those Starbucks lattes. I am also grateful to Katrina Denza and the wonderful staff at Weymouth Center for the Arts and Humanities for providing much-needed space and time to draft major parts of this manuscript. Shout-out to Lis Hamilton, who was my cheerleader during the final writing stages of this book. I will always think "Done! Check!" when I think of you.

LynDee Walker and Laura Ellen Scott were the first two people to read the book. I will be forever grateful to them for dropping everything and reading that messy draft and encouraging me to move forward with it. Thank you to the wonderful editor Caitlin Alexander, who made the book that much better as well.

Special thanks to Ed Aymar, one of my best writing friends, for always being supportive, generous and ridiculous just when I need it most. Other folks who offered simple gestures of generosity and kindness when they didn't have to include Paul Tremblay, Amber Sparks, Ben Chadwick, Christina Hogrebe, Linda Landrigan, April Kaminski and Alan Orloff. I'm grateful to my colleagues at ASCD for all their support and kindness, especially Anthony Rebora and Naomi Thiers.

Thank you to my delightfully witty and exceptionally attractive agent, Michelle Richter, for first believing in this book and taking all my paranoid Facebook messages with calm and grace. And my editor, Melanie Fried, who made this book better than I ever thought it would be. You are amazing at what you do.

I am fortunate to have a wonderful writing family, without whom I would be lost. So, much gratitude to all my friends who put up with my anxiety and craziness in this up-and-down business—I'm looking at you, Christopher Allen, John Copenhaver, Josh Denslow, Beth Fiencke, Tara L. Masih, Frances McMillen, Bernadette Murphy, Matt Norman, Helen Rye, Brandon Wicks and all my "family" at *SmokeLong Quarterly*. And endless thanks to Jennifer Egan, who I somehow am lucky enough to be able to call a friend and mentor and who always shines a hopeful light in the darkness.

And of course I need to thank my family. My dad, who always tells me I'm living right and doing what I believe in; my brother, Mike, who's probably the hardest-working person I know; and my aunts, who are basically my guardian angels.

My mom died just a few weeks before I sold this book, and my heart aches that I never got to properly celebrate with her over margaritas. Still, I know she's tipping her glass to me somewhere, somehow. I'd never be the writer or the reader I am without her. And I miss her.

Finally, thank you Art Taylor, my husband and best friend in the whole wide world and biggest champion. I'm grateful to share this crazy journey with you. And none of this would be worth it without our son, Dashiell, who brings more joy into the world than I could ever hope for.

ONE
NIGHT
GONE

TARA LASKOWSKI

Reader's Guide

**GRAYDON
HOUSE**

1. How does weather become a character in the novel? How do the seasons reflect the tone of each storyline?

2. What links or connections did you see between Maureen and Allison?

3. At one point in the novel, Clay tells Maureen, "Life isn't a game." How does this statement play out in the book? What types of games are being played? Who are the manipulators and who are the ones being manipulated?

4. What role does friendship play in the novel? How far would you go to protect your own friends?

5. Discuss Maureen's obsession with destiny. Was it ever a real, achievable thing, or just an ideal she holds onto to keep her going in life?

6. Discuss the class dynamics of Opal Beach. How do they compare to your own town or city? Were you surprised by the twist of what really happened to Maureen?

7. Did you ultimately forgive Tammy for her involvement with Lorelei? Discuss the idea that society treats women as

disposable. Is this something you see in the world around you? How might we fix it?

8. Were you satisfied with Allison's ending? Do you think she'll be able to avoid similar situations in the future?